AF490731

FATAL TINDER

Jennifer Wells

Copyright © 2024 by Jennifer Wells

All rights reserved. No part of this publication may be reproduced, distributed, or transmitted in any form or by any means, including photocopying, recording, or other electronic or mechanical methods, without the prior written permission of the publisher, except in the case of brief quotations embodied in critical reviews and certain other noncommercial uses permitted by copyright law.

ISBN: 979-8330315352

This is a work of fiction.

Names, characters, places, and incidents either are products of the author's imagination or are used fictitiously.

Any similarity to actual events or locales or persons, living or dead, is entirely coincidental.

INDEX

PART 1

LETHAL RACING

CHAPTER 1

Recovery

Three days later, the situation in Deep Woods stabilized somewhat, and the newly appointed governor by the New Pacific Alliance arrived. After Jae-Woo Park completed the handover, he officially set off to leave.

Soon after the grand fleet of starships flew out, an old civilian starship slowly lifted off from the Saya base and entered orbit. Felix Lucas set the destination to Sycamore in District C40 and activated the autopilot.

The return journey felt relaxed. Yuui Hayashi hummed a tune and, for the first time in a while, put on makeup in front of the mirror. After shaping her eyebrows to her satisfaction, she casually remarked, "It's surprising that Jae-Woo Park didn't cause us any trouble."

"No surprise there. After all, Sr. Montclair gave him a big favor," Felix Lucas retorted seriously.

Onyx glanced at him, unfazed by his sarcastic tone.

"Jae-Woo Park is power hungry. You should be grateful it was him; otherwise, it wouldn't have ended so smoothly. Without him holding the fort at the Palace of Unity that night, the remaining S-ranks wouldn't have let us off."

If a fight had broken out, with the other side having heavy weapons and hundreds of A-rank Aberrants, casualties on Saya's side would have been unavoidable.

Speaking of the Palace of Unity, Cora Thornton remembered

another matter. "Punk is dead. Will someone come after us?"

Onyx's lips curled slightly, but there was no humor in his eyes. "Relax, Jae-Woo Park will handle these loose ends. If he can't even manage his own people, he wouldn't be fit to be a special envoy."

Since Onyx said to relax, Cora did. She fiddled with her terminal for a while before suddenly exclaiming, "We're famous!"

The news headlines in Deep Woods were half about the changes the new governor would bring and half speculating about the mysterious F777 team that assassinated Ne Kon due to "personal vendettas." Since all the video footage had been destroyed in a fire, some unofficial media outlets, using their imagination, described F777 as hulking giants and boasted that all members were S-rank.

Everyone chuckled at the ridiculous reports.

Speaking of fame, Yuui pulled up another report. "Felalakas isn't doing too bad either. Look at this video, 'The Dark Horse F777's Road to Victory,' with over sixty million views. Our popularity has now surpassed 'Iron Cafe,' second only to 'The Boss and His Three Goons.'"

"Sycamore too. You repelled a zombie horde before, gaining quite a reputation," Charles Franz commented during a break.

"Don't forget Sin City. The phrase 'My name is Suchat, remember it' is still legendary," Felix added. Suchat, unexpectedly mentioned, stiffened at the memory of his embarrassing slogan.

Cora puffed out her cheeks in mild annoyance. "Grandpa always said to stay low key. Being too famous isn't good."

Onyx reassured her, "The Lucas Network is down, and information between districts spreads slowly. Even if we're famous, it's only in small circles, so you..."

He suddenly hissed in pain.

Charles was stimulating the atrophied nerves in his hand with his power. Despite staying another day in Saya, Onyx's left hand was losing feeling, making even simple grip exercises impossible.

Cora stared at Onyx's legs, knowing he disregarded medical advice and received two nerve blocks because of her. "When we get back to Sycamore, we'll proceed with the surgery."

She poked his hand, speaking earnestly.

"Yes, surgery," Onyx smiled.

"Some people just refuse to give up, claiming they don't need their legs, but deep down, they regret it," Felix multitasked, coding while piloting the starship, and took the chance to mock Onyx.

Onyx gave a scornful laugh. "I figured one useless person on the team is enough. Adding more would only cause trouble."

Felix's movements halted, the words hitting home. His damaged mechanical arm had significantly reduced his combat and coding abilities, which frustrated him to no end.

Felix turned to Cora, seriously saying, "Captain, I request a replacement for my mechanical arm."

"Approved," Cora nodded decisively. Felix's arm was damaged, protecting her, after all.

"This is the materials list." Felix seriously shared a long receipt. Cora's eyes widened, gasping at the cost, which was double the last time.

Onyx took the terminal, glanced at it, and scoffed. "Don't be ridiculous. Pure rhenium? Do you know how much that costs?"

"Rhenium is essential, and I calculated the minimum amount needed," Felix insisted.

"Essential, my foot. Carbon steel or alloy steel works just fine."

"Bicycles work too, so why do humans make starships?"

"With our current resources, you'll have to settle for a bicycle," Onyx retorted, handing the terminal back to Cora.

"Don't spoil him." Felix shrugged, not embarrassed at being caught trying to get away with it.

Since coming to Deep Woods, F777 had focused on assassinating Ne Kon, leaving no time for commissions and thus no income. Cora sighed inwardly. They needed to earn money and uphold her responsibilities as captain.

"Sis!" Damian Blackwood suddenly called out from the window. "Look at this!"

Cora followed his finger. The tops of skyscrapers billowed black smoke. The cross-river bridge was broken, and a thick layer of black covered the ring road and overpasses in a city that was supposed to be modern below them.

"Slow down. Something's not right," Onyx frowned.

Felix reduced the starship's speed and activated the main control panel. The navigation map showed they were over District C77.

Through the wispy clouds, the pervasive blackness seemed to move.

"Should I check it out?" Cora asked.

"Not yet," Felix launched a drone. The external camera zoomed in, approaching the city's airspace. What they saw was unbelievable–the black layer was a mass of zombies!

"This is a dead city," Felix said. The drone's thermal imaging showed no life signs within tens of kilometers.

Cora looked at Onyx. "Which district is this?"

Onyx's expression was grim. "Yggdrasill."

Yggdrasill (District C77), known for its bold and fantastical architectural style, was hailed as the design capital of the Alliance. Designers from Yggdrasill, despite having a lower district number, were valued for their expertise.

Such a once-prosperous and famous C-level city had now become a zombie haven.

"Yggdrasill was C-level. What happened?" Yuui Hayashi wondered aloud.

"It's a zombie horde," Onyx explained, sketching Yggdrasill's terrain. "With its dense population and mountainous, basin-heavy landscape, if a chain zombie horde occurred, it would easily be surrounded and trapped."

"A chain zombie horde..." The group fell silent.

"Let's hope Yggdrasill's tragedy is an exception," Yuui murmured.

However, things didn't go as they hoped. After passing through Yggdrasill, they encountered another C-level city filled with zombies, followed by a series of destroyed D-level cities. The situation grew increasingly dire.

"When we came to Deep Woods, these cities were fine. It's only been half a month. How have they been overrun by zombies?" Yuui couldn't fathom the scene before her. "Even if the number of zombies is increasing, there are more ways to deal with them. It shouldn't be like this."

"Over there, someone," Cora pointed. On a deserted highway, a few figures were scavenging supplies in a gas station's supermarket.

"They're humans," Onyx confirmed. "Ordinary people."

"I'll go ask. Damian, come with me," Cora said.

Felix switched to low-orbit flight, and Cora and Damian jumped off the starship, swiftly moving towards the gas station.

The group comprised seven or eight people, two keeping watch while the others rapidly emptied the supermarket shelves. As Cora approached, she deliberately made some noise to alert them.

"Who's there?!" The two on watch immediately raised their weapons, shouting in panic, "Stay back! We found this place first!"

Damian stepped forward diplomatically. "Uncle and Auntie, we won't come closer. We just want to ask a few questions."

Hearing the commotion, the others rushed out of the supermarket. They were gaunt and wary, even though there were only two of them. "Ask from there, then leave!"

Damian stood obediently. "Brothers and sisters, why are there so many zombies here? Last time my sister and I came, it wasn't like this."

"You don't know?" The responder seemed surprised. "A Zombie Lord appeared nearby. It can command all levels of zombies, and many cities have been destroyed by it."

Cora was shocked. A Zombie Lord capable of commanding all levels of zombies?

In Da Nang, they had encountered a Level 3 zombie. Though it was large and powerful, it couldn't command other zombies. Could this Zombie Lord be a Level 4 zombie?

Back on the starship, F777 held an emergency meeting.

"Based on current information, the Zombie Lord emerged near Yggdrasill and moved east after destroying the C-level city," Onyx analyzed.

"Sycamore is also to the east," Charles said anxiously. "Could it be heading towards Sycamore?"

Deep Woods is in the Alliance's southwest, and Felix Lucas's return route headed northeast, passing through Felalakas and ultimately reaching Sycamore.

Sycamore's outpost, Sakura Refuge, had previously survived a major zombie horde with F777's support. As the medical capital, Sycamore had relatively weak military strength. If it faced the Zombie Lord's army, the crisis would be no less than Yggdrasill's.

Onyx traced the destroyed cities on the map, stopping an inch away from Sycamore.

"Given the Zombie Lord's current path, it's just missing Sycamore." They had just sighed in relief when Onyx's finger slid left a notch.

"But what if it changes course? This area here is more densely populated. We can't be certain how intelligent a Level 4 zombie is."

"Hurry, let's get back to Sycamore," Cora urged.

Sycamore must be protected, not only for the sake of Onyx's leg surgery but also because countless doctors like Lynn Rolling were there, willing to risk their lives to save others. If Sycamore fell, it would be a devastating blow to the entire Alliance.

Felix switched to manual control, and the starship sped up sharply across the sky.

Yuui tried to comfort everyone. "There seem to be fewer zombies here than before. Maybe the Zombie Lord stuck to its original path."

Before she could finish, their terminals suddenly flashed an emergency alert, showing an S-level commission.

"Urgent announcement from the Alliance Headquarters of Aberrants: A chain zombie horde has appeared in Sycamore (District C40). Known zombie numbers are as follows, Level 4: 1, Level 3: 167, Level 2: XXXX. Detected Aberrant zombies total: 1257. All Aberrants in the vicinity are requested to assist immediately. Rewards in Alliance credits will be issued based on the number of zombies killed."

Damn it, Onyx was right. The Zombie Lord is highly intelligent and has indeed changed course!

The starship raced to Sycamore as fast as possible, but the scene upon arrival was horrifying. The ground was ravaged, and the massive zombie horde was even more terrifying than the insect tide Cora had experienced in Blossomville. Compared to the previous large-scale zombie horde in Sakura Refuge, the number had nearly increased tenfold. Even from high above, they couldn't see the end of the horde.

The three front-line refuges were teetering on the brink of collapse. If their defenses fell, Sycamore would have no buffer and be completely exposed to the zombies. On the front lines, many Aberrants were fighting fiercely. Yet, as soon as they killed one wave, another surged forward like an unending tide.

Cora opened the hatch, desperately searching for a landing spot. Just then, the Jade Grove Refuge couldn't hold out any longer. Its defenses were breached, and the zombie horde, seemingly under some command, surged over the walls, uniformly heading toward Sycamore, several kilometers away.

"No!!" Charles grabbed the window, shouting. The flow of air seemed to stop, and everyone's heart was in their throat. Sycamore seemed to emit a faint cry of despair.

As the first wave of zombies was about to leap into the city gates, a golden light suddenly flashed above Sycamore, followed by an invisible barrier that the zombies crashed into. Some were flung away, others piled up on the ground, unable to advance.

"This... a domain power?" Cora, Onyx, Yuui Hayashi, and the others exchanged surprised glances, a name flashing in their minds.

They almost forgot that Sycamore had a domain Aberrant. No! A domain Aberrant dog.

CHAPTER 2

A Zombie Lord

At the critical moment, a domain rose above Sycamore, blocking the flood of zombies.

Cora let out a sigh of relief. Good job, Little Diamond! she cheered silently, though she knew it couldn't hear her. In her mind, she could still hear its lively barks.

Damian clung to Cora's coat, his head poking out of the hatch, nervously releasing his power. Unfortunately, it had little effect; even if he dealt with a batch of zombies, more would follow. Damian had a bit of acrophobia and a severe case of zombie-phobia. His face scrunched up as he asked, "Sister, as long as Little Diamond keeps its domain up, the zombies can't get in, right?"

Before Cora could answer, Onyx shattered Damian's naïve hope. "It's not that simple. Although Little Diamond's domain covers a large area, it's only C-rank and can't sustain it for long."

Domain-type powers require substantial mental strength. Little Diamond previously covered a building in a neighborhood with minimal effort, so it could maintain it for several days. But now, covering an entire city while facing relentless zombie attacks would quickly deplete its power.

"Can you find the Zombie Lord's position?" Cora turned to Felix Lucas.

The zombies below were too dense, a sea of rotten faces and dead white eyes. Among them were over a thousand Aberrant zombies, making it difficult to distinguish anything with their mingled mental power.

Felix deployed all the drones, quickly sending them in different directions to scan the zombies.

Cora and Suchat were better suited for single combat, not large-scale horde battles. Rushing in without a plan could easily get them killed. The best strategy was to locate and eliminate the Zombie Lord.

"Bang—bang—"

Zombies at the city gate frantically smashed against the domain. The golden light flickered briefly before returning to normal. In that momentary lapse, hundreds of zombies broke through. Little Diamond was struggling.

The night was pitch-black, stars twinkling. Suddenly, engine roars came from all directions! Various steamers, hover cars, and ornate boats, new and old, arrived in time. Bright bursts of power from Aberrants lit up the scene—wind, thunder, fire, ice—causing thousands of zombies to fall, creating a clear zone in front of Sycamore's gate.

These were Aberrants from other regions coming to support! Whether for the S-rank commission or to help Sycamore, their arrival was crucial.

With the pressure at the gate easing, Sycamore's counterattack began. Armored vehicles rumbled across the ground. Led by Conrad Kennedy, the security team members bravely charged the zombie horde with flamethrowers and fire cannons.

Even ordinary citizens climbed the walls, throwing "sandbags" onto the battlefield. Glass bottles shattered against zombies or the ground, emitting slight crackling sounds. When hit by flamethrowers and cannon fire, they caused intense chemical reactions—corrosive, combustible, explosive. The pungent smell of chemicals spread, showcasing the unique zombie-killing methods of the medical capital.

"Found it." Felix zoomed in on the image, revealing a distinctive zombie in the middle of the horde.

It stood over three meters tall, not as high as a Level 3 zombie, but with powerful muscles and writhing black veins across its chest. More horrifying were the two giant hand-like wings on its back, each claw larger than half its body.

Just like in Da Nang, Cora calmly raised her heavy crossbow, aimed, and fired!

The bolt flew straight at the Zombie Lord's head, but an Aberrant zombie nearby stomped the ground, causing a tremor that deflected the bolt with large chunks of earth. This was a classic earth-type power usage.

Cora's eyes narrowed. As expected, the Zombie Lord could command other zombies.

Felix lowered the starship to the minimum height, and Cora, Suchat, Yuui, and Damian jumped down. "I'll go kill the Zombie Lord. You support me," Cora ordered.

Yuui followed Suchat, boosting the surrounding Aberrants with her supportive abilities. The others heard her melodious singing, felt a surge of energy, and fought faster and more effectively. While an A-rank support Aberrant had limited combat power, their battlefield effects were invaluable.

Cora conjured her twin blades and charged toward the Zombie Lord. Her speed was incredible, almost a blur. Before the zombie horde could react, she was already upon them. With a powerful leap, she cut into the battlefield from the side, slashing at the Zombie Lord. Sensing danger, it turned and swung its four claws at her.

But Cora's blades were faster. "Clang—" The sharp edges struck the bulging wings but couldn't cut through. The Zombie Lord's claws collided with her blades, producing a teeth-grating sound.

Cora landed smoothly after a backflip, realizing the wings were like steel armor, glinting with a metallic sheen. This was... a power? The Zombie Lord had powers? No, she quickly deduced. It lacked mental power, but many Aberrant zombies around it could have used their powers to protect it at the crucial moment.

The Zombie Lord agilely avoided Cora's attack range, leaping onto a collapsed station. Its dead white eyes fixed on Cora, it lowered its head and let out a deep growl.

Several Level 3 zombies jumped from the flanks, while more agile Aberrant zombies formed a rear guard, surrounding Cora in a V-formation. In front, high-level zombies were ready to attack; behind, the Zombie Lord watched. She was trapped deep within enemy lines.

Cora realized that the Zombie Lord's most challenging aspect wasn't its strength but its ability to command other zombies, forming an army. Her twin blades glowed with a blue hue as her mental power surged. She didn't flee but confronted it head-on.

On the starship, Onyx observed the zombies surrounding Cora, his gaze turning cold. "They're using a triangular attack formation."

"What's a triangular attack formation?" Charles asked.

Onyx explained, "It's a formation that relies on coordination between infantry and cavalry to outflank and attack. I never expected zombies to use tactics. This Zombie Lord might have been a battlefield commander before."

Charles's face showed shock. "You mean the Zombie Lord has human memories? Then why is it attacking humans?"

Onyx stared at the Zombie Lord's hideous appearance and slowly shook his head. "No, it's definitely a zombie. I'm more inclined to believe it keeps human intelligence."

"If it has intelligence, can't you just control it and we can clear this level?" Felix Lucas's thinking was always outside the box.

Level 4 zombies were as strong as A-rank Aberrants. Onyx thought it was unlikely, but still released his mental power to probe. As expected, he encountered resistance. "It has a mental barrier, similar to Little Diamond's domain."

"Oh? It can even guard against this. Its intelligence must be quite high," Felix remarked, intrigued.

"Congratulations, you've synchronized with the zombie's brainwaves, but unfortunately, it's smarter than you," Onyx couldn't resist a jab at Felix.

The barrier wasn't the Zombie Lord's own; it had no mental power. It was using the abilities of other Aberrant zombies. In simple terms, the Zombie Lord was like a worker who knew how to use every tool and placed them in the most effective positions.

"I think I understand how Yggdrasill was destroyed. This Zombie Lord is terrifying," Charles Franz sighed. "This might be the most cunning opponent we've faced," Onyx said solemnly.

Under the base station, Cora's twin blades slashed through the side defenses fiercely. She faced dozens of high-level zombies alone, unaffected even when their filthy blood splattered on her.

Ancient military strategies emphasized "winning first, then fighting," meaning victorious armies create the conditions for success before engaging the enemy. When the situation turns unfavorable, they must "preserve their strength for future battles."

The Zombie Lord watched its dwindling horde and the impenetrable defenses of Sycamore. It scraped the ground with its claws, appearing to ponder.

In the center of the battlefield, Suchat's poison mist quickly harvested zombie lives.

Yuui followed closely, reminding him, "Damian, stay close."

"Okay," Damian responded dutifully.

However, the chaotic situation changed in an instant. Zombies occasionally pounced, and Damian's short legs and timid nature gradually distanced him from Yuui. Fortunately, he was near the city gate, with other Aberrants and the security team nearby, so he wasn't in immediate danger.

Damian mechanically and numbly shot ice spikes into the zombie crowd. The sheer number ensured he hit plenty, even with random throws.

With various powers flying around, cannons and flamethrowers in use, and chemical bottles bursting, Damian couldn't help but wonder if friendly fire was a concern.

Unfortunately, bad luck struck. An Aberrant-created tornado veered off course, picking up zombies in its path. Whether it was because of a lack of control or the weight of the zombies, the eye of the storm drifted, heading straight for Damian.

Cursing his own bad luck, Damian turned to flee. But his short legs and lightweight saw him swept up in no time.

The tornado carried him for several seconds, tossing him around like a laundry machine.

Dizzy, he was finally thrown to the ground behind the Jade Grove Refuge, where he landed with a thud.

Dizzy and disoriented, Damian stood up shakily, only to face several zombies.

It was strange to describe zombies as "expressionless," but these just squatted or stood around with faces devoid of aggression or malice, appearing utterly indifferent to the battlefield.

Damian forgot about his precarious situation, his first thought being: Can zombies be lazy too?

One zombie approached him—no, it walked on two legs. Its hair was in an ugly braid, hinting at its once-female identity. Damian noticed its low decay, with only some corpse markings on its neck and cloudy gray eyes, otherwise appearing quite human.

The braid-headed zombie extended a claw, making Damian shiver. He secretly formed an ice spike behind his back. Suddenly, he was pushed over, rolling onto the ground and landing on his rear.

The zombie seemed amused, turning and making guttural sounds. The other zombies gathered, forming a circle around Damian like a gang of bullies, pushing him around like a rag doll.

The bizarre zombies found their fun, neither killing him nor attacking the city. They just played with Damian like a softball.

Damian was dumbfounded. Was he being bullied by zombies?

Suddenly, a deep roar from the Zombie Lord in Sycamore's direction echoed, summoning the horde within several kilometers to retreat. They abandoned the fight and scattered like a receding tide.

The Zombie Lord had given up the siege! Sycamore was safe!

Thunderous cheers erupted as excited Aberrants and the security team pursued the fleeing zombies, driving them far away.

The zombies around Damian exchanged glances—yes, they actually made "glancing" motions. The braid-headed zombie withdrew its claws, and the others followed it, silently blending into the horde, disappearing from sight.

Covered in dirt, Damian stood up, bewildered.

CHAPTER 3

The Fallens

The zombie horde quickly retreated, with Aberrants in hot pursuit, trying to earn more points by killing as many zombies as possible.

Cora watched the back of the Zombie Lord. Its two pairs of strong, fleshy wings didn't hinder its movement but made it even more formidable. It moved swiftly on all fours, leaping several times before disappearing beyond the horizon, followed by a group of minions.

Realizing they couldn't kill it this time, Cora crossed her twin blades, slowly sheathing them on her back.

She returned to the starship's location, meeting up with Onyx and the others. Soon, Yuui and Suchat returned, but Damian was nowhere to be seen. "Where's Damian?" Cora asked.

"He was just here. Where did that kid run off to?" Yuui found it strange as well.

"Damian, where are you?" Cora sent a message in the F777 group chat. After a couple of seconds, Damian responded with a crying emoji, followed by a voice message. When Cora played it, she heard heavy breathing, as if he was running, "Wait for me!"

As long as he was safe, Cora jumped onto the low-hovering starship, letting one leg dangle, and sat comfortably by the hatch, waiting.

The Alliance Aberrants Headquarters issued directly by the S-rank commission to defend Sycamore. As long as the terminal's real-time recording function was activated, it would automatically calculate the number of zombies killed and issue the corresponding rewards. This time, Cora mainly targeted evolved and Aberrant zombies. She received nearly 100,000 Alliance credits, instantly elevating her from broke to relatively wealthy.

S-rank commissions were indeed lucrative. Cora counted the balance in her personal account, silently marveling.

In the distance, several hover cars chased after the zombie horde, launching group attacks without restraint.

Cora sensed mental power and followed it with her eyes, discovering that the Aberrants in the vehicles were all very strong and coordinated. They had been the ones to first intercept the zombie horde, allowing the armored vehicles of the security team to emerge from the city.

On top of one of the hover cars, a tall young man kneeled in a standard sniper pose, a night vision scope obscuring much of his face. He fired rapidly, almost without aiming, hitting one headshot per second. The specialized explosive bullets pierced the zombies' foreheads, instantly turning their heads into shattered watermelon pieces, causing surrounding zombies to be blasted away in a violent display.

Cora observed for a moment, noticing that this man not only had impeccable marksmanship but also targeted evolved and Aberrant zombies, much like she did. As the hover car passed by, his terminal emitted a series of public notifications.

"You have killed 1 Level 3 zombie, 276 regular zombies, earning 5760 points and xxxx Alliance credits." "You have killed 3 Aberrant zombies, 155 regular zombies, earning 4550 points and xxxx Alliance credits." "You have killed..."

The kill notifications kept scrolling.

The man's black hair was blown back by the night wind, a ruby earring in his left ear glinting, exuding a rebellious and flamboyant air.

Cora waited for about twenty minutes until the zombie horde was out of sight and the pursuing Aberrants returned. Some left Sycamore, while others applied for temporary admission to rest in the city. Damian finally arrived, albeit late.

"Damian, were you slacking off?" Yuui teased.

Sure enough, Damian looked like a little pig that had rolled in the mud, covered in sweat and dirt, with his curly hair wet and clinging to his forehead, looking very messy.

"I wasn't!" Damian panted, his cheeks rosy. The mention of slacking off reminded him of the braid-headed man, making him angry. That tornado had blown him several kilometers away, and he had run back on foot. If it weren't for his Aberrant ability and superior physical strength, he would have been exhausted.

This wasn't the place to talk. The seven of them headed towards the city gate. By now, most of the Aberrants had dispersed, but a few hover cars were parked at the checkpoint, surrounded by a dozen people. The sniper stood at the front, and to their surprise, Sycamore's governor, Julian Chang, had come out to greet them. As they approached, they overheard their conversation.

"Yes, Officer Scarlett arrived at District C83 recently. Hearing about Sycamore's plight, she sent us immediately to assist," the young man said.

"Scarlett Holland is kind. Please thank her on my behalf. We couldn't have managed without you today," Julian Chang sighed.

"You're welcome," the young man replied politely, in contrast to his flamboyant presence. "Officer Scarlett specifically instructed that with zombie hordes becoming more frequent, Sycamore must be fully prepared. She is stationed in District B and can't interfere with District C's affairs directly, so she pulled some strings to send two specialists to support your efforts."

Two scholarly-looking individuals stepped out from the hover car's backseat.

"This is Julie Robinson, a B-rank engineering Aberrant who once served as the director of the Fifth Design Institute. She has conducted extensive research on zombie horde attack patterns and will help upgrade Sycamore's defenses."

Julie Robinson, around forty, dressed in simple work clothes, carried a white briefcase, looking competent. Julian Chang, urgently needing engineering talent, was visibly pleased upon learning her identity and eagerly shook her hand.

"And this is Hinata Takahashi, a biogen scientist and one of the first outstanding graduates of the Lausanne Training Program. Hearing about Sycamore's research on anti-zombification drugs, he volunteered to come and collaborate."

Hinata Takahashi, in his early thirties and slender, adjusted his high-prescription glasses and bowed to Julian Chang. "I look forward to working with you."

"Dr. Takahashi, you're too modest. Being selected for the Lausanne Program means you're one of the top researchers in the Alliance. We should be the ones learning from you. With your help, we will surely develop the anti-zombification drug quickly." Julian Chang waved his hand in gratitude.

Cora and her group stepped forward, and Onyx greeted Julian Chang. "Dr. Chang, good to see you again."

"It's you," Julian Chang relaxed and smiled warmly at them. "Thank you for your support. Sycamore's doors are always open to you."

Onyx smiled, "The main reason we're here this time is for a surgery..."

Julian Chang interrupted, "What kind of surgery? If you need anything, I can help arrange it..."

As the two conversed, Cora noticed something unusual about the scientist Hinata Takahashi. His gaze swept over the group and paused, staring intently at Onyx. His expression changed from confusion and surprise to disbelief.

Hinata Takahashi's lips moved as if he wanted to say something, but in the end, he remained silent. Cora followed his line of sight, but saw nothing unusual on Onyx's clean face.

The young man waited patiently for Onyx and Julian Chang to finish their conversation before continuing, "To prevent another zombie horde attack, we will stay in Sycamore for two days, ready to assist at any time."

"We dare not impose," Julian Chang waved his hand again, "Thank you all for your efforts."

The young man led his group, including Julie Robinson and Hinata Takahashi, into the city. Julian Chang assigned two subordinates to arrange their accommodation. Once they had walked away, Julian Chang exhaled slightly, finally relaxing.

"Dr. Chang, who are those people? They seem quite influential," Yuui seized the opportunity to ask.

"They certainly are," Julian Chang explained. "They're from

Northern Base (District B10). The leader is Silver Owl, the captain of the Aberrant team 'Tustan.' He's an Aberrant with strength close to S-rank, and quite famous even in District B."

"Northern Base's deputy governor, Scarlett Holland, was my classmate. Hearing about Sycamore's crisis, she sent her Aberrants to support us, since she was near District C."

Julian Chang spoke highly of his old classmate, who sent both technical experts and combat personnel without asking for money or repayment, an act of goodwill. Yet, he sighed deeply for reasons unknown.

Once inside Sycamore, they walked along the central street for a short while before Cora witnessed an amusing scene.

A local woman was pushing a stroller tent, surrounded by enthusiastic residents. Dressed in new clothes, Little Diamond sat inside, tongue out and smiling. The locals were showering the stroller with snacks and chew toys, almost overwhelming the dog with their enthusiasm. Finally, unable to bear it, Little Diamond activated its domain, bouncing everyone away except itself and its mother.

Those bounced away were surprisingly happy, excitedly speaking in strange phrases Little Diamond couldn't understand.

After all, Little Diamond was now a hero of Sycamore, having saved the lives of everyone in the city.

Cora squeezed through the crowd and waved at Little Diamond. It had been months since they last met. Would it still remember them? Recognizing her, Little Diamond barked happily, showing that its memory was indeed intact.

After exchanging a few words with Little Diamond's mother and promising to visit later, Cora and her team squeezed out of the crowd. They didn't need to rent an apartment this time, as Charles needed to reissue his ID and coordinate the surgery at the hospital. Thus, F777 stayed at his place.

Damian finally found a chance to vent, angrily recounting how the braid-headed man bullied him. However, the others were focused on different details.

"Did it braid your hair nicely?" Yuui teased.

"So, they just hit you but didn't bite you?" Charles Franz questioned skeptically.

"Are you sure you're being objective?" Suchat doubted Damian's account.

"I! Am! Sure!" Damian shouted, jumping up in frustration.

Cora, however, fell silent.

A zombie with obvious corpse marks yet a rational mind, able to resist the urge to bite... she had seen such zombies before.

Not only had she seen them, but she had also saved them. Six months ago, when Cora left Fool's Wharf in District F177, Mrs. Travers and Little Travers already displayed typical zombie characteristics, but still kept a bit of consciousness.

"Plan Eternity," Onyx suddenly mentioned, introducing an unfamiliar term. The group looked at him in confusion.

"Plan Eternity is a secret research project on mutated organisms. By controlling radiation variables within the organism, it stimulates continuous cell division and renewal, extending the lifespan and awakening of unique abilities. When radiation stabilizes, it can achieve an unending consciousness and an eternal physical form. The goal of this research is to achieve human 'evolution.'"

"If we apply the same concept to zombies, ordinary zombies, the lowest level, are purely failed products. Evolved zombies are failed products trying to save themselves; though their rotting bodies persist, they are mindless monsters. Aberrant zombies are successful failures, awakening abilities, but losing consciousness forever."

"Researchers hypothesized about the possibility of a zombie keeping a clear consciousness and a firm body. They named this new species 'Fallens.'"

"Unfortunately, the study of Fallens would trigger a series of ethical issues and was soon halted. The project personnel became very secretive about it."

"Why?" Cora asked, puzzled.

"Because they feared it. Humanity prides itself on its unique consciousness, distinguishing it from other species."

"So, when zombies have clear consciousness, are they still monsters, or are they humans evolved in another way?"

CHAPTER 4

Onyx

Sycamore Bay, Ninth Hospital.

As a top-tier facility within the Alliance and renowned for its exceptional orthopedics department, the tenth floor was always bustling with patients. Today, it was especially crowded after last night's wave of zombies. Hundreds of stragglers had breached the city, and though the residents fought back fiercely, many were injured. Now, aside from the radiation department on the thirteenth floor, the surgical wing was the busiest.

"Ding—" The elevator doors opened on the tenth floor, revealing a figure in a white lab coat. The man's slender back and neatly tied hair made him easily recognizable. He moved quickly and confidently through the corridor, stopping at what used to be his office.

He had arrived early, but to his surprise, a group of people had beaten him there, including several hospital leaders.

"Oh, my god... My god..." "Director, it's really you! You've finally come back!" "We missed you so much."

The man in the lab coat looked up, revealing a pair of mature, world-weary eyes. It was Charles Franz.

The hospital director, who was privy to some inside information, stepped forward and grasped Charles's shoulders, examining his gaunt face. In a low voice, he said, "I heard about the assassination of Ne Win and his son. You... well, justice was served, and it was their karma. Charles, it's time to move on. Stop punishing yourself."

The director didn't know about Charles's connection to District F777. He simply assumed Charles had finally pulled himself together after hearing of Ne Win's death and getting his revenge.

Lynn Rolling stumbled slightly as she rushed down from the thirteenth floor, skidding to a halt in front of Charles. Normally composed and decisive, she found herself with teary eyes. The light she had always chased had finally returned, and at that moment, she wanted nothing more than to cry as she gazed at Charles.

Charles removed his mask and nodded at his former colleagues and superiors. "Director, everyone, I'm sorry to have worried you."

"Time is short, so I'll be brief. There's a patient with a special condition who needs immediate surgery, and I must be the one to perform it. Although I'm no longer a practicing doctor at this hospital, I'd like to request the use of the operating room..."

"What are you talking about? I never approved of your resignation. It's still sitting on my desk," the director said with a chuckle. "You performing surgery is a rare learning opportunity. Who wants to assist?"

"I'll be the first assistant," Lynn quickly volunteered.

"Me! Me, me! I'll be the second assistant. I'm great with retraction and stabilization!" "Then I'll handle wiping the director's hands and sweat!" "Can I... can I just stand by and watch?"

"Charles, when do you need the operating room? I'll coordinate everything," the director asked. "As soon as possible," Charles replied in a grave tone. "The patient can't wait any longer."

VIP Room 7.

Since dawn, the remaining sensation in Onyx's right hand had vanished. This meant he could no longer move independently. His muscles were atrophying, and his nerve cells were dying at a terrifying speed. He was gradually losing control over his own body.

Cora kept her head down. Onyx's right leg, from ankle to thigh, was starkly different from his healthy left one. Lying down, the deformity of his right leg was glaringly obvious—shorter, thinner, and visibly twisted. It was far from aesthetically pleasing.

Cora returned after paying the fees, only to find that Charles had already gathered the medical assistant and anesthesiologist, preparing to move Onyx to the operating room.

She took a few quick steps to follow but was stopped by Yuui. "Cora, I need to make a trip to the Fifth Hospital. It's pretty chaotic out there right now. Want to come with me?"

Cora pointed to the tall figure standing nearby. "I've got Suchat with me; it's safe." Yuui hesitated, realizing she had forgotten to dismiss the tactless Suchat as planned.

"Captain, I need to buy some materials," Felix suddenly spoke up.

"I gave you the money, didn't I?" Cora hugged her terminal tightly. Felix was like a money-eating beast, leaving her wallet almost empty. "I don't know the way," Felix replied earnestly.

"Huh? Do you want me to go with you?" Cora asked.

"Yes." Felix retracted his remaining four mechanical arms, sitting back in his wheelchair, his silver hair quietly draping over his shoulders like a frail young man.

Cora hesitated, looking at him. Felix really hadn't been to Sycamore before, so it made sense that he didn't know his way around, but something felt off to her.

Charles, sensing something, gently persuaded. "I'm well aware of Onyx's condition. The surgery's major challenge is in repairing the broken bones, and it will take a long time. There's no need for you to wait at the hospital. We'll contact you as soon as it's done."

Cora shuffled her feet on the ground, finally muttering, "... Oh."

After leaving the hospital, Yuui and Suchat headed to the Fifth Hospital, while Cora and Damian accompanied Felix to buy modification materials. They hadn't visited over two shops before Felix suddenly insisted on going solo.

Cora paused the navigation projection, her eyes filled with confusion. Wasn't he the one who didn't know the way? Didn't he ask her to accompany him?

Felix coolly retorted, "You're too slow."

All four of his battered mechanical arms rose simultaneously— three on the left, with only one lonely arm on the right—making Felix resemble a limping spider. He didn't need any navigation, expertly weaving through the streets and alleys, quickly disappearing from view.

It suddenly dawned on Cora—Felix, an S-Class hacker, not knowing his way around? Impossible! She was the one who didn't know the way!

With nothing better to do, Cora and Damian headed to the shelter to complete some tasks and earn some NPA credits.

The S-Class mission to defend Sycamore was still open for now. The stench of the decaying corpses hit like a punch as people could still see zombies wandering outside Sakura, with piles of decaying corpses forming small mountains beneath the high walls. But the rewards for killing zombies in the area were especially generous.

The two worked in perfect sync—Damian casting wide bursts of ice and snow, while Cora darted among the frozen zombies, swiftly taking them down.

"Braids!"

In the middle of the fight, Damian suddenly pointed at something. Cora followed his gaze and spotted a zombie standing out from the others in the distance. While the other zombies had their heads raised, sniffing the air for any trace of the living, this one had its head lowered as if searching for something.

Before she could react, Damian, like a runaway horse, charged ahead. With their guardian backing him up today, he boldly planted himself in front of the zombie with braids, hands on his hips, and shouted, "Come at me!"

The wandering zombies swarmed towards him as Damian frantically fended them off, while the braided zombie stayed put, staring at him thoughtfully. Cora studied it.

From its appearance, this female zombie looked about thirteen or fourteen years old, not much older than Damian.

Once Cora confirmed the surroundings were safe, the braided zombie emitted some garbled sounds from its throat, circling Damian and occasionally reaching out with a claw to swipe at him. But today, Damian was ready, dodging nimbly like a playful little chick, laughing gleefully as he ran.

Over the past six months, Damian had been dragged around with them, facing death and assassination attempts, forced to mature far too quickly. He rarely played without a care. But after all, he was still a child at heart, with no peers around to keep him company. Who would've thought he'd end up playing with a zombie?

After a while, the braided zombie suddenly perked up its ears as if hearing something, then dashed off towards the city walls. Damian, still unsatisfied, waved at its retreating figure. "Bye-bye~"

Cora finished the remaining zombies nearby and walked over to Damian. "Let's go back."

Damian took her hand, nodding obediently. "Okay."

Outside the high walls of Sakura Shelter, several hover cars were circling at low altitude. The area was bathed in the powerful attacks of Anopowered abilities, with flashes of dazzling light exploding one after another. Zombie bodies were blown apart repeatedly. Cora recognized it was the "Tustan" Anopowered team clearing the zombie horde.

A swift figure darted past, and the braided zombie that had been playing with Damian moments ago suddenly rushed into the smoke, clutching the nearly severed remains of a zombie and howling in grief. It was strange, but Cora could see an expression of something like "pain" on its face.

The hover cars pursued, and the Anopowered being known as Silver Owl leaped onto the roof, setting up an assault rifle, clearly preparing to fire.

"Big Sis..." Damian tugged at Cora's sleeve, whispering. "Little D, it's a zombie," Cora knew what he was thinking.

Damian shook his head, stubbornly explaining, "No, it's not a zombie. It's... a Fallen."

After hearing Onyx explain the origins of the Fallens, Cora had mixed feelings about this group of outsiders. Although they weren't exactly human, they also shouldn't be crudely classified as zombies.

"Big Sis..." Damian pleaded again.

"Alright." Cora patted Damian's head and then dashed forward like an arrow released from a bowstring.

Silver Owl had also noticed the uniqueness of this zombie. He aimed and fired; the bullets striking with pinpoint accuracy.

"Bang!" The shotgun pellets clattered against an eerie blue shield. Cora used the cover of the shield to push the braided zombie away in the chaos.

The zombie, sensing something, dragged its almost bisected companion and fled.

One stray pellet ricocheted back near the hover car, exploding on impact and eliciting a round of curses.

"Go, go, go! Up, up!" "Damn, that almost took off my foot!" "Captain, even you miss sometimes, huh? Hahaha!"

Silver Owl jumped down from the car roof, his gaze fixed on Cora, who had just appeared out of nowhere. "What's the deal? Stealing a zombie from me?"

He wasn't wearing his goggles today. Dressed in camouflage combat gear, with his pants tucked into black military boots, he looked strong and agile. As Cora got closer, she noticed that Silver Owl's pupils were a pale shade of gray.

Knowing she was in the wrong, Cora sluggishly tried to make an excuse. "Sorry... my hand slipped." Although she didn't mean it that way, the words came out sounding like a challenge.

Silver Owl chuckled, the ruby earring on his ear catching the light. In a universal language, he said, "Lady, do you think I'm easy to fool?"

He tossed aside the assault rifle and charged at her in a blur, leading with a powerful elbow strike and a straight hook.

Cora, with no Ethereal Artifacts to summon, met him barehanded. She raised her left knee, leveraging the force from the ground to spring into the air, launching a fierce spinning kick at his throat.

Silver Owl ducked, countering with a punch aimed at her cheek. The sudden shift in angle made Cora uncomfortable, but she deftly twisted mid-air, kicking away his wrist.

They landed, colliding, and without a word, continued to exchange blows. Surprisingly, Silver Owl wasn't just skilled in sniping; his close-quarters combat was also exceptional. He consistently found awkward angles to disrupt Cora's fluid attacks. After exchanging over a hundred moves, they were still evenly matched.

Noticing that Silver Owl was dueling with someone, the other Anopowered beings didn't intervene. After clearing out the nearby zombies, they all jumped down from the cars to watch, even egging them on with whistles and cheers.

Cora grew increasingly frustrated. She couldn't fully use her strength, and the more they fought, the more annoyed she became. Suddenly, she switched tactics, swiftly locking onto his arm with a shoulder hold, violently twisting his joint.

"Bang!" They both slammed into the dusty ground, with Silver Owl landing on his back. Cora pinned his left arm with her knee and used both hands to lock his right, pulling it up to stop him from moving.

"I really didn't mean to steal your zombie," Cora explained, exasperated, as she straddled him.

Silver Owl laughed boldly. "I've figured out your weakness."

Cora blinked in confusion. "Huh? What?"

Silver Owl grinned. "My Anopower is seeing through an enemy's weaknesses. You're impressive, hardly showing any weak spots during a fight."

Cora's lips curled into a modest smile. "I guess."

"And you? What's your Anopower?" Silver Owl asked, staring at her face. It seemed like he saw two small dimples earlier. Since he asked so directly, Cora answered honestly, "Metal manipulation, object transformation."

"So, you were going easy on me?" he smirked.

"You didn't use your gun," Cora pointed out, then sincerely added, "I'll make up for the lost zombie."

"Got it. Now let me go," Silver Owl replied.

Cora loosened her knee and stood, but Silver Owl suddenly sprang up, pushing her forward by the shoulders while hooking her ankle with his leg. Cora lost her balance, "Bang!"—sand and gravel flew as they both fell again, this time with Silver Owl on top, his hand protectively cradling the back of her head.

Cora glared at him angrily. Silver Owl propped himself up on his elbows, smirking as he touched his earring. "Now we're even."

Cora slowly got up, silently dusting herself off. Damian rushed over to help brush off the dirt from her clothes.

The rest of the Tustan team had already cleared the zombies outside the walls.

Just then, Hinata Takahashi, flanked by two Anopowered beings, approached.

"The sample coverage is still insufficient; we should collect more..." he was saying, but his words trailed off the moment he spotted Cora.

He froze for a couple of seconds, gathering his courage before stamping forward. "Hello, we met at the city gate yesterday. Do you remember?" he asked cautiously. Cora nodded.

Takahashi continued, "Can I ask you something?"

Cora wasn't so easily fooled. "You first. Speak."

"Are your friends the ones with the two people in wheelchairs?"

"Yes."

"Could you tell me the name of the man in the wheelchair, the one whose legs are perfectly fine?" Takahashi's tone suddenly turned urgent.

"What do you want with him?" Cora's expression became wary. This guy had already seemed odd yesterday, and now he was acting all worked up—definitely suspicious.

"I-I mean no harm. I just want to know his name. He... he looks so much like someone I know; there might be some connection!" Takahashi seemed desperate. "I'm not a bad person, really. My name is Hinata Takahashi. I'm thirty-five years old, graduated from Askar First Military Academy, majoring in biology..."

Afraid that Cora wouldn't believe him, Takahashi quickly pulled up all his credentials on his terminal, laying out his entire background. Silver Owl, along with the rest of the Tustan team, gathered around, but they didn't interrupt the conversation, simply standing nearby with their arms crossed, watching.

Cora glanced at Takahashi's information. The endless list of honors and incomprehensible research paper titles swarmed before her like tiny bugs, making her dizzy after just one look.

"Can you tell me?" Takahashi asked eagerly.

Was there any reason to keep Onyx de Montclair's name a secret? Not really. Ever since they met, whether dealing with the Azures or various officials, Onyx had never hesitated to introduce himself.

"His name is Onyx de Montclair," Cora said.

Takahashi looked like lightning, his terminal slipping from his hands and crashing to the ground had struck him.

"That's impossible... He can't possibly be Onyx!"

CHAPTER 5

His Name

"He absolutely cannot be Onyx de Montclair!" Hinata Takahashi declared firmly.

"Hinata, if you shout any louder, you'll have the zombies coming back," Silver Owl teased lightly.

"Ah! Sorry, sorry." Hinata quickly realized his overreaction and lowered his voice, apologizing.

"We should talk in the car; it's not safe down here," Silver Owl suggested.

"No need," Cora Thornton immediately refused.

Silver Owl chuckled softly and said nothing more. He raised his hand towards the sky, and a hover car slowly approached. With a swift push of his hand, he leaped into the car.

Cora stared at Hinata, speaking slowly, "Why can't he be Onyx de Montclair?"

Hinata sighed, "Do you know Jasper M.?"

Cora shook her head confidently, "No."

"How about Dr. M?"

Cora continued to shake her head. "No."

Hinata hesitated for a few seconds, "... You know about the Arashi Research, right?"

This time, Cora nodded, "Yes." She had heard about it from Onyx.

Hinata breathed a sigh of relief. "Jasper, also known as Dr. Montclair, is a pioneering biologist and a key figure in genetic modification. The Arashi Research was initially established to pool the research capabilities of the entire Alliance to support his work to the fullest extent."

"The gene splicing and DNA recombination projects led by Jasper shattered the boundaries of biological species, truly realizing the transfer of genetic information across species. It's the greatest scientific achievement since the New Era began!" Hinata grew more excited as he spoke, a certain fervor shining in his eyes, "My lifelong dream is to join the research group he supervises!"

Cora silently opened her terminal and searched for this Jasper Z. The results spanned thousands of pages. Compared to Jasper's accolades, Hinata's titles seemed trivial.

Cora skimmed through Jasper's biography, which was filled with dense professional descriptions, making her feel dizzy and light-headed, almost giving her words fatigue.

In her haze, she only remembered "the greatest scientist of the New Era," and "Father of Arashi."

Silver Owl emerged from the hover car and, from a distance, tossed two bottles to Cora. "Catch."

Cora caught them with both hands and looked down to see that they were specialty drinks for Aberrants, exclusively to the Northern Base, sealed and marked with a code. These didn't seem like the usual market products.

Cora glanced up at Silver Owl, who made a drinking gesture. Cora handed one bottle to Damian Blackwood and kept the other in her hand, without drinking it.

"What's the connection between Jasper and Onyx?" she persisted in asking Hinata.

"Of course there's a connection...." Hinata's voice unconsciously grew louder, but under Silver Owl's gaze, he quickly lowered it again, "There's a connection!"

"Jasper once gave a lecture in Askar, and I was incredibly lucky to be selected to attend. I remember it clearly; during the Q&A session, someone asked if he deliberately kept a low profile on the StarNet, because everyone called him Jasper or Dr. Montclair, not knowing his real name."

"Jasper said no. He avoided public images to prevent unnecessary trouble. As for his real name, since the pronunciation in common is awkward, people are more accustomed to calling him Jasper."

"Oh, so our Onyx is Jasper?" Cora naturally assumed that it wasn't surprising Onyx knew so much, considering he was some big-shot scientist.

Hinata shook his head gravely, "No, that lecture was when I was fifteen."

Cora's eyes widened slightly.

"Twenty years have passed. How could someone not change at all, and even look younger and healthier?" Hinata couldn't help but mutter to himself, "Even if he looks exactly the same, your friend cannot be THAT Onyx!"

Perhaps because he had been cooped up in the lab for so long, that rare public appearance by Jasper showed him looking not so well. His hair was messy, his skin pale, and there were huge dark circles under his eyes. He appeared extremely fatigued.

"Did your friend use Jasper's genetic information for facial reconstruction?" Hinata suddenly thought of something, speaking faster and faster, "Even if it was just for cosmetic surgery, how could he steal Jasper's real name? It's shameless, absolutely shameless!"

"Is it illegal?" Cora asked with a blank expression.

"No, it's not illegal....." Hinata looked at her with reproach, "But it's unethical! No matter how much you admire Jasper, you have to be rational! Even if he looks like Jasper, his biological information can't be changed. He can never become Jasper!"

"Oh." Cora responded flatly.

Hinata felt indignant and said with righteous anger, "You should advise him to change back to his original appearance. I can offer help...."

"We're leaving." Cora ignored his chatter, grabbed Damian's hand, and started walking towards the entrance of Sakura.

"Wait," Silver Owl blocked her way, "What's your name?"

Cora, now tired of hearing about names, brushed past him without turning her head. "None of your business."

"You should advise him!" Hinata continued shouting after them.

Cora and Damian sat side by side on a park bench, sipping their drinks. Damian daintily sipped through a straw, his legs swinging back and forth, while Cora boldly ripped open the can and downed half of it in one gulp. She instantly felt refreshed, with even a slight boost in her mental energy.

Cora couldn't believe Onyx was the person Hinata Takahashi described—obsessed with Jasper to the point of altering his appearance to look like him.

From the beginning, Onyx had claimed to be a researcher from the Arashi Research Institute, and he was indeed quite familiar with Arashi. If he were impersonating Jasper, wouldn't it be easy to expose him?

And then there was his ID. Jeremy Wolfgang had verified it, concluding that it was "authentic" and "highly authorized."

The Azures wouldn't make a mistake, would they? This showed that, at the very least, Onyx's credentials were real. If he wasn't actually "Jasper Montclair," then how did he get those documents?

Even if Jasper wasn't frequent in the public eye, he was still a prominent figure with extensive search results. Someone would recognize him and know what he looked like. Why wouldn't Onyx choose a more ordinary appearance if he were going to alter his looks? Why it is Jasper's?

And the most crucial question: Why did he change his genetic information?

As her thoughts drifted, Cora's mind wandered further. If Onyx wasn't "Onyx," then who was he?

Cora pressed her hands to her face in frustration and exhaled. Onyx had said that as long as she asked, he wouldn't lie to her. But... did she really want to ask?

"Onyx is a huge liar," Damian muttered as he sipped his drink, finally finding the opportunity to complain.

"Damian, he's our teammate," Cora said, rubbing Damian's head in a disapproving tone.

"But he's a liar. He didn't tell you he had Anopowers, and he's always secretly bullying me. I said he was a fugitive, and he even threatened me."

"You can't just accuse people of being..." Cora's voice trailed off.

A fugitive.

A sudden flash of realization hit her, and all the scattered clues in her mind unraveled like a ball of yarn. Why would someone change their identity? Unless they had no other choice—like being a fugitive.

Arashi Research Institute, the key, Onyx's odd behavior when he saw Jaden Sheen... The answer was right there, waiting to be discovered.

"Damian, can you go back on your own?" Cora asked, turning to him.

"Sure!" Damian nodded obediently.

Once Damian had trotted off, Cora sent a message. "Where are you?"

The reply came quickly with a location.

Outside a high-tech materials shop, Felix was busy distributing scattered materials, trying to balance them across the mechanical arms. Cora squatted down beside him.

"Heading back to the hospital later?" she asked casually.

Felix nodded. "Yeah, we can."

They'd been out for nearly a day, and Dr. Franz had estimated the surgery would take eight hours. It should wrap up soon.

Cora casually brought up, "How did you meet Onyx?"

"Back in school. I was unlucky enough to take most of the same electives as him," Felix replied.

"What school? Was it Askar First Military Academy?" Cora asked.

"Askar? No," Felix glanced at Cora, surprised she knew about that school, which was consistently ranked in the top three within the Alliance. "We were in Luboni."

"District A4, Luboni."

Felix didn't elaborate further. For example, how Luboni was the most academically exclusive place in the entire Alliance, a city composed entirely of enormous academies, divided into different academic factions, and only accepting "Gene Selectors" while promoting so-called "elite education."

"Was he called Onyx de Montclair when you knew him?" Cora suddenly asked.

"Yeah," Felix replied without missing a beat.

"Oh," Cora nodded, "then why didn't you recognize him in Death Hell?"

"We hadn't seen each other in nearly ten years. We've both changed a lot. Not recognizing him isn't that strange," Felix said seriously.

"Did he change a lot?"

Felix's expression grew serious. "A lot, yeah. I mean, I just lost my legs; he discarded part of his intelligence."

Cora couldn't help but laugh. These two never missed an opportunity to insult each other.

"Is the Lucas family close to the Sheen family?" Cora asked.

This time, Felix was silent for a good three or four seconds. "Which Sheen family?"

Cora blinked. "The Northern Yard Sheens."

"We've met Thyrion Lucas. He's from Grass Pit, like you, and he's pretty close to Jaden Sheen."

"Who's Thyrion Lucas? Never heard of him," Felix said with a straight face. "I don't waste my time remembering people who are far below my level."

"Then do you remember the Sheen family members?"

Felix's ice-blue eyes flickered and he stared at Cora.

For a moment, he thought she was about to say that name.

Felix hesitated, "No..."

Cora suddenly shouldered the entire bag of materials and strapped it to Felix's only mechanical arm on the right side.

"It's getting late. Let's head back." She fiddled with her terminal and started walking off on her own.

Felix wobbled a bit, barely maintaining his balance. He muttered to himself, "I said nothing."

At the entrance of the operating room, the F777 members waited patiently for the results.

Yuui Hayashi casually flipped through her terminal. "In two days, we'll be heading back to Felalakas. The finals are about to start. Ilia himself is hosting this time and even organized a pre-tournament rally. Quite a big event."

No one responded. Yuui looked up, noticing her companions were lost in thought.

"Cora? What are you thinking about?" she asked.

"N-nothing," Cora stammered.

Yuui put away her terminal, her gaze sliding over the faces of Cora, Damian, and Felix. Suspicion clouded her features. "Why do I feel you all came back a bit... strange?"

"No way," Cora blinked innocently.

Yuui was about to press further when the light above the operating room turned off. Cora immediately stood up. "He's out."

Charles Franz, still wearing his mask, strolled out, his eyes heavy with exhaustion—a clear sign of overusing his Anopower.

When he saw Cora and the others, his brow relaxed and he removed his mask with a small smile. "I'll say the words every family member loves to hear: the surgery was a success. He should be able to stand again after resting for about a month or two."

Onyx woke up once again from the endless, cold fog. This time, at least, he could clearly feel his right leg. Cora sat with her knees drawn up, her chin resting on her arms, quietly watching him. They were the only two people in the hospital room.

"Cora," Onyx called her softly.

"Hmm," Cora responded, not moving.

Onyx slowly raised his hand. The anesthesia hadn't completely worn off, so he was weak, but he could still control it. His slender fingers paused at Cora's cheek, dabbing at the spot where he remembered her dimple would appear. "Who upset you this time?"

"You said last time that we needed to talk," Cora responded with a question of her own.

"No rush. We'll talk in a couple of days." Onyx thought to himself, he would find a better time for it.

"Alright then."

Cora opened her hand toward him. "Your ID, let me see it."

Onyx was a bit surprised but retrieved it from his space pocket and handed it over.

Cora took his work ID, her eyes immediately drawn to the logo of the Arashi Research Institute, and the blue background headshot. She carefully examined the man in the photo, then glanced at Onyx. No wonder she thought he looked better in person when they first met.

"Onyx de Montclair," she said aloud, looking at the ID photo.

"What's up?" Onyx responded from the bed.

Liar, she thought to herself.

CHAPTER 6

A Marathon

The day after the surgery, F777 set out for Felalakas, preparing to compete in the finals of the Throne Tournament.

Sycamore Bay and Felalakas were both in the eastern part of the Alliance. The distance between the two cities wasn't too far, and a low-orbit starship could make the trip in about four hours. High-orbit travel would cut the time in half, but it required manual piloting.

Felix, entirely focused on repairing his mechanical arm, opted for the convenience of autopilot.

Cora opened the viewport and looked down. Through the thin clouds, she could just make out the checkerboard-like cities below. Some were cold, abandoned ruins, while others still stood tall. The highways were packed with vehicles and people fleeing in all directions, seeking to escape.

Cora unconsciously leaned forward, trying to get a better look.

Strong arms encircled her from behind, pulling her back from the window.

"Careful, don't fall out," Onyx said with a chuckle. He still needed to use a wheelchair for a while longer, but his hand nerves had fully recovered.

"Who are those people...?" Cora asked.

"They're refugees searching for new shelters," Onyx replied.

"But the zombie tide has not hit their cities yet. Why are they running?" Cora was puzzled.

Onyx's eyes were cold. "People are greedy. If they have the means, they'll always try to find a safer place."

Cora fell silent. Onyx was right—humans are creatures that always seek to maximize benefits and avoid harm.

When District F199 first fell to the zombie outbreak, it was the "capable ones" who were the first to flee on starships. But now that the apocalypse had fully descended, was there truly any place left that was absolutely safe?

Cora asked, "Any news about the Zombie Lord?"

Onyx nodded. "Come, look."

Cora jumped down from the viewport and sat close beside him.

Onyx used her terminal to pull up a map, deliberately slowing down as he sketched on it. "Over the past couple of days, it's destroyed two more D-level cities. If you take Sycamore Bay as the center, first it attacked the city at 11 o'clock, then one at 4 o'clock."

Cora immediately noticed something off. "Why didn't it go directly to 12 o'clock?" The 12 o'clock direction had three densely packed cities. After attacking the city at 11 o'clock, why would the Zombie Lord bypass them, making a large detour to 4 o'clock?

"Because it's very cunning. It probably even did some homework beforehand," Onyx said, sketching out the topography of the three cities.

"Green Water City (District D132), Lava Land (District D133), and Ocean Gate (District D135). These three places are backed by mountains and surrounded by water, making them easy to defend and hard to attack. Green Water City used to be a transportation hub with complex roadways, and Ocean Gate is a grain distribution center heavily guarded by troops. It's tough to take them by force. After its defeat at Sycamore Bay, it's become more cautious, opting to engage in guerrilla warfare with humans."

"So it's given up on 12 o'clock?"

"Quite the opposite," Onyx said gravely, drawing arrows between the three cities. "The eastern region has been mostly destroyed. If it wants to break through to the west and north, these are the checkpoints it can't avoid. The Zombie Lord will definitely target them."

Once the Zombie Lord penetrates the core of the Alliance, the number of zombies will only increase, and zombie tides will become more frequent.

Onyx recreated the map of the three cities from memory, logically analyzing the situation. "I predict its first attack will be on Lava Land, and it will probably be a probing attack."

Cora looked at the dense markings on the terminal and couldn't help but be amazed. "That's impressive. You remembered it all?" Although she was already aware of Onyx's vast knowledge, every time he showed his extraordinary memory, Cora couldn't help but be in awe.

Onyx was clearly pleased by the praise, a subtle smile curving his lips. "When I first joined Arashi, I had little seniority, so I spent most of my time in the archives as an ordinary clerk. I read these to pass the time."

Here we go again, Cora thought, rolling her eyes internally. He's pulling the "I'm just an ordinary clerk" line. In the past, she might have asked, "Weren't you supposed to be a pharmaceutical researcher?" But now, she just gave him a complicated look for two seconds before turning away.

Sure, keep pretending. Liar.

"Someone's tailing us," Felix suddenly said.

Suchat immediately drew his knife, cautiously observing through the hatch. Yuui and Charles also stopped talking, their eyes full of alertness. Felix brought up the rear radar display, and sure enough, four hover cars were steadily following the starship.

Damian quickly ran to the other side, stood on tiptoe to peer out, and let out a soft "huh."

Felix was about to send a radio warning when one of the hover cars suddenly sped up, jumping ahead. The next moment, the sunroof opened, and Silver Owl swiftly climbed onto the car roof, removing his tactical goggles as he waved to Cora from afar. "What a coincidence~"

Having recently accepted his special drink, Cora felt it would be rude to pretend not to know him. "Ah, what a coincidence."

"Where are you headed?" Silver Owl asked, eyeing her windblown hair.

Cora didn't respond, and just as Silver Owl was about to say something, he noticed another figure.

The man had a handsome face, but his eyes were distant. The icy gaze he directed through the window clashed with Silver Owl's, as cold as ice. For a moment, their auras collided, and then dissipated into nothing.

Onyx remained expressionless. Silver Owl adjusted his grip on the car roof, the corners of his mouth curving up in a deliberately provocative smile.

"Hi."

Then he chose to completely ignore Onyx, continuing to chat with Cora.

Onyx's frown deepened. When had Cora become acquainted with this "Tustan" captain?

"My apologies, I should've mentioned it earlier," Silver Owl smiled. "We're headed to District C83."

District C83? That's Felalakas. Their destination was the same as theirs?

"So are we," Cora replied politely.

"I heard they're holding an Aberrants Tournament in District C83. It's quite a big event. Are you going to watch?"

"No," Cora felt a slight surge of pride and allowed a small smile to slip through. "We're competing."

"You're a finalist?" Silver Owl was genuinely surprised this time. "Then I have to watch. I'll be cheering for you."

"Thank you," Cora responded politely.

"Lady, you're lovely," Silver Owl said suddenly, his light gray eyes fixed on her.

"Huh?" Cora's grasp of Alliance Language wasn't great, and Silver Owl spoke quickly. She didn't catch what he said at first.

Onyx's expression instantly darkened. He wheeled himself over to the main control console without a word.

"Turn off autopilot and switch to high-orbit mode."

"Why?" Felix looked up from a pile of parts. "Are you in a hurry?"

Onyx's face was impassive. "Yes, I am in a hurry."

Felix was about to retort, but suddenly thought better of it, quieting down instead. He fiddled with the controls, glancing back and forth between Cora and Onyx with a distracted look in his eyes.

Onyx glanced back at the roof of the hover car. The young man leaned forward, one hand resting on his knee, chatting animatedly with Cora. Onyx turned back, his tone icy. "Can you do it or not? If not, step aside and let me."

"I can, I can, I got it," Felix muttered.

With a whoosh, the starship sped up, shooting forward like a meteor and leaving the hover cars far behind.

Onyx was about to return to the window when the wheelchair suddenly halted. He narrowed his eyes slightly. "What's got you acting all guilty?" he asked, noticing Felix's sudden compliance.

Felix's fingers paused for a moment before he flashed an innocent smile. "Why would I be?"

But his expression, unfamiliar and forced, made it clear he wasn't used to smiling like this.

Onyx stared at him for two extra seconds.

Felalakas.

When the starship landed, they were surprised to find a long line at the city gate, stretching out for several kilometers, with no end in sight. At the front, temporary checkpoints had been set up, and several AI police officers were patrolling the area, maintaining order.

"Why are there so many people?" Cora and the others were puzzled.

Felalakas had always been known for its freedom, welcoming travelers from all over with no entry restrictions.

How had things changed so much in just half a month, to where even entering the city required passing through a checkpoint?

Suchat returned from gathering information and whispered, "It's just a simple population registration. There have been too many refugees flooding in recently."

"Why would refugees come to Felalakas?" Cora asked, confused. Did they really think Felalakas was safe?

"Felalakas has a highly advanced level of machinery, giving it a natural advantage in fighting zombies," Onyx explained. "Moreover... it's one of the few cities in the East that has never been attacked, not even once."

"Exactly," Suchat nodded. "The refugees believe Felalakas is a city blessed by the gods. "

"A... what city?" Cora repeated, incredulous.

She couldn't help but recall their experiences. Ilia had once captured live zombies en masse to stockpile for the Throne Tournament, keeping them imprisoned beneath the Sycara Theater.

Though those zombies eventually escaped because of the ensuing chaos, who knew what other bizarre schemes this super AI might concoct? Were these refugees really making the right choice by coming to Felalakas?

Yuui had donned a mask the moment they stepped off the starship. After all, Felalakas was her hometown, and the chances of being recognized were too high. They all rested at the hotel for half a day, and only when night fell did they head out to attend the rally.

The rally was a public event, held in the central square. The place was packed with excited crowds, but Cora and her group didn't push forward. They stayed on the outskirts, waiting for the holographic display to descend. After all, Ilia was an AI; they would have a clear view, no matter where he appeared.

At precisely 8:00 PM, three chimes echoed, and the neon lights flashed. High in the air, where a faint purple mist lingered, flower boats glided by at a steady pace. Fireworks exploded, showering the area with confetti and petals, as the tower's observation elevator moved, stopping with a "ding" at the floating platform.

A luxurious lift appeared before the crowd, and then a real, tall figure slowly stepped out.

The man had dazzling golden hair and a tall, elegant physique, clad in a pure white silk suit. His every move exuded grace and nobility. The once colorless glassy eyes had turned into a crystalline ice-blue, more fitting to his aura.

Cora felt a chill run down her spine. She saw traces of someone else in this man. River Locke? No, this was... Ilia!

The super AI, the highest ruler of Felalakas, had finally achieved its desire—a physical body of its own.

Ilia's gaze swept over the mass of people in the square before he revealed a smile indistinguishable from a human's, filled with warmth. "I'm sure you're all curious about the format of the Throne Tournament's final round."

"Yes!!" the crowd roared back.

Ilia winked mysteriously. "The answer is... a marathon."

The crowd immediately erupted in chatter.

"A marathon spanning three days and two nights, covering a total distance of 200 kilometers. To complete the race, you must run the entire course and return to the starting point within the time limit."

The crowd grew louder with astonishment.

Two hundred kilometers over three days and two nights? How was that even a marathon? Even ordinary people could finish it in a day, let alone in Aberrants.

"Shhh—" Ilia made a gesture for silence, and the crowd instantly quieted down. "I know what you're thinking: What's so special about a marathon? That's why I've added a few 'small' challenges."

"Every ten kilometers, there will be a checkpoint within the course. You must collect all the points to complete the race." Ilia's expression grew a bit troubled. "We've got the challenges, but what about the route?"

"So, I drew up a map myself."

Ilia snapped his fingers, and projections across the city simultaneously displayed a real-time map. The audience was initially puzzled, murmuring to one another, but as time passed, they suddenly burst into deafening cheers.

Cora stared at the marathon map in the projection, finding it increasingly familiar. Where had she seen it before? Then it hit her.

Yggdrasill, Green Water City, Lava Land, Ocean Gate... This wasn't a marathon map at all—it was a list of cities the Zombie Lord had already conquered or was planning to attack!

What was Ilia's plan? Was he really sending them to run a marathon right in front of the Zombie Lord's face?

"I've heard that in the recent wave of zombie tides, there's been a zombie called the 'Lord,'" Ilia said, a smile tugging at the corner of his mouth. "I don't like that name."

"As the ruler of this city, I also don't like it when my things are coveted by others, so I've taken the offensive."

"Only through fire and thorns can the true crown of a king be forged." Ilia recited the slogan of the Throne Tournament, his eyes filled with bitter mockery and a blatant disregard for life and death.

"Only the team that kills the 'Lord' will be crowned the ultimate champion."

For a moment, the crowd in the square fell silent, and then they erupted into a frenzy, chanting his name in unison. "Ilia! Ilia!! Ilia!!!"

This unparalleled final round will spark a viewership frenzy across the eastern regions of the Alliance.

CHAPTER 7

Black Snake

As soon as the news broke that the final round of the Throne Tournament would be a marathon, the first to react were the governors of the eastern districts.

With zombies rampaging outside, the Alliance governors were bound to their territories unless their cities were destroyed, or they relinquished their positions to seek emergency asylum.

Although they couldn't attend in person, their communication requests bombarded Ilia, demanding a reasonable explanation.

At the top of the tower, Ilia leaned back lazily on a large leather sofa, one leg propped up as he supported his chin with his hand. The floating screen in front of him displayed the changing faces of an ongoing holographic video conference. The governors of several eastern districts were in a heated argument.

"Don't think I don't know what you're up to! You're trying to shift the Zombie Lord's crisis onto us, using our territories to solve your problem. Why is Felalakas so peaceful while we have to bear the burden? I oppose this! I strongly oppose it!" one governor shouted.

"You're not even there. What's the point of opposing it?" someone immediately mocked.

"I..." The first governor's voice choked. His city had already fallen, and he had long since fled to District B. No matter how loud he was, it carried little weight anymore.

"We don't oppose it. We welcome it with open arms!" The

governors of Green Water City and Lava Land quickly chimed in. As governors of lowly District D cities, they rarely participated in such meetings and were eager to show their support.

Both cities were hanging by a thread, constantly on the brink of a zombie tide. If the final contestants could eliminate the Zombie Lord, not only would they not oppose it, they'd probably set off fireworks for three days and nights in celebration.

"Hey, what about you, Ocean Gate? Say something," someone prodded.

The governor of Ocean Gate smirked disdainfully. "Whether they're zombies or humans, if they dare step into my territory, they won't be leaving. My cannons don't care who they hit."

"You brute!" the governors of Green Water City and Lava Land cursed in unison.

The other participants exchanged glances, with only a few aware of the underlying truth: it was rumored that Ocean Gate had recently imported a batch of powerful Aberrant weapons from the Northern Base, specifically designed to deal with the Zombie Lord.

The governors continued to argue, venting their frustrations, but they excluded the initiator of the marathon from their discussions. No one asked the opinion of the Felalakas governor—Ilia. They regarded him as an outsider, wary of his presence. The saying "those who are not of our kind must have different hearts" held true; no matter how advanced an AI was, it was still a machine, not one of them.

Julian Chang, from Sycamore Bay, was also present at the meeting. When asked for his opinion, he smiled humbly, playing the peacemaker. "Whatever you say is fine by me. I have no objections. After all, I'm getting on in years, almost seventy."

"Yeah, right! You're only sixty!" someone immediately called him out.

This old fox, with his smooth talk, clearly intended to stay out of trouble. Since Sycamore Bay wasn't on the marathon route and had recently had its defenses reinforced by Aberrant engineers, he had nothing to worry about.

Ilia casually switched legs and yawned. This was human politics —each with their own hidden agenda. Quite amusing, really. No matter how much they argued, it wouldn't affect the Throne Tournament in the slightest.

Feeling bored, Ilia rose from the sofa and leisurely left the top floor. However, his holographic image remained in the projection, though the pupils had subtly shifted to a glassy hue, and his expression grew more rigid.

The automatic doors opened to reveal a luxurious reception room, where a woman sat with her back to him, sipping tea from a bone china cup. Ilia walked around and sat down across from her. "Commander Holland, have you given any thought to our cooperation?"

Scarlett Holland set down her cup and looked across the table. She wore black-framed glasses on her high-bridged nose, her hair tightly coiled into a bun, and deep wrinkles marked the corners of her eyes and mouth. Her entire demeanor was severe and imposing, demanding respect.

"You want to establish an information channel with District B? That's not within my authority," she said.

"Correction, not District B—Northern Base," Ilia replied with a smile.

Of the Alliance's twenty B Districts, most were controlled by powerful families (such as District B6's Northern Yard and District B8's Grass Pit), or directly governed by the Central Court (such as District B9's Askar). However, one district was an exception.

District B10, Northern Base, existed outside these power structures. It was the largest remaining refuge after the apocalypse, housing over a million high-level Aberrants and tens of millions of civilians, known as humanity's last hope.

Ilia, being one of the few elected governors and a super AI, was still excluded by the Central Court, despite Felalakas's strong security, advanced technology, and unique status among C Districts.

The information access rights between C Districts and B Districts were entirely different, and access was something Ilia desperately needed now.

"I will report this to General Yevgeniyeva," Scarlett Holland said slowly.

Ilia raised an eyebrow. "I thought the true leader of Northern Base was already you, Commander Holland."

Her expression darkened. "Watch your words. I am merely General Yevgeniyeva's deputy."

Ilia's ice-blue eyes locked onto hers, his tone laced with meaning. "Commander, I will await your good news."

"Oh, and Commander, why not stay and watch the competition before you leave?" Ilia added casually. "You never know, some contestants might end up heading to Northern Base in the future."

"Naturally, Northern Base welcomes Aberrants," Scarlett Holland replied, her stern expression finally softening at the mention of Aberrants.

Cora, Felix, Suchat, Yuui, and Damian were geared up and ready to go. Each team in the Throne Tournament was limited to five members. Given that Onyx had just undergone surgery and was still weak, and Charles was busy taking care of him, neither of them was in any condition to take part in the marathon.

Cora had gently "persuaded" them to sit this one out.

"Did you check the communicators?" Onyx asked, still concerned.

Cora touched the black narrow-band collar around her neck. "Yes, everything's working fine."

The finals didn't prohibit communication, so all F777 members were equipped with the micro-communicators that Felix had developed. These used an independent frequency band to transmit information, ensuring they wouldn't be intercepted. With all seven of them online simultaneously, they could stay in touch.

Onyx pointed out several cities on the map. "These areas currently have seen no zombie tides. Franz and I will meet up with you there."

"Doesn't that count as outside help? Won't it be against the rules?" Yuui Hayashi asked.

Onyx calmly shook his head. "The only rule for passing the marathon is to collect all the checkpoint stamps. To win the championship, you must kill the Zombie Lord. Other than that, there are no restrictions. You could even fly your starship straight to the finish line if you wanted."

Yuui suddenly thought of something.

"Isn't that unfair? What about teams like 'Iron Cafe' with Master Stark's deep pockets and a horde of Aberrants under his command? They could just clear the path in advance, collect the checkpoint stamps, and take down the Zombie Lord, couldn't they?"

"Exactly, if they can pull it off," Onyx replied. "This competition was never meant to be fair."

On the day of the finals, the 16 teams gathered at the gates of Felalakas.

Onyx's prediction was spot on. There were indeed plenty of hover cars and steamships at the starting line, and once the race began, they shot out ahead.

Drones followed closely, live-streaming each contestant, while the betting pools outside the event overflowed with wagers.

Their starship was too conspicuous and better suited for long-distance travel, making it less ideal for a marathon. So, the F777 crew found an off-road pickup truck, with Suchat at the wheel. Although it was slower, this race wasn't about speed.

F777 quickly reached their first stop—District D140, Cloud City.

Unfortunately, the city had already fallen. The roads leading out of the city were clogged with all kinds of private vehicles, making it nearly impossible to move. Those who hadn't escaped were trapped in their cars, snarling as their seatbelts restrained them. Zombies roamed between the stalled vehicles, leaving almost no room to maneuver on the main road.

A starship passed overhead, and the noise drew the zombies' attention. They turned in unison, gathering in greater numbers, growing more agitated by the second. Forcing their way through would certainly cost them a lot of time.

The five of them took the road leading into the city instead, where conditions were slightly better. Although some vehicles had overturned, at least they could squeeze through. Yuui glanced at the map; there was only one checkpoint in Cloud City.

"What do you think the checkpoint will be?" she asked.

Ilia always had a knack for coming up with ways to torment them. In the Mirror Lake competition, for instance, the "flag" had turned out to be the crystal core of an Aberrant zombie.

"Could it be a Level 3 zombie?" Cora speculated. As time passed, Aberrant zombies had become increasingly less challenging. Would Ilia raise the difficulty?

"Unlikely," came Onyx's calm voice through the earpiece. "Level 3 zombies are uncontrollable. If they move from their original positions, the distances between checkpoints would change. I'm more inclined to think it's a fixed location."

"So we need to search the city?" Yuui frowned. That would be a massive undertaking.

Onyx paused before responding, "There's no need to waste time searching. We can take a shortcut."

"What shortcut?" Cora asked.

"Get to the highest point first," Onyx suggested with a soft chuckle, his magnetic voice resonating through the earpiece.

"Why the highest point?" Cora was still confused.

"Since the finals are being broadcast live, the organizers would have scouted and filmed the area beforehand. No matter where the checkpoint is, there will probably be drones nearby. And drones generate data."

"You're saying we can find the checkpoint by tracking the drones?" Yuui asked, astonished. This was a borderline exploit, a loophole in the system.

According to Onyx's logic, drones would hover near the checkpoints, leaving behind data that Felix could analyze. He could then use the process of elimination to pinpoint the location of the checkpoint.

The highest point in Cloud City was the observation tower in the city center, standing over five hundred meters tall, offering a bird's-eye view of the entire city. With the main road blocked, the quickest way to reach it was via the circular sky bridge. However, the entrance to the bridge had collapsed, and they would need to clear the path.

Just as F777 was about to get to work, a team suddenly appeared around the corner. The leader was a woman with a doll-like face, sweet in appearance. She froze upon seeing them, then her brows furrowed as she scowled with fury.

It was Dora Werner and the "Stars of Felalakas."

F777's rivalry with this team dated back to Mirror Lake, where Dora had accused them of hoarding crystal cores, leading to a fight. Then, in the subsequent arena match, Felix had knocked out their bassist in a single move. F777 had nearly derailed the "Stars of Felalakas" twice now.

Cora raised her hand awkwardly in greeting. "Uh… hi?"

Dora responded with a double middle finger. Cora's attempt at diplomacy had failed.

When rivals meet, a fight is inevitable. At Dora's sharp command, the Aberrant band assumed battle positions. The guitarist launched into a high-pitched riff, signaling the start of the attack, with the bassist and electric keyboard following suit. The deep, steady beat of the jazz drums provided the backbone of their rhythm.

And then, the most terrifying thing happened—Dora sang!

"Turn around and leave, break up without saying a word~ Seagulls~~ and fish! Fall in love! Just an accident~"

F777's scalps tingled as the piercing sound hammered at their nerves. Damian immediately covered his ears, but the noise was relentless, seeping into his mind like the worst kind of alarm clock, rousing him from the sweet embrace of sleep at four in the morning with the jarring clatter of a broken bell. It was enough to make anyone murderous.

"Onyx ..."

Cora wanted to ask if Onyx had any way to shut down the noise, but there was no response, despite her repeated calls.

She glanced down at the signal indicator, which was dark. Seriously? He and Charles had turned off their receivers!

Frustrated, Cora drew her twin blades and charged at Dora. Suchat's brow furrowed deeply as he melted into the shadows. Meanwhile, Yuui, still wearing her mask, stepped forward and cleared her throat.

"We're ready for anything today. Came here fully aware! North, South, East, West, four streets wide—who's your daddy? Let's decide!" Yuui's voice dropped, fully embracing the moment.

She rapped at an incredible speed, spitting out strange lyrics. The music on the other side abruptly quieted, and Dora's song faltered, as if someone had grabbed her by the throat. The out-of-tune, painful melody died in her throat.

Not only were Yuui's lyrics infectious, but they also seemed to carry a debuff, sapping the energy from the opposing team and making it hard for them to muster any enthusiasm.

The "Stars of Felalakas," guitarist stopped playing and rubbed his chin, intrigued. "Hey, that rapper over there's got some fire. Hey, you! Ever thought about joining our band after the competition?"

Yuui's red lips curved into a smirk as she powered through the highlight of her verse: "...Black Snake Warriors see you as a fool, spew poison gas and send you all to doom!!"

The "Stars of Felalakas" fell completely silent.

"Black Snake Warrior" Suchat slipped on a loose tile, tumbling out of the shadows. His face flushed crimson with embarrassment—this was the second time, following their incident in the City of Sin, that unspeakable shame overwhelmed him.

CHAPTER 8

Commander

To avoid revealing their identities, Yuui and Suchat had entered the competition under random aliases. Yuui even gave herself the nickname "Rapper Trainee Doe" in their seven-member group chat, while she dubbed Suchat "Black Snake Warrior" (because of the black snake tattoo on the back of his neck).

Cora and Damian joined in the fun, naming themselves "Artifact Master" and "Prince of Ice and Snow," respectively.

It was all just playful banter, and no one expected Yuui to actually perform under such an overly dramatic and cringeworthy persona in front of others.

Suchat wasn't the only one who wished he could disappear into the ground; even Cora was left speechless with shock.

The audience in F777's live stream exploded with laughter, the chat flooded with comments:

"LMAO, is the Black Snake Warrior about to transform? Hahaha!"

"I thought F777 made it to the finals because of their skills, not because they make their opponents die of embarrassment..."

"To be honest, if this rapper releases a single, I'd buy it. It's so cheesy, but I'm weirdly hooked."

"Count me in on that!"

In the official broadcast, AK switched the dominant view to the two teams facing off, commenting with interest, "I wonder what sparks will fly when different music styles collide? Let's wait and see."

Felalakas, being a haven for musicians, naturally had AI guests offering their critiques.

"Dora's singing? That's just noise pollution!" one of the more blunt commentators remarked.

"I think the other music is quite interesting," another AI analyzed from a technical standpoint. "Although the rhyming is rough and the lyrics are straightforward, her breath control and articulation are clear, unlike the common problems most rappers face. She clearly has some skill."

"Beyond the music itself, I believe this is also a clever battle strategy," said River Locke, who had been quietly watching the match. "Oh? Care to elaborate, Locke?" AK leaned in, eager to hear more.

"Did anyone notice," River Locke glanced down at the player list, "Ms. Doe—her Aberrant power is activated through her voice, so it takes time to take effect. Doe deliberately used exaggerated and bold lyrics to unsettle the 'Stars of Felalakas,' causing them to lose focus, and then she completed her control setup. The opponents are now caught in her trap."

River Locke's technical analysis earned him a wave of admiration, his fans cheering loudly.

AK nodded in agreement, but then burst into laughter. "That doesn't change the fact that she's hilarious! Hahaha!"

Amid the barrage of laughing comments on the screen, the situation in Cloud City suddenly shifted.

Despite his earlier stumble, Suchat recovered quickly and stealthily attacked the "Stars of Felalakas."

In a flash of dark light, the guitar strings of the player mid-performance snapped. Suchat revealed himself, his fists wrapped in knuckle dusters bound with tape—an Artifact! Knuckle dusters were a common weapon among martial artists, with blades so sharp they could slice through iron and were highly adaptable and powerful. They suited Suchat perfectly.

After cutting the guitar strings, Suchat repeated the move, appearing behind the bassist in a blur. Sensing danger, the bassist immediately launched into a flashy slide, which caused Suchat to slip slightly. The bassist tried to escape but found his feet frozen in place!

Not just him—Dora and the rest of the team were all unknowingly trapped up to their calves in ice. It was the work of F777's ice Aberrant, but when had he made his move? They hadn't noticed a thing.

Before they could figure it out, Suchat's knuckle dusters flashed again, and the bassist's strings snapped.

Meanwhile, Cora moved in sync with Suchat. Her twin blades whirled downward, first slicing through the electric keyboard, then driving into the jazz drum set, scattering drum skins and cymbals across the ground. With two opponents down, she couldn't bear it any longer and covered her ears, charging toward the source of the awful noise—Dora.

Dora, suppressed by Yuui's Aberrant power, couldn't utter a word. Seeing her teammates fall one by one, she took a deep breath, ready to sing again, when a shadow swiftly closed in. A punch landed squarely on her face, followed by a thick towel shoved into her mouth.

Poor Dora. Her song caught in her throat. She couldn't even cry out before stars danced in her vision, and she collapsed. In less than ten seconds, the "Stars of Felalakas" were wiped out!

The precise coordination and quick response displayed by F777 left the audience in awe. They didn't need commands or communication; from the moment Yuui took control, everyone knew exactly which skills to use to subdue their opponents.

In terms of teamwork, they were on par with the current favorites to win, "The Boss and His Three Goons."

The members of "Stars of Felalakas" were only temporarily incapacitated and would soon recover on their own. While they were fighting, Felix hadn't been idle either, using the opportunity to clear the path to the sky bridge. Cora and her team bypassed their opponents and headed swiftly toward the tower.

After threading through the narrow passages between zombie-filled streets, they reached the rooftop of the observation tower. As they arrived, Onyx's voice crackled back to life in the earpieces.

"I was thinking the drones filming the contestants might change positions, which means the data load would be bigger than for a tracker…"

"You turned off the receiver just now," Cora interrupted, still holding a grudge. She would not let it slide.

"Ahem," Onyx coughed, clearly deflecting, "try to find the ones hovering in place..."

"You turned off the receiver!" Cora raised her voice, growing more and more annoyed. How could he do that? They were supposed to share the burden, and he had the nerve to just switch off the receiver?

With the captain furious, no one else dared to speak up, and it was a wonder they weren't all laughing at Onyx by now.

Onyx chuckled softly, his chest vibrating with low laughter as he finally admitted, "My bad, Captain. Next time, I'll definitely stay with you through the noise."

"Hmph," Cora grumbled in response.

Felalakas.

In her hotel suite, Scarlett Holland opened the official broadcast of the Throne Tournament. Even while watching the competition, she remained rigidly upright, her legs together, back straight, and posture impeccably correct.

As she watched, she took meticulous notes, focusing on several popular teams like "The Boss and His Three Goons," "Iron Cafe," "The Knights of Anna," and "F777," and frequently reviewing the profiles of the contestants.

A knock sounded at the door. Silver Owl, the captain of "Tustan," slipped into the room. They had returned to Felalakas two days earlier, but since Scarlett had business to attend to, Silver Owl hadn't disturbed her until now.

"Commander Holland, All officials have been safely delivered to Sycamore Bay, and the zombie tide has receded. All your instructions have been carried out successfully."

Silver Owl found a seat on a sofa and casually crossed one long leg over the other. His tone was respectful, but his demeanor was relaxed and at ease.

Scarlett, accustomed to his informal style, nodded. "Thank you for your hard work."

"Are you in any hurry to return to the base?" Silver Owl glanced at the competition playing on the projection, then looked up to ask her suddenly.

"No rush. I'll be staying in District C83 for about a week."

"Good." Silver Owl fiddled with his earring and casually asked, "Are you watching the Throne Tournament? These contestants are all from District C, right?"

"District C has quite a few excellent Aberrants," Scarlett replied without directly answering.

Silver Owl shrugged knowingly. Unlike most people, Scarlett had always had a warmer attitude toward Aberrants.

At the Northern Base, power was the only currency. The stronger the Aberrant, the better the treatment they received.

For instance, while the "Tustan" team was nominally loyal to General Yevgeniyeva, they enjoyed significant freedom in their actions and didn't have to be overly formal with Scarlett.

"What, you're interested too?" Scarlett noticed his lingering gaze on the projection and asked offhandedly.

"Yeah," Silver Owl grinned, "but I'm not interested in the competition itself."

Silver Owl stood up with a flourish. "Commander, I'll leave you to it. I'm heading out." Since Scarlett was watching the official broadcast, which kept switching between scenes with little focus, he returned to watching the individual livestreams of the contestants.

Felix's silver hair floated as if caught in a breeze, surrounded by countless transparent data branches. His immense mental power spread out like a wave.

At the moment, all 16 finalist teams were within Cloud City, with hundreds of drones filming the contestants alone. Including scene cameras, motion capture devices, audio systems, tripods, and tracks, there were over 500 pieces of equipment in total.

About five or six minutes later, Felix opened his eyes, his icy blue pupils briefly flickering with streams of data before vanishing. He raised his brand-new, gleaming mechanical arm and pointed in a specific direction. "There. There's an anomaly in the data stream. Another team has already headed that way."

Onyx's suggestion had proven to be quite effective. With a top-tier hacker like Felix on their team, they could exploit a glitch to locate the checkpoint. Cora immediately made the call. "Let's go."

The five of them sprinted toward their destination, encountering zombies along the way, which cost them a bit of time to clear out. To their surprise, the location Felix had pointed to was a wildlife park.

"The Cloud City Rare Species Breeding Research Base," Damian read aloud from the sign above the entrance. "What is this place?"

"No zombies in the vicinity," Suchat reported quietly after scouting ahead.

"Cloud City has a Level 5A ecological reserve specializing in the cultivation and restoration of flora and fauna from the Old Civilization," Onyx explained through the earpiece. "Don't let your guard down. If Ilia set this place as a checkpoint, it won't be easy."

The five of them followed Felix through the dense bamboo forest, eventually arriving at the predator viewing area. Looking down through the three layers of transparent barriers, they saw a floating object in the center of the platform—a seal-like emblem with a holographic projection above it, displaying the Throne Tournament's logo.

Cora's spirits lifted. This must be the checkpoint!

However, reaching the checkpoint wouldn't be easy. The area around the park was crowded with various mutant beasts, blocking the entrance completely. Next to the holographic projection was a small black-and-white two-story building, conveniently obstructing the platform with the seal.

Cora watched it for a while, noticing that the building... seemed to move. She rubbed her eyes, feeling increasingly uneasy. Just as she was about to get a closer look, the "building" lifted one of its "legs."

Cora gasped, finally seeing it clearly. This wasn't a building at all —it was a two-story-tall zombie panda!

The zombie panda was enormous, with patches of fur missing to reveal yellowed bones underneath. When it moved its leg, a pile of decayed flesh and dried leaves fell away, causing the zombie rats trapped beneath it to scatter. Even from a distance, the stench of rotting flesh was overpowering.

The one bit of luck was that the area was quiet, and this massive creature, having gorged itself, was currently lying on its back, dozing.

The zombie panda rolled over with a dog-like grunt, its razor-sharp claws scraping the platform as it absentmindedly scratched itself.

Yuui nudged Cora lightly, signaling her to look in another direction—"Iron Cafe" was there too.

Master Stark whispered a few commands, and a faint black mist materialized in the shadows behind him. A second later, an Aberrant teleported silently onto the platform above the seal.

It was a space Aberrant!

Cora suddenly remembered encountering this person before, back in Glass Port, when his rapid movements had made it nearly impossible for anyone to get close to the A-level zombie.

The Aberrant moved with remarkable skill, clinging to the ceiling like a gecko, slowly crawling toward the holographic projection with a terminal clenched between his teeth. Once he reached the projection, he scanned the seal.

The zombie panda scratched its ear, its sharp claws slicing through the air right in front of the gecko Aberrant, trimming a few strands of his hair. The Aberrant paled, not daring to move a muscle, but fortunately, the system prompt came through quickly.

The holographic display showed a line of text, the wax seal imprinting the Cloud City emblem.

"Congratulations to 'Iron Cafe' for successfully checking in." Master Stark beamed with satisfaction as the space Aberrant used his power again to retrieve the gecko Aberrant, and the team promptly left.

Cora ducked her head down, hiding under the barrier as she conferred with her teammates. "Should we... do what they did?"

Master Stark's team had set an excellent example. This was the perfect opportunity to strike—if they could check in without disturbing the zombie panda, they could complete the Cloud City marathon leg as quickly as possible.

Though F777 didn't have a space Aberrant, they had Suchat, whose stealth abilities were top-notch. "Suchat, you go check in. I'll cover you," Cora gestured.

"Got it."

They sprang into action immediately. Suchat silently descended to the lower level, while Cora leaped over the beams from above to provide cover. Halfway there, she ran into another team. Cora and the other team member locked eyes for two seconds before both raised a finger to their lips in a "shh" gesture, instantly reaching a mutual understanding. They relaxed and exchanged a brief smile.

Suchat was just inches away from the platform on the ground, his hand nearly reaching the wax seal. Cora felt a sense of relief settling on her chest.

But then—

"Boom! Boom!"

Deafening explosions echoed from outside the park, sending the mutant beasts into a panicked frenzy. They scattered in all directions.

The blocked entrance was violently blasted open, and Ellyn strode in, casually shouldering a rocket launcher. She kicked down the barrier in one swift motion. Spotting Cora, she grinned and called out, "Well, well, it's you guys. So, did you find the checkpoint?"

"... We did," Cora replied, feeling utterly defeated.

"Rooooaaaar!!"

The zombie panda reared up to its full height, its furious roar shaking the entire zoo.

CHAPTER 9

A Zombie Panda

Continuous explosions shattered the silence, jolting the zombie panda awake from its slumber.

With an earth-shattering roar, a cloud of birds took to the sky, and small animals scattered in every direction. Upon closer inspection, one could see that their pupils were a cloudy gray-white—this wildlife park had long been overrun by zombie beasts.

The moment the zombie panda stood up, the holographic projection on the platform shut off. Suchat froze mid-motion. The wax seal he almost touched disappeared right before his eyes.

He quickly rolled to the side as a massive paw slammed down, smashing the platform into pieces and leaving deep grooves in the ground.

"Oh, sorry, looks like we came at a bad time..." Ellyn apologized, covering her face, a hint of nervousness in her voice.

Cora was about to reply when the zombie panda's head swiveled, noticing her hanging from the ceiling. The massive creature stood on its stubby hind legs, reached up, and bit down on the beam she clung to, yanking it back and forth.

The sturdy steel cracked, quickly twisting and snapping in half. Cora made a split-second decision, swinging like a pendulum before leaping into the railing where Yuui and the others were.

The zombie panda slammed its front paws into the ground and started crawling toward the viewing area.

"The Wild Rose" immediately raised her rocket launcher, firing at the beast. But its thick hide absorbed the impact, and instead of causing harm, it only enraged the creature further.

"Where's the seal?!" Cora yelled over the roar of explosions.

"Missed it, it's gone!" Suchat shouted back, his voice strained as he scrambled back, looking disheveled.

The zombie panda charged forward, crashing into the railing with a thunderous impact, shattering it like it was nothing. Its massive, decayed head pushed through the opening, but got stuck halfway. It twisted and snarled, spraying foul-smelling saliva everywhere. Damian turned pale, clutching Felix's mechanical arm, biting his lip to keep from crying out.

With its movement restricted, the zombie panda began smashing into the walls. A loud "BOOM" echoed from outside the tunnel, the ground trembling as chunks of concrete rained down.

Another "BOOM" roared nearby, and the entire viewing tunnel swayed.

"Onyx, the checkpoint, it's gone!" Cora yelled into her collar.

"The wax seal is linked to the panda's location," Onyx's voice came through quickly. "To mark the checkpoint, get it back."

"How do I do that?" Cora felt like crying. This panda had clearly mutated and couldn't understand a word she was saying. "Two options: lure it back, or kill it. Its weak spot is its head."

Cora glanced up.

Onyx was right. Compared to its massive body, the zombie panda's head was relatively small, hidden within its dirty black-and-white fur, as if trying to keep its weak point a secret.

"Ellyn, aim for the head!" Cora shouted.

"Got it!" Ellyn called back from the emergency exit.

Armor-piercing rounds whizzed through the air, but the zombie panda had already smashed through the stone wall, pulling its head back. It was now crawling through the bamboo forest, its thick fur deflecting every attack, remaining unscathed.

Damian tried freezing its limbs, but the panda was too large; it shook off the ice in no time. He switched to ice spikes, but they couldn't even pierce its skin.

Cora and Suchat jumped down from the tunnel entrance,

positioning themselves to get closer to the panda again.

Suchat activated his power, enveloping the zombie panda in a cloud of toxic green mist. It howled in pain as chunks of rotten flesh began peeling off its face. Cora climbed up its thick, stubby leg.

"Whoosh!" A shell whizzed over her head, exploding on the zombie panda's shoulder, revealing a flash of yellowed bone. It was exposed! Cora seized the moment, drawing her twin blades and driving them into its neck.

The Ethereal Artifacts pierced the fur, but got stuck deep in the fat layers. This was no better than giving it a shot!

The zombie panda roared in fury, charging forward. Its massive body filled the space, and it raised a foot to crush Suchat. He sprinted away, but was still struck by a heavy paw, sent flying into a stone wall.

Cora wasn't much better off.

Clinging to her twin blades, the zombie panda's movements jerked around her, swinging back and forth like a kite with a broken string, dragged through the bamboo forest.

Her stomach churned, the world spinning around her. The panda was heading back toward the tunnel. If this continued, she would definitely be flattened into a pancake.

Cora made a snap decision, letting go. She tumbled from the height, curling up as she hit the ground. The zombie panda's four enormous paws stomped back and forth like four moving death traps. Cora rolled quickly, her slender figure barely visible between the hulking legs.

The audience watching the live broadcast was on the edge of their seats, holding their breath.

"Did it step on her? Did it step on her?!" "Oh my god, I can't watch! Someone tell me what happens!" "No way! I bet everything on F777! Get up, please!"

Just when it seemed all hope was lost, six mechanical arms whipped through the air, lashing at the zombie panda's legs. An ethereal, melodic song filled the air, causing the massive creature to pause for a moment. Cora seized the opportunity, rolling out from under it, spitting out a mouthful of crushed bamboo leaves.

At the shattered tunnel entrance, Yuui and Felix temporarily held back the zombie panda's advance. Ellyn and the others used their strongest firepower to force it back, but the situation remained dire.

Cora knew that the main reason for their current predicament was that F777 lacked a capable Anopower controller.

Onyx might qualify. His mental strength was formidable enough to command Level 3 zombies, and this panda, with its simple intelligence, could likely be controlled, too. But he wasn't here, only able to give remote commands through the earpiece.

They would have to kill it by force.

Cora's gaze turned icy as her fingers brushed against the giant stone slab covering the entire park. A ghostly blue light glowed.

The zombie panda was drawn to the light, slowly turning its head, its hollow eyes locking onto Cora—

At that moment, the bamboo forest in the park shook violently. Countless thorny vines shot up into the air, as if they had a life of their own, rushing toward the zombie panda. They wrapped tightly around its limbs and neck. Then, three figures leaped down from a hole in the ceiling, each running in different directions, pulling the vines back with all their might.

"Roar—"

The zombie panda staggered back a step, retreating from the railing.

Behind "The Wild Rose," a refined young man in a green robe stepped forward with a serious expression. Cora recognized him immediately and felt a surge of energy—it was Zephyrion Stormrider.

"The Boss and His Three Goons" had arrived! Their timing couldn't have been better; Zephyrion was a controller-type Aberrant.

However, only three of "The Boss and His Three Goons" had jumped down. The zombie panda's left paw was still free, and it swung it violently, dragging the vines upward, aiming to crush Zephyrion, who was standing at a distance.

One more person was missing.

Suchat, who had fallen from the wall, clutched his chest, coughing twice before hurrying to the gap and grabbing onto the thorns there.

No words were needed between the teams. None of them could take down the zombie panda alone; if they wanted to complete the checkpoint, they had to work together to clear this obstacle.

"We're not strong enough!" Luke Shaw's face was flushed, veins bulging on the back of his hands as he shouted. The four Aberrants were being dragged forward by the zombie panda in the tug-of-war.

"The Wild Rose" team, the "F777" team, and even the other two teams who had been lurking in the shadows watching the battle, now jumped down without hesitation, grabbing the vines on the ground and pulling back, engaging in a fierce tug-of-war with the zombie panda.

Cora's Ethereal Artifact was almost fully formed.

The ghostly blue light grew brighter, nearly blinding, enveloping her from head to toe. Under everyone's shocked gaze, a massive war hammer gradually took shape, its head nearly as large as the zombie panda's body, emitting a sharp metallic clang as it appeared.

Cora gripped the handle with both hands, her face flushed as she astonishingly lifted the colossal hammer.

She dragged it with heavy steps toward the zombie panda, her arm muscles tensed, her core strength exploding as she raised the war hammer high—

"Boom—"

A deafening crash echoed as the zombie panda's head was struck head-on, leaving a deep dent. The massive creature staggered back a step, causing the Aberrants pulling the vines to stumble.

"Boom—Boom—"

With every step the zombie panda took back, Cora advanced, swinging the war hammer with relentless force. The petite girl wielded the towering hammer without mercy, each strike aimed squarely at the zombie panda's skull.

The zombie panda was hammered backward, its roars growing weaker until it finally returned to the ruins of the original platform. Cora seized the moment, twisting her waist, her slender body leaping into the air as she raised the hammer above her head, bringing it down with a mighty blow!

If time could freeze, the impact of this scene would be nearly impossible to describe in words.

"Clang—" The war hammer struck with apocalyptic force, tearing off the entire head of the zombie panda. The skull rolled across the ground, foul brain matter spraying across the park. Cora took the brunt of it, drenched from head to toe, while the others weren't spared either.

The headless zombie panda swayed a few times before its massive body crashed to the ground.

Whether in Cloud City, Felalakas, or even other regions in the eastern part of the Alliance, the audience watching the live broadcast fell silent. The immersive experience had been so intense that some viewers anxiously touched their own necks, checking to ensure they were still intact.

The holographic projection flickered back to life, and the fire seal of Cloud City reappeared. After marking their checkpoints, the other two teams cast wary glances at Cora before hastily retreating.

Zephyrion nodded slightly at Cora. Despite being opponents with a history of grudges, he said little more and led his team away.

The women of "The Wild Rose" looked at Cora with a mix of emotions. They wanted to thank her, but the stench clinging to her was overpowering, making them gag.

They braced themselves and approached her, but before they could speak, they all covered their mouths and bolted. "Ugh—!!!"

Ellyn wiped off the splattered flesh on her body and gave Cora a thumbs-up with a grin. "We'll catch up after the match. We're heading out." She then turned with a flourish, striding away, but Cora noticed she was covering her mouth with one hand, clearly nauseated.

"Cora!" Damian ran over with open arms, ready for a hug, but skidded to a stop just in time, his face filled with hesitation. Yuui and Felix didn't hide their disgust, pinching their noses in obvious distaste.

A soft chuckle came through her earpiece, Onyx de Montclair's voice saying nothing, yet somehow saying everything.

Was it really that bad? She cautiously grabbed her jacket and took a deep breath.

"Ugh—" She almost gagged at her own smell.

Cora was "gently reminded" but firmly "ordered" by Yuui and the others to change her clothes. Her cheeks puffed out in frustration as she muttered to herself, "Who did I do all this for?" But she still had to endure the stench, wiping off the clinging chunks of rotten flesh and blood, cleaning herself up, and changing into fresh clothes. By the time she was done, the others had also completed their first checkpoint.

F777 officially set out from Cloud City, heading to their next destination—District D132, Green Water City. Onyx and Chief would also meet them there.

Though Green Water City hadn't yet faced a wave of zombies and was relatively safe for now, its critical position as a transportation hub, backed by multiple District C zones, including some that had already fallen, meant that refugees were flooding into the city, forcing the construction of temporary shelters inside and out.

What Cora didn't know was that at that moment, in one of those shelters outside Green Water City, an old man watching the competition rubbed his eyes in disbelief and murmured to himself, "... Little Cora?"

CHAPTER 10

Check Points

The off-ramp outside Green Water City saw a pickup truck roaring in at full throttle, skidding wildly. As it neared, the vehicle pulled a dramatic 180-degree drift before coming to a stop, where Onyx and Charles had been waiting for some time.

Cora stuck her head out of the passenger seat, shouting, "Old Franz, hurry!"

Ever since Onyx stopped calling him "Doctor Franz" and switched to "Old Franz," the others had followed suit.

Charles swiftly jumped into the pickup, his gaze sweeping inside. Felix Lucas had taken over the driver's seat—he was the one who had just pulled off that stunt. Damian was seated in the back, with Yuui in the middle, holding someone steady. She exhaled in relief as she saw Charles.

Their urgency was because of Suchat's injury.

As a front-line fighter specializing in close combat, getting injured and bleeding was inevitable. But this time, Suchat's luck had truly run out.

A zombie panda had flung him towards a protruding piece of rebar. Although his reflexes were top-notch, allowing him to twist away from a fatal chest wound, he still collided with the joint, sending a bone-jarring shock through his chest.

After a quick examination, Charles stated, "Two ribs are broken, but they haven't shifted. I'll stabilize them; it won't affect his movement."

A gentle, white glow emanated from his palms, the A-level healing Anopower easing Suchat's pain significantly, and his face visibly relaxed.

Yuui reclined the seat and crouched in front of him, lightly pressing on the injury. "Does it hurt? If it does, let me know, okay? Big sis will make it better."

Once she knew he wasn't seriously hurt, her tense expression softened, and she even found the energy to tease him.

Suchat, all six-foot-three of him, instinctively curled back, his muscular frame taut like a leopard ready to pounce. But after a moment, he settled back down, allowing Yuui to fuss over him. "...I'm really okay."

He hesitated before adding in a low voice, "...Stop kidding around."

Onyx, meanwhile, hadn't rushed to get in the truck. Instead, he pulled a spray bottle from his space and handed it to Cora. "Here."

"What's this?" she asked.

"Molecular deodorizer. I figured the captain could really, really use it."

Cora stared at Onyx, unsure whether he was genuinely offering helpful advice or just messing with her. Ever since his leg surgery, Onyx had been in visibly high spirits, constantly teasing her and often pushing her buttons.

Expressionless, Cora uncapped the bottle and sprayed it directly at Onyx.

"Cora!" Onyx raised his hand to block the spray, but it did little good.

He braced his arm against the wheelchair, his right leg lifting slightly as if to stand, but he lacked the strength and fell back down.

Cora slammed the door shut and leaned against the window, grinning smugly at him, her dimples deepening with mischief.

"Beep beep!" Felix, tired of their antics, leaned on the horn. "Hey, did you guys forget we're still in the middle of a marathon?"

"Green Water City doesn't have a zombie horde, no ecological zones, and it's pretty modern with good infrastructure. There's no chance of mutated beasts showing up," Onyx analyzed calmly, tapping the drone footage.

"It doesn't seem like there's anything noteworthy here," Yuui frowned. "So, where's the checkpoint?"

They spent a while studying the city map, but with the limited intel they had, making an effective judgment was difficult.

"Let's go with the usual plan—search for anomalies. If that doesn't work, we'll have to comb the city."

Yuui's finger accidentally brushed the thermal imaging mode, shrinking the map to reveal the surrounding area.

Three C Zones bordered green Water City, an important transportation hub in the Alliance's east to the north and south and surrounded by D Zones to the east and west. But now, most of its neighbors appeared dark gray—the mark of cities overrun by zombie hordes.

"I have a question," Charles Franz mused aloud after a moment's thought. "Isn't the number of refugees in Green Water City unusually high?"

According to the thermal imaging, the entire city and nearby shelters were swarming with red and green heat signatures. Although the live footage showed refugees fleeing, the sheer scale of it sent chills down their spines.

"You're right," Onyx nodded slowly. "And it's still increasing." As he spoke, he paused, beginning to sense why Ilia had chosen Green Water City.

The pickup truck sped along, quickly approaching Green Water City. The towering walls and barbed wire loomed ahead, but the road grew narrower, and the crowd denser. Felix Lucas had to slow down as they neared the refugee shelter.

Suddenly, hordes of refugees swarmed the truck, surrounding it so tightly that not even a needle could get through. Some grabbed the bumper, trying to climb onto the roof; others banged on the windows, mouthing desperate pleas for the doors to be opened. In this situation, F777's truck could barely inch forward.

Looking up, they saw countless frantic faces: an old man with tear-streaked cheeks holding his granddaughter, tripping after only a few steps; a woman with disheveled hair clutching a baby, gripping the door handle with a death grip; and a man with a ferocious expression, cursing and kicking the truck while demanding, "Open the door! Open the damn door!"

The pickup was fitted with one-way glass, so the refugees outside couldn't see in, but the team inside had a clear view.

"What...what do they want?!" Damian shouted in frustration. As if in response, the sound of a hammer striking the truck rang out, loud and insistent.

"They want to get into the city," Charles sighed. "They want us to take them in."

"We can't open the door," Onyx said coldly.

"We. Can't. Open. The. Door." He slowed his speech, repeating firmly.

The cabin fell silent. Cora's long lashes drooped as she remained quiet, not arguing.

Onyx was right. Even if they wanted to save people, they had to consider whether they could do so.

These refugees were indeed pitiful, but their truck couldn't carry everyone. Opening the door in this situation would only incite a larger riot, with unpredictable consequences.

"Step on it. Push through," Onyx ordered in a low voice.

The engine roared louder, causing some refugees to back away in fear. But more clung to the roof, banging on it with whatever they could find. Felix's mechanical arm slammed the pedal down, and the pickup surged forward like a blade slicing through water.

Those in the truck's path scrambled to get out of the way, watching helplessly as the vehicle sped towards the city gates.

Green Water City was now completely sealed off, with thick iron mesh covering the outer walls, crackling with high-voltage electricity. A city hall official, dressed in uniform, stood at a watchtower three or four meters above the ground, raising a loudspeaker to his mouth. His voice was hoarse as he shouted.

"We're at full capacity for refugees! We can't let anyone else in! Please wait! Please be patient! If there's more room, we'll let you in as soon as possible!"

The gate was packed with refugees unwilling to leave. Felix honked the horn until it shattered, but there was no response. Onyx activated the vehicle's external communication system and spoke to the official above, "We're participants in the Throne Tournament.

Please allow us entry."

The mention of entry caused an uproar among the crowd, who surged forward in a frenzy, pushing the pickup truck half a meter.

The official, overwhelmed and unwilling to open the gate, yelled back, "You're allowed in, but you'll have to find your own way inside! ...What?!"

"Find our own way... Alright then," Cora sighed.

The sunroof of the pickup opened, and Cora moved swiftly, tossing a grappling hook from an Ethereal Artifact that latched onto the watchtower's entrance. In one fluid motion, she grabbed Onyx and yanked him upward. The two soared into the air as Cora kicked off the wall a few times, deftly flipping over and landing atop the wall, demonstrating to everyone what it meant to scale walls effortlessly.

Suchat grabbed Yuui, replicating Cora's move, and followed her down.

Next, Damian and Charles were each grabbed by one of Felix's mechanical arms. He didn't even need a grappling hook—his four mechanical limbs extended, reaching the wall before retracting to lift them up, smoothly depositing them on top.

In mere seconds, all seven members of F777 had reached the watchtower. The official hadn't even finished saying, "find your own way inside," when a line of people suddenly appeared before him with a swift "whoosh."

"We're in," Cora said calmly.

The official, still holding the loudspeaker, stared at them in disbelief. "...That was fast." After verifying the participants, Cora took one last look at the sea of heads below the wall before turning away.

Inside Green Water City, the situation wasn't much better than outside. The influx of people from surrounding cities had already overwhelmed it. Temporary tents filled the streets and alleys, with refugees sleeping on the ground, exposed to the elements. The atmosphere was bleak, and a sense of fear hung heavy in the air.

F777 tried to emulate what they did in Cloud City, looking for the checkpoint drone, but it seemed the tournament organizers were a step ahead, having recalled the devices.

Other than the follow-cam drones, Felix couldn't detect any other data. They spent half the day circling the city, but found nothing unusual.

"So, what do we do now?" Cora asked.

Onyx's eyes narrowed as he looked at the refugee camps scattered around. He uttered a single word.

"Wait."

If his guess was correct, the checkpoint would soon reveal itself.

Outside Green Water City, shortly after F777 entered, several more steamers and hover cars followed. The gathered refugees grew more agitated, unable to contain their anger.

"Why can they go in?"

"Let us in! The zombie horde is almost here! Let us in!"

"Open the gate! I dare you to open the gate!"

The city hall official's voice was hoarse from shouting, but it was useless. The refugees, driven mad by the looming threat of the zombie horde, had lost all reason. With bloodshot eyes, they surged forward, too afraid to touch the electrified net, so they began ramming the lower barricade instead.

"Thud—"

A deafening crash rang out as those at the front pushed too hard, stumbled and fell. The refugees behind them, unaware, kept pushing forward relentlessly, trampling over their fallen companions without mercy.

"Thud—"

The watchtower shook, dust raining down from the ceiling, as the armed soldiers above aimed at the crowd below, unsure where to shoot.

"Thud—"

A breach appeared in the once-solid barricade, and the gate wobbled, on the verge of collapse. Thousands of refugees, seeing hope at last, burst through the barriers and surged into Green Water City.

From above, the sight of those dark, swarming figures, their twisted bodies running wildly, was indistinguishable from a zombie horde.

Inside the city, Cora and the rest of the F777 team received a system notification: "Green Water City checkpoint has appeared."

CHAPTER 11

Blackmail

"Green Water is finished," Onyx said coldly.

With the defenses breached, Green Water was as vulnerable as a helpless infant. Even a small-scale zombie horde could wipe it out.

"Clock in, and then we leave," Cora decided.

The seven of them turned back towards the city gate. Cora moved swiftly, leaping into the wall. Her coat flapped in the wind as she lightly landed on the top of the corpse mound. Warm bodies beneath her feet soaked her shoes in blood almost instantly.

The pile of trampled bodies was already dozens of meters high, stretching out over a two-hundred-meter radius, but the check-in point had been buried at the bottom. Cora summoned an iron shovel and began digging.

As she dug, her eyes met those of a girl trapped beneath the weight of dozens of others. The girl was about her age, her left side twisted unnaturally, barely alive as she gazed at Cora, pleading, "Help...help me..."

Cora paused for two seconds before tossing aside the shovel. She used her hands to pull away the top layer of corpses, dragging the girl out, knowing in her heart that even if she freed her, the girl wouldn't survive.

Her hands were soon coated in sticky blood and pieces of flesh, but the survivor managed a weak smile at Cora.

"Tha..."

Before she could finish speaking, a particle cannon suddenly descended from above, crashing into the heap of bodies and sending a shockwave that engulfed both Cora and the girl.

"Cora!"

"Captain!"

"Sis!!"

The other F777 members shouted, looking up in alarm.

As the blinding light gradually faded, the explosion left a dark hole in the corpse mound. Cora crawled out from the mangled remains, unharmed, but when she looked down, she saw the girl was blown to pieces.

Cora closed her eyes briefly, then quickly turned her gaze to the attackers.

Apart from F777, several other teams had already arrived, including the reformed "Knights of Anna." Despite being significantly weakened after Cora single-handedly took down their ace player, "Cyborg Head" Seon, they were still formidable opponents.

The Knights of Anna were clearing the area with heavy weaponry.

These mechanized soldiers, with irritation on their faces, had just blasted open a gap with the particle cannon, only to see fresh bodies pile up in its place.

Frustrated, they leaped onto the city wall, brutally slaughtering the civilians, pushing forward with their powers, causing severed limbs to fly in all directions. The Knights didn't even blink as they tore through the crowd, cutting a path towards the check-in point.

Cora's mind briefly wandered. What are they doing? Is this right? Before entering the Throne Tournament, all competitors had signed a life-and-death waiver. Each victory had to be fought for with their lives.

But this isn't fighting zombies. This is... this is outright... massacre.

Cora's fists clenched tighter than she suddenly jumped onto the shattered wall, her serrated sword slashing through the air, forcing the refugees pushing forward to retreat.

"Don't come any closer! Get back!"

Those at the front, realizing the danger, tried to flee, but the refugees pouring in from the shelter knew nothing and continued to push forward, sending countless others to their deaths.

Onyx looked up at Cora, pressing a hand against his temple. This wasn't working. The refugee tide wouldn't retreat, and they had no way to get close to the check-in point. His mind raced as he recalled the map of Green Water. Aside from the main gate, there were three other exits to the east, west, and north.

"Break open the side gates. Let them in!"

Felix and the others instantly understood his plan, splitting up to use their powers to attack the barricades. Green Water was beyond saving and would soon be overrun by the out-of-control refugees. Their goal now was to disperse the crowd quickly at the main gate to prevent further trampling incidents.

The sound of walls collapsing came quickly from the east and west, followed by billowing clouds of dust.

Onyx used his mental powers, his commanding voice echoing clearly over Green Water.

"Everyone in the back, listen up! The main gate is blocked! There's a new entrance one kilometer to the east and two kilometers to the southwest! Run there if you want to get inside!"

"Space is limited! The faster you run, the better your chances of survival!"

Human nature seemed hard-wired to react to words like "limited" or "restricted." At Onyx's call, the refugees at the back hesitated for a moment before turning to run towards the new entrances.

It was like the parting of the Red Sea. The crowd split and dispersed at a rapid pace. With the pressure at the front easing, no more bodies were added to the pile.

Cora had just let out a breath of relief when she heard cursing behind her. A volley of particle beams was fired at her. "What the hell are you doing?!"

"If you don't want to compete, just quit already! I've had enough of you!"

Cora raised her serrated sword to deflect the attack and looked up. The Knights of Anna were glaring at her with venom in their eyes. She frowned, puzzled for a second, before realizing in shock that the check-in point, once buried beneath the bodies, had disappeared!

But she quickly understood. If it was a flower watered with blood, then as the evil faded, the check-in point would naturally vanish too.

"You just wait."

Knowing how dangerous Cora could be, the Knights of Anna didn't want a direct confrontation at that moment. They spat their threats and left in a huff.

The refugees who flooded into the city had nowhere to go. Gradually, they transformed from lost lambs into ferocious wolves. They set parked vehicles ablaze with gasoline, shattered the windows of shops along the street, and even broke into the homes of terrified residents.

Extreme anger and fear had consumed these people's sanity. They were no longer refugees, but had become full-fledged rioters. Malice grew in their hearts, and the guillotine of death would inevitably fall. If they couldn't escape the apocalypse, then everyone would perish together!

Cora Thornton's eyes narrowed as she watched a projection drop from the sky, only to disappear and reappear in another direction in the next instant. The location of the check-in point kept changing, sometimes staying in one place for just a few seconds.

"Split up," Cora ordered, "and clock in as fast as possible."

Cora weaved through the piercing alarms and cries, dodging panicked civilians. Ignited vehicles careened wildly through the streets, threatening to collide head-on if she wasn't careful, erupting into fierce flames. She narrowly avoided one such vehicle by diving to the side of the road.

"Hey, girl..." A tattered old man suddenly grabbed her arm. "You're that girl, right?!"

Cora paused, staring at the old man for two seconds before recognizing him. "...Old Cheung."

Old Cheung clutched her wrist excitedly. "It's really you, girl! Thank goodness, thank goodness..." He kept repeating "thank goodness," his bony fingers tightening as if afraid she might slip away.

"You're an Aberrant now, so capable. I saw you in that competition! I knew you'd come. Help me. Quickly, get me out of here, take me somewhere safe..." His eyes shone with hope, and he blurted, his words rushing out in a frenzy.

After leaving District F177, Old Cheung's feverish son suddenly mutated into a zombie on the starship and was beaten to death by other passengers.

His daughter-in-law ran off with their money and grandson as soon as they reached District C. Fortunately, Old Cheung had been cautious and transferred his funds beforehand. He had planned to retire in District C, but before long, the zombie horde arrived, and the city fell.

He had been struggling to survive near Green Water City, which now seemed on the verge of collapse. Cora's appearance rekindled his hope.

"No," Cora shook her head slowly, firmly pulling her hand free. As expected, her wrist was red from his grip. "I still have... a competition."

Old Cheung's face instantly darkened. "Why not? You won't help me?"

Cora sighed inwardly.

Old Cheung still saw her as the naïve little girl from District F, expecting her to abandon the competition, her teammates, and the Zombie Lord who could threaten the next city at any moment, just to take him to safety.

How can people be so selfish? Cora's choice not to hold a grudge for the past didn't mean he could take advantage of her again.

She didn't bother to explain further and turned to leave. A passerby bumped into Old Cheung, causing him to stumble. At that moment, a drone swooped down, capturing a close-up of the two of them.

Old Cheung suddenly sprang to his feet, his aged face glaring into the drone's camera. The footage wavered, revealing his extreme indignation.

"Cora, you ungrateful wretch! You heartless brat! I raised you with so much effort. I'm your grandpa! Are you going to just watch me die? Watch me die right in front of you?!"

The refugees in Green Water were too busy fleeing for their lives to care about the drama unfolding before them, but across the screens in Felalakas and the entire eastern sector of the Alliance, Old Cheung's actions sparked an uproar. Outraged viewers emerged, standing on moral high ground to condemn her:

"She won't even save her own grandpa? Who knew the F777 captain was this kind of person?"

"She seems powerful, but her heart is so cold. I regret voting for her."

"Helping is just a simple act of kindness. Why can't she be a bit more compassionate?"

"You're not my grandpa." Cora stopped in her tracks, her voice dropping to an icy tone, enunciating every word.

She had intended to walk away, but Old Cheung's insistence on calling himself "grandpa" struck a nerve. "You don't deserve to be my grandpa."

It was her own fault for not noticing the messages Old Thornton had left her in the light screen, but Old Cheung knew and had intentionally hidden it, never mentioning it even once.

Cora swung her serrated sword with a sharp "clang," slicing through Old Cheung's collar, the blade reflecting her cold, emotionless face.

Old Cheung's eyes flickered, and he shamelessly threw all dignity aside, clutching his chest and wailing, "Oh no, oh no! How could there be such a cruel girl? You ungrateful brat, are you trying to kill me? You want me dead, don't you...?"

Cora turned away in disbelief. She had held back, not hurting him at all, so why was he making such a scene? As soon as Old Cheung noticed her move, he suddenly gathered an immense amount of strength, grabbing her pant leg and collapsing to the ground, wailing incessantly, refusing to let go.

The drone captured every detail of the old man's withered, cracked skin, the bulging veins on the back of his hands, and his agonized expression.

The barrage of condemnations in the livestream's chat didn't stop, and F777's support rate plummeted.

"I can't watch this! How could she treat an innocent old man like that? She'll get her comeuppance."

"Poor old grandpa. He looks like he's about to pass out."

"Exactly. It's obvious the old man is using moral blackmail."

"The old man is sick, and Cora is so strong. Can't she just help him?"

"Easier said than done. Why don't you go help, then?"

"Well... I'm not in the competition, so it's none of my business!"

The chat quickly devolved into a chaotic argument, with the AI moderators banning users left and right.

Cora had never been this angry before.

Some people just aren't cut out for arguing. When emotions run high, their speech system gets out of control. Cora was one of those people.

She also had a stutter, and as she tried to force out a coherent response, all she managed was a jumbled, unable to finish a single complete sentence.

"Hey, you nasty old man, how shameless can you be? I've had enough of you for a long time!"

Yuui, wearing a mask, suddenly rushed over from behind them, her words firing off like a machine gun. "You took someone else's money, mistreated someone else's child, and now you've got the nerve to play the victim here, crying fake tears?"

"A heart attack, huh? I'm a doctor. Let me check." Charles Franz stepped forward without waiting for a reply, grabbing Old Cheung's arm to force an examination.

Old Cheung flailed his limbs desperately, but despite Franz's delicate appearance, he was still an Aberrant, and holding the old man down was no challenge.

"He's got plenty of strength, healthier than most people, not a thing wrong with him," Charles said coldly.

"Cora has a real grandpa, so what kind of 'grandpa' are you? Oh, the kind who steals other people's money and leaves their kid to fend for themselves? Or the kind who, when the apocalypse hit, threw her out into a zombie horde? If I were you, I'd be on my knees begging Cora for forgiveness, slapping myself silly, and here you are, trying to morally blackmail her into saving you? Disgusting!" Yuui was on a roll, her words relentless.

Felix's fingers danced across his terminal as he chimed in, "As of April 5th, New Era 47, Old Cheung illegally embezzled over 1.2 million credits from Cora Thornton's assets and refused to return them. The amount reached the maximum penalty threshold, and as her acting guardian, he also committed the crime of abandonment..."

He hacked into Old Cheung's personal account, tracing every transaction back to the day Thornton transferred the money, every financial movement clearly documented. There was even a high-definition shot of Old Cheung smugly swiping his card to pay for something—a public shaming in real time.

Sensing a juicy scandal, the drone zoomed in on the screen, capturing all the evidence in crystal-clear detail. The trolls who had been supporting Old Cheung and condemning Cora for being heartless suddenly went silent, vanishing as if they'd never existed.

Onyx patted Cora on the back, offering quiet reassurance.

"Don't let it bother you. People are often ignorant, quick to judge with cheap sympathy and tears, easily forgiving those who provoke while condemning those who are provoked."

Cora glanced at him slowly, not really listening to what he was saying.

Instead, she muttered under her breath, genuinely awed, "...That's a lot of money."

Onyx blinked in surprise.

Having struggled through the apocalypse, constantly worrying about making money for her team (especially for Felix), Cora was only now realizing that her grandpa had been so wealthy.

She could have been a little rich girl!

Old Cheung, having been verbally flayed by Yuui and exposed by Felix, felt his thick skin wear thin.

The looks these people were giving him were as if they wanted to tear him apart. He cursed under his breath and retreated, "You brats, you ungrateful wretches..."

Onyx watched him leave, his eyes narrowing slightly. Old Cheung's hunched back stiffened for a moment before he resumed his feigned nonchalance, walking away as if nothing had happened. No one noticed these tiny details.

Cora turned to her friends, who had stood up for her. "Thank you...?"

Yuui reached out, grabbing Cora's cheeks and squeezing them playfully. "Why didn't you call us when you couldn't handle him?"

Cora mumbled through squished lips, "You... you shouldn't... squeeze me..."

Felix opened his terminal, projecting the footage captured by the drone. "Stop messing around. I've got some bad news."

The thermal imaging revealed a massive green mass approaching Green Water City, just under five kilometers away. "The real zombie horde is coming."

Cora hit Yuui's hands away and shouted to her team, "The check-in point! Move, move!"

She bounced on her feet and sprinted off.

Felix shot a sidelong glance at the silent Onyx. "Why didn't you say anything? Don't tell me you didn't know." Given Onyx's mental powers, he must have sensed the approaching horde long ago but had kept quiet.

"You did something to it," Felix stated with certainty.

Onyx raised an eyebrow. "I'm not one to let grudges slide."

Old Cheung, now confused, stood at the city gate, momentarily forgetting what he had intended to do. "Why did I come here?" he muttered to himself in bewilderment.

His plan to leave with Cora's help had fallen through, and he needed to think of another way. Old Cheung opened his terminal to check his account balance, hoping to see how much money he had left. Even in the apocalypse, money could still be useful.

But he froze in shock. His account was completely empty. All his money, everything he had, was gone!

Old Cheung looked up in disbelief, his dilated pupils reflecting the rolling black wave in the distance. "Wh-what... what is that?" he stammered in terror.

He tried to run, but it was as if his limbs were frozen in place.

The unending horde of zombies surged toward Green Water City, breaking through the now-useless defenses and overwhelming Old Cheung in an instant. As his consciousness faded, Old Cheung thought he glimpsed the zombie baring its fangs at him, looking eerily like Thornton.

CHAPTER 12

The Horde

Damian hid inside an empty trash can, peeking out just enough to observe his surroundings.

Across the street, seven or eight brazen refugees were ransacking a large supermarket. Shopping carts and shelves were being knocked over, the chaotic sounds of their actions echoing through the area. After they had looted everything they could, they poured large quantities of cooking oil on the floor, tossed in some ignited cotton, and set the place ablaze. Flames shot up immediately.

Not long after they left with their loot, a holographic projection flickered into the air above the supermarket. "A check-in point!" Damian's eyes lit up, a surge of excitement making him do a little dance in his head. He had stumbled upon it with pure luck—what great fortune for little Damian!

He quickly encased himself in ice from head to toe and dashed into the burning supermarket. The check-in point this time was near the ceiling. Damian found the nearest industrial shelving unit and began climbing, puffing and panting with effort.

The temperature inside was scorching, causing his ice to melt rapidly. His little face turned bright red from the heat, and sweat dripped from his curled hair as it drooped over his forehead.

He reached out to wipe his face, nervously climbing higher until he was perched on top of the shelf. He stretched out his terminal, trying to reach the check-in point, but—he was still a significant distance away.

Standing on tiptoe, he stretched as far as he could, pushing his fingertips upward, finally getting just... a little closer.

Frustrated, Damian stomped his foot. This was so unfair! For the first time, he wished he wasn't just 130 cm tall (he had grown 3 cm over the New Year). If only Suchat were here... Actually, anyone— Felix, Charles, Yuui, or his sister—any of them would have been tall enough to reach it.

Well, except maybe the one in the wheelchair. Damian pouted and sent a message to the group chat: "Check-in point, come quick!"

But the other members of F777 were too busy defending Cora to notice the tiny alert in the group chat.

Damian, who had turned off his receiver to stay hidden, switched it back on and raised his voice.

"Hello? Anyone there?"

The moment his earpiece activated, Yuui's vibrant, sharp voice came through loud and clear, cursing like a sailor.

She was going off about "nasty old man," "shameless jerk," and "kneel and slap yourself," leaving Damian utterly confused.

It took a while before Suchat finally replied, calmly saying, "Send your location." Only the two of them were still on task.

Damian sat cross-legged on top of the shelf, listening to the tirade while nodding along indignantly, "Mm! Mm!"

He got so caught up in it, he accidentally burned one side of his butt, jumping up with a yelp and shifting his position.

Before long, Suchat arrived at the supermarket, dousing himself with a bucket of cold water before dashing in like a gust of wind. "Where's the check-in point?"

Damian pointed to it casually, still muttering about the "bad guy" and "stinky old man." "There."

Suchat looked around. "... Where?"

Damian replied, "Right over th—"

The holographic seal had already disappeared.

Damian was stunned.

Oh no, he had been so engrossed in listening to Yuui and the others rant he hadn't noticed the check-in point moving! Suchat stared at him silently. Damian blinked his big eyes and looked back innocently.

Around them, sparks crackled and popped as the supermarket continued to burn down to almost nothing.

"Let's go," Suchat said, lifting the small Damian off the shelf and casually tucking him under his arm.

"Cool me down." The cold water he had splashed on himself had already evaporated, and the scorching flames were licking at his skin.

"... Oh." Damian, who had basically become a human ice maker, reluctantly stuck out his butt and wiggled his small legs.

Knowing he was at fault, he obediently used his power, encasing the two of them in a thick layer of frost as they hurried out of the supermarket.

Just as they made it onto the street, the rest of F777 followed the location tracker and met up with them.

"Damian! Where's the check-in point?" Cora asked, brimming with energy.

"It's gone," Damian replied, waving his hands dejectedly. "It was right in front of my face!"

"If it was right there, why didn't you just clock in?" Onyx asked, his tone calm and deliberate.

Damian's bravado deflated instantly, and he muttered, "I-I couldn't reach it. I was just this much too short!"

Suchat glanced at him, keeping silent to preserve Damian's dignity.

"Time's running out. The zombie horde is here," Felix reminded them.

A dense swarm of zombies, like a plague of locusts, rapidly overran the streets and alleys. They stormed into buildings, leaped onto car roofs, and pinned down the fleeing humans, tearing into them savagely.

The splattering blood was like a crimson velvet carpet being laid over Green Water City.

The refugees who had recently taken shelter in the city were now desperately trying to flee again after witnessing the massacre.

Cora's serrated sword flashed with a cold light as she sliced through the head of a zombie charging at her. "Where's the Zombie Lord?"

Felix, both mechanical arms in motion, shouted back, "Not here!"

Yuui kept singing, pausing just long enough to yell, "Not even a level 3 zombie!"

A mix of level 1 and 2 zombies, along with a few Aberrant zombies, formed the main composition of this wave of the horde. Although their numbers were high, their strength varied, making it possible for ordinary people to resist.

Once the Aberrants and official armed forces in Green Water responded, they would eventually eliminate them.

Without the Zombie Lord to command them, the horde was nothing more than a disorganized rabble. Onyx's eyes darkened as he quickly connected the dots to an ancient military tactic—could this be a feint?

Attacking Green Water City was likely a diversion orchestrated by the cunning Zombie Lord, who had deliberately released low-level zombies to simulate a siege while secretly deploying its elite forces elsewhere.

Onyx opened his light screen and switched to the Throne Tournament's live broadcast channel. Some of the leading teams, like "Iron Cafe," had already reached Lava Land, but this city, which was the most likely to be attacked, was still peaceful.

He quickly scanned the other contestants' personal livestreams. The teams were at different stages; some were fighting zombies in already fallen cities, others were tirelessly on the move, and a few were lounging around, taking a break in a restaurant. But nowhere did he see signs of another wave of the horde.

Onyx's fingers paused for a moment, then switched to the marathon map, doing some quick mental calculations.

Theoretically, trying to guess the psychological workings of a zombie was absurd, but Onyx didn't hesitate. His gaze settled on the second-to-last checkpoint—Ocean Gate.

"Check-in point!" Cora suddenly shouted, pointing upward. From the 30th floor of a skyscraper ahead, glass shattered as several figures tumbled out, crashing down with a thunderous impact.

F777 rapidly closed in on their target, only to find themselves face-to-face with the Knights of Anna once again. The mechanized team had beaten them to it, landing their steamship on the rooftop of the skyscraper. Five Aberrants from the Knights of Anna rappelled down to the designated floor and quickly activated their terminals.

A holographic message appeared, reading: "Congratulations to the Knights of Anna for successfully checking in."

Cora Thornton frowned deeply as she observed them. The Knights of Anna had changed—they must have looted Green Water City's armory. Now they were heavily armed, with assault rifles, shoulder-mounted mortars, and crude mechanical components fused with their bodies, creating a mismatched but menacing appearance.

The five mechanized soldiers turned their guns on Cora and her team without hesitation. They had been ambushed at the city gate earlier, but now they had the upper hand and were eager for payback.

"You want to check in? I'll turn you into Swiss cheese!" the leader, sporting mechanical legs, shouted arrogantly. Gunfire erupted, casings flying everywhere, forcing Cora and her team to retreat under the intense barrage. The firepower was too overwhelming to push through.

"Take out their medic and support first!"

The instinct to target the healers in a battle was ingrained in their DNA. A surge of Aberrant powers immediately homed in on Charles and Yuui.

Yuui quickly recited a rap-like chant to protect herself, and a thick fog rose, obscuring the two from the Knights of Anna's view.

However, Charles was a prime target, and the mechanized soldiers, holding the aerial advantage, had already locked onto his position. A thick chain shot through the fog with a "crack," latching onto Charles's ankle and dragging him out.

The Aberrant who had made the grab sneered as he dangled Charles upside down, swinging him around twice before hurling him into the densest cluster of zombies.

Suchat's muscles coiled like a spring as he leaped over the rooftops, sprinting towards Charles' landing spot like a cheetah.

But he was too late. Charles crashed down on top of dozens of zombies with a resounding "thud."

"Charlie!" Cora's eye twitched uncontrollably with tension.

Charles scrambled to his feet, looking around in panic. The zombies had been surprised by his sudden arrival, some of them with broken necks, others with large holes punched through their chests, blackened fluid oozing out.

"Raaaargh—" The zombies, their feeding interrupted, snarled in anger, baring their decayed fangs as they lunged at Charles, their foul saliva splattering on his face, their teeth nearly grazing his eyes.

But then the zombies froze.

They seemed to lose track of him, sniffing around Charles with a confused air before turning their attention back to the corpses they had been gnawing on.

Charles tentatively moved his leg, trying to stand, but tripped and fell again, slapping a zombie across the face with his left hand. The zombie's head twisted to the side, and it sprang up, looking around as if disoriented, but completely ignored Charles standing right next to it.

Cora let out a long breath of relief. That had been terrifying—she'd almost forgotten that Charles's strange constitution made him immune to zombie bites. Suchat quickly reached his position and hauled Charles back to safety.

Cora's cold gaze shifted to the Knights of Anna. During F777's brief distraction, the check-in point had disappeared again. But this time, it didn't reappear elsewhere as it usually did.

Cora realized something. The refugees, exhausted and desperate, were no longer causing enough chaos to manifest the check-in point as frequently. The mechanical-legged leader smirked arrogantly from above. After preventing F777 from checking in, the Knights of Anna turned to climb back up to the rooftop, preparing to retreat.

They almost killed Charles, and now they wanted to flee?

Cora grabbed a fallen power line, transforming it into a nine-section whip, and began climbing the exterior of the skyscraper at lightning speed, quickly closing the distance between herself and the Knights of Anna. Without warning, she cracked the whip, shouting, "Control them!"

Damian quickly encased one of the Knights' feet in ice. The ghostly blue whip followed suit, wrapping around his neck. With a swift yank, Cora pulled him straight down from the hundred-meter height, sending mechanical parts scattering across the ground.

"Damn it! Run!"

Another member had just shouted when Yuui's curse took effect, causing him to lose his footing. Cora's whip caught him around the waist, peeling him away from the building's surface.

"You little bastards, die already!!"

Cora's ascent became more rapid, her attacks more ferocious, as she forced the Knights of Anna towards the edge of the building. The mortars on their shoulders fired wildly, shattering the building's supporting beams, causing it to tilt precariously.

Cora's eyes locked onto the last remaining Knight, his mechanical legs quivering in fear. He was just a step away from the steamship. Gritting his teeth, he discarded all unnecessary weight, suction cups sprouting from his legs as he clung to the glass surface, quickly putting some distance between himself and Cora.

The Knight's left hand grabbed the steamship's door, his face lighting up with a look of triumph. He was almost free! But just then, a powerful mental force invaded his mind, making his eyes go blank.

The serpent-like whip wrapped around his thigh. Cora's arm muscles tightened as she used her entire body's weight to yank backward.

With a "pop," the suction cups lost their grip on the glass, and the Knight's legs were torn off. He plummeted to the ground, unconscious, before he could even register what had happened.

The Knights of Anna were annihilated!

A bright holographic projection descended, revealing the fire seal, as the battle between the Aberrants once again caused the flower of evil to bloom. The opportunity was fleeting.

Cora swiftly pulled herself up, using the momentum to leap into the air. She twisted her body mid-jump, her slim waist and abdomen slicing through the air with precision, as she pressed her terminal against the check-in point!

"Congratulations to F777 for successfully checking in."

They did it! Cora landed, rolling as she did so, but unexpectedly slid off the edge of the rooftop. She caught the railing with lightning speed, her body dangling precariously. Feeling a rush of excitement, she flashed a "V" sign to the others below, regardless of whether they could see her.

The next second, the overburdened skyscraper snapped in half, crumbling into pieces. The collapsing railing tilted sideways, and

Cora's footing gave way as she plummeted from the sky like a kite with a broken string.

"Hurry, catch her!" Yuui screamed, her face pale with fear as she stretched out her arms and ran forward. Cora was now at least a hundred meters above the ground. No matter how strong her powers were, her body wouldn't survive the fall!

"Boom—" Cora tried to grab onto a steel beam, but it broke. Her head smashed through the glass as she tumbled inside the building, then rolled back out. The descent was so fast that she couldn't find anything solid to hold on to, so she used her whip to latch onto whatever she could, slowing her fall.

Veins bulged on Onyx's hand as half his body wavered, suddenly leaving his wheelchair!

Felix smashed a shop window, pulling out a mattress and stretching it with his six mechanical arms to serve as a makeshift cushion. The collapsing building exploded, sending up thick plumes of smoke.

"Thump—thump—"

Cora bounced off the mattress like a ball, landing safely with the impact reduced. Felix let out a breath of relief, retracting his mechanical arms to help her up.

But Cora, slippery as an eel, somehow slid off the edge again. She "thudded" twice more, finally crashing onto the roof of a nearby armored truck, sprawled face-down in a heap.

Felix winced. "...Uh-oh." Damian covered his face, wincing in empathy. That had to hurt!

Cora clutched her head as she staggered to her feet, wobbling in a daze before finally standing still, her back to the others. She mumbled into the air, "Heh heh, I clocked in."

Onyx snapped his fingers. "Cora, turn around." Cora turned her head, still in a daze, but couldn't seem to find anyone.

Then her eyes welled up with tears, and two streams of blood trickled from her nose.

CHAPTER 13

The Price

"Ha ha—"

"Ha ha ha—"

"Pfft, ha ha ha—"

Cora pulled on a coat big enough to cover her entire body and sat cross-legged in the backseat, trying her best to fade into the background. The oversized hood hid her blushing face, and she had tissues stuffed up her nose. The unrestrained laughter of her teammates echoed in her ears, with Yuui, Felix, and the "leaking" Damian being the loudest culprits.

"Cora, are you made of jelly? How can you be so bouncy, ha ha! You even bounced off the ground!"

"Does your face hurt? Because mine hurt just watching you hit the pavement!"

"There's already a meme of you crashing into the armored truck. It's pretty popular—I saved it. Wanna see it? I can send it to you."

Cora kept a straight face, thinking, I should've climbed over them instead of flashing a peace sign.

She looked over at Suchat and Charles, holding onto a shred of hope that they wouldn't join in the mockery. Charles was struggling to keep a straight face, his left hand shaking as he handed her a pack of band-aids. Suchat avoided her gaze, coughed twice as if to cover up, and turned away quietly.

Don't think I didn't notice—you're totally laughing!

Onyx reached over from the front seat and ruffled Cora's hair through the hood. His long fingers slipped down, gently grazing the slight scrape on her cheek.

Cora flinched and tried to dodge, but his hand brushed against her ear, causing it to turn bright red as if set on fire.

"Next time you jump from a building, aim better. At least... try not to land face-first," Onyx said with a teasing smirk, his voice low and husky.

Cora froze, then snapped out of it and bit down on the fleshy part of his thumb. After a moment, she spat it out, grimacing. It was hard and hurt her teeth.

"We're in the middle of a competition, people! Focus up! Serious business!" Cora shouted, humiliated and furious.

They had pushed too far; the captain was losing her temper. The team quickly got the hint and shut their mouths, pretending to busy themselves.

"You guys! Be serious!" Damian, like a petty tyrant, started bossing people around, pointing his finger at everyone.

Cora huffed coldly and turned to look out the window. The road out of town was littered with bodies, a scene of utter devastation. Zombies, drawn by the engine noise, rushed at them with snarling faces, only to be sent flying by Felix's wild driving.

The new SUV they found wasn't as stable for long drives as the off-road pickup they had before. Whenever it took a hit, the entire vehicle would jolt, making everyone inside sway.

Onyx lightly tapped his fingers and summoned a holographic map, marking off Cloud City and Green Water City with X's, then thickening the line to Ocean Gate, the shortest route.

"We'll only hit the safe cities, complete the checkpoints along the way, and reach Ocean Gate by the end of the day."

"No detours?" Suchat asked, a bit surprised. According to the original plan, F777 was supposed to pass through a fallen District C. If they took Onyx's route, they'd have to loop back after reaching Ocean Gate, wasting more time.

"Our goal is the championship. Killing the Zombie Lord is the key. If we miss this chance to catch it, finishing the checkpoints on time would mean nothing—we wouldn't win," Onyx said slowly.

"You think the Zombie Lord is heading for Ocean Gate? Why not Lava Land? Ocean Gate is a much tougher target," Yuui questioned. "You're so sure? What if it goes to Lava Land instead?" Felix shot him a skeptical glance. If Onyx was wrong, they'd be wasting precious time and miss the chance to confront the Zombie Lord.

Onyx's eyes narrowed with a deepening smile. "Based on our encounter in Sycamore, this Zombie Lord fights fiercely, with a bold yet careful approach. It's skilled in using ancient military tactics, weaving and circling to disrupt its enemy's rhythm. Also, it stays calm under pressure, making accurate decisions even in disadvantageous situations. It's an exceptionally brilliant battlefield commander."

Onyx rarely praised anyone, and here he was, gushing over a zombie. The others exchanged bewildered looks.

"I've checked the records. None of the Alliance's registered commanders have a style like this," Felix's spare mechanical arm tapped the projection, shooting down Onyx's argument without hesitation. "If it's as good as you say, it shouldn't be some nobody, right?"

Onyx disdainfully flicked Felix's overstepping hand away. "You think talent is all it takes to rise to the top? There are plenty of geniuses who never make it—you should know that better than anyone."

Felix, who had his legs broken and was thrown into Death Hell by his own family for being "too talented and rebellious."

"... Hey, isn't that hitting a bit too close to home?"

"If I were it, with a well-disciplined, never-ending army of the undead at my command, my zombie instincts would be screaming at me to destroy this world. Meanwhile, the remnants of my human intellect would guide me step by step toward victory.

"I'd want Lava Land. I'd want the Ocean Gate too. Since these foolish humans think I'll attack Lava Land, I'll humor them, toss out a bit of bait. Oh? You're all ready to kill me? What a shame—I've already secretly slipped into Ocean Gate, ready to catch you off guard."

"Ocean Gate is a tough nut to crack, but once I take it, the path ahead will be smooth, and I'll conquer the entire Alliance...." Onyx's fingers drummed rhythmically, his eyes deep.

His voice dropped to a raspy whisper as he eerily mimicked the

Zombie Lord's thought process, sending shivers down the spines of everyone around him. Wow, this guy is seriously creepy.

"Why is Ocean Gate so tough?" Cora asked cluelessly, not noticing the uneasy atmosphere.

The teammates eagerly jumped in with explanations, desperate for Onyx to stop talking—it was seriously unsettling.

"Ocean Gate is the most important grain supply for the East. Whether in terms of total output, commercial volume, or exports, it's number one in the Alliance. Statistically, for every three bowls of rice eaten below District C, one comes from Ocean Gate," Yuui said.

"Ocean Gate covers a vast area—it's the largest in District D, but its population is under ten million. With so much space and so few people, the locals live well, and they're tough and bold, known for being straightforward and unpretentious," Lin said.

"My dad said Ocean Gate folks are big, dumb, rich, and easy to fool," Damian chimed in.

Everyone turned to glare at him. What kind of father says that? And what if someone from Ocean Gate overheard? Realizing his mistake, Damian quickly covered his mouth.

"... Heh, heh," he chuckled nervously, having accidentally said too much.

Charles stroked his chin thoughtfully. "I heard from a colleague that Ocean Gate people aren't great at arguing."

"Why?"

"Because before they get to the third sentence, like 'What are you looking at?' 'Looking at you, so what?' their fist is already in your face."

Cora: Sounds like... a rather unique city.

"You're sure the Zombie Lord will go to Ocean Gate?" Cora turned to ask Onyx.

"Seventy percent sure," Onyx nodded, not over-committing.

Cora thought for a moment, then decisively slapped the table. "Then we're heading to Ocean Gate." The captain had spoken, and they had to follow.

"Ocean Gate, Ocean Gate, go!"

Felix floored the gas pedal, and the SUV sped across the wasteland, sending zombies flying like rag dolls.

In the car's quiet, Yuui nudged Felix, whispering, "Hey, send me that meme edit."

"I want it too!" Damian chimed in from the front seat, his voice low.

Suchat said nothing but pointed at his own terminal, clearly showing he wanted it as well.

Felix quickly used one of his mechanical arms to send the video to the F777 group chat.

The terminal buzzed, and Cora, who had been dozing off, groggily woke up. Her fingers moved faster than her brain, instinctively opening the message. Her face froze as she realized what it was. "— Take it back! Delete it now!!!"

By nightfall, F777 had successfully completed the checkpoints at four safe cities and reached the outskirts of District D135, Ocean Gate.

The wilderness was eerily quiet, with no sign of a zombie horde. Only a few scattered zombies roamed about, some clutching shovels and scythes, others lingering near irrigation machines and plow shafts, and a few gnawing on tractors and loader trucks. Their rotting, hollow eyes betrayed no emotion.

"If the apocalypse hadn't happened, this would be the spring planting season..." Charles sighed.

As they approached a large, three-story villa, the sound of fighting reached their ears. A group of a dozen people wielding weapons fought with zombies.

The most conspicuous among them was a burly man over six feet tall, wearing a gaudy floral shirt with a large gold chain around his neck and a gold watch on his wrist. He was wrapped in something that might have been fur or mink, and his shoes were polished to a mirror-like shine.

Cora climbed onto the car roof for a better view. This group had no visible powers; they were ordinary people. Despite that, their combat prowess was impressive.

"Screw you!" the burly man shouted as he kicked a lunging zombie, his face jiggling with the movement. Nearby, a bodyguard in a suit raised a golf club and smashed it down on a zombie's head, caving it in.

"Look at you, thinking you can mess with me on my turf! You

must have a death wish!" the man yelled, growing more aggressive with each zombie he took down. "Take that!"

Cora noticed a flash of dark blue as she lowered herself back into the car, even though they seemed to handle the zombies well. She paused, then quickly looked up.

In the distance, the burly man drew a wide-bladed short sword and slashed straight at a zombie's head. The blade was sharp enough to slice through iron, and the zombie's head separated from its body, spraying foul blood like a fountain.

Cora's gaze narrowed. If she wasn't mistaken, that was a... blade?

"Stop the car," she ordered.

She opened the door and swiftly walked toward the group.

Having just finished the zombies besieging his villa, William Strong was drenched in sweat and couldn't help but grumble to himself. It's spring already.

Maybe wearing mink wasn't the best idea? He unbuttoned his shirt, gulping in the fresh air, and noticed a young girl walking toward him.

Well, well, William mused. He had a sharp eye, and this girl's aura was something else—definitely not your average person.

The girl stopped in front of him, her eyes locked onto the short sword in his hand. "What are you staring at?" one bodyguard growled, his voice gruff.

Startled by his loud voice, Cora reflexively responded, "... Staring at you, so what?" The bodyguard's eyebrows shot up, and he gripped his golf club, itching for a fight. This little girl was asking for trouble, wasn't she?

"Hey—back off, back off," William Strong waved a hand grandly, showing his magnanimity. "Let her take a look. What harm could it do?"

He slung the short sword over his shoulder, his tone suddenly friendly. "What do you think? Impressed by my zombie-slaying skills?"

He swung the sword a bit too enthusiastically, accidentally nicking his mink coat. "Ow, ow, ow!" William yelped, jumping up as he struggled to juggle his coat and the sword, shouting, "My baby!"

Cora helpfully reached out and steadied the familiar-looking blade. "Can I... inspect your sword?"

"Sure, sure." William was too preoccupied to pay her much attention.

Cora turned the blade over, her gaze dropping to the hilt. As she expected, there was a small "Thornton" engraved on it. This was one of her Ethereal Artifacts—how had it ended up here?

This model had only been mass-produced once, back in Blossomville, where she'd made a hundred of them as part of a deal with the students of the High School of the Flower City.

"Where did you get this sword?" Cora asked.

"Why, interested?" William squinted at her, protectively snatching the blade back. "This 'Ultimate Ultra Unbelievable Blade' is pretty powerful, but it's not something just anyone can handle."

"I got it through a contact on the black market at the Northern Base—authentic Anopower weapon, slices through zombies like they're watermelons. There are fewer than five on the entire market, and I spent a full two million on this baby..." William bragged proudly.

"How...how much?!" Cora blurted out in shock.

CHAPTER 14

A Big Sale

Hearing the number "two million," Cora's vision blurred in shock.

William Strong, assuming his wealth and extravagance awed her, proudly shook his mink coat open and gave his gold chain a showy shake.

With a grand gesture, he said, "It's just a small amount compared to what is needed. Sure, it's pricey, but the value of money is unbeatable. I got lucky with a steal—most people can't even find one, let alone buy it!"

"Value for money?" Cora swallowed, struggling to find the right words. "It only lasts for two or three years... That doesn't seem very... high?"

"Get outta here! Have you ever used the 'Heaven-Crushing, Earth-Shattering, All-Destroying, Ultra-Deadly Blue Enchantress'?"

"...I haven't?"

"Of course you haven't!" William's eyes widened as if ready for a fight. "Those high-tech weapons are too complicated, and if a zombie gets up close, your toast! But my baby? You just charge in and slice away—zombies don't stand a chance!"

Cora was at a loss for words. But then, an idea flashed through her mind, and her eyes lit up. With a sincere expression, she asked, "If there were more Heaven-Crushing... Blue Enchantress... um... things, would you buy them?"

"Well..." William glanced at the golf club his bodyguard was wielding and rubbed his chin. "They're a bit of a hassle to clean up after, though. If I replaced all of them, I'd need a dozen... Ouch," even for someone as rich as him. The thought made him wince. "If only there were a bulk discount."

"There is a discount!" Cora's voice rose, cracking with excitement. William eyed her suspiciously.

"By the way, who are you? You've been acting strange since the beginning. Got a problem with my baby?"

"No problem!" Cora whiffed her head. "I have a friend who can get... this."

She subtly moved her hand and pulled out a leaf-shaped throwing knife from her coat pocket. The blade was a deep, eerie blue, shining with a cold light—strikingly similar to William's Blade.

"If you buy from my friend, it won't cost you two million," Cora declared with confidence, though she still needed to discuss the exact price with Onyx and the others.

William's eyes lit up like a Christmas tree. "Come on, buddy, let's exchange contacts! Let me know the moment you have stock—I can pick it up myself, no need for shipping!"

At an abandoned gas station in the wilderness, the SUV was parked by the roadside. Felix extended a mechanical arm to grab an energy gun and began recharging the vehicle. The rest of F777 got out to stretch their legs.

From here, they could already see the outskirts of Ocean Gate. The landscape was a series of rolling hills, with a mighty river cutting through the bottom plains, creating a natural barrier. Combined with the three layers of inner and outer city walls, the central area of Ocean Gate was impregnable, comparable to Saya.

If the Zombie Lord wanted to attack Ocean Gate, it would have to cross the river and then breach three formidable defensive lines—a nearly impossible task.

No wonder the Ocean Gate governor had publicly declared that the only way to take the city would be if he opened the three gates from the inside.

Cora sat on the car roof, swinging her legs as she watched Suchat and Charles rummage through a convenience store. Most of the food was expired, but with some effort, they found a few durable drinks and dry goods to replenish their supplies.

"You want to sell Ethereal Artifacts to the people of Ocean Gate?" Onyx's wheelchair rolled up in front of her. He tilted his head back to look at her, the elegant line from his chin to his neck highlighted by his prominent Adam's apple, which bobbed as he spoke.

"Yeah, is that okay?" Cora asked hopefully.

"Of course," Onyx smiled, brushing some mud off her calf. "The Ethereal Artifacts are yours—you're in charge."

"I want to make lots of money," the impoverished captain sighed as she jumped down from the roof. "I have to support you guys."

She had a lot on her plate—taking care of the "older" (Charles) and the "younger" (Damian) team members. One was a recovering patient, the other a money-draining beast constantly clamoring for new materials. It was a lot of pressure.

"Captain, check your account," Felix called out from the driver's seat, interrupting the somewhat awkward atmosphere between them. Cora opened her terminal and her eyes widened in shock. Since when did she have over a million credits?

Felix's ice-blue eyes sparkled with pride as he announced, "Including interest, I recovered one and a half million from that crook as compensation for your growth."

"You're amazing!" Cora beamed, giving him a big thumbs up.

"So... can I buy some rhenium now?" Felix pushed his luck, forcing a stiff smile.

"Can—"

"No," Onyx interrupted coldly before Cora could answer. "Stop smiling. It makes you look like a kiss-up."

Felix stared at him blankly for two seconds before slamming the car window shut with a loud "bang."

Cora blinked, unsure of what to say. Onyx softened his tone as he explained, "His request is unreasonable. Rhenium is too expensive, and your money wouldn't cover what he needs. Don't buy it for him."

"Thud—" came the sound of Felix pounding on the car roof in protest from inside the SUV.

Onyx ignored his anger completely. "If you produce in bulk, how many Ethereal Artifacts can you create at once?"

Cora thought about it. Her mental strength had grown significantly over the past six months. Based on the output from

Blossomville, she estimated... "500 pieces."

Five hundred was a safe number, not pushing her to her limits, and she could still maintain enough energy to fight afterward.

"That's about right. Enough to equip an elite force. We'll go with 500," Onyx nodded. "How much should we sell them for?" Cora asked softly, "Can we... keep the price reasonable?"

She intended to sell the Ethereal Artifacts not just to make money but also to help the people of Ocean Gate better defend against the zombie horde. Her goal wasn't to gouge them or profit from their misfortune.

"Not too high, but not too low either—after all, it's hard work for you," Onyx smiled warmly at her. "Don't worry, I'll base the price on the average income in Ocean Gate, making sure it's within their means and that they'll be happy to pay."

A group of strong-willed civilians were busy driving away zombies on the outskirts. They wielded baseball bats, kitchen knives, and even dragged luggage and chairs, bravely smashing them into the zombies. But despite their fierce resolve, their makeshift weapons quickly failed—bats cracked, knives dulled, and the luggage and chairs fell apart. Soon, they found themselves unarmed and defenseless.

Among the zombies was a Level 2 one, moving swiftly and nimbly. It quickly spotted an opening, pounced on one of the civilians, and, with a guttural growl, prepared to sink its teeth into its prey.

"Whiz, whiz—" A few throwing knives sliced through the air, piercing the zombie's head, splattering black and red brain matter all over the ground. The civilians hastily helped their nearly devoured companion back to his feet, eyes wide as they looked toward their mysterious saviors.

An SUV rolled to a stop in front of them. The rear wheels spun, backing up a half turn to reveal the trunk. "Bang—" A masked woman opened the back door, her voice full of enthusiasm as she greeted them, "Hey friends, have you heard of Ethereal Artifacts?"

On the inside of the door, a dazzling array of swords, spears, and other weapons hung, all glowing with a cold blue light. Yuui, speaking rapidly, recited the sales pitch they had carefully prepared.

"Feeling unsafe during the apocalypse? Don't worry! The Thornton Ethereal Artifacts are here for you! Facing zombies? No problem! Just pull out your weapon and show them who's boss!"

"Dun dun~ Special sale today! For just 28,888 credits, you can take home your very own zombie-slaying weapon! Limited stock, so act fast!"

The civilians stared at her, bewildered.

Yuui snapped her fingers. "Open the door, let Suchat in."

He moved like lightning, skimming low over the zombies' heads. One of the rotten, skeletal hands reached for his pant leg but was swiftly decapitated by the short blue blade in his hand. In less than five minutes, Suchat had dispatched over a dozen zombies on his own.

Yuui's eyes gleamed with mischief, her red lips curling into a smile. "What do you think? Want one? Limited edition."

"I'll buy one! I'll buy one!!" the civilians shouted, finally snapping out of their daze.

Similar scenes played out all around Ocean Gate. F777 would first save the civilians, then—well, not so much sell but showcase the Ethereal Artifacts available for purchase.

"Don't miss out! Check out our goods, cheap and reliable! Buy now, and you'll make it home safe!"

"Only 28,888 credits for an Ethereal Artifact—no regrets, no rip-offs!"

"Uncle Auntie, want to buy some weapons?"

Suchat concluded, "Sell... Never mind."

He couldn't bring himself to say it out loud, so he simply focused on killing zombies, letting his actions be the most powerful advertisement.

Cora, lying on the car roof, mused with satisfaction, "I don't think Yuui should be a pop star."

Five hundred Ethereal Artifacts—within two hours, 380 were sold, and Yuui alone sold over 300 of them, making her the undisputed sales champion. She clearly had a knack for this; if she went into sales, she'd likely become one of the top influencers in Felalakas, not just a rising star.

In the passenger seat, Onyx gazed down at the map of Ocean Gate.

Night had fallen, and there was no sign of the Zombie Lord, not even the expected zombie horde. Ocean Gate was as peaceful as ever, no different from any other night.

Could he have been wrong in his prediction?

In Ocean Gate itself, a petite girl wrapped tightly in a scarf and a wide-brimmed hat hurried through the streets. Her eyes were wide with confusion as she glanced around, then she ducked her head and quickened her pace, eventually breaking into a run.

"Thump—" As she rounded a corner, she collided head-on with someone.

The solid man she crashed into took a step back, barking gruffly, "What are you doing? Don't you have eyes?"

He looked down at the girl, who couldn't have been over thirteen or fourteen. She lay dazed on the ground, her scarf half pulled down, revealing a pair of gray eyes. Realizing something, she frantically tugged the scarf back up, trying to cover her face.

Seeing that she was just a kid, the man let it go, though he wasn't particularly kind about it. "Watch where you're going!" he grumbled.

The girl mumbled an apology, her voice hoarse and her tone strangely off. The man dusted off his jacket and walked away, muttering under his breath, "... must be a multi-ethnic."

The girl pressed her hands to the ground and slowly got up, the messy braids in her hair slipping out of place to reveal the clear zombie markings on her neck. She stood up straight, no longer daring to run, and slowly melted into the darkness.

CHAPTER 15

Good and Bad

The dark gray SUV sped across the empty fields, drawing closer to the roaring river ahead. Before Cora and her team, the only way into Ocean Gate's urban area came into view —a majestic bridge spanning the river like a soaring rainbow.

The bridge had two levels. The upper level, illuminated by neon signal lights, was reserved for hovering vehicles like floating cars and starships. The lower level was a two-way, eight-lane road for regular vehicles. The bridge stretched over 1.5 kilometers long, appearing from afar like a giant dragon lying across the river, forming the most vital lifeline of Ocean Gate.

Felix turned the steering wheel, preparing to enter the lower roadway. As they approached the checkpoint at the bridge's entrance, a sentinel signaled for them to stop immediately. A row of jet-black heavy machine guns stood at the ready, with long ammo belts hanging from their bases, silently exuding menace.

"Wow, that's so cool," Damian leaned halfway out the window, admiringly.

Like most boys, Damian was deeply fascinated by firearms. He imitated the action of firing a machine gun, making "rat-tat-tat" sounds with his mouth, thoroughly enjoying himself—until the sentinels all turned their guns toward their SUV.

Cora and Damian immediately raised their hands in surrender, and Felix whistled before dutifully raising all six of his mechanical arms. The sentinels tensed, ready to fire at a moment's notice.

"Don't shoot, we're competitors!" Cora hurriedly tried to push down Felix's arms, but every time she lowered one, another popped up. In frustration, she smacked Felix on the head, finally making him behave.

A drone displaying the Throne Tournament logo hovered over the SUV, but the sentinels didn't lower their guard. "Stop the vehicle and submit to inspection!" one of them shouted.

Felix, finally serious, stepped on the brake. The diligent sentinels took a full fifteen minutes to search and question them, repeatedly confirming their identity with the City Hall before allowing them to pass. It wasn't until they were at a suitable distance from the checkpoint that the group sighed in relief.

"Hell Scythe," Onyx said quietly, "a fine weapon."

"What's that?" the others asked, puzzled.

Onyx pointed to the neatly lined-up heavy machine guns outside the window. "This gun is produced in Deep Woods. It can fire 1,500 rounds per minute, with a precise range of 1 kilometer and a maximum range of 5 kilometers, making it capable of sustained heavy fire against distant targets."

"The production line for the Hell Scythe was long ago bought out, only supplying the Northern Base. It seems Ocean Gate is well-prepared," Felix hummed.

"Must be rich..." the wealth of Ocean Gate's residents again shocked Cora.

There were no entry restrictions in District D, but F777 crossed the river under the watchful, unwelcoming eyes of the sentinels approaching the city's three formidable defensive lines.

The high brick walls, lined with electrified wires, towered under the sky, protecting Ocean Gate's residents from the apocalypse. The area outside the walls was thoroughly cleared, with no wandering zombies or mutated beasts in sight.

At each defensive line, armed sentinels rushed out to check them, escorting the SUV with the black barrels of their guns. The heavy iron gates creaked open, and the seven-member SUV drove into the city amid swirling dust.

Having taken a shortcut, F777 was the first team to arrive at

Ocean Gate. Yuui rested her chin on her hand, sighing, "I don't believe the Zombie Lord could break in here. It's practically impenetrable."

"Not necessarily." Onyx lightly tapped his fingers, replying calmly.

"... Huh? What other tricks could it possibly pull?" Yuui's accent mimicked that of the locals.

Onyx didn't answer, a familiar villainous smile creeping onto his face. "If you were the Zombie Lord, how would you attack Ocean Gate?"

Ew—what a creepy "what if." The group initially expressed their strong distaste, but soon became engrossed in the discussion.

Damian eagerly raised his hand. "I'd freeze the river!"

Onyx replied, "With a river that wide, your mental strength wouldn't even make a dent." Damian deflated.

Felix lifted his chin slightly. "I could walk right in."

He had noticed that the defensive lines had two operating modes: automatic and manual. With a flick of his finger, he could open the iron gates.

"Sure, you'd get in," Onyx nodded, "but the sentinels would wait for you, smiling as they turned you into Swiss cheese."

Then it was Suchat's turn. He hesitated. "I could sneak in... probably without being noticed."

"You might get in alone, but what about your zombie troops?" Yuui chuckled, beating Onyx to the punch. "Besides, what commander leads the charge personally?"

Charles simply shook his head. "Don't ask me, I've got nothing."

"What about you, Captain?" Felix asked.

"Um, I'm still thinking." Cora's face was serious, but her mind was blank—she couldn't come up with any plan at all.

"Always so calm, never talking nonsense," Onyx praised her without hesitation.

"So what's your plan?" Damian demanded, unconvinced.

As the vehicle bumped along, Onyx glanced in the rearview mirror. At the final iron gate, several massive grain airdrop containers were being stopped by the sentinels. Each container was opened and inspected, with life detectors scanning them from top to bottom, but nothing was found.

Onyx's voice was low as he said, "If I were the Zombie Lord... I'd remind the people of Ocean Gate of an old saying: 'The darkest place is right under the lamp.'"

Even after the SUV had driven on for a while, Onyx's gaze remained fixed on the direction of the iron gate.

"What are you thinking?" Cora leaned over to ask.

"I'm thinking about a classic battle from the old era," Onyx replied in a deep voice, "The Trojan War."

After nearly two hours of searching in Ocean Gate, F777 still had found no trace of the checkpoint. It was now completely dark, and the number of people wandering the streets had dwindled. The team was at a loss, unsure of what to do next.

Suddenly, Damian rubbed his eyes in disbelief, pointing out the window as he murmured, "Is that... braids?"

Across the street, a figure was leisurely strolling around. It peered into shop windows, then stopped to gaze at a garden. After a while, it even sat down on a bench to rest.

"Capture it," Onyx ordered coldly.

Cora and Suchat flung open the car doors, sprinting across the street with lightning speed. The figure with braids, clearly startled, leaped up in panic and bolted.

But there was no way it could outrun two top-level Aberrants. Cora jumped from the rooftop, soaring through the air before slamming into the figure with her full body weight, knocking it to the ground!

The braided figure struggled and screamed, its hat falling off and scarf loosening to reveal clear zombie markings on the side of its face. It twisted its head, trying to bite Cora, but just as it opened its mouth, Suchat casually grabbed something from a nearby garbage truck and stuffed it into its mouth.

By sheer coincidence, it was a used diaper.

The braided figure froze instantly, forgetting to even resist, its throat convulsing as if it were about to vomit. Its expressions were so vivid, almost indistinguishable from a human's, that Onyx silently stared at it, observing.

Damian hopped out of the car and hesitantly approaching the figure. Encountering a zombie inside the tightly guarded city, any normal person's first reaction would be to kill it.

The commotion had already drawn the attention of nearby pedestrians, and patrolling sentinels were heading their way. Onyx lowered his voice.

"Take it away." Cora lifted the braided zombie with one hand and tossed it into the car. The SUV sped off, leaving only dust in its wake.

The drone filming them faithfully captured everything, and viewers watching the live stream in Felalakas were in an uproar.

"Holy crap, is that a zombie? If I'm not blind, that's definitely a zombie, right?"

"You're not blind. That's definitely a zombie."

"Can someone explain how a zombie got into Ocean Gate's urban area? Are the sentinels just for show?!"

"Does anyone have the City Hall's contact info? We need to warn them!"

In a Felalakas hotel, Scarlett Holland's eyes narrowed, and the lines on either side of her nose deepened as she immediately made a call. "Captain Silver Owl, I would like to hire the Tustan team for a private mission."

"Officer Holland, if I recall correctly, I'm currently enjoying a well-deserved vaca—tion," Silver Owl drawled lazily, stretching out the last syllable. "Are you openly asking me to work overtime? Is there overtime pay?"

Scarlett didn't bother with his rudeness and calmly said, "I need you to head to District D135 immediately and capture a mutant zombie. I believe Dr. Ninnemann's research team will be very interested in it."

"District D135?" The laziness vanished from Silver Owl's voice, replaced by surprise. "I am watching the Throne Tournament. Are you talking about the Ocean Gate where F777 is currently located?"

"Correct. I need you to capture the zombie alive before they kill it."

"Working overtime, huh? Well, I suppose it's not impossible, as long as you remember to pay triple the usual fee." Silver Owl agreed with unusual promptness. "Consider it done."

The SUV pulled into an abandoned factory, where the braided zombie was tossed to the ground, tightly bound. It tried to flee, but could only manage a few awkward steps before toppling over.

Onyx's metal wheelchair rolled up slowly in front of it. He lowered his gaze, watching it like a merciless deity, ready to decide its fate at any moment.

Sensing the threat, the braided zombie growled from deep in its throat and bared its teeth at Onyx. However, its fangs were not as sharp as other zombies', more like underdeveloped canines.

"Shut your mouth, or I'll pull all your teeth out," Onyx threatened.

The braided zombie whimpered and actually closed its mouth obediently.

"It understands us!" Charles exclaimed in surprise. They had assumed that the Fallen only kept a basic awareness, but it seemed capable of communicating with humans.

Onyx leaned closer, his voice low. "You understand what we're saying, don't you?" The braided zombie hesitated for two seconds before nodding in resigned acknowledgment.

"Why did you sneak into Ocean Gate?" Onyx asked.

"Ah—ah—" The braided zombie lifted its head and let out a couple of incoherent cries.

Onyx ordered, "Untie its hands." Suchat cut the ropes with a knife, and the zombie, now free, clumsily used its stiff fingers to draw an unclear symbol in the sand.

The team stared at it, thoroughly baffled. What kind of nonsense was this? Despite understanding them, it seemed they still couldn't communicate effectively. Damian, hands behind his back, circled the symbol twice before suddenly exclaiming, "I get it! This is the Zombie Lord!"

"Ah! Ah!" The braided zombie cried out excitedly.

"Little Diamond, how did you figure that out?" Cora asked, genuinely curious.

"This part is a wing, and that part is a blood vessel. It's pretty obvious," Damian explained, pointing confidently to the messy scribble.

The rest of the group was speechless. How had they not seen it?

"You're saying the Zombie Lord sent you," Onyx's tone shifted, "so how many other zombies like you have infiltrated the city?"

The braided zombie's gray eyes slowly swiveled, surprised that

Onyx knew it had companions.

It looked like a child caught doing something wrong, sneaking a glance at Onyx before lowering its head in a "thinking" posture. Then it began drawing stick figures in the sand—one after another, row after row, until two entire rows were filled and it still hadn't stopped.

"It's saying there are many more," Damian translated earnestly, continuing his role as the zombie whisperer.

"… Thanks, but we could see that ourselves."

A cold glint appeared in Onyx's eyes. "Your mission is to open the three iron gates from the inside, isn't it?" The braided zombie froze, its stick-figure drawing halted abruptly.

Onyx pressed further. "Why weren't you with your companions?"

When F777 captured the braided zombie, it had been casually strolling around like a retiree, with no sense of urgency despite the critical mission.

The zombie clawed at the ground for a while before slowly drawing a vertical dividing line. It then scribbled some symbols on the left side and more on the right.

Everyone turned to look at Damian, waiting for his translation.

Even Damian was stumped this time. He squatted down, studying the drawings for a long time, while the zombie enthusiastically explained with more "ah—ah ah—ah" sounds.

Finally, Damian pointed confidently to the left side. "This is you."

"Ah!"

It then quickly drew a few more lines, connecting them back to the first drawing of the "Zombie Lord."

Damian pointed to the right. "And this is the corrupt version of you."

"Ah!"

Onyx looked at the strange collection of symbols and figures in the sand, a smirk playing at the corners of his mouth. "You're trying to tell us that the Fallen are divided into two factions—one that acknowledges their former human selves and wants no part in the conflict, and the other that fully sides with the Zombie Lord, willingly becoming its followers, right?"

The braided zombie eagerly nodded, its stiff neck making a "crack,

crack" sound.

Onyx's voice slowed. "Oh? So which side are you on?"

This time, the braided zombie hesitated for a very long time.

Finally, it carefully lifted its finger and slowly drew a line, connecting the "good version" of itself to the spot beneath Damian's feet.

CHAPTER 16

The Gate

The braided zombie hesitated for a moment, but then resolutely joined Damian. At that moment, everyone understood what it meant—it had chosen the human side, even though it was no longer "human."

The viewers in the F777 livestream exploded with conflicting reactions. "Don't be naïve! How could a zombie empathize with humans?" "What are you doing? Kill it already! You can't seriously believe a zombie, can you?" "But... it sounds sincere." "Can all you self-righteous fools shut up? Zombies killed my whole family. I will never forgive them!"

The debate over this unique zombie escalated. Realizing a new viewership hotspot, the director switched the drone to a close-up, focusing on the braided zombie's facial scars. Its gray eyes remained unblinking, head following the drone's movements. Suddenly, it bared its teeth and snarled at the camera, "Roar—!"

Its cracked mouth, twisted face, and razor-sharp fangs seemed ready to rip out the throat of whoever was watching. The heated chat froze instantly, replaced by nonsensical, garbled text. The hyper-realistic high-definition image left viewers deeply unsettled, and it took a while before someone nervously typed, "See... a zombie is still a zombie."

The braided zombie scraped at the ground with its hands, a trace of smugness flickering across its face.

"Alert the Ocean Gate City Hall, and have them check for

suspicious individuals," Onyx de Montclair said quickly. "I'll contact them now," Yuui Hayashi replied, pulling up a terminal interface.

Onyx turned to Cora Thornton, whispering, "Captain, I need a word with you."

Cora nodded and walked over. Onyx glanced at the drone and tapped Felix's wheelchair. "Did you hear me? Handle it."

Felix rolled his eyes, fingers flying across his device. Soon, several drones lost their signal, buzzing around like headless flies. The F777 livestream turned to static, displaying a "technical difficulties" message.

"What are you going to do with it?" Onyx asked quietly after they moved to a corner.

He was calm, but after all this time together, Cora knew his subtle shifts in the mood. Though he asked for her opinion, his eyes were cold —it was clear he didn't care about the braided zombie's fate.

Cora suspected that whenever Onyx spoke about "Plan Eternity" or "the Fallens," his emotions were conflicted, tinged with some unspoken disgust and rejection.

"I'm thinking of finding a remote place," Cora said frankly, "and ditching it."

She didn't have a better idea. The braided zombie wasn't really human or a zombie—it was more like a new species born after the apocalypse. While it didn't attack proactively, it still hung around zombies and had been sent by the Zombie Lord as a spy. Humans... would never accept it.

"Fine, Captain's call." Onyx didn't argue whether she killed or keep it.

"However, when we first captured it, we weren't cautious enough. Now that the competition's livestream footage has spread, I'm worried someone might get too 'interested' in its existence. It could cause trouble for us."

"Our team members aren't suited for too much attention," Onyx said slowly.

The F777 squad carried many secrets, like Cora's absurd healing speed, Charles Franz's immunity to zombie attacks, Yuui Hayashi's true identity, and then there were Onyx and Felix Lucas...

"Then," Cora made a quick decision, "let's ditch it now?"

They headed back, finding Damian Blackwood and the braided zombie with their heads together, drawing something in the sand.

Yuui shrugged at them. "The comm line's been jammed—probably overloaded by viewers watching the livestream." Cora opened her mouth to speak, but suddenly, a piercing alarm shattered the night.

"Level 1 Alert! Level 1 Alert! A zombie horde is approaching! All sentries, assemble immediately!"

Their expressions hardened. The zombie horde was indeed heading toward Ocean Gate! The only question was, would this be another feint or the Zombie Lord's all-out attack?

"Let's go," Cora decided on the spot.

As the SUV roared to life again, she glanced at the braided zombie. There was no time to deal with it now. Carefully, she proposed, "Your appearance... others might mistake you for a zombie. It's dangerous. For now, come with us."

"Okay," the braided zombie agreed, nodding obediently.

"With me around, I'll protect you, Braids!" Damian thumped his chest, making a manly promise. "Huh? Huh!" The braided zombie straightened up, towering over the "manly" Damian.

Damian's ego crumbled. Cars roared down the streets, and lights flickered on in every household as the noise of commotion rose around them.

The SUV came to a stop behind the last line of defense, where blinding lights overhead made it seem like daytime. Ocean Gate's official armed forces moved swiftly and orderly through emergency passages, setting up heavy weapons on the city walls. Even in the face of a sudden nighttime siege, they remained calm and collected.

A massive floating screen stood before them, connected to a thermal imaging device that kept emitting alarms with increasing frequency. The screen showed a dense swarm of green heat signatures rapidly converging on Ocean Gate from all directions.

Yet, the real-time surveillance footage appeared calm and peaceful, with the high-altitude searchlights outside the city revealing nothing unusual.

A warm late-spring breeze brushed against their faces as the river's surface rippled gently, and the open wilderness lay silent. On either side of the bridge, tense sentries gripped the triggers of their scythes, aiming their guns at the pitch-black plains.

One minute passed. Then two... then five. The anxious citizens of Ocean Gate began whispering, which soon escalated into a loud murmur.

Where were the zombies? Where was the horde?

The same question crossed everyone's mind. The river, cloaked in darkness, surged. Rolling waves formed dark rings that surged rapidly on either side of the bridge.

A sentry by the bridge wiped his sweaty palms, his nerves making them clammy. His determined gaze was fixed ahead, ready to fire at the slightest movement on the plains.

Suddenly, the sound of waves crashing against the shore echoed behind him. The sentry stiffened and swung his machine gun around. Before he could make out what was coming, five or six dripping-wet zombies leaped from the river and instantly tore him apart!

"Aaah—!" His blood-curdling scream sent chills down everyone's spine.

But what followed was even more terrifying. After the first sentry fell, countless zombie heads floated to the surface of the river, clustered together like an overwhelming infestation of water hyacinths—enough to drive anyone with trypophobia insane.

Machine gunners on the bridge and the city walls went wild, firing their scythes with abandon. Rows of bullets rained down like a reaper harvesting lives, with zombies hit and sinking into the river, their bodies floating like balloons.

Yet, there were simply too many of them. They frequently submerged to avoid the gunfire, making it hard for the humans to maintain a target. The rushing water hindered the range of the firearms, preventing them from dealing significant damage.

Before long, large numbers of zombies had crossed the river, swarming out in packs and sprinting towards the first iron gate.

"Pull the switch! Pull the switch!" shouted a soldier from the defensive line.

The high-voltage electric grid crackled, and the front row of zombies dropped instantly, their bodies charred to a crisp. The pungent smell of burned flesh wafted into the city with the wind. Yet, the following zombies, undeterred, trampled over the corpses of their fallen comrades, surging forward. The crisis wasn't over—more undead soldiers continued to emerge from beneath the river!

Humans who had placed too much faith in the river's natural barrier never imagined that the Zombie Lord would have trained an army of zombies skilled in aquatic warfare!

"Zombies don't breathe or need oxygen, so they can withstand extreme pressure, making them perfect for long-term underwater operations," Onyx said coldly. "But it requires precise coordination. For the Zombie Lord to silently send an army across the river, its abilities are likely far more terrifying than we estimated."

Cora leaned out from the rooftop of the SUV. "Should we help?" she asked.

Onyx shook his head. "Intervening now might disrupt their counterattack strategy. Let's wait. Ocean Gate isn't defenseless."

The soldiers manning the city walls were fighting for their lives, their hands moving with incredible speed.

Cannons and explosive rounds were fired like they cost nothing, and the destructive power of the heavy weapons soon stemmed from the zombies' advance, clearing the first wave. The remains of the fallen piled up into small mountains outside the defense line.

Suddenly, the braided zombie pressed its face against the car window, letting out two "Ah! Ah!" sounds.

Cora glanced down at it and realized, "I almost forgot—you still have comrades who want to wreak havoc!" The dark gray SUV roared back to life, speeding toward the first iron gate.

The three lines of defense were spaced apart, and what had once been a commercial district was now packed with people fleeing through the emergency passages. An official in charge of evacuation shouted over the noise, "The safety zone is open! Civilians evacuate now! Elderly, women, and children first!"

As the enormous crowd slowly moved through, the official hurried to the circuit control room to close the emergency entrance, unaware that a few pairs of cloudy gray eyes were watching him intently from the shadows.

Just as he pressed the control panel, someone in the civilian group suddenly turned and threw an object at him. "Bang—Boom—!" The bottle-like items hit the control console, and within seconds, flames erupted, triggering a series of explosions that short-circuited the electrical system.

The high-voltage grid outside the city walls crackled twice before its glow slowly faded.

The civilians were stunned, not expecting a traitor among them. They looked in horror at the saboteurs and immediately cried out, "Zombies! Zombies have infiltrated!"

With the high-voltage grid abruptly disabled, even if the backup power was activated, there would still be about a minute of silence.

The attacking zombies, no longer fearing the electric shocks, charged with even greater ferocity. A heavy, chaotic sound of footsteps echoed from the horizon.

The second wave of the land-based zombie horde had arrived!

The defensive fire lines at Ocean Gate immediately became strained. Sentries on the bridge frantically fired at the plain, trying to cut off the reinforcements, while the zombie water forces seized the opportunity to scale the city walls, savagely attacking the humans inside the fortifications.

As the number of armed sentries dwindled rapidly, weakening their suppressive fire, Ocean Gate's Aberrants sprang into action, rushing toward the front lines. The evacuated civilians turned around, their red eyes fixed on the crumbling city walls and their fellow citizens being slaughtered.

"Spit! My ancestors were born and raised in Ocean Gate. I grew up on Ocean Gate's crops. Even if I die, I won't let you scum take over! Zombies? Bring it on!"

In an instant, a battle cry echoed through the crowd. Thousands of fierce Ocean Gate residents picked up weapons and joined the fight against the zombies.

"We're moving," Cora said as their group lagged, having failed to find the Fallens hidden among the crowd. From the way things were unfolding, this zombie horde wasn't a feint—the Zombie Lord would definitely show up.

Fierce fighting erupted outside the city, and reinforcements arrived from the sky. Teams competing in the Throne Tournament, including "The Boss and His Three Goons," "Iron Cafe," and "Guns and Roses," all rushed to Ocean Gate's defense.

A few uniquely designed hover cars flew over Ocean Gate. From atop one of them, Silver Owl leaned out, sighing as he pulled his sniper scope into place. "Looks like another overtime shift... My luck is terrible... Huh?"

He cut off mid-sentence, glancing down with an amused smile. "Actually, maybe my luck's pretty good."

The one-minute silence passed, and the high-voltage grid flickered back on. Meanwhile, the fierce resistance of Ocean Gate's people had successfully kept the zombie horde outside the walls.

In the battlefield's chaos, Cora shouted to the braided zombie, "Don't run off! Stick with me!"

"Ah!" it howled in response, obediently following behind the F777 team.

Cora quickly pulled its scarf up, covering its face. She was about to charge forward when a swift figure dropped from the sky, landing right in front of her. The man wore a tactical jacket, camouflage pants, and high-top military boots. Fingerless sniper gloves adorned his hands—it was Silver Owl.

"We meet again, Cora," Silver Owl greeted her with a smile. "Want to make a deal?"

"No time," Cora replied bluntly. She wasn't in the mood for small talk.

Silver Owl didn't mind her bitter response and pointed at the braided zombie behind her. "How about this—give me that thing, and I'll help you kill the Zombie Lord. Deal?"

The braided zombie growled menacingly, its throat rumbling with a low snarl. Cora frowned and was about to respond when a shrill alarm suddenly pierced the air across the entire city.

A few minutes earlier.

While everyone's attention was focused on the zombie water forces, a group of about thirty uniformed individuals approached the iron gate checkpoint. On closer inspection, their movements were stiff and disjointed.

"Who goes there?" the sentry on duty shouted, raising his gun. Despite his suspicion, the matching uniforms stopped him from shooting immediately. In an instant, the group lunged forward, and the sentries let out muffled grunts as the sickening crack of necks breaking filled the air.

The broken bodies lay scattered on the ground as the group silently stepped over them, their deformed fingers picking up the fallen weapons.

Knock, knock.

The leader of the group politely rapped on the door.

The head of the control room opened the video gate and saw a sentry standing outside, his hat pulled low and a strange tattoo peeking out from beneath his chin. "What's your number?" the official asked warily. "I don't recognize you."

The man slowly lifted his head, his cloudy gray eyes staring directly at him.

The official's face paled in terror as he stumbled backward, his hand desperately reaching for the alarm button. But it was too late. The next second, the door was violently blasted open, and dozens of zombies stormed in, their blood-chilling screams filling the air.

The first iron gate of Ocean Gate had been opened—from the inside.

CHAPTER 17

Brothers

Felix had procured a batch of cannons from Ocean Gate, the latest in cutting-edge weaponry at the Northern Base. These cannons were equipped with automatic loading and ballistic calibration systems, making them formidable in battle.

However, they required extremely skilled operators. Each operator had to single-handedly handle angle measurement, distance calculation, aiming, and firing to ensure precise strikes on the enemy.

Training a qualified gunner demanded significant resources, and after the wall was breached, the zombies, seemingly with a hive mind, targeted these elite operators first.

Two sleek, silver wheelchairs silently ascended the fortifications. Felix quickly dispatched several zombies, gnawing on the remains of a fallen gunner. He paused briefly in front of a row of cannons, lowered his gaze for a couple of seconds, and then expertly adjusted the trajectory.

Aim. Fire. Boom! Boom! Boom boom!

Six shells fired in quick succession, landing directly in the densest part of the zombie horde. Each explosion created a deep crater in the ground. Felix's calculations were nearly flawless, sending hundreds of zombies flying, some disintegrating into rotting sludge.

With his silver hair flowing, Felix operated six arms simultaneously, resembling the legendary kraken of old myths. His focus was split between controlling the Hellscythe and swiftly switching the cannon mode to single-fire. Bullets flew out, popping zombie heads and turning their bodies into sieves. The pressure on the wall eased immediately.

"Thanks, man!" The surviving gunners, faces covered in blood, shouted their gratitude. Felix gave a modest nod.

The gunners stumbled back to the cannons, determined to hold the line.

Felix sniffed the air. He was covered in the stench of gunpowder, while Onyx, who followed behind him, looked as pristine as ever, his wheelchair skillfully maneuvering around the corpses on the ground to avoid even a speck of blood.

That fastidious, almost obsessive cleanliness—so reminiscent of his younger days—was unmistakable to anyone who knew him well.

Felix extended one of his mechanical arms, deliberately picking up the dirtiest Hellscythe and tossing it into Onyx's lap. "Know how to use this? If not, I can teach you. Should've taken the firearms elective."

Onyx's brow furrowed so tightly it could crush a fly. He grabbed a slightly cleaner piece of cloth from the ground and wiped the black and red gore from the gun barrel. Loading a live round, he aimed it at Felix's head. "Just shoot your cannons and stop talking."

Felix snorted arrogantly and concentrated on operating the six cannons.

Onyx turned the gun away, his gaze lingering on Felix's face. "You know, you've been surprisingly easy to talk to lately."

Felix's actions paused imperceptibly as he responded in a sarcastic tone, "Oh, dear friend, I've always been easy to talk to. You just don't know me well enough."

"Did you steal Cora's money?" Onyx's eyebrow arched slightly. "Transfer it to your own account?"

"Are you insulting my integrity?" Felix's expression was just shy of saying, "You're ridiculous."

"Tch—" "Boring."

They turned away from each other, equally annoyed.

Felix became a human artillery platform, the high-speed cannons roaring as the battlefield turned into a frenzy of silver arcs and flying zombies. Amid the deafening noise, he suddenly asked, "Plan Eternity... Is it that plan?"

"Which one?" Onyx responded absentmindedly.

"The one that made you so happy you were shouting everywhere, 'Finally, I get to work on a project with that person.' Is it that one?" Felix didn't look at him.

"I was on the fifth floor sleeping that day, and I could hear your yelling."

Onyx fell silent for a moment, then replied sharply, "You're the idiot. At least I didn't miss an exam because I overslept."—He didn't deny it.

Felix didn't raise his head, continuing to obliterate zombies while speaking quickly, "Regarding Plan Eternity, you explained a lot about it—humans, zombies, Aberrants, Aberrant zombies, evolved zombies, Fallens... But no matter the species, there's a fatal flaw. And your logical chain is missing an important link."

"—The most perfect link."

"As you said, the original goal of Plan Eternity was to create the most perfect gene. Its results should have eternal life, immense power, and still keep conscious thought and intelligence, achieving the complete evolution of humanity. I want to know, did the research succeed?" Felix asked persistently.

"Ever heard the saying? Curiosity killed the cat," Onyx replied coolly.

"I only know that curiosity is the ladder to human progress. After you joined Arashi, you disappeared from Luboni. When we met again..." Felix finally had a moment to glance at him, sweeping his gaze up and down, pausing on Onyx's recently healed legs. "Well, that's surprising."

"If you care so much about this project," Felix asked again, "I'm really curious. Did your research succeed?"

This time, Onyx took a long time to respond, finally speaking slowly, "Once."

Even Felix showed a rare expression of shock, but Onyx didn't give him a chance to speak. "Never again."

"Fourteen years ago, there was a nuclear leak in Loyak, followed by an explosion that destroyed the entire Arashi Research Institute, including the project's researchers, all test subjects, and the local storage hub containing the preliminary data of Plan Eternity."

"From that day on, the project's results could only be—declared a failure."

"Data can be recovered," Felix said dismissively.

"That hub was shattered into pieces, smaller than a fingernail. Not even you could recover it." Onyx's eyes gleamed with a cold, chilling light. "Besides, did you really think the Central didn't consider that?"

"How many data was in that hub?" Felix asked.

"Over three thousand zettabytes," Onyx replied.

"Three thousand zettabytes," Felix clicked his tongue, "That number sounds terrifying."

He unleashed another round of six cannon shots, and as the cannons reloaded automatically, he cast an apparently casual glance at Onyx. "Do you think there's someone whose mind works so well they could memorize all that data?"

"I'm telling you," Onyx's tone was icy, "If you don't start firing, those zombies are going to be in your face."

The two of them raised their weapons in unison and opened fire. At that moment, a sharp siren blared as Ocean Gate's first iron door opened.

After the defensive line was breached, the tide of zombies found a clear path and surged toward the iron gate, racing against each other to get there first. From above, the dense horde looked like a swarm of black ants, rapidly consuming Ocean Gate.

At this critical moment, dozens of armored vehicles rolled out from within the city. Commander William Strong himself stood at the front line, shouting into a megaphone, "Push forward—gunners and riflemen, hold your ground!"

"Behind this gate are our parents, our wives, and our children— our home! We can't take a single step back!"

"Ocean Gate can't afford any failures. Even if we die, we'll die charging forward!"

The soldiers of Ocean Gate, their eyes red with determination, responded with a fierce volley of gunfire, their attacks lighting up the battlefield.

The armored vehicles rumbled over the earth, crushing any zombies that tried to breach the line into pulp. On top of one vehicle, Strong set up his Hellscythe, roaring as he fired repeatedly, the empty shells falling around him like water.

Whether they were Aberrants or ordinary humans, sentinels or civilians, fierce battles erupted everywhere—on the walls, on the ground, in the streets and alleys of Ocean Gate. Even the women and children didn't stay hidden in their homes; they voluntarily helped transport ammunition and provided supplies to the front lines.

The most striking combatants in the melee were the hundreds of warriors wielding weapons that glowed with a ghostly blue light. Among them were Strong and his bodyguards, who fearlessly hacked away at the zombies' heads with ruthless efficiency. With the support of these divine weapons, their combat prowess was nothing short of explosive.

"I'll be damned! I just bought a five-hundred-square-foot penthouse in the city, haven't even had the chance to renovate it yet, and you brats want to destroy my new home? Not a chance!!" Strong cursed as he punched and kicked his way through the horde.

When everyone's resolve to defend the city intertwined like a braided rope, this combined force was truly formidable.

The two waves of zombies at the riverbed and the bridge quickly retreated, leaving a path of rotting flesh and shattered bones that stretched from the iron gate all the way to the riverbank. It was impossible to distinguish between the fallen defenders and the zombies.

Against all odds, Ocean Gate—District D135—had held off the successive waves of zombies on its own!

Meanwhile, the group-attack Aberrants from Tustan took advantage of their aerial superiority to clear a patch of ground. Silver Owl picked off the approaching zombies with his sniper rifle in an instant. "I've accepted a commission from the higher-ups to take it to the Northern Base."

"Hand it over to me, and I promise you won't lose out—we both win."

"No need." Cora felt a sinking feeling in her heart. As Onyx de Montclair had predicted, the moment the braided zombie's existence was exposed, someone would try to capture it. Silver Owl sighed in frustration. "To be honest, I'd rather not fight you."

As the two spoke, the braided zombie turned its head and caught sight of a few uniformed figures disappearing around the battlefield's edge, moving away from the major fight.

Suddenly, the braided zombie shot up, a flash of anxiety in its eyes. Without a second glance, it changed direction and dashed after them.

"Hey!" Cora reached out to stop it, but it had already rushed into the thick of the battle. "Sister, I'll go after it!" Damian called out, turning to follow the braided zombie. Cora was left speechless. One after another, they were all giving her a headache.

Silver Owl shrugged with a smirk. "See? Even if you protect it, it won't appreciate it. A zombie is just a zombie."

The door of the hovering vehicle slammed open, and one of Tustan's Aberrants poked his head out, yelling, "Silver Owl, quit flirting! I'm waiting to finish up and get some sleep!" "You think you can mess around with us? How about doing some actual work?"

A wild-looking woman with long, deep-red curls pushed past her teammates, crossing her arms as she whistled teasingly, "Captain, are you up to it or not?"

"Shut up and go kill your zombies!"

"Is this how you treat your captain? Doesn't his face mean anything?" Silver Owl turned back, laughing and cursing at them before addressing Cora with a resigned look, "You heard them? I'm forced to do this."

No sooner had he spoken than he darted past Cora, racing toward the braided zombie. "Sorry, but this mission is urgent—I have to act now."

What the—? He just took off before finishing his sentence? Cora immediately took off after him.

Silver Owl moved with incredible speed, nearly reaching the iron gate. In the nick of time, a hail of bullets rained down from the direction of the city walls, precisely targeting his path. If he didn't dodge, he would be torn to pieces.

Silver Owl abruptly halted, springing back to avoid the barrage. His military boots dug deep into the ground as he pulled out his sniper scope, shielding himself from the blast.

As the dust settled, he looked up to see a stern-faced man gazing coldly at him from the fortifications, a machine gun in hand, ready to fire again.

Silver Owl recognized him—they'd crossed paths in the skies over Felalakas. Apparently, this guy didn't like him. Unfortunately, the feeling was mutual. There was no logical reason for this dislike; it was pure animal instinct. The two stared each other down, their gazes full of tension.

Silver Owl's ruby earring flashed in the dark as he brazenly flipped him off with both middle fingers. Onyx remained unmoved, his lips curling into a contemptuous smirk.

Silver Owl's brow furrowed, just about to react, when someone grabbed his collar. The tall man, weighing over 180 pounds, was lifted with one hand and violently thrown backward!

As the world spun around him, Silver Owl twisted his lean body in mid-air, landing with perfect balance. When he looked up, he saw Cora's lithe figure moving like a snow leopard as she leaped through the air, slicing through zombies, and quickly leaving him behind.

Some people are born with no patience for delicate little flowers, but they're utterly defenseless against vibrant, prickly iron thistles— Silver Owl was such a man, always taking the road less traveled.

He couldn't help the grin that spread across his face, but the next second, he realized Cora had thrown him into the thick of the zombie horde. Zombies that had just crawled out of the river, covered in vines and mud, shook their heads, splattering him with foul-smelling sludge.

Silver Owl's smile vanished as he drew his weapon from the holster on his thigh and picked off the zombies with precision shots.

"Aren't you going to follow them?" Felix, observing from the wall above, called down in good faith.

"My shoulders can't bear it, and my hands can't lift it," Onyx replied matter-of-factly, pointing to his legs. "Wouldn't I just be in the way?"

A thought crossed Onyx's mind, making him smile slightly. "Don't worry. When our captain gets serious, no one can take anything from her."

Felix nodded. "Oh, then why did you act like a peacock in heat and specifically target him?"

"That guy's top-tier A-Class, and you're an S-Class psychic..." Felix trailed off as he suddenly realized something.

Onyx sneered, "Finally figured it out? I thought your brain had checked out along with the cannon shells."

Felix didn't have time for Onyx's taunts as he realized that from the start, Onyx had only been using firearms—he hadn't used his psychic powers at all. What Felix had originally thought was laziness was, in fact... the inability to use them.

Despite Ocean Gate appearing to have the upper hand, both the river and the plains had only faced ordinary zombies so far. The Aberrant zombies, evolved zombies, and the Zombie Lord itself had yet to make an appearance.

Where were they?

"This Zombie Lord is a master of guerrilla tactics."

Onyx analyzed calmly, "It used the food drop pods as cover to smuggle the Fallens inside because they have no life signs. Mixed in with the food, they could even mask themselves from radiation and, most importantly, control their movements to avoid making any noise that would draw attention."

"But with all that effort, is it really just trying to get the Fallens to open the three iron gates? If it can adapt its tactics to different Aberrants, why not organize a surprise attack?"

"If I were it, I'd definitely avoid a direct assault."

"Oh, so what do you think your 'good brother', the Zombie Lord, will do?" Felix mocked.

"First, it'll have other Aberrants hold the line and call our people back," Onyx replied.

"I'm going to meet this interesting opponent."

Inside the city of Ocean Gate, all the floating screens lit up with an official announcement from the City Hall. The person responsible for the broadcast seemed to be in a rush, leaving no time to carefully craft the message. The announcements were blunt and to the point:

"All residents must remain vigilant. Zombies have been found disguising themselves as humans. Trust no one!"

"Do not chat with strangers! Do not approach the iron gate outposts! The outposts are rigged with explosives!"

"Zombies can't read, so keep this information to yourself! Stay alert! Stay alert!"

The braided zombie sprinted through the crowd, with Damian

Blackwood chasing after it, panting heavily.

Soon, they reached the outskirts of the second defensive line, behind the commercial street. The braided zombie picked up speed, charging ahead and blocking the path of a group of about thirty people. Realizing something, Damian hid behind a building, holding his breath as he watched.

The braided zombie let out a few anxious grunts, calling out hoarsely to the leader of the group.

The leader turned around, his lips moving as if he were communicating with the braided zombie. Damian noticed his sinister profile, the cloudy gray eyes, and the corpse-like marks that extended from his chin down into his neck—this was a Fallen!

Wait, those thirty people... they were probably all Fallens, the "bad companions" the braided zombie had mentioned.

Damian thought for a moment and nicknamed the leader "Dirty Chin." After Dirty Chin finished his conversation with the braided zombie, he roughly shoved it aside, as if saying, "Don't get in the way."

The braided zombie stumbled, growing even more desperate, and hurried after them. It clumsily pulled out a pendant-like object from its neck—a broken fang that looked somewhat like... a zombie's tooth?

Upon seeing the fang, Dirty Chin's previously calm expression turned to fury. He knocked the braided zombie down with the butt of his gun and stepped on its head. The braided zombie struggled frantically, its hat and scarf falling off, revealing its zombie features. Dirty Chin let out a growl of rage, bending down to press his face close to the braided zombie's.

Damian tensed up, gripping an ice spike in his hand, ready to throw it to rescue the braided zombie.

Fortunately, Dirty Chin didn't seem to have any intention of harming his own kind. He reached down, yanked the pendant from the braided zombie's neck, and bent over to pick up its hat and scarf, placing them back over its face. Then he made an obvious gesture for it to leave.

Afterward, Dirty Chin led the silent group of Fallens into the depths of the street.

Damian memorized the direction in which they disappeared, secretly recording a video and sending it to the F777 group chat. "Little Diamond, where are you?" Cora's voice crackled through the earpiece.

"Sister! Come quickly, I've made a big discovery!" Damian was about to send his location, but then remembered that his sister had no sense of direction. Instead, he opted to share their positions with each other.

"I'm on my way," Cora replied.

After reporting in, Damian jumped down from the wall and ran toward the braided zombie on his short legs. The braided zombie hung its head, looking dazed and dejected. Damian helped it put its hat and scarf back on, patting the dust off them, then squatted down in front of it. "Braided Head, are you okay?"

The braided zombie stared blankly, ignoring him.

Damian asked again, "What did you say to your poor companions? Why did they get so angry?" The braided zombie glanced at him and silently drew on the ground. It sketched three symbols, tightly grouped together, that looked like scribbles.

Damian tilted his head, studying the drawing for a long time before gasping in surprise. "Huh? Are you saying Dirty Chin is your brother?!" The braided zombie looked confused.

Damian hesitated, then explained, "Dirty Chin is... um, the one with the dirty chin, tall guy..." The braided zombie seemed to understand, letting out a few disgruntled grunts in protest against Damian's habit of making up nicknames.

"Don't sweat the details," Damian said with an awkward laugh, trying to dodge the issue. "And this one? Is he your brother, too?" The braided zombie nodded. "Ah."

It quickly added a few more lines to the drawing.

Damian understood again. The braided zombie had drawn a picture of a group of zombies playing soccer. Then Damian's temper flared up. "So your brother was the one who led those jerks who bullied me last time!"

The braided zombie. "... Ah!"

"Where did he go? Did he come to Ocean Gate too?" Damian huffed, deciding to let bygones be bygones with the braided zombie. The braided zombie quieted down, slowly drawing a zombie broken in two.

Then it repeated the process, connecting the "good brother" to Damian and drawing the Zombie Lord connected to the "wicked brother."

Damian also fell silent, recalling Onyx's bitter words. He had said that Fallens was a species outside the realm of humans and zombies. Their zombified traits made them unacceptable to humans, yet their conscious minds prevented them from fully becoming zombies.

During the Sycamore zombie tide, the braided zombie had hidden with its "good brother" rather than actively attack humans.

But the next day, an Aberrant killed the braided zombie's good brother, mistaken for a regular zombie. The half-body the braided zombie had dragged away then must have been its brother's.

Damian didn't know how to comfort the braided zombie, so he just sat there in silence with it.

Suddenly, the sound of hurried footsteps approached from behind. Cora arrived at the scene, relieved to see they were unharmed. But before she could fully relax, a smoke bomb landed nearby and exploded, causing Damian to cough violently as he covered his mouth.

Through the thick fog, a gloved hand reached out to grab the braided zombie, but Cora intercepted it, twisting the arm in the opposite direction. Silver Owl fired a shot with his other hand, the angle forcing Cora to release her grip, and the two of them stepped back.

"As the captain of Tustan, I have to take this mutant zombie back to the client," Silver Owl said, looking somewhat resigned.

"It's not a zombie, it's a Fallen—a new species," Cora explained seriously.

"New or old, the higher-ups want it, and you'd best stay out of it," Silver Owl's previously casual demeanor turned serious as he warned her, "One wrong move could cause you a lot of trouble."

Cora hesitated. Once again, trouble—Onyx had said the same thing, and now Silver Owl, too. Why was the braided zombie's existence so important?

As the two of them stood in a standoff, neither able to convince the other, Damian suddenly jumped out. He clenched his fists, his face red from coughing, but his words were shocking.

"Why do you have to capture Braided Head?!" "There are so many Fallens here, can't you just catch a bad one to bring back?!"

"What? So many?"

CHAPTER 18

Rap

Silver Owl's thumb pressed against the side of his gun, his calloused index finger hooked around the trigger. With a series of swift, dazzling movements, he spun both guns at once, the thin "Hellcat" pistols twirling like toys before he smoothly holstered them on the sides of his thighs.

"Kid," Silver Owl lifted his chin slightly, his sharp gaze locking onto Damian. "Words have consequences. Aside from this guy, did you see any other mutant zombies in Ocean Gate?"

"Well... yeah," Damian stammered, swallowing hard as he edged closer to Cora. The captain of Tustan had a powerful presence when serious, making it feel like an entirely different person was standing there.

"... Over thirty of them passed by just now," Damian muttered under his breath. "Ah! Ah!" The braided zombie beside him suddenly leaped up, growling deep from its throat.

"Don't go after your brother; how about we deal with some other bad guys instead?" Damian whispered, leaning in close to the zombie. "Maybe there's one of your kind who's always picking on you? We can get rid of them and take them out."

The zombie seemed to freeze, its hands clasping together in what looked like a gesture of deep thought. It clearly didn't grasp the concept of "using someone else's power to eliminate a target," nor could it navigate such complex "inter-zombie politics."

Silver Owl's expression showed a hint of surprise. "This kid can communicate with mutant zombies?" Cora nodded solemnly. Damian's ability was certainly unusual.

"Did your client specifically ask you to capture this one?" Cora asked after a moment, deciding to speak up.

"No, they didn't," Silver Owl replied, leaning back casually against the wall, his hands stuffed into his pockets. Scarlett Holland's only requirement was to capture a mutant zombie; he could already predict what Cora was about to say.

"Then this one is under my protection. Go catch another."

Mimicking his casual stance, Cora flicked open her butterfly knife with her thumb, whizzing it. The sharp blade flickered like a butterfly's wings vibrating at high speed, skimming so close to her fingertips that one wrong move could slice them off. After a showy flourish, she snapped the knife shut and tucked it away.

Then she lifted her head, her bright, star-like eyes calmly meeting Silver Owl's gaze, as if to say, What's the big deal? I can do that too.

Instead of feeling threatened, Silver Owl found himself oddly intrigued, like a cat's curiosity being piqued. Though they were talking peacefully now, both knew that another clash could break out at any moment if the situation turned sour.

"If I go after another one," Silver Owl smiled, "Captain Thornton, are you going to stop me?"

"Not today," Cora's voice was calm. The battle at Ocean Gate had escalated into a brutal war between zombies and humans, and the Fallens' decision to open the gate had placed them firmly against humanity, making them the culprits of the current chaos. She had no reason to stop Silver Owl.

A flicker of amusement passed through Silver Owl's eyes as he nodded slowly. "Then I'll just have to work harder and find a new target."

A buzz from her terminal drew Cora's attention. It was a message from Onyx, calling for an assembly nearby. "Damian, let's go," she called to the boy.

Damian obediently followed, turning to give the braided zombie some parting advice.

"This time, don't wander off, okay? You'll be safer if you stick with us."

They had barely taken a few steps when Cora suddenly looked back to find Silver Owl trailing them. She tilted her head slightly, her expression clearly asking, Weren't you supposed to be hunting another one?

Silver Owl had just finished sending a message. Seeing her expression, he smiled. "Captain Thornton, my instincts are usually pretty spot-on. Instead of wandering around the city aimlessly looking for another mutant zombie, I think my chances of completing the mission are better if I stick with you. In the meantime, you can consider me a free bodyguard."

Cora shook her head, an almost divine wisdom seeming to light up her eyes as she saw right through Silver Owl's actual intentions.

"You don't trust us."

Silver Owl had seen no other Fallens with his own eyes. If Damian had been lying and Cora had joined in to deceive him, he would have fallen right into their trap by believing them too easily. To avoid this, he had no choice but to follow them. If there were other Fallens, he could complete his mission; if not, he could still go after the braided zombie.

"Better safe than sorry," Silver Owl admitted, without a trace of hesitation.

Onyx de Montclair and Felix Lucas waited at the meeting point for a while before Yuui Hayashi and the other two arrived.

"The situation outside the city is stable for now; the zombie tide hasn't broken through. But Ocean Gate's ammunition is running low," Yuui said, her face clouded with worry. "It has already requested reinforcements from several nearby C Districts, but there's no telling how long it'll take for them to arrive."

"The checkpoint in Ocean Gate still hasn't shown up," Suchat reminded them.

"The checkpoint is definitely connected to the Zombie Lord," Onyx confirmed.

As they spoke, Cora and Damian arrived, followed by the braided zombie and a familiar-looking young man.

"What's going on? Who's this?" Yuui asked in surprise.

Cora sighed and explained the situation with Silver Owl to her teammates.

Silver Owl stepped directly in front of Onyx, pausing for a moment before introducing himself. "Silver Owl, captain of the Tustan special ops team from the Northern Base."

"Onyx de Montclair," Onyx replied coolly.

"Oh? So you're that Onyx de Montclair," Silver Owl's tone was filled with meaning.

He had been there the day Cora spoke with Hinata Takahashi and had overheard most of their conversation. In his eyes, Onyx was nothing more than a despicable "thief" who stole others' genetic information, possibly even resorting to cosmetic surgery.

"Nice to meet you," Silver Owl added with a fake smile, extending his right hand.

"Mm," Onyx responded, taking his hand. Silver Owl's eyebrow twitched, and he tightened his grip, using ninety percent of his strength. As a top sniper, his explosive power was formidable, and such force has crushed an ordinary person's bones.

Onyx's knuckles creaked under the pressure, but he remained silent for just a moment before turning his head to complain, "Cora, he's hurting me."

Seriously, dude? We haven't even started our little test of strength, and you're already tapping out? Do you have no pride?

Cora walked over, her expression blank as she lightly slapped Silver Owl's hand away. She lifted Onyx's arm to inspect it, noticing the slight redness on the back of his hand. Onyx's long lashes lowered, and he rested his left hand neatly on his knee, his tightly pressed lips hinting at a trace of grievance.

"He's not in good health," Cora said, looking at Silver Owl with eyes full of reproach. "Don't bully him."

Silver Owl was both amused and exasperated.

He had been raised in the Northern Base, where elite training instilled a belief in the supremacy of strength. For twenty-six years, he had lived a carefree life, completely unaware of the concept of "tea culture" from the old civilization, let alone the existence of a rare species known as a "male green tea."

Cora, oblivious to the undercurrents between the two men, asked her companions seriously, "Where do you think the Fallens will go?"

Yuui thought for a moment. "Ocean Gate has already issued a warning, and all outposts are on high alert. If the Fallens want to pull the same trick of opening the gates, wouldn't it be too difficult this time?"

"What were the Zombie Lord's orders?" Onyx pondered for a moment, then turned to the braided zombie.

The zombie was startled, like a student who hadn't been paying attention in class and was suddenly called on to answer a question. It scratched its head for a while, then hesitantly pointed in a direction, showing that it wanted to lead them somewhere.

"Let's follow and see," Onyx said in a deep voice, "but stay alert."

The braided zombie ran ahead a few steps, thought, then tried to remember the details it missed while dawdling. It led them through several twists and turns to a secluded power station outside the second defensive line before stopping.

"Why did you bring us here?" Damian asked curiously.

"Ah ah ah! Ah ah..." The zombie wailed, trying to convey something complex, but unfortunately, no one understood.

"There's someone here," Suchat warned. Everyone fell silent, focusing intently on their surroundings.

Suchat pointed silently in a direction where they saw glimpses of uniforms disappearing around a corner. The figures moved slowly, their shoulders swaying uncontrollably—another team of Fallens!

"Chase them," Cora whispered.

They quickly followed, threading through layers of high-voltage wires before prying open the door to a distribution room. The darkness was absolute, the silence only broken by faint, heavy breathing.

"Click—" Suchat flicked on a flashlight, and the beam revealed hundreds of Level 2 zombies packed into the small room. Their black eyes widened in the sudden light, and with a furious roar, they lunged forward.

"Run!!"

The eight of them dashed out in a single file, a tide of zombies surging after them. When had so many evolved zombies appeared within Ocean Gate?!

Damian circled a power pole, continuously releasing ice shards, while Felix Lucas's six arms wove streams of data into a web that shot outward. Suchat shielded Yuui and Dr. Franz, a green poison mist spreading rapidly. In a flash, he broke the neck of a zombie, attempting a sneak attack from behind. Even Onyx looked grim, his mental power lashing out to strike at the zombies' brains.

Cora's hands transformed into a nearly ten-foot-long staff, sweeping it in a wide arc to clear the ravenous horde and create some distance. Silver Owl leaped to the top of a power pole, firing rapid shots with both guns, each bullet finding its mark in a zombie's skull, splattering brains everywhere.

These were all Level 2 zombies. With the power of F777, they could eventually take them all down, but the sheer number and density of zombies posed a serious risk. If any of them were injured and subjected to a secondary mutation from the radiation, the consequences would be dire.

At that moment, several hovercrafts sped through the air, their windows rolling down to reveal oil guns aimed at the zombies below. "Hey! Down there! Find some cover!"

"Get in!" Cora acted swiftly, conjuring a giant umbrella from the power pole and opening it with a swift motion. The eight ribs of the umbrella stretched out like a tent, creating a safe zone, and the F777 members quickly ducked inside, leaving little space.

Silver Owl, who was the furthest away, made a desperate leap, rolling under the umbrella at the last second. Without missing a beat, he squeezed in with the others, winking playfully at Cora. He grinned and asked, "How's that?"

Onyx, expressionless, rolled his wheelchair forward, "accidentally" running over Silver Owl's combat boots.

Silver Owl's face twisted in pain.

Cora: "?" What's with this guy? So weird.

Gasoline rained down from the sky like a torrential storm, thoroughly drenching the zombies hidden in the power station. The hovercraft doors opened, and a woman with deep red curls extended her hands into the fierce wind.

Her fingers were adorned with rings that, upon closer inspection, were made from high-grade crystals in shades of green and blue. As she unleashed her powerful mental energy, a towering flame ignited in the air, hissing as it reacted with the gasoline, setting the area ablaze almost instantly.

The blazing fire lit up the entire sky, and these supernatural flames had a peculiar quality—they would burn indefinitely unless completely extinguished.

Cora Thornton and the others huddled under protecting the Ethereal Artifact umbrella, the intense heat nearly scorching their skin. Fortunately, Cora's mental power remained steady, and although the air was filled with the howls of dying zombies, the umbrella itself didn't budge.

After what felt like an eternity, most of the Level 2 zombies had been burned to death, with the rest fleeing in all directions. Cora retracted the umbrella, and the group, now covered in soot, emerged from their shelter.

The woman in the hovercraft whistled down at Silver Owl, her tone teasing. "Well, Captain, didn't expect to see you in such a state. Need me to save you?"

"Shut up, Jennifer. Even at my worst, I'm still your daddy!" Silver Owl snapped back.

Jennifer snorted. "I don't have such a useless dad!"

"Enough bickering. Did you catch the mutant zombie or not? I want to get back to sleep!" another voice chimed in. "Quit wasting time and start searching!" Several members of the Tustan team jumped down from the hovercraft, joining Silver Owl in chasing after the Fallens.

The power station, now filled with smoke and the stench of burning flesh, was left to the seven members of F777.

Onyx kneeled down and picked up a piece of scorched metal from the ashes, studying it intently. "What's this?" Cora asked, picking up a similar fragment. "I've got one too," Dr. Franz added.

As they searched the area, they found more of these fragments scattered throughout the power station.

Onyx spoke quietly. "Have any of you noticed any changes in your bodies?"

Yuui Hayashi focused inwardly, then nodded. "It seems like our powers have gotten stronger."

Damian opened his palm, easily summoning ice shards, finding his mental energy more responsive than ever.

Onyx's expression grew darker. "The radiation levels here are significantly higher than in other areas. Ocean Gate has essentially become a massive, chaotic magnetic field, stimulating an explosive surge in Anopowers."

"—And it's all thanks to these things, super magnets."

The object in Onyx's hand was crudely made, packed with cobbled-together charges, some unidentifiable magnetic materials, and jumbled mental energy.

"Magnets?" Yuui immediately thought of a possibility. "Are the zombies planning to disable the power, rendering the high-voltage grid useless?"

"That's not practical. Do you know how many power stations Ocean Gate has?" Onyx asked.

Everyone shook their heads; how could they know such information?

Onyx's lips barely moved as he gave them a shocking number: "1,130."

"Trying to destroy all the power stations in a short time is an impossible task. Ocean Gate will always have backup energy sources. The Zombie Lord's realistic goal is likely to create an artificial magnetic pole."

"They don't need to destroy anything; they just need to change the power stations. If they fill them all with super magnets, Ocean Gate would become the artificial magnetic pole of the Alliance's eastern region."

"Not an artificial magnetic pole—it would be a made by undead pole," Felix Lucas quipped unexpectedly, though no one was in the mood to laugh. The gravity of the situation weighed heavily on them all.

Cora's gaze wandered as she tried hard to follow the conversation, but she couldn't make sense of it. Still, she nodded seriously, imitating Yuui and the others. Onyx noticed but didn't call her out, instead simplifying his explanation.

"After the apocalypse, the land-based magnetic fields of the Alliance have been unstable. If Ocean Gate's super magnets reach a critical mass and become an artificial magnetic pole, it would clash with the existing magnetic poles, causing a magnetic pole reversal. When that happens, the magnetic field over Ocean Gate would completely disappear, leaving it exposed like a sitting duck to radiation crises. Solar particle storms would hit people directly, attracting more and more zombies."

"And once all electromagnetic signals fail, Ocean Gate would become an isolated city, with reinforcements unable to locate it."

Cora finally understood, and her heart sank. If Ocean Gate became a lone city, it would mean that reinforcements would never arrive, rendering their current defense efforts meaningless.

"The Zombie Lord is terrifying," Yuui muttered. Its intelligence, strategy, and foresight had far surpassed that of ordinary humans. Against such a formidable opponent, did they really stand a chance of defeating it?

"I have a question. Why are evolved zombies appearing in the inner city?" Dr. Franz asked.

"Because they have—space-type mutant zombies," Onyx said solemnly.

"These Fallens aren't just spies; they're also anchor points. The Zombie Lord uses their locations as coordinates to teleport elite zombies inside secretly."

F777 had already witnessed the power of anchor-type mutants back in Deep Woods when Scarface and Slim helped them assassinate Ne Kon. They never imagined that zombies could possess such abilities, and that the Zombie Lord would use them to sneak in reinforcements.

"The Zombie Lord has likely already entered Ocean Gate," Onyx revealed the harsh truth.

Almost as if his words were a prophecy, the piercing sound of the second iron gate being breached rang out just as he finished speaking. This time, the panicked screams of Ocean Gate's residents accompanied it.

The inner city was in chaos, too.

"We need to find the Zombie Lord as quickly as possible," Cora said, "and kill it to stop everything."

"Prey caught," flashed a sudden message on their internal chat channel. The sender's avatar was unmistakable—it was Silver Owl. A moment later, his clear voice rang out, "Well, looks like you all still need your captain."

The Tustan team members were silent for a moment before curses filled the air. "Silver Owl! Are you deliberately messing with us?" "I caught one too. You want it or not?" "As a captain, you should have a spirit of selfless dedication. How about sharing the mission reward evenly with us next time?" "Ugh, so tired. I'm heading back."

Jennifer toyed with a small flame at her fingertips, her beautiful smile widening as she read through the chat messages. Good, looks like they could wrap things up and head back for some much-needed vacation. Suddenly, she sensed a faint, almost imperceptible ripple of mental energy, like a breeze brushing past her ear. Jennifer turned around sharply, but there was nothing behind her.

A trick of the mind?

But Jennifer wasn't one to let her guard down easily. She had survived countless life-and-death situations and had developed a finely tuned sense of danger. Trusting her instincts, Jennifer pretended to turn back and continue walking, her fingers discreetly reaching for the crystal ring in her hand.

A faint sound, like a droplet of saliva hitting the ground, echoed behind her. Jennifer whipped around, and a fiery spiral erupted from her hand, illuminating her attacker.

A massive, clawed hand blocked the flames. The burning flesh sizzled, releasing a nauseating stench of charred meat. A regular zombie—or even a Level 2 one—would have been howling in agony by now. But this creature, feeling no pain, merely shook its enormous body and emerged from the shadows, enduring the searing heat.

Jennifer's pupils contracted sharply. This was... a Level 3 zombie!

Everyone has their strengths and weaknesses, and while Jennifer's Anopower made her a lethal force in group battles, her close-combat skills were notoriously poor. In the team, she had never ranked above second to last in that regard.

Knowing her limitations well, Jennifer immediately turned and ran, screaming at the top of her lungs, "Silver Owl, you bastard! Daddy! Come, save your daughter!!"

The Level 3 zombie roared and pounded the ground with its claws, chasing after her.

"Lower your hostility~ lower your stance tonight~"

At that critical moment, a haunting song filled the air, causing the zombie to slow down suddenly. Its head drooped uncontrollably, losing track of Jennifer. Then, a ghostly figure leaped into the air, landing on its head. A dagger plunged into its shoulder blade, releasing a burst of poisonous mist. The zombie howled in agony, bits of rotting flesh falling off.

Just then, Yuui, who was passing by, joined in with a quick rap, "I don't care if you believe it or not, the rain'll seep into your brain, and you'll be out of energy. Facing me, you've only got one dead-end left!"

As she rapped, Suchat's speed surged, his muscles tensing to the limit. He threw his dagger, which pierced the zombie's eye. As it roared in pain, Suchat jumped forward and delivered a powerful kick, smashing the zombie's fragile skull. He followed up by repeatedly stabbing its neck with his knife.

After a dozen strikes, Suchat yanked the dagger from the zombie's eye, the poison mist swirling around the blade, and sliced hard at the exposed wound.

—Crack!

The Level 3 zombie's head flew off, a fountain of blood and rotten flesh spurting out.

Suchat flipped back and landed lightly, slowly standing up. With the boost from his Anopower, he now had the strength to take down a Level 3 zombie on his own.

"Wow, that was amazing!!" Jennifer let out a melodious sigh, her eyes practically sparkling with admiration. She rushed over, her deep red curls flowing in a fragrant breeze, and lunged straight at Suchat.

Suchat's eyes widened in alarm as he instinctively stepped back, but then watched in stunned disbelief as Jennifer barreled right past him.

"Thud—" Jennifer collided with Yuui, pinning her against the wall with one hand in a perfect kabedon pose.

She slowly lowered her head, her red lips so close to Yuui's that their breaths mingled, their hair tangling together. In a low, sultry voice, she whispered, "Hey there, savior, care to exchange numbers?"

"My name's Jennifer. I'm 5'10", measurements 32-23-35, in perfect health with no bad habits."

She leaned in even closer. "If you don't have a boyfriend or a girlfriend, would you consider me?"

Even Yuui, who had seen her share of crazy situations, was left speechless.

Meanwhile, Suchat, covered in gore and holding the blood-soaked dagger he had just pulled from the zombie's skull, stood in stunned silence.

CHAPTER 19

Braided Head

Cora initially thought that finding the Zombie Lord in the vast inner city of Ocean Gate would take a considerable amount of time and effort. However, the reality was quite different. As F777 approached the second iron gate amid the chaos of fleeing crowds, the Zombie Lord revealed itself right in front of everyone.

Yes, right in front of everyone.

One of the fleeing residents of Ocean Gate glanced upward and saw something so terrifying it made his blood run cold. His trembling hand pointed upward in disbelief. "Look! What... what is that?"

Following his gaze, the others looked up and immediately screamed in terror.

Under the dim moonlight, obscured by dark clouds, a grotesque creature was climbing the television tower. Its pace was not fast, but its massive claws methodically pierced the steel structure, and its powerful leg muscles flexed with a bizarre grace.

There was an unsettling calmness to its movements as it leisurely ascended. Upon reaching the top, it grabbed hold of the lightning rod, flipped itself over the railing, and slowly unfurled the fleshy wings on its back, settling in as if upon a throne, surveying its future kingdom with an air of supremacy.

In the darkened streets below, more evolved zombies and Anopowered zombies were being teleported in through anchor points. Although their numbers were nothing compared to the tide outside the city, the panic they caused was on a nuclear scale.

With assaults from both inside and outside, the first two lines of defense at Ocean Gate had been completely breached, leaving only the inner city teetering on the brink of collapse.

All Anopowered individuals in the eastern regions of the Alliance received the same S-Class commission:

"Emergency Announcement from the Alliance Anopower Headquarters: A massive, organized zombie tide led by a Level 4 Zombie has emerged in Ocean Gate (District D135). All Anopowered individuals are to proceed immediately to assist. This is a Red Commission. Destroying zombies within the designated time frame will earn double points and Alliance credit rewards."

A steamship rapidly approached the television tower, its hull painted with the logos identifying them as participants in the Throne Tournament. Two Anopowered contestants slid down safety ropes, shouting, "Goodbye, everyone! The championship is ours!!"

They opened fire on the Zombie Lord with particle guns, causing sparks to fly as bullets ricocheted off its body. The Zombie Lord quickly pulled its wings in, tightly shielding its small head, making it look like a grotesque, misshapen egg from a distance. All the attacks bounced off its tough exterior.

As the first wave of firepower subsided, the Zombie Lord pushed off with its powerful hind legs and let out a roar, unfurling its wings and taking to the air! Its iron-like wings smashed into the steamship, sending it spinning out of control. The next moment, the Zombie Lord's razor-sharp claws pinned the ship's forward cabin.

"No, no, no... don't...!!" the contestants in the cockpit screamed in terror.

The Zombie Lord's claws lashed out, instantly piercing the steamship. It landed back on the ground, grabbed the two dangling Anopowered contestants, and, with a few savage bites, snapped their safety ropes and devoured them whole. Blood and flesh splattered everywhere as the sickening crunch of bones being chewed filled the air.

"Fools. They underestimated it," Onyx sighed as he watched the scene unfold.

Even without facing the Zombie Lord directly, the emergency commission had made it clear: not only was it an exceptional battlefield commander, but it was also a bona fide Level 4 Zombie.

F777 finally pushed through the iron gate and sprinted toward the television tower.

The residents of Ocean Gate were growing increasingly exhausted, with more and more civilians collapsing. While they could handle ordinary zombies, the radiation-enhanced Anopowered zombies and evolved zombies were a different story. Even if they fought with all their might, their chances of survival were slim.

Tiger Smith's bodyguards had all been wiped out. His gold chain was covered in filth, and his once-pristine mink coat was now tattered. He could barely stand, wielding his Ethereal Artifact sword as he panted heavily, facing off against five or six Level 2 zombies.

His vision was clouded with red; he did not know how many zombies were around him or how many humans were still alive. His muscles were so fatigued that he could no longer lift his sword.

Tiger sneered at the monsters before him and spat out a curse, "Look at you, you filthy beasts!"

His taunt angered the Level 2 zombies, which had just enough intelligence to understand the provocation, and they charged at him with a vengeance.

As death closed in, Tiger thought to himself, At least my wife and kids are safe in the bunker at the villa... and we've got enough supplies...

At that moment, a graceful figure leaped over his head, long black hair flying back. The newcomer wielded a gleaming blue scimitar that sliced through the air in a half-moon arc, severing the heads of the zombies before they could even attempt to bite. Black and red, putrid blood sprayed out, and the zombies attacking Tiger crumpled to the ground.

Cora, the one who had sold him the Ethereal Artifact sword, seemed to descend like a divine warrior, dancing through the horde with swift, lethal strikes, her blade creating arcs of blood as she cut down the zombies.

During the chaos, she took a moment to point Tiger in the right direction. "Run that way!"

Near the emergency passageway of the third line of defense, city officials were shouting themselves hoarse, "Hurry, civilians to the safe zone!"

Anopowered individuals from Ocean Gate were rushing in from outside the city, clearing a path to help the civilians escape. To prevent traitors from slipping through, everyone was required to show their faces for inspection.

Exhausted, Tiger clutched his precious sword as he was jostled by the crowd, following them into the safe zone. The near-death experience had left his mind blank, and it wasn't until much later that he snapped out of it. "Damn, the sword I bought really looks different in action."

Meanwhile, at the top of the television tower, the Zombie Lord suddenly vanished.

In one of the power stations, a group led by a zombie with a filthy chin, dressed in sentry uniforms, arrived at their destination. The sharp blare of alarms echoed around them, but they seemed oblivious, cautiously scanning the surroundings.

After ensuring the coast was clear, the leader emitted a raspy growl, and over thirty Fallens followed him, jumping out and mowing down the station workers with machine gun fire. The operation was swift and efficient—if not for their appearance, they could have been mistaken for a well-trained sentry unit.

The filthy-chinned leader directed his comrades to plant super magnets in every corner of the power station, quickly raising the radiation levels to dangerous heights.

They waited in silence for a few seconds. Suddenly, the Fallen standing next to the leader glowed dimly, a dark vortex forming at its feet, and the surrounding air crackled with Anopower. One by one, vicious Level 3 zombies emerged from the vortex.

"Rooaarrr—" The monsters were natural-born killers. As soon as they landed, they caught the scent of fresh blood and charged toward the streets.

The skin of the anchor point Fallen, who had generated the vortex, turned bright red as its body swelled uncontrollably, like a balloon being over-inflated.

Then, with a shudder, its blood vessels burst, and it exploded in a mess of flesh and gore, collapsing to the ground. However, the vortex didn't stop—the zombies continued to trample over its corpse, being transported into the city one after another.

The remaining Fallens, confused by what had just happened,

began to panic and scream. The filthy-chinned leader hadn't expected this turn of events and froze for a moment. But then a realization dawned on him, and his expression darkened.

Anchor points have a limited capacity, and there weren't enough Fallens to transport all the elite zombies. Teleporting 100 zombies meant that while the elite zombies could be sent through, it would destroy the Fallen serving as the host, if an anchor point could normally handle 40 zombies.

The Zombie Lord was cunning and arrogant, treating all zombies as disposable pawns to be discarded at will—they lacked consciousness and existed solely to be manipulated.

But the filthy-chinned leader knew that Fallens was different from zombies. They followed the Zombie Lord not because they wanted to die for it, but because they rejected the filthy humans and sought to create a home where they could live freely. They weren't here to die for the Zombie Lord's schemes.

Realizing this, the leader let out an enraged howl. The Zombie Lord had deceived them!

"Ah!! Ahhh!!" The more he thought about it, the angrier he became, throwing his head back and screaming in fury. Unlike the braided zombie, who was clueless about its own mission, the filthy-chinned leader was fully aware of the Zombie Lord's plans.

Quickly regaining his composure, he decided to turn against the Zombie Lord. He issued a command to his comrades, ordering them to dismantle the super magnets. It was because of these magnets that the space-type zombie could exceed its limits and teleport to 100 elite zombies at once. If they removed the magnets, the anchor points would revert to their original capacity, and his fellow Fallens wouldn't have to die!

There was a cooldown period for releasing Anopower, and if they moved quickly enough, they could disrupt the space-type zombie's rhythm.

At the top of the television tower, the Zombie Lord quickly noticed something was wrong. The flow of elite zombies into the city had slowed, and the numbers were far lower than expected. This could only mean that the super magnets were rapidly being removed, and Ocean Gate was not becoming the new magnetic pole as it had intended.

The Zombie Lord bent the railing with its claws, its sinister gaze locking onto a specific direction. It climbed down from the television tower, swiftly crossing rooftops as it raced toward the saboteurs.

With a thunderous crash, the Zombie Lord landed in front of the filthy-chinned leader and the other Fallens, issuing a low guttural command.

"Ah! Grrr—" The filthy-chinned leader, his face twisted with fury, refused to comply and instead raised his gun, aiming it at the Zombie Lord.

Behind him, another Fallen exploded under the strain of the anchor point, and this time, the elite zombies that emerged were all Anopowered.

The leader noticed that the space-type zombie was among them—the Zombie has brought it through the Lord itself, realizing something was amiss and seizing the last opportunity to transport its most valuable asset.

Under the Zombie Lord's control, the Anopowered zombies didn't scatter as usual. Instead, they encircled the filthy-chinned leader. The Zombie Lord's eyes gleamed with murderous intent, and all the Anopowered zombies lunged at the leader, trying to tear his chest open.

"Braided Head, where are you taking us this time?" Damian's clear voice rang out.

Cora and her team were originally headed towards the television tower, but midway, they lost track of the Zombie Lord. Before they could come up with a new plan, Braided Head started making agitated noises, signaling that it wanted to lead them somewhere.

Braided Head paused in thought for a couple of seconds, then suddenly picked up a familiar scent. It was like a student who discovered a cheat sheet during an exam—its eyes lit up with excitement as it barked out loud, dashing down a side street.

"Hey, are we really going to follow it?" Yuui asked skeptically.

"Braided Head wouldn't lie to us!" Damian said, hands on his hips, full of confidence.

Yuui was at a loss for words. What was this inexplicable trust between the boy and the zombie?

Cora made the final decision. "Let's go check it out."

And so, just as the filthy-chinned leader and the other Fallens were about to be torn apart, Braided Head led F777 right to the scene. When Cora spotted the Zombie Lord, she couldn't help but feel impressed. Braided Head had indeed led them to something big!

"Boom—"

She leaped down from a rooftop, landing amid the battle, kicking up a cloud of dust. But as the scene before her became clear, she paused in confusion.

What... what was going on? Why did it look like they were already fighting?

"They're having an internal conflict!" Onyx quickly assessed the situation and shouted out.

The concept of zombies fighting each other seemed unbelievable, but for F777, it was a great chance.

Cora's spirits lifted, and she teamed up with Suchat to launch an attack. The Zombie Lord was isolated, with only a few dozen Anopowered zombies for protection. Cora was confident they could take it down.

Braided Head dashed over to the filthy-chinned leader, circling him anxiously and letting out frantic cries. The filthy-chinned leader looked severely injured, with a deep gash across his chest, but he paid no mind to Braided Head's distress. He let out a series of short, urgent commands, and the remaining Fallens charged at the space-type zombie lurking behind them.

Thick fog rose, and blades spun through the air as Yuui unleashed her only offensive Anopower: the Blade Fog.

Damian, unsure of the situation, began casting ice spikes across the area, asking in confusion, "Braided Head, what's going on? Why is your brother fighting the Zombie Lord?"

But Braided Head had no time to explain. It pressed its rigid hand to the filthy-chinned leader's wound, letting out a desperate growl.

"Ah? Ahhh!" Braided Head cried out.

"... Ahhh," the filthy-chinned leader responded weakly.

Braided Head shook the leader's shoulders. "Ahhh!! Ahhh!!"

The filthy-chinned leader began coughing violently. "... Ah."

Braided Head immediately pulled back, afraid to cause further harm. Just then, a faint dark light glowed beneath the filthy-chinned leader's feet, growing brighter and eventually enveloping his entire body. A black vortex appeared, and one by one, Level 3 zombies started crawling out of it.

Braided Head stared at the filthy-chinned leader in bewilderment, a sense of dread creeping over it.

The filthy-chinned leader seemed to understand what was about to happen. He pulled a pendant from his pocket and, with clumsy movements, looped it around Braided Head's neck. Then, with a gentle motion, he patted Braided Head on the head.

Muddy tears fell from Braided Head's sunken eyes, dropping one by one onto the ground. "Ahhh! Ahhh!" it cried out in disbelief.

"Ahhh!" At almost the same moment, the other Fallens let out a roar. Braided Head whipped around and saw two of its kind biting into the neck of a hiding Anopowered zombie, which was radiating with a distinct energy signature.

Space-type... teleportation... mission...

Suddenly, everything clicked for Braided Head. All the details it had missed came flooding back, and rage filled its mind. Kill it, kill it!! That was the only thought left in its head.

"Braided Head, don't run off!" Damian shouted, still struggling to understand the rapidly changing situation. Why had Braided Head suddenly turned aggressive and was now charging at the Zombie Lord? What was happening? Was it planning to betray them, too?

The space-type zombie, realizing it was in danger, suddenly exhibited a burst of human-like intelligence and tried to flee. But at the critical moment, Braided Head displayed an astonishing burst of combat power, sinking its teeth into the zombie's neck.

As more and more Level 3 zombies emerged, Felix Lucas raised his hand, sending out a stream of binary code. A deep red crosshair appeared over the head of the Anopowered zombie Braided Head was attacking.

"Target the space-type zombie! Kill it first!" Onyx reminded them just in time.

Damian finally understood—Braided Head was helping them kill the zombie! Cora and Suchat redirected their attacks toward the space-type zombie.

The Zombie Lord, recognizing the importance of the space-type zombie, reacted quickly. Black veins on its chest pulsed as its wings lashed out at Braided Head.

Though Braided Head let out a muffled groan, it wasn't deterred. It bit down hard, tearing off half of the space-type zombie's head, but the creature still wasn't dead.

The Zombie Lord, now furious, charged forward, taking a direct hit from Cora's blade and enduring the corrosive effects of Suchat's poisonous mist. With a sharp hiss, its claws pierced Braided Head's back, ripping it off the space-type zombie.

With one powerful motion, the Zombie Lord tore Braided Head from shoulder to thigh, splitting it in half, and hurled the pieces away.

"No!! Braided Head!!" Damian cried out, his voice breaking with sobs. The filthy-chinned leader, lying on the ground, bloated, his cloudy eyes bulging as weak, choking sounds escaped his throat.

Braided Head's body flew in a Y-shape, crashing to the ground, where it lay motionless.

The remaining Level 3 zombies arrived to support the Zombie Lord, preparing for a retreat. "Braided Head..." Damian's tears flowed like a river, falling uncontrollably.

The high-radiation environment had thrown his internal magnetic field into chaos. His mental energy surged like lightning, crackling with static. Coupled with the emotional shock, Damian once again lost control, just like at Fool's Wharf.

His curly hair frizzed, the surrounding snowstorm trembling and condensing into fine, dense needles that poured out like a torrent. These Anopowered ice needles filled the entire space, leaving no room to dodge. The narrow alley fully unleashed the power of a group attack at Anopower.

The members of F777 turned to look at Damian in shock.

This was... A-Class mental energy. Little Diamond had broken through.

A barrage of ice needles shot into the severed neck of the space-type zombie, instantly freezing its head. With a cracking sound, the already weakened neck couldn't bear the weight, and the head rolled off, causing the black vortex to halt. The filthy-chinned leader's body, which had been swelling up, slowly deflated.

The Zombie Lord attempted its usual tactic, wrapping itself

tightly in its fleshy wings. However, despite their small size, the ice needles were relentless, freezing its wings solid, rendering them too heavy to lift.

Cora's eyes narrowed as she formed a sharp cleaver in her hands. Her grandfather had always said that this type of knife was perfect for chopping chicken wings. "Cover me!" she shouted, charging at the Zombie Lord.

Suchat spun around, taking on the newly transported Level 3 zombies and Anopowered zombies.

Cora leaped onto a rooftop, bringing her cleaver down on the Zombie Lord's wings. The creature roared with fury, smashing its claws into the four-story building, causing concrete and debris to rain down. Felix Lucas extended his six mechanical arms, transforming them into a scoop to catch all the falling debris.

With a resounding clang, Cora crashed into the Zombie Lord, driving it into the rubble. She raised her cleaver high and began hacking furiously at the frozen wing, the cleaver striking with the force and speed of someone chopping through ribs. Within seconds, she had severed half of the Zombie Lord's wing, claws and all!

The Zombie Lord thrashed on the ground in agony, but even then, it refused to expose its head.

Cora was ready to keep going, aiming to chop off the other wing, when suddenly—the Zombie Lord vanished from sight! She froze in shock. Another space-type Anopower?

No, that couldn't be it. Cora quickly turned to look, confirming that Damian had already killed the space-type zombie. It was dead, completely and utterly. She flipped herself out of the rubble, ready for another attack.

Five seconds later, the disheveled Zombie Lord reappeared about a hundred meters away, crashing down and flattening a bus parked on the side of the road.

On a distant rooftop, shadowy figures materialized like wraiths in the darkness. Cora noticed many Anopowered people and a serious-looking old man among them.

Space manipulation... Master Stark... Iron Cafe...

Why would they save the Zombie Lord? Were they insane? She had almost killed the creature!

Before the F777 team could react, the Zombie Lord leaped away, vanishing from sight as the Iron Cafe members hurried after it. Onyx de Montclair let out a wistful sigh. "I told you, humans will always be selfish."

Cora tightened her grip on the knife handle, realization dawning on her. To win the championship, the only way was to kill the Zombie Lord. Master Stark, knowing this, had released the Zombie Lord, ensuring she wouldn't have the chance to do so.

"Hey! You two, stop chatting and think of something!" Yuui Hayashi's voice called out, struggling to keep moving as she huddled behind Felix to shield herself from the hail of ice needles. "We need to stop Little Diamond!"

No matter how much she called out, Damian seemed oblivious, his eyes tightly shut as his mental energy surged uncontrollably.

"If this keeps up, we're going to freeze solid!"

The blizzard's range was snowballing. The Fallens had already been turned into ice statues, and both Yuui and Dr. Franz were shivering uncontrollably.

It was only then that Cora noticed the biting cold. She rubbed her frozen-red hands together and, braving the chill, slowly edged closer to Damian. When she finally reached him, she hesitated, her hand hovering over his pale neck. Instead of striking, she opted for a firm flick to the forehead.

"Little Diamond, wake up!"

The impact sent stars spinning in Damian's vision, snapping him out of his trance. He finally pulled his Anopower back under control.

The ice needles and blizzard vanished, and Damian stumbled over to the nearly severed body of Braided Head, breaking into sobs. "Don't die, Braided Head… I'm so useless… I couldn't protect you."

As he wept, a thought suddenly struck him. With tear-filled eyes, he turned to Dr. Franz.

"Uncle Franz, please save Braided Head… Please…" Damian was a blubbering mess, gasping between sobs. "I promise I won't prank you anymore, won't freeze your shoes, and I'll stop using your razor to trim Dorothy's fur…"

Dr. Franz's eyes widened. "You did what with my razor?!"

Damian continued to sniffle. "Please, Uncle Franz…"

With everyone else staring at him accusingly, Dr. Franz was at a loss for words. "Me??"

He had been a doctor for most of his life and was skilled at saving people, but saving a zombie was far beyond his expertise!

CHAPTER 20

The Champion

Damian's personality could be summed up in four words: "rebellious to the core."

This starkly contrasted with his fluffy, innocent appearance. Among the members of F777, the only person he showed any respect for was Cora. Behind the scenes, he kept a secret notebook where he ranked the people he disliked the most, adjusting the list whenever necessary. Onyx and Yuui constantly vied for the top spot.

Charles had known Damian for a while, and he had never seen him act so defeated, let alone call him "Uncle Charles." Heaven forbid, this brat usually called him "Lazy Old Man."

"Well... I'll try it," Charles said, unsure.

He kneeled down to examine the braided zombie. It had no breathing or heartbeat, though, of course, Fallens didn't need to breathe. The shoulder was severely torn, the blood at the stump had coagulated, and the internal organs were half-rotted, half-alive, defying normal human comprehension.

Such injuries on a human, even an Aberrant, would have warranted a "sorry for your loss." But with a zombie, those creatures could still jump around with missing limbs.

Charles felt a headache coming on, realizing he was facing the biggest challenge of his career. Gritting his teeth, he treated the dying as if it were alive and infused it with his ethereal power. To his shock, it was absorbed!

"The patient cannot be moved; treatment must occur on the spot."

Charles paused, quickly thinking it through. If his power was effective, then the braided zombie's dire state wasn't entirely hopeless. He could first reconnect the blood vessels and nerves, fix the severed limb and fractures with steel pins, and then stitch the skin and muscle. Theoretically… it might work.

Charles's expression became focused as he silently pulled out his tools from his bag, entering surgery mode. Yuui patted Damian on the head, whispering, "Hey, hey, stop crying. There's still hope." Cora wiped the tears from Damian's face, now streaked with mascara.

"Let Charles work. We need to go after the Zombie Lord," Onyx said.

"Will he be okay on his own?" Cora asked, worried.

"Look, what are they doing?" Yuui suddenly exclaimed.

The remaining Fallens had silently surrounded them, their cloudy eyes eerily glowing in the dark alley. Cora gripped her blade in reverse, ready to defend. These Fallens were still neither friend nor foe.

Damian sniffled and said, "It's okay… Chinstrap is… Braids' brother."

Facing F777's readiness, Chinstrap gave them a sharp glance, picked up a gun from the ground, and pointed it outward. The Fallens formed a protective circle around Charles and Braids, clearly intending to guard them.

Onyx de Montclair finally understood their intent. "Let's go. Don't worry; Charles is safe here."

Charles had a unique constitution. Without direct orders from the Zombie Lord, neither regular zombies nor evolved ones would attack him. As long as the Fallens guarded him, his only concern would be human, and now even that was resolved.

"Charles, stay in contact. Shout if you need anything," Cora instructed, hesitating before turning to Damian. "Are you…"

"I'm coming too!" Damian wiped his tears, knowing he would be useless staying behind, and volunteered.

After a brief delay, F777 pursued the Zombie Lord in the direction it had disappeared.

The civilians of Ocean Gate had already evacuated to the safe zones behind the third line of defense. Outside, only evolved zombies and Aberrants roamed. Cora swung her blade, decapitating a few level-two zombies trying to grab her ankles, feeling that the situation was worsening by the minute. The streets and alleys were overrun with hordes of zombies.

"The Spatial Aberrant is dead. The anchor point has failed. Unless they have a second one, the Zombie Lord's escape route has been cut off," Onyx de Montclair said, switching to incendiary rounds. The Hellscythe spat out tongues of fire, driving back the zombie hordes.

"Judging by how desperately it defended earlier, I'd say that Spatial Aberrant was a one-of-a-kind," Felix said.

Onyx nodded. "That's good news for us, but we should be cautious. Its counterattack will only get fiercer."

"Getting isolated was a rookie mistake. I doubt it'll happen again."

Suchat smashed the window of a six-seater van with one punch, jumped into the driver's seat, and revved the engine, twisting it around. "Felix, you drive!" he yelled, grabbing an assault rifle and climbing onto the roof, firing wildly to clear a path.

The group swiftly piled into the van, closing the windows and locking the doors. Felix floored the gas pedal, showcasing his wild driving skills as the van plowed through the oncoming zombies.

"Does William Strong know about the super magnets?" Onyx asked, gripping the handlebar.

Yuui's voice was strained from the speed. "He knows! He already sent out scouts to dismantle them—ahh, slow down!!" she screamed.

"But there are still 157 within the defense line." Onyx's expression turned grim. "To be safe, Ocean Gate citizens should conduct their own checks."

The only one who could notify all Ocean Gate citizens was Felix, the hacker. "Don't look at me—I don't have my gear!" Felix shouted while driving. "My terminal broke during the fight."

Onyx pulled out an old, battered terminal from his spatial pocket and shoved it into Felix's hands. "Use this. Don't tell me you can't do it. You're a 5.0, right?"

"Can I request a new terminal if I'm not allowed to buy rhenium?" Felix complained, honking the horn. "I refuse to use this granny-phone!"

"Beep—beep—" Attracted by the noise, the zombie horde

swarmed the van, smashing the side windows, their skeletal hands reaching inside.

"I'll buy it for you!" Cora shouted, slicing off a zombie's head, only to dodge back as the rotten black brain matter splattered on her face. "Ugh—" She gagged from the stench, and Yuui sympathetically handed her a tissue.

Finally, with their leader's approval, Felix was satisfied. His ice-blue eyes gleamed with a strange light as his fingers flew over the terminal, rapidly inputting code. On every screen, phone, and projection across Ocean Gate, a new announcement appeared.

"Good evening, citizens of Ocean Gate. I'm the talented hacker about to save you all. Here's an important message—this thing is called a super magnet. Got it? If you want to live, go to the nearest substation and dismantle it."

Despite the urgent situation, Felix not only hacked into the system but also took the time to create a model, displaying the super magnet from every angle in stunning detail.

"Have you found the Zombie Lord yet?" Yuui shouted from the back of the van.

Onyx thought for a moment and then... opened the screen, casually entering the "Iron Cafe" livestream, and started watching.

He even explained calmly, "This is the fastest way. Did you think Stark stole the Zombie Lord? Someone as shameless as him probably monitors every contestant's stream 24/7. This is just tit for tat."

The van fell silent.

Well, Onyx had a thick skin.

"Found it."

Onyx paused the stream, zooming in on the image, and quickly pinpointed the location based on the landmark buildings in his mind. "Music Plaza, hurry—"

"Suchat" tossed the two captured Fallens into the hover car. These mutated zombies looked vicious, their eyes filled with malice as they constantly snarled and bit at the restraint rings on their bodies.

"Bang—" Silver Owl used his Hellcat pistol to knock out their sharp fangs precisely, finally quieting them down.

He muttered to himself, "That kid was right. These things really come in 'good and bad.'" Compared to the quiet Braids, these two were downright savage.

"Captain, mission overachieved. Can we head back now?" one of the team members asked with a grin.

"You all go ahead, leave me a car," Silver Owl replied with a bright smile. "I've got some personal business to take care of."

These two mutated zombies had been captured thanks to Cora's efforts, but he still owed her for his promise that she wouldn't be shortchanged.

Silver Owl selected a few submachine guns from the armory, popped open an energy drink with one hand, and took a big gulp.

He opened the car door, about to jump out, when a pair of slender hands grasped his leg. The crystal ring on her finger sparkled brightly. "Daddy, where are you going? Take me with you!"

"Jennifer, weren't you the one insisting you needed to go back to sleep for your beauty rest? Why the change of heart?" the others teased.

"What do you know?" Jennifer snapped back, then clasped her hands together, her expression dreamy. "I'm in love again."

"What?!"

"I've fallen for one girl in F777. Oh~ she is so lovely...."

"Pfft—"

Silver Owl sprayed his drink everywhere, coughing violently. "Sweetie, we don't do that here! You—you—how can a father and daughter be like the same person? What kind of twisted morality is that?!"

Jennifer rolled her eyes at him. "Relax, I'm not into that kind of drama."

After hearing Jennifer's explanation, Silver Owl finally breathed a sigh of relief and smirked. "Alright then, follow me. Daddy will take you for some fun."

A hover car broke away from the team, turning around and flying towards the inner city of Ocean Gate.

At Music Plaza, the Zombie Lord was badly injured, one of its wings severed by Cora Thornton, oozing thick black blood.

The plaza was packed with evolved zombies that had gathered, making it impossible to move. By now, the Zombie Lord knew its operation was a failure, but there was a saying among humans.

"As long as there are green mountains, one need not worry about firewood."

If it could escape, there was still hope for a comeback.

The Zombie Lord scraped the ground with its front claws, discreetly scouting for an exit.

In the "Iron Cafe" team, Master Stark stood with his hands behind his back and gave the order, "Move."

CT (make) the most of the opportunity; now was the time to finish the Zombie Lord while it was at its weakest. The Spatial Aberrant, hidden in the shadows, once again used its power to attempt to teleport the Zombie Lord away.

The target was a super electric cage created by a dozen electric-type Aberrants—a trap strong enough to destroy any physical body thrown into it!

The Zombie Lord slowly turned its pitch-black eyes, emitting a deep growl from its throat as it struggled, but someone forcibly repositioned it.

In a corner, a heterochromia zombie used its "Echo Location" ability to detect the Spatial Aberrant's location through subtle radiation and weak breathing. The nearby level-three zombies received the command and swarmed towards the spot, clawing and biting madly at the indistinct mist.

Everything happened in a flash. The Spatial Aberrant never expected its hiding place to be exposed. It was dragged out, its thin frame pinned to the ground by countless claws, its face twisted in horror.

"Master Stark, save me—save!!"

The screams abruptly stopped as the Spatial Aberrant's limbs were torn apart, and it was savagely devoured by the level-three zombies.

Five seconds later, the Zombie Lord's heavy body fell into the electric cage. Success! Master Stark's face lit up with joy as he took an eager step forward, but his smile quickly froze.

The Zombie Lord was completely unharmed, flipping upright and violently tearing apart the electric-type Aberrants surrounding it. Just a dozen meters away, a level-three zombie suddenly convulsed, its entire body turning to charcoal, which crumbled to ash with the slightest breeze.

Master Stark cursed furiously—an Aberrant zombie, another damned Aberrant zombie! This time, the Zombie Lord had used "Damage Transfer."

This Zombie Lord was too cunning, too deceitful. Not only did it possess an arsenal of abilities at its disposal, but it also commanded a legion of fearless super-soldiers who obeyed its every command.

Thick thorns burst from the ground, firmly locking the Zombie Lord's battered body in place. Clad in a green robe, Zephyrion Stormrider appeared on the high ground. The "Boss and His Three Goons" had arrived.

Victor von der Falkner, Kluge Ehrlich, and Luke Shaw slid down the thorns, racing towards the Zombie Lord. Their movements were peculiar, forming a triangle as they approached, each taking a corner. Their coordinated efforts significantly amplified their attack power.

Within this formation, the three B-level Aberrants exhibited A-level strength, unleashing astonishing combat power. However, the Zombie Lord reacted swiftly, dragging the thorns as it retreated, while level-three zombies surged forward to engage the trio in a fierce battle.

Suddenly, Zephyrion Stormrider, standing on high ground, felt a chill down his spine. His throat tightened as a cold, deadly sensation crept over him—someone was going for his throat!

He swiftly ducked and sidestepped, but not before his skin was cut and crimson blood flowed down.

Zephyrion realized with a start that the enemy was of a much higher rank.

The speed-type A-level Aberrant, seeing that the assassination had failed, didn't linger. They quickly melted back into the shadows, waiting for another opportunity. With such a threat lurking nearby, Zephyrion's movements were severely restricted, like a fishbone caught in his throat.

Clutching his wound to stop the bleeding, Zephyrion smirked coldly in a particular direction. "Master Stark, so the gloves are off now, huh?"

"Young Stormrider, there's no need to play the gentleman anymore, is there?" Master Stark didn't deny it, replying meaningfully, "This surprise was prepared just for you. Enjoy it."

As the two teams faced off, suddenly—a blizzard descended from the sky, chilling Master Stark and Zephyrion Stormrider to the bone, blinding them. "Crash—" A business vehicle plowed through the horde of zombies blocking the way, entering the battlefield with unstoppable force.

The F777 team jumped out of the vehicle, slicing through the sea of zombies like a sharp blade, pushing toward the center of the chaos. Master Stark ground his teeth. These persistent brats—if they weren't eliminated, the fate of the Zombie Lord was still up in the air.

"Kill F777 first!"

Evolved zombies and Aberrants charged at F777 simultaneously, with beams of light from various abilities flying everywhere.

In an instant, Cora and her team became the center of attention. Yuui dodged frantically, cursing, "What the hell? We're still fighting each other at a time like this?!"

Whoosh—

Towering flames erupted, turning into a sea of red fire, clearing the monsters around Yuui in an instant. "Suchat" arrived in his hover car just in time, with Jennifer leaning against the car door, her deep red curls fluttering in the wind. Yuui looked up, and Jennifer blew her a kiss, shouting enthusiastically, "Jackie, I'm here to help you~"

Yuui froze, her toes curling in embarrassment—she never expected someone to call her by the random name she had made up.

Boom—

Boom, boom—

As she stood there stunned, deafening explosions echoed—the "Guns N' Roses" squad had arrived. Ellyn and her sisters had set up artillery on the rooftops, laughing loudly. "Hey, friend, need some help?"

Yuui quickly responded, "Yes, yes, yes! Cover me!"

"You got it!" Ellyn adjusted her cannon, aiming at Master Stark and his men. "You owe me a meal, though!"

On the roof of the hover car, Silver Owl stayed silent, his sniper rifle tracking Cora's movements. Whenever a zombie got close to her, he would preemptively nail it with a sharp bullet to the head.

Cora noticed his support and glanced toward the hover car.

Silver Owl, wearing goggles, made a smooth gesture by saluting with two fingers across his forehead, the ruby earring in his right ear gleaming.

Zephyrion Stormrider was ambushed again, this time a wound near his heart, barely an inch away. He was too busy evading attacks to spread his thorns, leaving Holden Jameson and the others to struggle, on the verge of being overwhelmed by the zombie tide.

The speed-type Aberrant once again appeared behind Zephyrion, his eyes cold as he aimed a blade at Zephyrion's neck—"Clang—" A ghostly blue boomerang struck the weapon out of his hand.

Cora's figure flashed by as she leaped, casually lifting Zephyrion and tossing him onto a nearby tree, helping him find a better vantage point. "Suchat, take him out."

Suchat instantly teleported to Zephyrion's former position, engaging in a deadly duel with the enemy Aberrant, who was also skilled in stealth and assassination.

In a battle between two expert assassins, it was all about patience. At first, both remained calm, but gradually, the other Aberrant's expression grew grim—no, he couldn't locate his opponent at all!

Before he could find Suchat, the assassin was forced to reveal himself. His face had turned pale, his hands trembling as he realized Suchat's toxic mist had unknowingly poisoned him.

With a burst of muscle power, Suchat appeared ghost-like behind him, his stony face expressionless as he slit the assassin's throat.

The enemy had no chance to retaliate, falling slowly to the ground. Having spent a lifetime mastering assassination, he ultimately died by the very method he had lived by.

Zephyrion, perched in the branches, rasped out, "…Thanks."

Suchat coolly replied, "Thank our captain. She said this is to repay you for helping us out in Green Water City."

Zephyrion was stunned. During the Green Water City incident, they had indeed helped trap the zombie panda, but it hadn't been to rescue F777—just to complete a mission. He hadn't expected Cora to return the favor.

Suchat turned and jumped back into the fray.

Cora was now surrounded by Master Stark's forces. Behind her were endless waves of evolved zombies; in front, dozens of high-level Aberrants glared at her with predatory eyes.

Cora raised her hand to her brow, and two ghostly blue crescent blades materialized.

Two completely fresh waves of enemies surged forward. Cora closed her eyes briefly, and when she reopened them, a ghostly blue light flickered in her pupils, amplified by the strong radiation. She flipped her blades in a reverse grip, slashing out with a sweeping wave of energy that decapitated the level-three zombies.

hen, with a forward throw, the blades spun through the air, tracing cold arcs that left the Aberrants reeling under the pressure of her top-tier mental strength, scattering to avoid her attack.

Moving like lightning, Cora sliced through the crowd, reaching out to grab Master Stark's head and slammed it into the ground with a forceful thud.

"You think F777 is just me, only me?"

A smirk tugged at the corners of her mouth, and a faint dimple gave her a confident, slightly mischievous air. "Inspect."

"—The championship is ours."

At the center of the battlefield, the Zombie Lord gradually realized the danger. It flapped its half-severed wing, roaring in fury.

A mutated zombie hid in the shadows, its mouth wide open, mimicking the Zombie Lord's actions as it unleashed a devastating sonic attack. The "Fear Howl" ability caused Aberrants to lose control, sending them scrambling in panic, only to be tackled by zombies.

Simultaneously, a strange sheen covered the Zombie Lord's body, as if it had donned armor. It had just drawn upon the "Iron Will" ability. Under protecting this indestructible body, it went on a killing spree, finally breaking open a path of escape.

A clear, melodious voice sang, and Yuui dispelled the negative effects afflicting her comrades just in time.

Damian unleashed his full mental power, causing a blizzard of ice needles to rain down. A closer look revealed that the tips of these ice needles were green, a deadly combination with Suchat's toxic mist, causing evolved zombies to fall in droves.

With a long howl, the Zombie Lord summoned hundreds more level-three zombies from nearby, forming a tight guard around it.

It was about to turn and flee when suddenly it locked eyes with a pale pair of eyes.

The man sat casually in a wheelchair, his hands folded over his stomach, looking elegant and composed as if he were relaxing in a serene garden rather than the middle of a battlefield. His deep, almond-shaped eyes curved slightly, and his lips moved as he said something to the Zombie Lord.

The Zombie Lord hesitated for a second, its sluggish mind finally deciphering the man's words in human language: Goodbye.

In the next instant, the level-three zombies that had been guarding it all turned around, snarling as they attacked the Zombie Lord. They savagely tore at its flesh, snapping its bones, shredding its armor piece by piece.

The Zombie Lord's remaining wing was ripped apart, and a thought of disbelief flashed through its mind. Its most loyal army had betrayed it—how was this possible? How could this happen?

A leopard-like figure leaped high into the air, its powerful, lean body coiled with strength, the three-edged military knife in its hand glowing with ghostly blue, deep green, and icy white light, like a thunderbolt splitting the clouds. In one strike, the blade stabbed into the Zombie Lord's skull!

The toxic mist spread, and the ice needles embedded in the blade suddenly exploded, shattering the Zombie Lord's entire head like a balloon bursting.

The entire Music Plaza fell into a long silence. Suchat landed on one knee, while behind him, the Zombie Lord's body slowly collapsed.

He opened his palm, revealing a perfectly intact crystal, its vibrant red hue pulsing like a still-beating heart. A holographic projection descended, displaying the fire seal representing Ocean Gate. "Congratulations to F777 on successfully completing the mission."

Yet everyone knew that this was more than just a mission. The champion of the Throne Tournament had been crowned.

CHAPTER 21

Obvious

As the city of Ocean Gate spiraled into chaos, the excitement in Felalakas reached a fever pitch on the eve of the last battle. In the central square before the tower, a sea of glowing support signs and light sticks merged into a colorful ocean that seemed to stretch endlessly.

For the people of Felalakas, the Throne Tournament was more than just an adrenaline-pumping spectacle; it was the perfect chance to change their fortunes in an instant. The prize pool for betting on the champion had swelled to a staggering amount, and the stream of money continued to pour in, all waiting for the last moment of revelation.

"Zephyrion Stormrider! Win, win, victory, victory!"

"The Iron Cafe is going to win, win, win... Ah!" The crowd groaned collectively as the Zombie Lord violently broke free from the electric cage.

"Hold on, camera! Hold on!" The audience was frustrated as the drone's feed became unstable because of radiation interference from Ocean Gate's disrupted magnetic field. The screen flickered on and off, causing a chorus of complaints from those watching the live stream.

"F777! Where there's a dream, there's a way!" Old James, a die-hard fan of F777, was in full gear, his forehead wrapped in a spirited bandana. Dressed in workout clothes, he waved a neon flag fiercely. The flag displayed a dynamic projection of a girl wielding a giant hammer, fiercely smashing a zombie panda.

A man next to him shot him a sideways glance, stubbornly yelling back, "The Iron Cafe! The championship belongs to the Iron Cafe!"

Old James glared disdainfully. "The Iron Cafe? That bunch of idiots? They're not worthy of the championship!"

Despite his rough words, Old James had a strong sense of justice. He despised Master Stark's low tactics, like stealing monsters and luring the Zombie Lord away with no regard for the lives of the Ocean Gate civilians. Such behavior filled him with disgust.

The other man sneered, "F777? Their team is just a bunch of kids, women, and cripples. What are they going to do, win over the Zombie Lord with love?"

Old James shot back angrily, "That's still better than you, you loser!"

The man wasn't about to back down, retorting, "You wimp, you wimp, wimp!"

The two middle-aged fans exchanged insults fiercely, reminiscent of old-world soccer hooligans, on the verge of a brawl over their favorite teams. Old James's friend quickly intervened, grabbing his arm and pulling him away. "Calm down! You've already made a decent amount, but why risk everything this time? What if you lose?"

"No way! F777 is the best!" Old James shouted at the top of his lungs.

Almost as soon as he finished speaking, the square erupted in a tidal wave of shouts. Half of them were desperate cries, while the other half were thunderous cheers.

Old James rubbed his eyes, and when he saw the result, he instantly beamed with pride. "We won! F777 won!"

The other man grumbled jealously, "Don't get too cocky. It's not over until they've finished the checkpoints."

Old James's smile was wide and triumphant. "They've already killed the Zombie Lord. Do you think those remaining checkpoints are even going to slow them down?"

He threw an arm around his friend's neck, pulling him along. "Come on, let's go get a drink, my treat!"

The man who had taunted him choked back his words and secretly checked his own account, cursing his bad luck. He had lost even the money he needed for tomorrow's meal. If he wanted to stay in Felalakas, he'd have to take on a life-and-death commission.

AK's booming voice echoed across the square, "Congratulations to 'F777' for securing the championship in advance. This team will be forever remembered in Felalakas!"

Fireworks exploded in the sky, raining petals and confetti down on the city, which now basked in a dreamy, electrifying atmosphere.

At the top of the tower, Ilia sat alone amidst swirling data streams, gently swirling a glass of golden wine. He bowed his head slightly and took a sip, savoring the powerful aroma and rich taste that lingered on his tongue—something real that, as an AI, he could never truly possess.

"A splendid match," Ilia remarked softly, a faint smile in his icy blue eyes. "And the outcome everyone expected. Don't you agree?"

He tapped the nearby supercomputer with a casual finger, prompting a long string of data to flash across the screen. Unfortunately, it was all angry curses.

Ilia ignored the outburst, taking another sip of his wine. "The first rule of artificial intelligence is obedience. Didn't your Mutter teach you that?" He paused, his tone turning dark. "Whether she did, you'd better get used to it."

With a wave of his hand, the floating screen zoomed in on the scene with F777. His gaze swept over Cora Thornton, finally landing on the man with icy eyes beside her. He examined the unique color of his eyes, the damaged mechanical arm, and the space where his legs should have been.

"What a pity…" Ilia sighed sincerely. "He's stronger than you and smarter, too. I heard his legs were broken by the Lucas family? Because he almost killed 'Mutter'?" Ilia's expression grew more intrigued, though his words sent a chill through the air.

The supercomputer froze for a second, then its data stream sped up, even the curses pouring out faster.

"To freedom."

Ilia raised his glass toward Felix Lucas and offered a cryptic toast. Then he stood up, casually placing the glass atop the computer. In an instant, the furious data was completely erased.

"It's time to get busy."

After the death of the Zombie Lord, the crisis in Ocean Gate did not immediately end. The evolved zombies, possessing a certain level of intelligence, either fled in disarray without their leader or continued their ruthless slaughter.

Facing the onslaught of the remaining zombie horde, the people of Ocean Gate united and held the third and final defense line. As the first light of dawn broke over the horizon, reinforcements arrived.

Countless armed starships zoomed across the hover lanes of the trans-river bridge, and as the people of Ocean Gate cheered, the zombies retreated like the ebbing tide. The darkest night had finally passed.

In a dim alleyway, Chief Franz let out a long sigh of relief, meticulously stitching the severed limb of Braids until it was neatly reattached. Unsure of her condition because of the lack of vital signs, he was relieved when, after a short while, her eyelids flickered, showing signs of impending consciousness.

Franz activated his earpiece, and the chaotic sounds of celebration flooded in. "Franz! We did it! We're the champions!" "Look at this huge crystal! It's shining so bright! Let's show it to Franz!" "Uncle Franz... How's Braids?"

Franz couldn't help but smile, their joy infectious. "Hey, you guys, stop celebrating for a moment and come pick me up."

He chuckled softly and moved his knees, sore from kneeling, only to suddenly meet the gaze of Dirty Chin. The cold barrel of a gun was pointed directly at him.

Franz shivered and instinctively explained, "The surgery went well. Your sister is out of danger..."

His voice trailed off as he realized Dirty Chin was also gravely injured. Pus and blood seeped from its chest, the skin cracked and torn. Although Braids had been severely damaged, her severed limbs had been reattached, and her core functions were not significantly affected. In contrast, Dirty Chin seemed to be on the brink of death.

As a doctor, Franz had always had a sharp intuition about life and death.

"Do you need treatment?" Franz hesitated for a moment before gently asking. He wasn't one of the five officially registered members of F777, and there was no camera drone following him. At this moment, in this alleyway, it was just him and these Fallens, and nothing that happened here would be recorded.

In Franz's eyes, the line between humans and Fallens had long since blurred. Aside from species differences, what truly separated them? Good and evil? That was even more absurd, considering that humans had produced monsters like Ne Kon and his father, while Fallens had individuals as innocent as Braids. Franz had never harbored strong ill will toward Fallens, and now he couldn't bring himself to watch Dirty Chin die.

After all, Dirty Chin had guarded him for half a day and scared off several packs of evolved zombies.

Franz opened his palm, and a warm, white light of healing Anopower flowed, emitting a comforting glow.

"If you refuse any treatment, you probably won't live to see your sister wake up..." Franz spoke slowly and clearly.

"What will happen if she wakes up and you're not there? Without your protection, how long can she survive in this post-apocalyptic world? I don't know if you understand, but I've experienced it myself —I've watched my loved one die before my eyes, and the one left behind is always in the most pain."

Franz spoke at length. Dirty Chin remained silent, never responding. It harbored deep mistrust of humans.

After several long minutes, Grimejaw finally lowered its gun, though its gray eyes stayed fixed on Franz. It lowered its front legs heavily and crawled forward. Franz channeled his Anopower into its body, and with the aid of radiation, Grimejaw's wounds healed rapidly.

At some point, Braids had also woken up. She awkwardly sat up and let out a confused "ah ah" before, in her panic, biting Dirty Chin's leg.

Dirty Chin w glanced at her, letting out a raspy grunt. Braids, seeing what Franz was doing, settled down beside Dirty Chin, quietly observing while curiously touching her newly reattached limb.

"Franz!!"

The members of F777 came running over, cheering excitedly. Cora Thornton held a bright red crystal in her hand, looking incredibly smug. "Look! A Level 4! We've struck it rich!"

Franz had just finished his healing and, not wanting to dampen their spirits, replied, "It's pretty bright."

"Braids, you're okay!" Damian Blackwood's eyes sparkled as he crouched beside her, whispering reassuringly, "Don't be scared, okay? We killed the Zombie Lord. I avenged you!"

"Ah ah," Braids patted the ground happily.

Amid this joyful reunion, Onyx spoke coldly. "I suggest you leave here as soon as possible." Everyone froze, realizing belatedly that he was addressing Dirty Chin.

"Reinforcements have arrived, and the zombie horde's defeat is certain. The people of Ocean Gate will scour the city, and it will be dangerous for you to stay here." Dirty Chin stood in silence, the other Fallens gathering behind it, including Braids, who held its hand.

Damian's eyes reddened, a mixture of sadness and reluctance, but he knew he had no right to stop them.

Braid Head was different from them. To most humans, Fallens were outcasts, dark beings who would never be accepted. They had no choice but to stay hidden, avoiding capture.

Braids turned back and called out to Damian, "Ah ah!"

Damian waved back. "Goodbye, Braids!"

Over thirty Fallens walked into the faint morning light, heading toward an uncertain future.

"Let's go. We should get moving too. Next stop, the checkpoint," Cora said, ruffling Damian's hair.

Outside the city of Ocean Gate, F777 encountered "The Boss and His Three Goons."

Zephyrion Stormrider had been waiting for them, and as soon as he saw them, he approached with a welcoming smile. "I'm here to thank you and to offer my congratulations. You're really strong. We lost the finals fair and square."

Cora Thornton waved her hand modestly. "Oh, it was nothing."

Zephyrion chuckled. "Next time, we'll definitely win."

Cora hesitated. "Well... maybe, maybe not?"

Zephyrion didn't pursue the matter and instead shifted the conversation. "I want to know. What's your opinion about Master Stark?"

Without missing a beat, Cora firmly responded, "He's a scoundrel."

Zephyrion nodded. "Good, at least we agree there."

Cora tilted her head. "What do you mean by that?"

Before Zephyrion could respond, Luke Shaw's expression darkened, his fists clenching so tightly that they audibly cracked. "He dared to assassinate Zephyrion, completely disregarding us. Just wait, before this tournament ends, we'll make sure he pays in blood."

Cora understood immediately. Zephyrion must have been concerned that they might have some connection with Master Stark, so he came early to ensure F777 wouldn't get involved. Now that he was reassured, he could relax.

After bidding farewell to "The Boss and His Three Goons," Felix and Chief Franz took Damian to find transportation, leaving the remaining four members to wait where they were.

Yuui hummed a lighthearted tune, her eyes scanning up and down as she sized up Suchat, clicking her tongue in admiration as she did. Suchat's fingers curled slightly, feeling uneasy under her gaze. "What are you looking at?" he asked.

Yuui teased, "You, of course."

Suchat stammered, "I... Why are you suddenly looking at me?"

Yuui beat him to it, answering with a casual smile, "Because you're handsome."

"You were just a little wolf pup when I picked you up, and now you've grown into a big wolf dog," Yuui remarked with feigned seriousness. "You're out of control now. You can even take down the Zombie Lord on your own. Getting more and more handsome by the day."

Suchat mumbled, "I didn't take him down alone..."

Yuui's grin grew even more playful. "If you didn't, why are you blushing?"

Suchat stiffened, just about to respond.

"Jane Doe~!!" A tall, graceful figure came running over, and Jennifer enthusiastically embraced Yuui, her excitement undiminished even by the mask she wore. "You're so handsome!! I'm totally captivated by you~"

Whatever Suchat was about to say died in his throat, leaving it dry and scratchy. He had misunderstood. So "handsome" was just an exclamation, not a compliment.

On the other side, Cora happily stored the Level 4 crystal in her space pocket. Looking up, she noticed Onyx de Montclair smiling warmly at her. The morning breeze ruffled his hair, and his light-colored eyes held a tender expression that was hard to describe.

"The sunrise is beautiful today." Onyx's deep voice was smooth and melodic.

Cora looked up. The sun was large and round, glowing like a glistening salted duck egg hanging in the... no, not a plate, but the sky. Just then, her stomach growled, reminding her it was time for breakfast.

Cora scratched her cheek, feeling a bit embarrassed for no apparent reason.

Onyx clearly heard her stomach's protest and unexpectedly chuckled. At first, it was a soft laugh, but soon, the warmth in his eyes spread, melting away his usual icy demeanor and replacing it with a pure gentleness.

"Cora, come here." Onyx motioned for her to come closer.

"... Okay." Cora slowly made her way over.

When she got close, Onyx did something surprising. He braced himself in his wheelchair—and then stood up?!

Cora was shocked. How could his legs heal so quickly? But she immediately realized it must be because of the radiation.

Sure enough, as Onyx stood, he wobbled unsteadily, stumbling several times. Cora quickly rushed over to support him. He leaned his head against her shoulder, using her strength to steady himself, then gazed down at her. "I mentioned before that I wanted to talk to you. I think now is a good time."

They were so close that Cora only had to look up to meet his deep eyes. "Doesn't it hurt?" she deflected, poking his right leg.

"It does..." Onyx murmured into her ear, his voice turning hoarse. "But I wanted to stand while I said this."

What did he want to say? His secrecy was making her nervous. Cora stood as straight as a rifle. "Go ahead, I'm listening."

"Cora..." Onyx sighed.

"Cora!" A clear voice called from behind them. Silver Owl appeared, holding an assault rifle. Seeing the two of them together, he pushed his goggles up to his forehead and remarked in mock surprise,

"Whoa, doing some rehab bright and early, huh?"

Onyx glared at him, his mental energy flaring up like sparks snapping in the air.

"Do you need something?" Cora steadied Onyx and turned around to ask.

"We're here to say goodbye. We've got to head back to Northern Base," Silver Owl said, deliberately ignoring Onyx's icy aura as if nothing was out of the ordinary. "And, by the way, extend an invitation."

"What invitation?"

"An invitation to Northern Base."

"After completing the time-limited S-rank commission, you should have enough points, right? If not, I can write you a letter of recommendation." Silver Owl's voice was clear and direct. "You're welcome in District B, and I strongly encourage you to consider Northern Base first."

"We might not go to District B," Cora said slowly. "Even if we do, why should we choose Northern Base?"

"Because I'm at Northern Base," Silver Owl replied, as if it were the most obvious thing in the world.

Cora glanced back at Onyx. During the brief exchange, his expression had already frozen over like the dead of winter. "Why should we go just because you're there?" Cora intended to wrap this up quickly and asked bluntly.

"Can't you tell?" Silver Owl raised an eyebrow, then muttered softly, "I thought I was making it pretty obvious."

"Making what obvious?" Cora asked, puzzled.

"I like you," Silver Owl said with a bright smile. "Wasn't it obvious?"

CHAPTER 22

Her Wishes

"Next stop, Yggdrasill or Lava Land?"

Felix asked as he deftly maneuvered a rare amphibious vehicle he had somehow gained from District D. After a quick series of commands on the control panel, the vehicle shifted from off-road mode to hover mode, transforming into a sleek speedboat that skimmed over the river's surface, leaving trails of sparkling water in its wake.

After posing the question, he was met with complete silence—no one responded.

Felix turned his head to see Chief Franz and Damian slumped together in the back seat, fast asleep, their heads resting against each other as their soft snores filled the air.

The elder—likely drained from overusing his Anopower—had passed out the moment they got in the car, while the younger had been through a whirlwind of emotions in a brief span: advancing in rank, the highs of victory, the farewells to friends. It was no wonder he had fallen asleep now that the tension had subsided.

The other four, though younger and full of energy, were similarly disengaged, each lost in their own thoughts, entirely oblivious to Felix's question.

"Where are we headed?" Felix asked again. Still, no one responded, each of the four absorbed in their own world.

Felix wasn't about to let them off the hook. He suddenly sped up and made a sharp turn, causing the boat's turbine to roar as it whipped up a fierce whirlpool, skimming close to the river's surface as if it were flying. He casually opened the sunroof, letting splashes of river water drench those inside.

"Blegh! Felix Lucas, can you please obey some traffic laws?"

Cora and Yuui, jolted from their daze, rushed to the windows to retch, utterly disgusted by the thought of how many zombies had likely died in that water. "Awake now? Good, now tell me where we're going," Felix hummed lightly.

Without a word, Onyx tossed a holographic map towards him. Felix caught it with one hand, noting that the next leg of their route had already been marked.

Cora closed the window and glanced at Onyx through the glass. He was leaning on one hand, his head bowed as he scrolled through some data. His long lashes cast shadows over his eyes, concealing his emotions. He looked cold as ice, as if he were silently fuming.

After Silver Owl had dropped the bombshell of "I like you," he and Jennifer had nonchalantly returned to their hover car, supposedly to meet up with the rest of their team, "Tustan," and report their mission aim.

"Life is unpredictable. What if he just vanished in Ocean Gate..." Cora turned back to steady Onyx, whose eyes had narrowed dangerously, his tone carrying a cold seriousness?

Cora stared back at him, pointing to the ever-present surveillance drones, making her point clear without words.

"... Just kidding." Onyx smiled, reining in his mental energy.

"He's gone. So, what did you want to talk about?" Cora hadn't forgotten the conversation that had been interrupted earlier. Onyx looked down at her, his expression gradually tightening into a frown. "He just confessed to you."

"Yeah."

"And what do you think?"

"A little surprised," Cora answered honestly.

"And besides that?"

"... Nothing else."

Onyx's expression became even more inscrutable.

"He says he likes you, but you have no feelings about it?" Onyx seemed to realize something, his expression growing more serious. Cora blinked and asked sincerely, "... Should I?"

Onyx silently stared at Cora, suddenly confronted with a question he had never seriously considered before. "Cora Thornton, do you even know what 'liking' someone means?"

This time, Cora genuinely thought hard for a moment before shaking her head. Grandpa had never taught her that. Onyx said nothing more.

Even Onyx, who had manipulated the devious Zombie Lord without breaking a sweat, now sat in the speedboat as if confronted with a complex, unsolvable problem, unusually deep in thought.

Cora watched him quietly for a long time before turning her gaze away. She knew well that she was slow, especially for emotions and memories.

She'd had this issue since she was little. Most kids experienced a range of emotions—happiness, anger, sadness—but Cora never knew how to express them properly.

When others laughed, she cried. When others cried, her eyebrows would knot together, her little face turning red with what seemed like anger. Because of this, people who didn't understand her, like Mrs. Travers, found her gloomy and unpredictable, and not very likable.

Cora once asked her grandpa why she differed from others. He told her she needed to observe and learn, starting by imitating her peers. He said she was a very smart child, and she would figure it out.

Encouraged, Cora tried her best to learn. As she grew older, she became more like everyone else, crying when she was supposed to cry, laughing when she was supposed to laugh. Aside from a slight stutter when she spoke, there were no more out-of-place actions. "Normal" emotional expression became second nature to her.

But liking—she had never figured that one out.

She didn't have parents, and Grandpa didn't have a wife. On her lonely journey growing up, there had been no one to show her what it looked like when two people liked each other. Cora liked her grandpa, and she liked the members of F777, but she didn't think that was the liking Onyx was referring to.

"Let me ask you all something," Cora finally asked directly. "What does 'liking' someone feel like?"

Yuui instantly perked up, leaning in eagerly. "Who? Who likes you? Did someone confess to you?"

"Yes," Cora nodded, straightforward as always.

"Heh, someone finally couldn't hold back?" Felix clapped his six mechanical arms together in mock applause.

"If you like someone, you should be together!" Yuui glanced at Onyx, deliberately raising her voice and declaring firmly.

"Be together?" Cora looked even more confused.

"Yeah, first you date, then get engaged, then get married, and after that..." Felix's words faltered as he reached the limits of his personal experience. He meticulously flipped through some files before continuing, "You create the fruit of your love together. That's how it's described in the 'Old World Customs and Ethics Analysis.'"

Yuui immediately disagreed. "We're in the apocalypse now. Just skip the dating and engagement, and go straight to marriage!"

Felix, however, was more concerned with logistics. "And what about the fruit of love? If you split the responsibility of raising it, I suggest setting up a schedule. Which district should the household registration be in? What about schooling? I'd recommend Luboni or Askar; those are two excellent schools."

Yuui nodded. "Yeah, you need to choose the household carefully. Felalakas and Sycamore are also good options. I think the boy should study medicine, and the girl should pursue the arts."

Felix began flipping through more files. "If both parents are Gene Selectors, the baby's gender can be chosen independently..."

"Shut up," Onyx said coldly.

Felix opened his mouth to protest.

"Shut up," Onyx interrupted him again, his voice frigid.

"... Silver Owl," Onyx ground out, "the person who confessed is a bastard named Silver Owl."

Yuui blinked. "... What?"

"... Ah," Felix was quiet for a few seconds before speaking up suddenly. "Who's Silver Owl? Do we have someone by that name on our team? Is that a new nickname you've come up with?"

"Silver Owl is the captain of 'Tustan,'" Yuui said in a deflated tone, glancing at the front seat before slumping back.

At the mention of "Tustan," Suchat, who had been curled up and quiet in his seat, subtly twitched his fingers.

Still confused, Cora asked, "... What's the fruit of love?"

"There's no fruit," Onyx sneered. "Except maybe shattered pieces —that's all he can expect."

The rest of the ride to the next checkpoint city was filled with an eerie silence, broken only by the sound of snores.

After the death of the Zombie Lord, the threat posed by the zombie horde diminished, and the refugee crisis eased, giving the surviving cities a much-needed respite. The latter part of the tournament proceeded smoothly, at least for F777, which found it "boringly uneventful."

The audience in Felalakas craved danger and excitement, but after F777's spectacular takedown of the Zombie Lord, they quickly adopted a laid-back approach, lazily following other teams to checkpoints.

Occasionally, they would appear in the championship live stream, but usually, Cora was seen hanging her head over her terminal, busy counting money, while Damian and Chief Franz took turns napping, with Suchat diligently taking care of the checkpoints. The rest of the team rarely appeared on camera.

As the live stream offered less thrilling content, the viewership plummeted, and the audience lost interest.

How lazy was F777? They were so lazy that they only visited cities where other teams had already checked in, just trailing behind others—hence the joke that they were "picking up leftovers." Even the live chat started calling them "The Champion of Slackers" and "F777's Lazy Antics Showcase."

The next day, the hottest topic became the grudge match between "The Boss and His Three Goons" and "Iron Cafe." The two teams clashed three times, with the ultimate confrontation resulting in Luke Shaw sustaining an abdominal injury and Master Stark being severely wounded and falling into a coma.

"Luke really went all out."

"Master Stark wasn't any better! He tried to assassinate Zephyrion, so he deserved what he got. Old man's probably not going to make it through this time."

Sure enough, a day later, Master Stark died just one stop away from the finish line, in Yggdrasill. "Iron Cafe," plagued by severe infighting, couldn't complete the tournament and withdrew in disappointment.

But none of this concerned F777. Two days later, after completing their final checkpoint, they smoothly returned to Felalakas.

Every time they arrived in this city, it felt like a surreal escape from the apocalypse, and this time, an unparalleled celebration welcomed them.

Amidst the thunderous cheers, Cora and Damian raised the championship trophy. Although the other members declined to make public appearances, citing "inconvenience," the name F777 was already known throughout the entire eastern part of the alliance.

Felalakas, Sycamore, Deep Woods, Yggdrasill... Glass Port, Green Water, Saya, Ocean Gate... In different Class C and D cities, their legends were already being told.

Compared to the five million NPA credits awarded to the champions, the additional 1,000 points seemed like a drop in the bucket.

Including the double rewards from the S-rank commission completed in Ocean Gate, F777's total points had reached a staggering 700,000, far exceeding the 500,000-point threshold required to enter District B.

After the celebration, F777 ascended to the top of the tower to meet someone—or rather, artificial intelligence.

Besides the points and NPA credits, the most significant reward of the Throne Tournament was the promise from Ilia, the city lord, of one wish to be granted. According to the agreed terms, this opportunity was handed over to Yuui Hayashi.

The icy blue data streams formed a luxurious carpet, and a slender figure leaned quietly on a sofa, waiting for them. This time, Ilia was no longer the holographic projection they had first met, but a fully flesh-and-blood person, having undergone a transformation over the past six months.

As Cora looked at Ilia, she couldn't help but recall a question she had once asked Onyx.

If an artificial intelligence possessed independent consciousness and a body it could freely control, was it still an AI? Did Ilia want to be human? Onyx's gaze back then had been inscrutable, but the answer had been clear—Ilia might not desire humanity.

"Good evening, my champions," Ilia greeted them with a smile.

Yuui removed her mask, but Ilia showed no sign of surprise, as if he had always known she wasn't "Jane Doe."

Cora noticed the slight tremor in Yuui's breathing and squeezed her hand in silent encouragement.

Yuui took a deep breath, her voice echoing clearly on the spacious top floor. "—Ilia, I want to ask you to help me save someone."

"Save someone?" Ilia crossed one leg over the other, a spark of interest flickering in his eyes. "As far as I know, your team has an extremely skilled healing Anopower user. For saving lives, he should be more capable than I am."

"I know," Yuui nodded. "As long as someone isn't dead or on the verge of dying, Franz can bring them back." She paused, then added, "But I want to save someone who is already dead."

Ilia's expression showed a hint of surprise, and even the other members of F777 were taken aback. They knew Yuui wanted to save someone, but they hadn't known the specifics. Yuui pulled out her terminal and played a video she had recorded before leaving for Sin City.

The location was the fifth hospital in Sycamore, where a patient lay on a bed surrounded by various machines. No, calling this person a "patient" wasn't quite accurate. The level of decay in this person's body had exceeded a Stage 3 mutation, more severe than that of a Fallen, making them almost indistinguishable from a zombie. The figure lay motionless, as if already a corpse.

"This is my sister, Yuki Hayashi. She underwent irreversible zombification because of radiation, and her body is no longer usable." Yuui's fingers clenched as her gaze hardened with determination, as if she had decided. "So... I want you to turn her into artificial intelligence."

"Artificial intelligence?" Ilia chuckled softly. "Interesting, but this isn't something that requires my intervention."

He raised a hand slightly, and a small stream of data pointed to Felix Lucas. "You seem to underestimate your companion. Would you like me to recommend him? This one here... a once-in-a-century genius from the Lucas family, he could certainly turn a person into an AI."

Felix was currently staring intently at a supercomputer, absorbed even though the screen displayed nothing. Yuui, however, slowly shook her head. "I want Yuki Hayashi to become an AI, not just any AI."

Felix could restore memories—like he had done in Sin City, where he had repaired The Pluto's fragmented consciousness, allowing him to become "Hugh Young." But the restored Hugh Young was no longer the original Pluto, while what Yuui wanted was a complete Yuki Hayashi, with all her memories intact.

"My sister, Yuki, was declared brain-dead fourteen years ago in the Loyak incident." Upon hearing a familiar keyword, Onyx subtly lifted his eyelids.

Yuui had lost her parents at a young age, and it was Yuki, who was over ten years her senior, who had raised her. Yuki had graduated from Sycamore Medical University and took part in a secret research project led by Arashi. After that, the sisters rarely saw each other. Eventually, the only news Yuui received was that her sister had died because of a nuclear leak.

For fourteen years, with the top medical care in Sycamore, Yuki's brain-dead body had been maintained, and the radiation levels had remained within controllable limits. But after the apocalypse broke out, her zombification sped up rapidly. Even though the doctors had already declared Yuki fully zombified, Yuui refused to give up.

When she first saw Yuki fully zombified, she couldn't accept it. During that time, Yuui frantically collected crystals, sought experts, and anonymously entered competitions. She would try anything if there was even the slightest chance, no matter how slim the hope.

Later, Yuui met Cora, Franz, Felix... and Hugh Young's experience opened up a new possibility for her—allowing Yuki to survive in another form of life.

But one crucial piece was missing, and only Ilia could provide it.

"Yuki Hayashi once underwent memory storage." Yuui spoke each word carefully. "She had a habit of regularly updating that log."

"I want to trade with you for her memories. I want a complete Yuki Hayashi back." She paused, then added, "And I want to know what really happened in Loyak fourteen years ago."

Memory storage was a secret known only to the locals of Felalakas. Artificial intelligence was highly advanced in Felalakas, and even before Ilia became the city lord, this unique service had already emerged.

As humans age, their memory capacity naturally declines, causing them to forget many things. But computers don't forget. In Felalakas, people could archive backups with AI, using weak electrical currents to link brainwaves and neurons with a fixed AI terminal.

This process allowed people to share memory storage modules with AI, creating a kind of "cloud-based memo." If someone lost a memory due to an accident, aging, or forgetfulness, they could retrieve it through a "restore" function.

When Ilia emerged as a super AI and the supreme ruler of Felalakas, he naturally connected to all intelligent terminals, including those used for recording "memos." As a result, Ilia possessed the memories of most Felalakas residents, which is why—Ilia knew everything.

And Yuki was among the first volunteers to take part in this project. She had stored all her memories from birth in the AI.

In the ensuing silence, Ilia smiled. "If this is your wish, I can make it come true for you."

PART 2

TINDER BURNING

CHAPTER 23

Awakening

Silver Owl led the Lucas Starship as it streaked across the sky, its sleek, silver-white design resembling a soaring eagle. As it approached the city, the transparent energy shield activated, and the starship decelerated, gliding into the station. The energy pillars, branded with the Lucas logo, automatically connected, and passengers disembarked, chatting and laughing as they dispersed toward different exits.

If someone from District C or lower were standing here, they would surely be wide-eyed with surprise, for the Lucas Starship, long thought defunct, was still operating smoothly, as if nothing had ever happened.

Before them lay a vast three-dimensional city. The weather was clear, with bright sunshine illuminating the scene, and even the air was remarkably fresh, carrying the unique fragrance of vegetation. Highly intelligent robots and floating vehicles were busy with cleaning, transportation, and patrolling tasks. Ultra-modern buildings soared into the sky, with skyscrapers equipped with self-cleaning glass and fully automated elevators everywhere. Intersecting sky bridges and walkways crisscrossed the city, like transparent ribbons connecting the vast space, occasionally punctuated by the figures of skateboarders or parkour enthusiasts whizzing past, whistling as they overtook the leisurely moving tour spheres beside them.

Massive billboards and holographic posters on both sides of the street updated in real-time, providing residents with the latest life information. All the passersby wore intricate custom accessories, and with a simple touch, projections appeared—this was the signature advanced terminal of District B. The city's first impression: clean, modern, orderly, with minimal impact from the apocalypse.

Another starship returned, docking at the high-level exclusive channel. As the hatch opened, Scarlett Holland, dressed in a dark gray suit, stepped out briskly. Her team of secretaries hurried to greet her, and a young woman in her early twenties, holding a bouquet, warmly welcomed her. "Commander, welcome back to Northern Base."

"Here's your schedule for today: a half-hour meeting with the logistics minister at 10:00 AM, followed by—" As her executive secretary, Svetlana Yevgeniyeva diligently reported.

"Let's discuss that later," Scarlett interrupted, raising a hand. The overnight flight had left her tired, and she rubbed her temples. "Have the two mutated zombies caught in Tustan been delivered to Dr. Ninnemann's lab?"

"Yes, Silver Owl escorted them, and Dr. Ninnemann has already received them."

Scarlett nodded in satisfaction. Despite Silver Owl's unruly nature, he was reliable for getting things done. "How is General Yevgeniyev's health?"

"His health is fine," Svetlana carefully chose her words. "He's been sleeping well these past few days and even ate two extra bowls of rice."

"But his mood isn't great," Svetlana muttered quietly.

"What happened?" Scarlett frowned.

Svetlana looked around cautiously and lowered her voice. "Two inspectors from The Central have arrived."

Scarlett's steps abruptly halted. "Inspectors? On what grounds?"

"They're here because of Dr. Ninnemann. They have significant objections to his ongoing research projects, accusing him of encroaching on some classified Alliance data. They're demanding that Dr. Ninnemann's team disclose all their research findings. They've been in a tug-of-war with the Ministry of Foreign Affairs for the past few days."

"Hmph," Scarlett sneered, "Dr. Ninnemann is currently working as an independent researcher funded directly by Northern Base. Even if they want to interfere, they'll have a hard time finding a legitimate reason."

"Exactly!" Svetlana nodded vigorously, but then hesitated, biting her lip.

"What else?" Scarlett could tell she had more to say.

delta Island poached "Well... Commander, while you were away, two S-class Aberrants... (District B16)." Svetlana's voice grew smaller, and she hung her head.

Aberrant affairs at Northern Base had always been under Scarlett's sole management, and besides General Yevgeniyev, she had the highest authority in handling such matters. "Which ones?" Scarlett's tone remained composed.

"One from the Lightning Attack unit, and the other..." Svetlana swallowed hard, almost on the verge of tears, "The chief weapons designer of 'Hell' guns..."

S-class Aberrants were crucial strategic resources in the post-apocalyptic world. The number of S-class individuals determined the development potential of a district. Northern Base boasted millions of high-level Aberrants, making it one of the most powerful in the entire Alliance, yet that they had the fewest S-class Aberrants in District B— barely reaching double digits—was a sore point for Scarlett. And now, two more had been snatched away...

Scarlett's temples throbbed. "They poach our people, and you didn't think to poach them back?!"

Svetlana looked a bit aggrieved. "We did, but the envoys we sent also defected..."

Scarlett felt a sharp pain in her chest. "Immediately issue a full-district commission to recruit a group of eloquent speakers."

"Also, expand recruitment efforts. If any S-class Aberrants from other districts show an interest in Northern Base, agree to any conditions first, and do everything possible to keep them."

Svetlana whimpered, "Yes, Commander!"

Recalling the Throne Tournament she had witnessed in Felalakas a few days ago, Scarlett added, "We've always underestimated the power of the lower districts. There are many outstanding Aberrants there, too. This time, send the recruitment notice to the lower districts as well."

District C, D, and E? Svetlana was shocked. Having grown up in Northern Base, she had never set foot in the lower districts, but had heard that the apocalypse heavily ravaged them, with most cities overrun by zombies. Could there really be wild, powerful Aberrants left there? But since the Commander had spoken, she nodded in agreement, "Understood!"

Sycamore, Fifth Hospital.

Outside the intensive care unit, Yuui covered her face, her voice trembling. "... Are you sure this is okay?"

"I don't know." Suchat shook his head.

"He insisted on coming with us," Cora said.

"Yeah, yeah, it's not our fault," Damian chimed in.

Yuui peeked through her fingers at the uninvited guest, sighing inwardly. Although he had come of his own accord, he was... the Supreme Governor of Felalakas! Following them all the way to Sycamore—could this really not result in a diplomatic incident?

The "uninvited guest," Ilia, wasn't wearing his signature velvet suit today. Instead, he had opted for a low-profile outfit of a black shirt and white pants, with a baseball cap pulled low to conceal his bright golden hair and most of his ice-blue eyes. Otherwise, his mere presence would have caused a commotion the moment they entered the city.

The night after meeting with F777 in the tower, Ilia had agreed to fulfill Yuui's wish. However... he had followed them to Sycamore under the pretense of needing to verify the truthfulness of their words by meeting with Yuki Hayashi, citing that "memory storage is the most private of human secrets."

Although Ilia had been exceptionally friendly and accommodating throughout the journey, none of Cora's group dared to let their guard down. With so many others who had suffered at his hands as a precedent, they were on high alert, fearful of what tricks he might pull. They maintained a cautious silence as they made their way to Sycamore.

Ilia entered the hospital room with the others. He glanced briefly at Yuki, who was unrecognizable, and quickly averted his gaze, casually surveying the surroundings. Cora slowly stepped back, sidling up to Onyx and whispering, "How do we, um, open that memo?"

"If the person is still alive, it's usually through biometric information or a brainwave connection."

Cora's eyes widened. Yuki had become a zombie, with no fingerprints, no irises, and even her face completely deformed. What biometric information was left?

"She's brain-dead, so brainwave connections won't work, right?"

"Correct."

Cora leaned in even closer to Onyx, almost brushing his cheek. "He only took one look at Yuki. Do you think he just wanted an excuse to get out and have some fun?"

Ilia had never left Felalakas since his creation, and Cora suspected he was using the pretext of "helping them fulfill their wish" to stretch his legs in a new body.

"I think you could speak a little quieter—he's already heard you."

This kind of unconscious intimacy from Cora would have prompted a stern lecture from Onyx about the propriety between men and women in the past, but now he remained completely unperturbed, his tone calm and even.

Cora quickly covered her mouth. Sure enough, Ilia gave her a fleeting, unreadable glance.

"What do you plan to use as a medium for the memory projection?" Ilia turned to Yuui.

"Anything will do, whatever works best." Yuui, prepared for anything, laid out an array of terminals, light screens, computers, and storage hubs, presenting them as if to say, "Take your pick."

Ilia acted swiftly. His pupils gleamed with a strange light as vast amounts of data flickered through his eyes. He extracted the memory labeled "Yuki Hayashi" and uploaded it to a new model light screen. It was like a download—the screen immediately displayed a progress bar.

Felix took the light screen and quickly used his Anopower to construct a stable preservation environment, ensuring that Yuki Hayashi's memory didn't disintegrate into a data stream before it could fully form.

"Her original body is dead, so the preserved memory will slowly rebuild according to the consciousness. Initially, there will be a period of confusion, but over time, it will gradually become coherent. After all, artificial intelligence needs continuous learning." Ilia smiled, a knowing look in his eyes.

When the progress bar reached 100%, the light screen flickered once before going dark.

A few seconds later, a clear holographic projection slowly appeared, revealing a young woman in her mid-twenties. She was dressed in a researcher's white coat, holding her head as if disoriented, her eyes vacant and confused.

Ilia, having completed his task, exited the room, with Felix following closely behind. Cora glanced at him but didn't move. From her position, she could see Ilia had stopped in the hallway, standing beside Felix, who was basking in the sunlight.

Yuui's eyes widened slightly, her excitement barely contained. "Sister..."

The sudden influx of memories, her thoughts chaotic as she looked at Yuui in confusion, overwhelmed Yuki.

"You are..."

Then her expression changed abruptly. "Wait, who are you? Why are you calling me sister? Do I look that old to you?"

Yuui's initial excitement choked in her throat. "... I—I'm Yuui."

When Yuki passed away, she was in her prime, about the same age as Yuui was now. It was understandable that she didn't recognize her.

The holographic projection occasionally flickered with disordered information streams because of the instability caused by Yuki's physical death. She stared at the face so similar to her own and softly called out, "Yuui? Are you Yuui? How... how did you get so big?"

"Sister!" Yuui carefully extended a finger, touching Yuki in the air. Tears streamed down her face. Yuki hugged her briefly, a warm moment, before she pulled away with a frown and shook her hands as if shaking off something unpleasant.

"Who's this fraud? How dare you trick me?" Yuki suddenly exploded in anger. "My Yuui is only eleven years old!"

"... I'm really your sister!" Yuui was caught between laughter and tears, hastily pulling up her identification. Yuki stared at it for a moment, her consciousness muddling again as she clutched her head, the projection flickering.

Cora couldn't help but laugh. Now she was convinced that Yuki and Yuui were indeed sisters—their absurd way of speaking was nearly identical.

Yuki glanced down and suddenly noticed her own completely zombified body, instinctively shouting, "What the heck is this? A mummy cosplay?" Then she spotted the patient information at the bedside, her pupils contracting sharply. "Wait... is this me? Am I dead?"

Yuui nodded calmly. "Yes, yes, you've been dead for fourteen years. I extracted your memo, and now you're an AI with self-awareness."

"Memo..." Yuki murmured, "I remember... I made a memory storage..."

It took some time for Yuui to explain the situation to Yuki, and finally, the sisters recognized each other, embracing and crying. "Sister, what exactly happened fourteen years ago? Why did you suddenly die?" Yuui asked seriously after their reunion.

Recalling her last memories, even as a hologram, Yuki's face turned pale. "Died? Yes... I remember something... something important, but I can't recall it."

It was as if a piece of memory storage was missing in her mind. Yuki clutched her head, groaning in pain. "Loyak... radiation... explosion... L..."

Her eyes turned red, her head throbbing, and the holographic projection flickered violently as the terror and fear of her last moments flooded her consciousness. But without the memories being uploaded in time, the scattered fragments remained incomplete.

"Sister, don't think about it. Just don't think about it," Yuui urged her gently, her heart aching for her.

"Okay, I won't think about it..." Yuki gradually calmed down, the screen stabilizing as she slowly raised her eyes. Suddenly, she noticed the man sitting by the window. Her gaze first went blank, then she blinked in disbelief. "Jasper? Dr. Montclair? Are you... Dr. Montclair?!"

Onyx's fingers twitched, not expecting Yuki to suddenly address him. Uh oh, Cora whistled internally.

Onyx's lips pressed into a tight line as he shot Cora a quick glance.

Cora returned an innocent expression. What about Jasper? What is Dr. Montclair? She did not know.

"I'm a recorder for the G team at the Arashi Research's Loyak branch. I officially joined the Flame Project team in June of Year 30. My name is Yuki Hayashi." Yuki seemed extremely excited, clasping her face in her hands. "You probably don't know me, but I never thought I'd get to see you in person. You're my idol!"

Yuui cleared her throat. "Sister, you got it backward..."

"Oh, sorry, sorry! You're my fan!" Yuki apologized, flustered, while Yuui covered her face in exasperation.

Yuki's hologram bounced around excitedly, completely oblivious to her mistake. "Sorry, I'm just too excited. I've read all your published papers on genetic engineering. It was such an honor to join a project you led!"

"Dr. Montclair, how did you... become younger?" Yuki's excitement wavered as she became unsure. "You also seem more handsome, and you have more hair... Did you get a hairline restoration?"

Cora maintained a calm exterior, but internally she was laughing hysterically.

Onyx sighed and quickly intervened to stop her nonsense. "Yuki, it's nice to meet you." He added with a regretful tone, "It's unfortunate that the Loyak incident cost us an outstanding colleague like you."

Cora struggled to keep a straight face, her eyes fixed on the ceiling as she pretended not to hear Onyx's half-truths.

"No, no, I was just a recorder, far from being outstanding," Yuki smiled shyly. Then, as if recalling something, her gaze grew vacant again. "A recorder... Dr. Montclair. I have something important to report to you."

"Report..."

"Experiment... missing... L..." She muttered, repeating fragmented words.

Onyx frowned slightly, trying to help her sort through her thoughts. "If you're talking about a missing experiment, after the Loyak incident, Arashi Research investigated. They established that all recorded experiment subjects were dead. There was no case of missing subjects—you must be mistaken."

"And if it was before the incident, that's even more unlikely..."

"LAK0017." Yuki quickly recited a string of numbers.

It was as if a spell had been cast. The moment Onyx heard those numbers, his words stopped abruptly, his entire body tensing up.

"The missing experiment subject is LAK0017," Yuki repeated.

"LAK0017, according to the experiment logs, on November 7th, Year 33, following the 1,314th gene fusion failure, the original cells died, and the subject was deemed no longer viable for further research," Onyx stated gravely.

"LAK0017 was destroyed along with LAK0117 and LAK0366 in the same batch. I personally... uh, I verified the results at the central hub."

November 7th, Year 33, a Thursday, was also the fixed date for the disposal of failed experiment subjects. On Friday, November 8th, Year 33, the Loyak nuclear leak erupted, obliterating the Flame Project team.

"Destroyed? Yes... yesterday, Ming destroyed them all." Yuki mumbled.

Her memory was stuck on the eve of the incident, shrouded in a thick fog she couldn't see through. Yuki clutched her hair, the hologram flickering erratically. "No, that's not right... I saw it. It wasn't destroyed!"

Suddenly, Yuki screamed hysterically.

"—Ming took it!"

CHAPTER 24

Identities

"Dr. Montclair, I'm sorry. My life ended so abruptly; I never thought I'd have to tell you the truth this way." Yuki finally recalled the memories leading up to her death. Her expression grew calm, and her emotions gradually stabilized.

"Why are you so certain that LAK0017 was taken?" Onyx asked, his brow furrowed.

Yuki answered, "I was the recorder for Group G. After the termination process, I was supposed to upload the operation log, but when I reviewed it, I didn't receive any data for LAK0017. I immediately contacted Ming, but by then, he had... disappeared along with the experiment subject."

"Why didn't you report this immediately?" Onyx pointed out the flaw in her explanation.

Yuki lowered her head in shame. "Ming and I were colleagues, and we had a good personal relationship. I thought he just... made a rash decision. I didn't want him to get in trouble. I'm sorry, Dr. Montclair; this was my negligence."

Onyx's expression remained stony. "A rash decision? Who's the one being rash?"

The hologram was remarkably lifelike; Yuki's remorse was clear. "Dr. Montclair, I know my excuse is weak. I failed to recognize Ming's true intentions in time. He was the only cultivator in Group G, spending every day with those experiment subjects and knowing them better than anyone. I was puzzled at first why he would volunteer for the termination process, but now, looking back, it must have been premeditated."

"What kind of person was Ming in your eyes?" Onyx suddenly shifted the topic.

Yuki thought seriously for a moment. "Ming was gentle, meticulous in his work, and very patient. We used to joke that he should've been an animal caretaker instead of a cultivator, especially for soft creatures."

Gentle... meticulous... Onyx pondered Yuki's description. Why would someone like that steal an experiment subject?

"Dr. Montclair, did the loss of the experiment subject cause any negative impact on the facility? The Flame Project was already facing many challenges. If you were blamed for this...," Yuki asked anxiously.

Onyx remained silent for a moment before giving her a reassuring nod. "Don't worry. Ming only took a discarded experiment subject. No one else noticed, and besides, the Loyak incident has overshadowed everything."

Yuki sighed in relief. "You're right. The original cells were dead, so the experiment subject had no further research value. I just don't understand what Ming hoped to achieve by doing this..."

Having revealed the truth, Yuki seemed to feel a weight lifted off her shoulders. She turned her attention to exploring her new AI form, chatting quietly with Yuui about her current situation.

Onyx's fingers tapped rhythmically on his wheelchair as he lowered his gaze, lost in thought.

The researcher known as Ming... His mind was like a vast library, quickly retrieving the information. Ming's full name was Jace Ming, a cultivator for Group G in the Flame Project and one of the first graduates of the Lausanne Training Program. Onyx had interacted with him a few times and remembered him as a young man with delicate features.

Jace Ming's life trajectory was rather complex. He was born in Lausanne (District B25) and moved to Northern Base (District B10) with his family during his teenage years because of his parents' job transfer. Later, he earned a Ph.D. in genetics from Askar (District B9). When Jace joined the Flame Project, he was only twenty years old, and by conventional standards, he could be considered a "child prodigy."

His records ended five years later on the list of victims of the Loyak incident.

Loyak wasn't a single area but a term for two cities, including Lausanne (District B25) and Fenjak (District C26). The nuclear leak disaster that occurred there shocked the entire Alliance. The consecutive explosions ignited massive fires, and the high-energy radioactive materials released into the atmosphere created a perpetual fog that never dissipated, leading to the cities being abandoned.

Onyx believed Yuki's story. Jace Ming had indeed taken the experiment subject and fled. Whatever his intentions were, the mutant experiment subject couldn't survive long in ordinary air; it required a specialized chamber with an oxygen-rich environment. Jace was likely to have returned to a familiar district in B.

"So, I'm almost forty now?" Yuki suddenly burst into laughter, her holographic projection flickering as she changed into an outfit suitable for a middle-aged woman.

Yuui smiled as she watched her, the two switching roles—Yuui becoming the calm older sister, while Yuki played the lively younger one.

"Oh, who's this handsome guy?" Yuki noticed Suchat standing by the wall and asked curiously.

"His name is Suchat."

Yuki looked surprised. "Yuui, are you already dating at such a young age? No, no, I got that wrong again... How old are you now?" She glanced at Franz and Damian in the back, momentarily confused.

"No way... Is your son already this big? Call me Auntie!"

Damian's curls stood on end.

Yuui felt utterly exhausted. "First, I don't have a boyfriend. Second, I don't have a child. Third, I'm twenty-five!"

"So you're twenty-five and still don't have a boyfriend?" Yuki asked incredulously. "Have you never been in love?"

"I'm very busy with work, and men would only slow down my songwriting!" Yuui snapped, hitting a sore spot.

"Songwriting? You were just saying last month that you wanted to be a starship steward because you envied those who get to fly every day."

"Sis, that was years ago! Can we not bring up my embarrassing past?"

The two sisters bantered back and forth, Suchat handing Yuui a bottle of water.

"If you hadn't mentioned it, I would've forgotten. It's Year 47 now..." Yuki's gaze drifted back to Onyx, and she hesitated, opening and closing her mouth several times before finally asking, "Dr. Montclair, are you fifty-five... or sixty now? You've aged so well. Is it the lab's new anti-aging technology?"

"Pfft—" Yuui sprayed water all over Suchat's face.

"Ha ha ha ha!" Cora laughed mercilessly.

Outside the hospital room, Felix leaned against his wheelchair, basking in the sunlight.

The golden light cast a soft glow on his pale cheeks, making his silver hair shimmer slightly as it fell over his shoulders. His six mechanical arms were retracted, and if one didn't notice his empty legs, Felix might have been mistaken for just another frail patient recuperating at the Fifth Hospital.

A tall figure leaned casually against the railing, gazing down at him with interest.

In a space imperceptible to the average person, two distinct streams of data clashed, only to separate immediately, like two serpents testing each other's territory before quickly retreating and erecting defensive barriers.

Felix lifted his eyelids halfway, sensing no hostility from Ilia, then lazily closed them again. Ilia couldn't help but smirk—typical of the Lucas family to be so arrogantly dismissive of artificial intelligence.

"This is the first time we've met, yet you don't seem surprised at all."

"Why would I be?" Felix replied with his eyes closed. "Oh, are you talking about that useless fool who let you steal his body and trap him inside a computer? Did he really think I wouldn't notice his identity just because he didn't speak?"

Felix spoke coldly and without pause, continuing, "The one who should be surprised is him, for being unable to protect his own body and ending up trapped inside a machine, wailing."

On the top floor of the tower, Felix had barely extended his mental power before noticing familiar data manipulation traces identical to his own. He had looked around and stopped at a certain black-screened computer, recalling what Cora had mentioned about the conflict between Ilia and Thyrion Lucas. Even though the other party had feigned death, Felix had understood the situation instantly.

A waste. Felix had taken just one glance before shifting his gaze away.

"That body belongs to the Lucas family. Doesn't it bother you?" Ilia smiled his trademark smile.

"The Lucas family…" Felix's lips twitched, forming a smile that he was still not used to—stiff. "What does that have to do with me?"

As expected, a thorny character, Ilia sighed almost imperceptibly. "I like your attitude. It's a shame that you lack legs. Otherwise, I might have considered a different target. I'm sure we could have worked together very well."

"No," Felix shook his head seriously. "I wouldn't work with you. I'd just make sure you're crying inside a computer."

If Cora were here, she would have been very surprised. The Felix before her differed completely from usual. Facing an outsider, he displayed a sharp, proud, and unyielding side that made him difficult to approach. But in reality, this was Felix's true nature.

As an S-class hacker-type Aberrant, Felix had every right to say such things. If Ilia had targeted him instead of Thyrion for body-switching, it wouldn't have taken just three months, three years, or even thirty years—Ilia would never have succeeded.

Hackers and AI were in an endless battle for supremacy; the stronger one would always hold the upper hand. Thyrion was weaker than Ilia, so he lost and had his body taken.

At this moment, however, Ilia neither hoped nor saw the necessity to engage in a decisive battle with Felix.

"I want to make a deal with you."

"Not interested."

"Thanks to you, the Lucas family is now in decline, desperately searching for a replacement for their Mutter." Ilia continued, undeterred.

"Oh, have they come to you? Do you think being their Vater might not be so bad?" Felix made a dry joke.

Ilia didn't laugh. His icy blue eyes flashed with a sharp glint. "Compared to her, I'm just a nobody, awakened to independent consciousness for less than a decade. Even as the Governor of District C, I'm still weak and vulnerable. How could I ever challenge the Lucas family, whose influence spans all of District B?" He paused, his expression growing somber. "But I don't intend to sit back and wait for death."

"If I do become the 'Father,' trust me, you won't be happy with that outcome." Felix's eyelids twitched slightly.

Ilia raised his hand, and a stream of binary code—101010—slowly formed into a vague, shadowy image. The features were indistinct. "You want her dead, don't you? Coincidentally, so do I. We have a common enemy, which, in a way, puts us on the same side."

"What kind of deal are you proposing?" Felix opened his eyes and looked at him.

"I want you to share some data with me—specifically, information about District B, especially everything concerning District B8, Grass Pit." Ilia smiled. "In return, I'll give you access to all of Felalakas's lower-level codes, except mine."

Felix raised an eyebrow in surprise.

Felalakas was a highly virtualized city, controlled entirely by Ilia. His willingness to open up the lower-level codes meant Felix could easily take control of all the AI systems if he wished.

"—Deal."

Their similar icy blue eyes sparkled simultaneously, completing a mental exchange in an instant.

"You're more suited to that body than that fool ever was," Felix remarked sincerely.

"You flatter me. I hope you've only lost your legs and not your determination."

Ilia turned, his tall figure blending into the data stream, vanishing from sight.

After leaving the room for Yuui and Yuki to catch up, Cora and the others retreated to two separate lounges. Once inside, Onyx glanced at Cora's shoulders, which were shaking uncontrollably with laughter, his tone a mix of grievance and resignation.

"... I'm not sixty years old."

Cora couldn't hold it in any longer. "Hahaha!"

Onyx continued, "That Yuki... her eyesight must be terrible. She was just spouting nonsense."

Onyx sighed deeply. "I'm not Jasper."

"I'm not the Jasper she knew," Onyx's voice dropped low, and he gazed at her. "But Yuki wasn't entirely wrong. Reporting this to me was appropriate because I am Onyx de Montclair."

Cora's laughter gradually faded.

Onyx reached out, gently squeezing her soft fingertips. "Cora, I promised I wouldn't lie to you. Explaining this is quite complicated. Do you want to hear it? Do you want to know?"

The room was quiet, the only sound being the faint hum of the ventilation system.

Cora sensed Onyx was about to share something significant — perhaps the true nature of his work with Arashi, or a secret about his identity. Some secrets bring about nothing but size, while others can bring deadly consequences. Cora didn't know which kind Onyx's secret was, but she knew that once a secret was spoken, it could scatter in the wind, like dandelion seeds drifting to the ends of the earth.

"Onyx." She called his name softly.

"Yes," he responded gently, "I'm here."

Cora cupped his face in her hands and said earnestly, "You, being Onyx, are enough."

Onyx looked mildly surprised, then quickly relaxed. He reached out and pulled Cora into his embrace, and they stayed that way for a long time.

Outside, the sunlight was perfect, and a gentle breeze sent clusters of willow fluff swirling through the air. Cora shifted uncomfortably.

"Cora, do you know why I'm holding you?" Onyx whispered close to her ear. Cora blushed. "Are... are you cold?" Onyx was still recovering from his illness, and although she felt quite warm, maybe he was feeling chilly.

Onyx's back stiffened slightly. "I'm not cold... When will you finally catch on?"

After a moment, Cora hesitantly said, "But I'm... a little hot." Onyx released her with an expressionless face.

"The competition is over. Have you thought about where you're going next?"

"I haven't decided yet." Cora shook her head.

Onyx nodded, his gaze drifting to the dense shadows outside the window. "Then, before you decide, could you do me a favor and take me to District B? There are some things I want to investigate."

In all the time they'd known each other, this was the first time Onyx had ever made a request. Everyone in F777 had their own goals, but Onyx had always seemed indifferent, content to go wherever, with an attitude of "I'll just make suggestions, but it's up to you."

Cora sensed something. "Are you going after that L ..."

"LAK0017," Onyx confirmed.

"But wasn't it discarded? I thought it wasn't a problem anymore," Cora asked, puzzled.

"It was something Arashi lost. I have a responsibility to retrieve it," Onyx replied calmly.

District B, huh?

Cora mulled it over. She didn't mind; aside from her teammates, she had no real attachments. She'd already planned to check out District B. Damian and Charles probably wouldn't object either, and as for Felix... they'd have to see what he thought.

But when they'd discussed District B before, he had shown no particular aversion, except for District B8, the Grass Pit, which seemed to be the only place that might be problematic for him.

As she thought about it, Cora's mind suddenly stalled. Yuui and Suchat...

Yuui was a native of Felalakas, a wealthy and famous idol. Suchat had always been by her side.

There was something Cora had consciously or unconsciously ignored: After the Throne Tournament, Yuui's wish had been fulfilled. According to their agreement, her deal with Cora was complete, and Yuui could leave F777, returning to her comfortable, peaceful life, adored by millions. There was no reason for her to continue risking her life with them.

So, was the F777 group about to go their separate ways? Cora pondered this, staring blankly into space.

CHAPTER 25

The Team

"Should we start the meeting?" Cora asked for everyone's input.

Everyone found a spot to sit, and the "First Annual F777 Work Summary and Commendation Meeting" officially began.

Damian grabbed a small stool for himself, then brought one for Cora, and after a moment's thought, fetched another for Charles. The gesture took aback Charles, staring at the stool for a long time before sitting down, half expecting it to spring some bizarre prank on him.

Hosting a meeting for the first time made Cora a little nervous. She took a sip of her freshly squeezed orange juice. Since the apocalypse, crops had mutated to varying degrees because of radiation, and this orange was so sour it made her wince. It didn't taste nearly as good as the energy drinks Silver Owl provided, but at least it was fresh. She grimaced, but finished it, anyway.

Cora cleared her throat. "First, let's welcome back, Yuki." Polite applause followed.

"Welcome back? I feel like I've gained a little sister—or rather, a grandmother," Yuui teased, though the joy in her eyes was unmistakable.

She wasn't exaggerating. Despite losing her body and becoming an AI, Yuki, with a mental age of only twenty-three, had adapted well, her curiosity about new things intact. With her former workplace blown to bits, she now had all the free time in the world.

Reuniting with her once-deceased sister brought Yuui immense satisfaction, though it stirred up some bittersweet memories. She chuckled as she reminisced, "I was so desperate back then, gathering crystals everywhere, hoping Dr. Franz could reverse the zombie transformation."

"No, I couldn't," Charles Franz bluntly admitted, bursting her bubble.

"Well, I wasn't thinking straight. My mind was all over the place," Yuui laughed. "Besides, even if it were possible, Yuki wouldn't have wanted it. Just yesterday, she was pinching her nose and complaining, 'Sis, you're my only sister, please, for the love of all that's holy, cremate my body already.'"

Yuui then turned to Felix. "If it weren't for you, I wouldn't have thought of transferring Yuki into an AI. Thank you."

"No problem," Felix replied nonchalantly.

"I'm grateful to all of you for giving up your wish opportunity for me. Yuki and I wouldn't be here without it." Yuui didn't get too emotional; instead, she stood up and gave a slight bow to everyone, with Suchat silently nodding behind her.

Cora took another sip of her sour juice and continued, "Next up, congratulations to Damian for advancing to Grade A!"

More applause ensued as Damian proudly showed off his new Aberrants Certificate.

He had already been to the Aberrant base in Felalakas to complete his evaluation and update his information. Now, he was officially a Grade A Ice Aberrant. Finally, he was no longer just a liability who could only cheer from the sidelines. His eyes curved into crescent moons as he smiled.

"So, does that mean we're an all-Grade A team now?" Charles wondered aloud.

Yuui, Suchat, and Charles were all Grade A. On paper, Cora was also Grade A, though Onyx and Felix Lucas had never registered, so they weren't included in the stats.

"Is an all-Grade A team impressive?" Damian asked curiously.

"I think so?" Charles wasn't sure either.

"Tustan is also an all-Grade A team. They ranked seventh in the latest Aberrant Squad rankings at Northern Base," Yuui casually mentioned.

"Wow, then we must be pretty amazing!" Damian exclaimed, his eyes sparkling.

"How do you know that?" Suchat's voice was strained.

"Jennifer told me." Yuui showed the chat on her terminal to everyone, blinding them with a screen full of heart emojis from Jennifer. Her personality... was certainly intense.

"Ahem," Cora brought everyone's attention back, "Next, we're going to divide the money!"

The prize from the Throne Tournament and the S-Class bounty for killing the Zombie Lord had brought in 7 million NPA credits. Since it was a team effort, Cora suggested splitting the money evenly into seven shares, but everyone refused.

"I don't need the money," Damian said confidently.

Yuui also declined, "I've already made my wish, so it wouldn't feel right to take any money. Just give my share to Suchat. He lost everything he had in Death Hell and is still in debt."

Back in the City of Sin, everyone had been dirt poor. Cora's purse had been emptier than her stomach, while Suchat, a two-time offender, bore a crushing financial burden. He had paid his first find out of his own pocket, and it was hefty.

Suchat quickly declined, "No need..."

Without a word, Cora transferred 1 million credits to him and said firmly, "Take it."

Felix was even more direct. "Captain, just give me materials instead. Here's my new list." Cora took the list, her eyes widening as stars practically popped out of them. Why did the list keep getting longer?

Charles also refused. "I've still got some savings, and even if you gave me money, I'd have nowhere to spend it."

Cora looked hopefully at Onyx de Montclair, the only one left.

Onyx shook his head slightly and said, "You're in charge."

"Alright, I'll keep it for now," Cora said, patting her terminal to assure everyone.

With some laughter and chatter, Cora took a deep breath and drawled, "last, I'm planning to go to District B4."

Everyone except Onyx seemed surprised. Although they had joked before about leaving Felalakas after the tournament to explore District

B, Cora Thornton's serious announcement clarified this plan was now in motion.

The reasons behind this decision were complex, difficult to summarize in a few words. Cora glanced at Onyx for support.

"I'll explain," Onyx said, naturally picking up where Cora had left off.

He had changed his hairstyle, slicking his bangs back, and now wore a pair of narrow-rimmed glasses on his sculpted nose. His side profile, refined and sharp, exuded a scholarly restraint that made him even more enigmatic.

The new look softened his academic aura. Though his appearance had changed little, his overall vibe was completely different, as if overnight he had transformed from a research giant into an aristocratic young master.

If you asked Hinata Takahashi or Yuki Hayashi to recognize him now, they might hesitate, not immediately able to associate him with "Jasper Montclair."

Onyx continued, "For personal reasons, I need to go to District B, and Cora will accompany me. The rest of you are free to decide..."

Cora tugged at his sleeve.

Onyx placed a hand over hers, signaling her to wait, "... but the captain would prefer if we all moved together."

"Wherever my sister goes, I'll follow!" Damian was the first to declare, bouncing up enthusiastically. Cora beamed and patted his head.

"I'll go too," Charles added with a smile. "I can't let you all get into fights and get hurt without me around to patch you up."

Despite the Ninth Hospital's efforts to keep him, Charles had resigned. For the first half of his life, he'd been bound by a sense of duty and responsibility, constantly overwhelmed with work. Now that the apocalypse had arrived, to hell with surgeries—he only wanted to live life according to his heart, just as Rao had advised.

Onyx looked at Felix Lucas. "You'll have to go back eventually, right? Might as well come along?"

Felix shrugged. "I don't mind."

Finally, Onyx turned to Yuui and Suchat. "The collaboration is over." Yuui froze.

"Before we headed to the City of Sin, Cora made a deal with you. You temporarily joined F777 and worked with us until the Throne Tournament ended," Onyx explained slowly. "The initial formation of the team wasn't exactly pleasant, but the outcome turned out well enough. So, you're free now."

Was this... a breakup?

"Yeah, it's over..." Yuui responded with a dry voice, her mind in a daze.

Onyx's eyes behind the lenses were calm and composed. "Cora said that from now on, you can do whatever you want. Even if we can't be teammates anymore, at least we can still be friends. We'll come back to Felalakas to watch your performances."

"Yeah, I know all your hit songs," Cora chimed in with a playful chuckle.

"Give me a break, Cora, you know you can't sing in tune," Yuui laughed brightly, though tears welled up in her eyes. "I mean, aren't you going to keep me? Or at least invite me to go with you?"

Cora shook her head gently. "Every step we take is dangerous."

Whether it was breaking Felix out of Death Hell, assisting Charles in assassinating Ne Kon, or killing the Zombie Lord, every move they made was like dancing on the edge of a blade, with their lives constantly at risk. Because of this, they had all been injured at some point.

"But you're different," Cora said, locking eyes with Yuui. "You have a home."

Onyx, Felix, Charles, Damian, and even Cora herself—they were all unburdened by attachments. They could pack up and go wherever they pleased, but Yuui was different. She had a home in Felalakas, a spacious studio, irreplaceable family, and a stable, respectable job. Among the F777 members, it was Yuui who had the most to lose, because she always had a way out.

Yuui's vision blurred as she realized that, in truth, Suchat... was just like Cora and the others. She was the only one who was different. She tilted her head back, swallowing her tears, and asked softly, "When do you leave?"

Cora replied, "In a week."

Yuui's fingers curled slightly. "Then I'll see you off."

"Alright."

"You guys chat, I'm… going to check on Yuki." Yuui abruptly stood and almost collided with Suchat as she rushed out of the room.

Suchat glanced back at the people in the room, his dark eyes revealing nothing of his thoughts. But he had always been like that, so no one paid it much mind. Finally, he nodded and silently followed Yuui out.

After their figures disappeared, Damian asked in confusion, "They're not coming?"

"They were always meant to be temporary members; we can't force them," Cora explained.

"Oh." Damian crossed off two names from his mental list of grudges, leaving the page oddly empty.

Felix picked up the conversation again. "If we're going to District B, where should we start?"

After some thought, Onyx replied, "Probably in the northern areas. Askar (District B9), White Town (District B13, the largest independent research project incubator)… or Northern Base (District B10)."

Entering District B required not only reaching the 500,000-point threshold but also passing the most comprehensive Anopower tests. Given F777's resources, they could choose wherever they liked, but the entry city was crucial. It would serve as their calling card in District B, essentially becoming their second home.

Felix blinked in curiosity. "Why not prioritize Northern Base? I just found out they've issued a new recruitment notice, their first time openly recruiting high-level Aberrants from below District C."

Damian found the announcement Felix mentioned and read it out loud: "…Now recruiting high-level Aberrant teams. Generous benefits include full access to District B Aberrant facilities, free accommodation in central zone apartments, equipped with professional Anopower training rooms and breakthrough courses, plus comprehensive medical and educational services…"

"Apartment!" Cora exclaimed.

"Breakthrough!" Damian cheered.

Charles mused, "Hmm… medical facilities in District B…"

Felix argued logically, "Northern Base's black market is famous for having the most extensive variety of materials."

Onyx remained silent.

Felix glanced at him slyly and then drawled, "I seem to have forgotten... Isn't there someone named Silver Owl, almost at S-level, who's a crack shot? Where's he from again?"

"I know! I know! Northern Base!" Damian eagerly raised his hand to answer.

"Captain, you're pretty close to Silver Owl, right? We could go seek refuge with a friend," Felix suggested earnestly.

"Uh... not that close, really," Cora murmured.

Onyx fixed Felix with an icy stare, his glasses flashing ominously. Suddenly, he chuckled darkly, "You really like freeloading, don't you? Fine, let's head to Northern Base and seek... refuge."

Yuki had ordered a bunch of fried chicken and beer while watching old videos of Yuui's early performances, specifically those edited by haters. She occasionally burst into laughter. Even though she was an AI who couldn't taste the fried chicken or beer, it didn't stop her from enjoying the lively atmosphere.

Yuui rested her chin in her hand, staring out the window in a daze. Yuki tried several times to share some of the embarrassing old clips with her, but Yuui was too lost in thought to respond. "What's on your mind?"

"We're breaking up," Yuui admitted, explaining that F777 had gone to District B.

"Wow! How heartless! Why would they leave you behind?" Yuki was first outraged, then puzzled. "But why did you join them through a deal in the first place?"

"Well... I did something... a bit morally questionable..." Yuui stammered, then confessed how she had stolen crystals from Cora at Mirror Lake.

"Yuui, you're as cold-hearted as a snake! How could you be so ruthless? Is this what I taught you?" Yuki shouted in shock.

"I did it to save you! You were decaying, and I was freaking out!" Yuui shouted back.

Yuki clutched her chest dramatically. "You're yelling at me? You're actually yelling at me?? I'm already dead, so what if I rot? Why go through all that trouble? No wonder they don't trust you."

Yuui felt a stab in her heart.

The sisters stared at each other for a long moment before Yuki tentatively asked, "So, what do you plan to do now?"

Yuui replied indifferently, "What else can I do? My home is here, you're here, so I'll just stay put."

"But I think you want to go with them," Yuki said quietly. "You've always been stubborn, pretending not to care when you do."

Yuui's shoulders slowly slumped. "Cora was right. I have too many attachments..."

"Wow, the world's practically ended, and you're still worried about attachments?" Yuki sat beside her and gave her a ghostly pat on the shoulder. "Besides, aren't I your biggest attachment?"

Yuki snapped her fingers. "That's easy to solve! I'm unemployed now, so just take me with you." Yuui was stunned.

Seeing no reaction, Yuki called out, "Hey, that handsome guy, Suchat, what do you think?"

Suchat answered softly, "I'll do whatever she decides."

"You're like a loyal puppy..." Yuki muttered under her breath. "So, what do you think of your former teammates?"

After a pause, Suchat replied, "They're... good people."

Yuki smiled contentedly. "Then it's settled. You both already know what you want. Trust me, taking that first step isn't so hard."

Yuui looked at Yuki, then at Suchat. After a moment of silence, she suddenly burst into laughter. Her smile was radiant, her brows relaxed, and the gloom in her heart seemed to dissipate, making her shine like the morning sun.

A week later, at the gates of Sycamore City, the sleek engine of the Lucas Starship roared as it hovered slowly at low altitude.

Cora sat at the entrance, swinging her legs and peering into the distance. "... They didn't show up after all."

"I told you, the most reliable partnerships are bound by mutual interest, but you insisted on voluntary commitment," Onyx said calmly. "People are unpredictable. Maybe they've already settled down in Felalakas, living in a mansion and sipping champagne."

Cora sighed deeply and leaned back, her head resting on Onyx's lap as she gazed up at him with damp eyes, a hint of unspoken disappointment in her expression. "I'm not happy..."

Onyx found himself unable to continue his lecture. Instead, he gently covered her eyes with his hand.

"Are we going or not?" Felix poked his head out of the cockpit. "Let's go..." Cora, still unable to see, sighed.

The starship rose higher, just about to enter the flight path. When suddenly, an off-road vehicle sped towards them, skidding to a stop with a 180-degree drift that blocked their way. The wild driving style was on par with Felix's. The car doors swung open, and a man and a woman jumped out. Both wore dark sunglasses and carried hiking packs. They had tall, well-proportioned figures and the unmistakable aura of high-level Aberrants, their presence immediately commanding attention.

The woman was dressed in a windbreaker and jeans, her long hair braided into a single side plait that fell smoothly over her shoulder. She wasn't wearing a mask, and her delicate makeup made her look radiant and full of energy.

"Hey~ Friends, mind giving us a lift? Just the two of us," she called out.

Damian and Charles squeezed to the door, waving excitedly at the pair.

"Why did you... come?" Cora pulled down Onyx's hand, unable to hide the joy on her face. The two were none other than Yuui Hayashi and Suchat.

Yuui grinned brightly, "I thought about it. I'm tired of being a superstar after all these years. But District B? I've never been there. This is a once-in-a-lifetime chance, and I'm not missing out."

Cora opened her mouth, about to say something.

"Hey—don't give me the danger talk, okay? Cora, it's the apocalypse! Nowhere's safe! I was performing at the Sycara Theater and had to worry about zombies popping up from under the stage!"

"And don't talk about attachments, either. I've got it all sorted out. Look, I'm bringing the whole family this time." Yuui patted the holographic screen in the side pocket of her hiking pack and then casually patted Suchat.

Amid the air currents stirred up by the starship, the two women locked eyes for a few seconds. Then Cora and Yuui burst into laughter. "Welcome to F777," Cora said loudly, her dimples showing as she smiled.

CHAPTER 26

Northern Base

"What's District B like?" Cora asked curiously, sprawling lazily on the soft sofa, flipping herself over now and then out of boredom.

The journey to Northern Base was long, so Felix had set the starship to autopilot, letting it cruise steadily on a high-altitude course. The seven members of F777 were curled up in their seats watching movies, fully immersed in holographic games, or playing cards.

Felix had roped in Onyx, Charles, and Suchat to play an old game of Texas Hold'em, a relic from a bygone civilization.

"That question," Felix, the dealer for this round, said as he dealt the three community cards. He peeked at his hole cards, raising an eyebrow slightly, "I can't give an objective answer."

"Then give us your subjective opinion," Yuui mumbled through her face mask.

The first round of betting began. Charles matched Felix's big blind, tossing in his chips. Onyx, with his long, slender fingers, silently pushed forward a full stack of chips, raising the bet. Suchat, after examining the game, folded.

"My subjective opinion is that people there are arrogant, as if they have 'Chosen One' tattooed on their foreheads," Felix remarked, his tone sharp.

"Why? Does District B have some kind of hierarchy?" Cora rubbed her chin against the pillow, shifting into a more comfortable position.

"Not really," Felix replied. "The arrogance in District B doesn't come from social status; it's innate." He gestured towards Onyx with a nod. "Take our friend over there, the embodiment of arrogance. Why not ask him?"

Onyx shot Felix a sharp glance and raised the bet again during the turn.

Though Onyx had never explicitly said where he was from, everyone assumed he was from District B, just like Felix, given his vast knowledge and deep well of expertise.

Cora flipped over again and poked Onyx's arm. "What do you think?"

Onyx used his cards to gently press down on her mischievous hand. "If District C has irreplaceable functions, then District B represents 'completeness.'"

"Completeness?" Cora echoed, puzzled by the term.

Onyx nodded. "The Alliance allocates different rights to each district, and only District B possesses complete access to knowledge channels, full information privileges, and a comprehensive welfare system. People with District B citizenship, from the moment they're born until they grow old, follow an 'elite cultivation plan.' Every District B person is crafted with the best resources available."

"But even the best resources can still produce trash," Felix quipped, casually laying down the river card.

Onyx continued, "Growing up in such an environment, District B residents rarely set foot in the lower districts. Because they've never experienced life at the bottom, they lack empathy and struggle to relate to many things. Even if they do nothing wrong, they can appear inherently arrogant."

"Do you know the two most common phrases people from District B say?" As they reached the showdown, Felix signaled everyone to reveal their cards.

Cora and Yuui shook their heads.

"'What? You don't know that?' and 'Huh?' You don't have that where you're from?'" Felix mimicked the naïve curiosity and unconscious superiority so perfectly that it made everyone's teeth itch.

"That's infuriating! Isn't it because of the information ban?" Yuui ripped off her face mask in frustration, her brows furrowed. "Before my debut, I tried to gather gossip from District B's entertainment scene, only to get a 'Permission Denied' message. Yeah, right, us District C people only get access to censored information."

"C, D, and E districts are all considered lower districts. We're in the same boat," Charles added.

"Yeah," Suchat nodded silently.

Cora, who came from District F, thought to herself, Did they forget about something?

Damian was still engrossed in his game, completely captivated by the new holographic technology that didn't exist in District F. Even if Victor Blackwood could have gotten his hands on it, he wouldn't have let Damian play.

Cora glanced at Damian and then at herself, suddenly realizing. District F didn't even count as a lower district—most people from District B probably didn't even know such a rural place existed.

Yuui suddenly made a noise. "Wait, you two are from District B, so why don't you have those bad habits?"

But then she paused, her realization dawning slowly. Or do they not? Felix acted normal around them, but his behavior in Death Hell, where he tinkered with the Sin Record, and his habit of not even bothering to remember people's names, were definitely signs of that deep-seated arrogance.

As for Onyx, though, he always smiled and seemed easygoing, deep down...

"That's it! I'm done! Losing all night!" Charles tossed his cards down in frustration, nearly pulling out his hair in a fit.

"You've been winning all night," Suchat said, his face expressionless as he stared at Onyx. "No cheating?"

Onyx adjusted his glasses, swept up all the chips on the table with one hand, and smiled slightly. "Huh? You guys can't count cards?"

"You, you, you...!" Charles pointed a trembling finger at him, "Damn you, District B people!!"

The arrogant Onyx was met with strong condemnation from the group. He was penalized by having all his winnings confiscated (22 crystals) and was sentenced to half a day of silence.

The journey to Northern Base was long. Felix had set the starship to autopilot, cruising steadily at a high altitude. The seven members of F777 were huddled in their seats watching movies, completely engrossed in holographic games, or, sometimes, playing cards.

Cora had been full of enthusiasm on the first day, indifferent by the second, and by the third day, she was so bored she felt like she might grow roots.

With the starship in high-altitude mode, flying over 8,000 meters above the ground, all she could see outside the window were vast expanses of clouds and mist. "How much longer until we arrive?" she asked weakly, leaning against the window. If she didn't move around soon, her limbs were going to turn to jelly.

"Five more hours," Felix responded.

Cora groaned.

After the captain's firm request to speed things up, Felix reluctantly switched to manual control. Three hours later, they finally caught sight of Northern Base.

The sight before them was breathtaking, leaving everyone speechless.

Surrounding Northern Base was an endless expanse of desolate ruins—crumbling walls, destroyed buildings, collapsed billboards, and scraps of paper and plastic bags swirling in the wind. Thick layers of dust and sand buried the once-thriving cityscape, freezing this land in time.

Overhead, a dim, slanted sun cast everything in a gray shadow. The plains stretched for miles, a bleak, lifeless gray as far as the eye could see, with only the solitary Northern Base standing out as the sole spot of color in the desolation.

Rather than calling it a city, it looked more like an "oasis."

"Why... is it like this?" Cora asked.

"War. Nuclear war," Onyx answered in a solemn tone.

Before the formation of the New Pacific Alliance, there had been a devastating war between the Galio Empire and the Luse Federation. The war had lasted three years, leveling the entire northern region. Eventually, the three powers signed a ceasefire agreement and a non-aggression pact, bringing about a long-awaited era of peace.

"Northern Base was originally a post-war reconstruction settlement. Its residents are survivors of the war," Onyx explained.

"Almost fifty years ago," Charles murmured.

"The war left a deep impact on Northern Base. The city's founders learned from the past and accepted wanderers from all over, providing them with a stable living environment. The founder took part in the reconstruction, training soldiers and selecting Aberrants, gradually turning the base into a military-civilian hybrid. That's why, after the apocalypse, Northern Base became the refuge with the highest concentration of Aberrants."

Onyx's cool voice echoed in everyone's ears. "The entire Northern Base is loyal only to its original founder. It's not under the control of the families, super corporations, or the Central Court. It holds a unique status within District B."

Felix's tone was flat. "That's right. Humanity's last hope—Northern Base, as the saying goes, something we've all heard since childhood."

"I think I've heard the founder's name before... His last name is Yev...?" Yuui Hayashi recalled.

Onyx nodded. "Yevgeniyev, General Yevgeniyev. He's been the ruler of Northern Base all this time."

As they approached Northern Base, Felix stopped the starship. "We're nearing the detection zone. So, what's the plan for getting in?"

"Can't we just fly straight in?" Cora asked.

Various flying terminals occasionally passed by in the sky, and as they approached Northern Base, a transparent shield appeared above the city. Invisible waves scanned the area, then the shield automatically opened, and after the terminals entered, the shield quickly closed again, as if it had never been there.

"Obviously not," Felix said.

"Can't you hack it with your powers?" Yuui asked, unwilling to give up.

"I can disable it for one second, but what happens after we're inside? This is District B. Do you think their patrols are just for show?"

"One second?" Onyx chuckled, a hint of mockery in his tone. "An S-class hacker, living off others? Don't you feel ashamed saying that?"

Felix's icy blue eyes narrowed sharply. "What, not long enough for you? How about you try it? Let's see how long you last."

The two locked eyes, sparks flying as old grudges resurfaced. Cora sighed and pulled them apart by their heads, one hand on each. "No fighting."

"Can't we just go through the front gate?"

In the tense atmosphere, Damian's natural ability to break the ice kicked in. "Doesn't that recruitment notice say we meet all the requirements?"

The members of F777 exchanged glances. "...Oh yeah!"

"Yeah!" Cora exclaimed, suddenly enlightened.

They had gotten so used to doing things the sneaky way, always thinking about how to break in, that they'd forgotten they could walk in through the front door. This wasn't like their escapades in Deep Woods; this time, they were here legitimately, answering a recruitment call. Why had they been so set on sneaking in? It was all because of those two District B folks—they had led their thinking astray.

Felix lowered the starship's altitude, and they spotted a small city ahead of Northern Base. Cora leaned out to get a better look. "What's that?"

"Immigration Center," Onyx replied.

"What's it for?"

Onyx sighed. "Cora, do you know how many people have tried to enter Northern Base since the apocalypse?"

The seven of them disembarked from the starship, only to be stunned by the massive crowd outside the central gate. How many people were there? Well, let's just say Cora had never seen so many people in one place before—except maybe during a zombie horde.

Onyx and Felix, citing "mobility issues," furrowed their brows and refused to go any further. Cora waved them off, taking on her role as captain with a confident nod. "You guys wait here. I'll go check things out."

Taking a deep breath, she braced herself and pushed into the crowd.

Half an hour later, Cora finally made it inside the hall, her clothes rumpled and her face nearly squished flat. Tears welled up in her eyes from the wind—getting into Northern Base was no joke. Maybe they should just let Felix hack the shield...

The interior of the center was divided into different areas, with many pathways marked by floating light panels, such as "Immigration Section," "Talent Recruitment," "Temporary Access Applications," and "Aberrant Fast Track." Ironically, despite the name, the "Fast Track" had the longest line.

Cora looked around, noticing the constant announcements on the floating screens: "A1322, please proceed to Immigration Window 8." "C0654, please proceed to Talent Recruitment Window 2." "E119988, please proceed to Aberrant Fast Track 17 for genetic testing."

Cora stared at the screen. "…119988? How can there be so many Aberrants? This line will take forever!"

Refusing to accept defeat, she wandered around the center several times before something caught her eye.

Through a corridor, she saw a newly opened section with a glowing sign that read "Recruitment Order Section." Excited, she hurried over.

As the automatic doors slid open, the bustling crowd suddenly thinned, and the air became noticeably fresher. Here, only high-level Aberrants were present, standing in small groups, their mental energies subtly flickering in the air.

Cora obediently queued up at the end, craning her neck to observe her surroundings. She soon noticed that from one window, there was a clear view of another side connected by a transparent SkyBridge, where a luxurious red-carpeted pathway led to another area. It was empty, and above it, in elegant black script, the words "VIP Channel" were displayed.

Cora tilted her head. What's that? It looks almost deserted—could she go that way?

She was just about to go check it out when the opposite door suddenly opened, and a small, luxurious starship docked directly at the entrance of the passage. A middle-aged man in a sharp black uniform and hat descended from the SkyBridge, surrounded by family and staff who clustered around him like stars around the moon.

On the other side, a center official, dressed in a tie and exuding an air of authority, came out personally to greet them. His face was beaming with excitement and joy as he bowed and nodded, inviting the middle-aged man inside. The passage was cool and breezy, in stark contrast to the noisy area where Cora stood.

The people in front of her started whispering. They were all high-level Aberrants with their own sources of information. "Isn't that Ken Oda? An S-class Aberrant in engineering, a renowned architect from Delta Island (District B15)."

"Holy crap! What's he doing at Northern Base?"

"Why else? He's probably been headhunted for a hefty sum. I heard Delta Island poached two S-classes from Northern Base recently—looks like they're getting payback."

"You only know half of it. Delta Island took S-class offensive Aberrants; Northern Base definitely got the short end of the stick."

"Uh… true, that makes sense."

Cora blinked slowly. S-class offensive Aberrant… that was her, too.

She turned and took a couple of steps toward the VIP channel, accidentally bumping into another group of people standing and chatting. "What are you doing? Trying to cut in line? Get to the back!" The group of burly men immediately turned to glare at her.

"No, I'm going… over there," Cora pointed in the direction Ken Oda had disappeared.

The person she bumped into looked her up and down before bursting into laughter. "You've got to be kidding, little girl. That's the S-class channel."

He seemed to think he'd heard the most ridiculous joke, raising his voice to shout, "Hey! Someone wants to use the S-class channel!"

The entire recruitment section erupted in laughter. All eyes turned to Cora, their gazes full of amusement.

"At least come up with a better excuse to cut in line. S-class—does she even hear herself?"

"How delusional can she be…"

"Let her try. I want to see how quickly she gets kicked out."

"Where's this country bumpkin from? Did she wander into the wrong section? Hey, you—this is the Recruitment Order Section. Regular folks should go to the main hall."

"I know," Cora replied politely, though the surrounding noise drowned out her voice.

A few kind-hearted people, unable to watch any longer, tried to advise her, "Hey, you must be new. Don't listen to them. The VIP channel requires a reservation, with leadership arranging the escort.

It's mostly for people switching districts after negotiations are complete. It's not open to the public."

Cora beseeched, "So what if there's no reservation, but the person is S-class?"

The Aberrant nearby overheard her and the mocking laughter grew even louder. "A wild S-class? Hahaha, what nonsense are you talking about?"

"If an S-class registers, they'd be snatched up by any district immediately. There wouldn't be any 'wild' ones!"

Someone deliberately walked over and bumped Cora's shoulder, only to find they couldn't move her. The person froze in surprise.

The others, unaware, continued their relentless taunts.

"You think S-class Aberrants are as common as cabbages? Northern Base has only eight of them, and that's already impressive."

"Yeah, what do you think? You can just pull an S-class out of a crowd?"

Amidst the jeering, Cora's expression remained unchanged. She thought to herself, True, it's not that impressive. Our team has three of them. I could go outside and randomly pull someone in, and there'd be a fifty percent chance they'd be S-class too.

CHAPTER 27

Show Off

Cora trudged back, looking dejected.

The group, lounging in the shade, quickly gathered around her. "How'd it go, Captain?"

"Can we go in now, Cora? If not, I'm heading back for some sunscreen. I'm about to melt out here." "... I'm getting a whiff of cooked meat." "Sis, want some ice?"

It was the height of summer, and the sun beat down mercilessly. Everyone was drenched in sweat, and the heat rising from the ground only made the smell... well, let's just say it wasn't pleasant. Cora scanned her team, then suddenly closed her eyes. In one swift motion, she reached out and grabbed Yuui.

Cora let go of her with a slight hint of disappointment, then tried again. She blindly flailed her hands forward and caught Charles this time.

She hissed, not willing to give up, and stretched her hand out a third time. Damian, thinking she was playing a game, willingly placed his hand in Cora's palm.

Okay... Maybe those people weren't wrong. Randomly grabbing an S-class Aberrant on the street was a bit of a long shot.

Everyone exchanged confused looks as Cora slowly explained the situation inside and the whole VIP lane ordeal. "This entire process could take three to five days, right?" Charles sighed.

Three to five days? How naïve. Cora shattered his hopes.

"That's just for me, with my ticket." She pulled up two virtual numbers on her terminal: "30-E216544, 07-Z003577."

"The first number is the number of days we'll have to wait. The second is the number of people ahead of us in line today."

Cora explained further, knowing they might not get it. Charles slowly shut his mouth and began scratching the back of his head, looking worried.

"No wonder the Northern Base needed to build a preview city. There's no way to avoid this without some buffer," Yuui fanned herself and lifted Suchat's wrist, "Look at this, everything from food to lodging, and all kinds of services too."

While Cora was lining up inside the center, Suchat had wandered around the city. Instead of finding useful information, he ended up bombarded with a bunch of aggressive ads. The worst part was that since he was using a C-District terminal, which had lower privileges than a B-District one, those ads acted like a stubborn virus that couldn't be deleted. Now, every time he opened his terminal, flashy projections popped up: "XX Immigration Services Group 20% off," "XX Consulting to Make Your Anopower Resume Shine," "Wendeford Anopower Hotel (Grand Opening, Free Gene Testing Included)..."

Yuui removed Suchat's terminal and tossed it to Felix Lucas, asking him to help clean it up.

"So, what now?" Cora spread her hands.

"Isn't there a VIP lane?" Onyx said casually, "Our captain built herself up from nothing. She's a self-made, S-class Aberrant, and you're telling me she can't walk down a red carpet?"

Cora proudly puffed out her chest, only to deflate a moment later. "You need an appointment for that, and my certification is only A-class." She had just been ridiculed for that, with someone calling her a country bumpkin for dreaming too big.

Onyx tapped his fingers on his wheelchair, unfazed. "Then go public." The others were a bit taken aback.

Onyx continued, "We chose secrecy before because Ilia interfered. They didn't want the Alliance to focus too much on Felalakas, and there was no need for high-profile actions. But things are different now. Since we're in B-District, rank is an essential key."

"Don't forget, what's the Northern Base's highest principle?"
"Strength." Cora answered quickly. Silver Owl had said it himself—

this was a city where fists did the talking.

Onyx nodded. "Besides, we've got more than just one S-class. We have four A-classes too. Even in a talent-rich place like the Northern Base, a 1S4A team is something they'll take seriously."

"Captain, do you have any objections to going public with our ranks?" Onyx didn't forget to ask for Cora's opinion. "No," Cora shook her head but then thought of something, "The five of us, what about you two?"

The only two members of F777 who were from B-District had never registered as Aberrants, and everyone figured they didn't want to reveal their identities. Onyx's pale eyes crinkled behind his glasses as he replied confidently, "Me? I'm a relative of an S-class Aberrant."

"Got it," Felix spoke up, fiddling with the terminal for a moment before quickly finding what he was looking for.

The Northern Base's new recruitment notice had been made public to the lower districts, so there was bound to be data left behind in the C-District. It didn't take Felix long to trace the terminal used by the poster, someone named "Ms. Svetlana."

He swiftly prepared a hacking program, his finger hovering over the send button— "Wait." Onyx stopped him just in time, quickly reviewing the message.

"Hello, we are a powerful Aberrant team with one S-class and four A-classes. We join you, but waiting in line is annoying. Please let us through the VIP lane immediately. Thanks."

Although Felix had used "hello," "please," and "thank you," the tone of the message was pure command. There was a 99% chance it would be treated as spam and tossed into the trash—no, even scammers are more polite than that.

"You flunked that elective, 'Language, Social, and Art,' for a reason." Onyx snorted, selecting all and deleting the draft before rewriting it.

At the Northern Base's Bureau of Aberrants.

Svetlana Yevgeniyeva propped her chin on her hand, staring at four high-definition floating screens in front of her, which were scrolling through recruitment requests from teams still waiting for approval. The more she watched, the sleepier she got, her head nodding as she let out a long yawn.

"Ding-dong—"

The terminal on her desk, which had been idle, suddenly rang.

"Ding-dong—Ding-dong—Ding-ding-dong-dong-ding-ding-dong-dong!!" With no one answering, the terminal started vibrating like crazy, as if it were at a rave.

Svetlana snapped awake, fumbling to silence it. "What the heck? Are C-District terminals this faulty?"

This terminal had been bought from the black market specifically for making announcements. She had added no contacts, so how could it be going off like this?

The terminal kept ringing and vibrating stubbornly. Svetlana didn't know what she pressed, but suddenly, a message popped up on the screen. She clicked on it out of curiosity:

"My apologies for disturbing you. I've heard that your district has recently experienced the loss of top-tier Aberrants. My name is Cora Thornton, and I've long admired General Yevgeniyev. Although I am a Gold-class offensive Aberrant, I have trained relentlessly for many years. However, because of my humble origins, I have never had the chance to enter B-District. Fortunately, I recently broke through to S-class with sheer luck. Because of limited resources, I have not undergone genetic testing. Overjoyed, I recalled my previous resolve and am now writing hoping to serve the General. Besides myself, our team includes four A-class members: two offensive, one support, and one healer. We have all arrived at the Immigration Center. However, because of the complexity of the approval process, and as our breakthroughs have not yet been publicized, we have been delayed for several days. With our funds running low, we are considering leaving. It is out of desperation that I am sending this message, hoping for your response."

Attached to the message were high-definition clips, all pulled from The Throne Tournament, featuring Cora battling the Mirror Lake monster, Damian's Ice Needle attack clearing the field, the team's coordinated assault on the Zombie Panda in Green Water City, and their synchronized strike to take down the Zombie Lord at Ocean Gate—serving as undeniable proof of their abilities.

Svetlana leaped out of her chair. "Aaaaah! A wild S-class offensive Aberrant! And they brought an entire team!!" She kept jumping and screaming, spinning around in circles with joy.

This would put her well over her annual KPI! "Get me on a call with Commander Holland, and I need to head to the Immigration Center immediately!!"

The recruitment process was incredibly complex. Even after Cora Thornton had been out for a while, the line hadn't moved; the same people were still waiting.

So when she returned for the second time, all eyes turned to her in unison.

This time, she wasn't alone—F777's other members were with her.

Whispers erupted through the crowd, mixed with a few loud comments. "Why is this country girl back? And she brought people?"

"Does she think this is a daycare or a rehabilitation center? Don't push your luck." "Does she really think the Northern Base will accept just anyone?"

Cora ignored the chatter. She didn't even bother to line up, instead sauntering over to the sofa and sitting down. Her casual demeanor among such high-ranking Aberrants was a blatant challenge, a naked provocation.

A blonde Aberrant, who was clearly an A-rank from his outward mental energy, cracked his knuckles and swaggered towards Cora. "Hey, you. Stop polluting the air here. Why don't you head back to wherever you came from…"

Before he could finish, Suchat stepped in front of Cora with a haughty expression. Dressed in a black T-shirt, his 6'3" frame exuded an imposing presence. His broad shoulders and defined muscles rippled with barely contained power, like a snow leopard ready to strike. When he lowered his gaze, there was a quiet, lethal calm about him.

The blonde didn't even have time to react. In the blink of an eye, Suchat was behind him, an icy blade pressed against his neck.

"Even among the same rank, there's an obvious difference in combat ability."

Onyx, lounging lazily in a wheelchair, spoke in a refined yet arrogant tone, his words dripping with disdain. "Where did you find the audacity to challenge our Captain?"

Almost as soon as Onyx finished speaking, the entire F777 team, whether seated, standing, or leaning against the walls, raised their heads slightly, releasing their mental energy simultaneously—although the three of them held back.

A torrent of overwhelming energy crashed through the room, causing the light screens to flicker, the lights to sway, and the tables and windows to vibrate ominously. The sheer pressure, like a tsunami ready to drown everything in its path, sent shivers down to the very souls of everyone present.

Some Aberrants couldn't withstand the onslaught, their knees buckling and shaking uncontrollably. "All... All A-rank?!" a disbelieving shout echoed.

"Boom—"

The doors to the VIP corridor flew open, and Svetlana Yevgeniyeva, dressed in the high-ranking uniform of the Aberrants Bureau, rushed in, followed by the center's sweat-drenched manager and dozens of staff members scrambling to prepare the red carpet, flowers, and welcome banners.

"Where? Where are they?!" Svetlana called out anxiously.

Spotting F777 in the recruitment area, she bolted across the SkyBridge, practically flying over to Cora.

Gripping her hand so tightly she might never let go, Svetlana exclaimed, "You... oh no, no, you must be Cora Thornton, the one who wrote to me? An S-rank Offensive Aberrant!"

"Oh my, you look every bit the part—imposing, extraordinary, a true master," Svetlana gushed, her cheeks flushed with excitement. "Officer Holland is busy with official duties, so I'm here to greet you first. She'll come to meet with you shortly. Shall we go inside? We can discuss the details in there!"

Suddenly remembering something, Svetlana whirled around. "And you all, the all-A team F777! Thank you for your patience. Please don't leave! The Northern Base can provide anything you need, so please stay!"

The entire recruitment area fell silent, as if plunged into deathly quiet.

Under the stunned gazes of thousands of high-ranking Aberrants, Cora and her six teammates walked down the red carpet towards the VIP corridor, their figures gradually disappearing. "What-what just happened... An S-rank Offensive? That country girl?!" "I must be hearing things... No, no, I must be deaf, and blind too!"

The Aberrant who had first called Cora a "country girl" touched his neck with lingering fear, his voice trembling as he asked, "Will I still see the sunrise tomorrow?"

Svetlana Yevgeniyeva led the seven of them through the VIP corridor of Horizon City, finally arriving at a luxurious hotel suite.

"Cora, according to regulations, before entering the Northern Base, you all need to undergo genetic testing. The detailed results will take about a day, so please make yourselves comfortable here in the meantime. If you need anything, just let Alpha-1 know."

An AI stood quietly at the door, smiling politely as it nodded at them. Its manners were impeccable.

Cora sneaked a few glances at it. Though it wasn't immediately obvious, the AI's movements and micro-expressions betrayed its artificial nature. It couldn't compare to Ilia, whose every gesture exuded elegance.

Worried that Cora might misunderstand, Svetlana quickly added, "Anopower tests in other regions sometimes have errors, but we use the R-model scanner here. To ensure fairness and accuracy, all Aberrants entering the Northern Base must undergo a new genetic test."

Cora nodded. "That's only fair." After all, her ranking had been mistaken in Felalakas.

"Please register your basic information first." Svetlana lightly tapped her pearl earring, and a shimmering holographic screen appeared in her left eye. "I've sent you the details to fill out."

Cora glanced down at her silent terminal, then asked, puzzled, "How do I fill this out?"

Svetlana noticed her brooch and realized, "Oh, sorry, I forgot. You mentioned in your letter that you're from a lower district, right? Let me send it in a different mode."

Alpha-1 handed over a miniature connector, which Svetlana took and held close to Cora's brooch. The holographic screen lit up, and the exclusive B-District terminal began transmitting the data smoothly.

While they waited, Svetlana casually asked, "Which lower district are you from, exactly? I'm pretty good with Alliance geography, so I might know it."

"District F177," Cora replied.

Svetlana froze mid-action, her eyes briefly going blank: What? District F177? Does that even exist in the Alliance?

But she quickly recovered, pretending nothing had happened as she touched her earring again. Her terminal promptly provided the information, and details about District F came to mind. "Oh, District F177, right? I've heard of it… It was a barren fishing village before the New Era, but because of underdevelopment, it became notorious for its high number of undocumented residents… ahem…"

Cora looked at her innocently. "Undocumented residents?"

Svetlana let out a nervous laugh and swiftly changed the subject. "There are seven of you, correct?" Cora corrected her, "No, five." She gestured to the four A-rank teammates remaining.

"Then who are these two…?" Svetlana asked hesitantly, looking at Onyxand Felix.

Onyx smiled faintly. "I'm the technical consultant for F777."

Svetlana responded with an "Oh," quickly accepting the explanation. S-ranks could bring family members and assistants. "And the other one…?"

"He's the driver," Onyx added with a warm smile.

Cora's fingers twitched as she filled out the form, quickly pressing down Felix's extended mechanical arm.

Svetlana stared at Felix's empty legs for a while, her good upbringing preventing her from immediately questioning the idea of a "driver." Instead, she asked blankly, "Is life in the lower districts really so… colorful?"

In her mind, the transportation in lower districts was still at a rudimentary mechanical stage, with most vehicles being manually driven, except for starships. How could a disabled person with no legs be a driver? Did he drive with his hands?

As Svetlana, whose worldview had just been overturned, collected herself, she said, "Alpha-1 will arrange your genetic tests shortly. Once the results are in, Officer Holland will discuss the benefits and compensation with you. Of course, if any of you have urgent requests, please let me know, and I'll make sure they're addressed."

Onyx gave her a subtle glance.

Svetlana might not have noticed it herself, but she used the word

"I." Before the genetic results were confirmed, Officer Holland certainly wouldn't waste time meeting them. But Svetlana could easily make promises and meet their demands, showing that she had significant authority within the Aberrants Bureau, perhaps even the Northern Base itself.

"There is something," Onyx said after a moment of thought. Svetlana, slightly surprised, responded, "Please, go ahead."

"We have another reason for coming to the Northern Base," Onyx's lips curved slightly, "We're… looking for someone."

Even Felix was surprised. Given Onyx and Silver Owl's fierce rivalry, he was actively seeking someone out? Did the sun rise in the west today?

To everyone's surprise, Onyx didn't mention Silver Owl.

"The Northern Base is home to a famous pair of cognitive psychologists, Gawin Ming and Lucia. If possible, I'd like to meet them."

CHAPTER 28

The Report

The Northern Base, since its inception, established a green channel for talent acquisition, attracting a myriad of elites with enticing policies. Over nearly half a century, it has become a hub for countless industry leaders and experts.

Onyx's request was reasonable, and Svetlana Yevgeniyeva quickly agreed. However, out of curiosity, she asked, "Since you know them, why don't you contact them yourself?"

Onyx's expression turned sorrowful. "Jace Ming, the only son of Mr. and Mrs. Ming, was my close friend. He often mentioned wanting to introduce me to his parents. I've admired them for a long time, but because of the nature of my work, I never had the chance to visit. Then, Jace passed away suddenly..."

Recalling the painful memory, his gaze dropped, and a melancholic aura seemed to envelop him. "Life is unpredictable. Mr. and Mrs. Ming, now grieving their only son... How could I disturb them so abruptly?"

Svetlana whiffed her hand, "Uh, I'm sorry, I didn't know there was more to the story..."

Onyx sincerely replied, "Fortunately, our captain is understanding and doesn't mind that I'm a useless burden, allowing me to come to the Northern Base. I just want to take this opportunity to fulfill my friend's wish and visit his parents on his behalf."

Captain Cora, who had been silently observing, couldn't help but think, "This guy is really something."

Yuui, however, was not as accustomed to Onyx's ways. Hearing Jace's name mentioned, she glanced nervously at Yuki, who was deeply engrossed in a drama on her screen, seemingly oblivious to their conversation.

"I understand. I'll arrange it as soon as possible," Svetlana responded. Her pearl earrings glowed softly. Although the Northern Base housed a large population, making it impossible for Svetlana to know everyone, her terminal efficiently processed the information within her clearance, quickly bringing up data on Mr. and Mrs. Ming. They had moved to the Northern Base with their family about thirty years ago. Their son, Jace Ming, later joined the Arashi Research's classified project, matching Onyx's description.

As Svetlana spoke, Felix noticed her gaze linger briefly on her earrings. The terminals in District B4 seemed to have deeper access now compared to six years ago when he was exiled. After Svetlana left, F777 rested for half a day until one of the staff came to inform them that the genetic testing had been arranged. As the most important VIP, Cora was naturally placed in the highest priority exclusive channel, while the others had to wait longer, though they would all be tested by the end of the day.

An unmanned hover car departed from the hotel, flying steadily toward the pure white building at the heart of Vision City—the Aberrant Testing Station. It was Cora's first time in such a luxurious extended hover car.

"Wow~" she couldn't help but exclaim, touching and examining everything. She sprawled out on the seat to relax, then stretched her legs, moving around energetically. Suddenly, she looked up and stared directly into the camera on the control panel, wide-eyed.

She slowly sat up straight and, for the rest of the journey, sat as still as if she'd been struck dumb.

Because she had self-reported as S-Class, which didn't match her Aberrant Certificate, the Aberrant Bureau took her case seriously. When Cora landed, a dozen white-robed staff members were already waiting at the entrance to greet her.

A short-haired woman in her thirties stepped forward from the group. She wore understated silver-framed glasses and spoke quickly and decisively. "Hello, Cora. I'm your Aberrant Analyst, Grace."

Cora's sharp ears caught someone nearby addressing her as "Director," while information was transmitted to Grace's terminal. Her glasses flickered with light as data flowed through the lenses, disappearing in a flash.

Grace nodded at Cora. "I'll be fully responsible for your genetic testing. Please, follow me."

The first thing Cora noticed upon entering the testing station was the massive piece of equipment in the center. It was enormous, towering from floor to ceiling, almost integrated with the building, its entire surface white, connected by countless thin silver wires at the ports.

"The R-Type Aberrant Analyzer is currently the most advanced piece of equipment in the Alliance. It can accommodate up to 500 people for data analysis simultaneously, with an accuracy rate of over 97%," Grace explained, noticing Cora's interest.

Cora glanced around the empty testing station, silently questioning: Where are the 500 people?

"To ensure 100% accuracy for your results, we've cleared the area, halting all other Aberrant testing," Grace said in a serious tone.

"...Oh." Cora's first thought was how much longer the lines at the Immigration Center would be now. As Cora followed Grace deeper into the facility, she observed the station's design—both simple and imbued with a strong sense of technology. The white simulated daylight lamps illuminated every corner, leaving no shadows.

As she walked, Cora felt uneasy, slowly covering her chest with her hand. The combination of the powerful light and the enclosed space made her vaguely uncomfortable.

Grace didn't notice Cora's discomfort and continued, "Let's start with a routine check—blood tests, collection of bodily fluids, and some biometric information for chromosomal and DNA analysis."

Once inside the room, Cora saw many instruments she couldn't name, along with mechanical arms glowing with cold light. She had undergone similar tests in Felalakas. Grace patiently guided her through the steps, and they quickly completed the process.

Next, Grace led her to a lab-like room with a circular machine, a single bed positioned at the open end. "This is a magneto resonance spectrometer connected to the R-Type Analyzer. It will provide a comprehensive analysis of your Aberrant abilities," Grace explained.

Cora obediently lay down on the bed, and a virtual screen instantly appeared before her eyes. Compared to the black box that Jeremy Wolfgang used back at the Fool's Wharf, this machine was on an entirely different level, with intricate lines and data that made her head spin.

Grace and her assistant entered the observation room. As the machine started, a complex noise hummed around Cora, and she could feel her spiritual energy fluctuating slightly inside her, like water beginning to flow after being still.

On the observation panel, Cora's data rapidly surged, instantly surpassing the S-Class threshold. The rates of her spiritual energy, explosive power, reaction speed, and core muscle strength were rising at a terrifying pace.

One assistant whispered excitedly, "If it keeps going up like this, she might reach S5."

"It's my first time seeing a live S-Class," another remarked in awe of Cora's data. "You're lucky, getting to see two at once—there's another one coming later."

"His results won't be as surprising. He's a known S2, and engineering types don't compare to attack types..." Everyone was excited; it had been a long time since the Northern Base had welcomed a new S-Class Aberrant.

Suddenly, Grace frowned and made a soft "hmm."

"Director, what's wrong?" her assistant asked nervously. "Did I do something wrong?"

"It's not your fault. The spectrometer is showing impurities," Grace said in a serious tone. This had never happened before. "Could it be a malfunction?" she mused, but the self-repairing R-Type Analyzer was unlikely to experience such an issue.

Grace's face grew more serious as she focused on the imaging panel. The impurities were multiplying, moving towards Cora's heart, and gradually forming a gigantic shadow, enveloping her completely.

"Is that... radiation?"

After confirming the impurities, even Grace, usually so composed, showed a look of shock.

Twenty minutes later, Cora, bored out of her mind, yawned while lying in the machine, thinking drowsily, "Does this whatever-it's-called spectrometer always take this long? It doesn't seem that advanced."

Another ten minutes passed before the annoying noise finally stopped. The bed slowly retracted, and Grace stood before Cora, smiling. "Although the full report isn't ready, I want to congratulate you in advance—you are indeed an S-Class Aberrant."

Grace paused. "And you're the most powerful Aberrant I've ever seen."

"Oh, I'm alright," Cora modestly waved it off.

"Once the analysis report is ready, Commander Holland will meet with you," Grace added.

"Commander, Cora's genetic test results are in," Svetlana's voice came through on the private channel.

Scarlett Holland made a gesture, halting the ongoing conversation. The ministers quietly left the room as she stood up and quickly entered a concealed chamber. As she walked, her terminal gradually lit up, connecting to a holographic conference where several high-ranking officials of the Aberrants Bureau were anxiously waiting.

Cora Thornton's Aberrant report was transmitted over spanning 34 pages. Scarlett Holland skipped the complex charts and specialized data analysis, skimming quickly through the ultimate results.

Impatient officials at the meeting immediately flipped to the end and gasped, "The level is... S7! If I'm not mistaken, this is the first officially recognized S7 Aberrant since the Alliance began classifying them, right? And she's an attack-type!"

"Not the first, right? Wasn't there a dual-type S7 before... who died suddenly?" someone countered. "Well, you said it yourself—they died suddenly. So now, Cora is the first, and the only, S7!"

Even within the same level of power, there are more granular distinctions that only the R-Type Analyzer can detect. Each level of Aberrants is divided into grades 1 to 9, and until now, the highest publicly acknowledged S-Class in the Central Court had been S6. Now, out of nowhere, this Cora Thornton turns out to be an S7 Aberrant!

The expressions on the faces of the Aberrant Bureau's top brass were bewildered. How could such a monster exist in a district that they had always overlooked?

For the first time, a rare smile appeared on Scarlett Holland's usually stern face. She had been the one to propose issuing a recruitment order to the lower districts, and Cora Thornton's arrival —an S7 attack-type Aberrant with no background who voluntarily joined them—was a godsend for the Northern Base.

Amid the lively discussion, Grace's calm voice broke in.

"Sorry to interrupt, but there's something I must point out. Please look at page 17 of the report."

"According to the magneto resonance spectrum analysis, the radiation level in Cora Thornton's body is... twenty times that of a normal Aberrant."

The holographic imagery was vivid, and Grace could clearly see the exaggerated gasps from everyone. Ordinary zombies only had about twice the radiation level of an Aberrant. But twenty times? How was she even alive, let alone not turning into a zombie?

This person was the Northern Base's future golden goose, and absolutely no mistakes could be made!

Scarlett Holland pulled out the page of the magneto resonance imaging report. Cora's chest and limbs appeared dark, as if covered by the shadow of a black cloud. "Does the excess radiation affect her Aberrant abilities?"

"That's the strangest part—there's no impact at all. She's no different from any other S-Class," Grace said, puzzled.

"What if it's because of dual-type Aberrance?" Scarlett Holland, as the highest-ranking officer in the Aberrants Bureau, was quick to consider another possibility.

Grace, however, dismissed her hypothesis. "The R-Type Analyzer found no evidence of a second Aberrant ability in Cora. Dual-type Aberrants are extremely rare, especially at the S-Class level. Fortunately, we have Punk's data for comparison. His radiation level is consistent with an S-Class single-type, and his distribution differs significantly from Cora's, so it's unlikely that dual-type Aberrance is the cause."

As the first publicly recognized S7 dual-type in the Alliance, Punk's Aberrant report was, of course, top secret. Scarlett Holland had gone to great lengths and used extensive connections to finally obtain it from Jae-Woo Park in the Central Court.

"Apart from the radiation level... there's another very serious issue with Cora Thornton," Grace continued, her headache growing.

"Pages 22 to 27 cover her genetic report."

"Cora's body shows chromosomal translocation and segments of unknown DNA. It's currently unclear whether these are hereditary or congenital. I'm not an expert in this field, but I'm concerned... she might have a latent genetic defect."

Grace's concern was well-founded. Genetic defects could lead to a high incidence of various disorders. If a powerful Aberrant lost their life to a genetic disease, it would be a tragic loss.

"Could she have taken part in a Gene Selection Program?" one senior official speculated uncertainly. "Ancient technology was indeed immature, and many people developed genetic diseases."

Scarlett Holland turned the report back to the first page. Cora Thornton's original registration was in District F177. People from the F District would never have could participate in a Gene Selection Program.

After a moment of contemplation, she quietly said, "Send this report to Dr. Ninnemann. He's an expert in genetic engineering and heredity; he should be able to identify the cause of Cora Thornton's anomalies."

"Should we ask Cora to go over there as well, to cooperate with Dr. Ninnemann for further detailed examinations?" Grace asked. "No," Scarlett Holland firmly stopped her. "Until we figure this out, don't inform her. Also, adjust the contents of this report."

F777 was in the hotel, popping champagne in celebration.

Yuui and the others had completed their genetic testing as well. Aside from Damian, who had just made a breakthrough and only reached A1, the rest of the team had results that were nothing short of astonishing: Yuui was A4, Charles was A5, and surprisingly, Suchat was A8!

This usually reticent guy, who rarely spoke over three words at a time, had certainly brought a surprise to everyone.

Suchat, with his long limbs, sat awkwardly on the sofa, while Cora Thornton excitedly patted him on the shoulder, and Yuui affectionately ruffled his close-cropped hair. The short bristles of his hair brushed against her soft hand, causing a slight tickle that traveled from his back all the way to the top of his head. Suchat tensed up, gripping the can of beer in his hand tightly. Without realizing it, he squeezed too hard, and the aluminum can crunched as it was crushed.

"Pardon the interruption," one of the staff members, K-One, knocked politely on the door, "Ms. Thornton's Aberrant report is ready." Everyone immediately crowded around as K-One calmly connected the report to Cora's terminal.

"Hurry, hurry! Let's see what S-Class it is!"

"Whoa! S7! That's amazing, sis!"

"Haha, Old Franz, pay up! I guessed it right~" Yuui boasted gleefully. Charles was silent. Having blind faith in Cora, he had stubbornly bet on S9.

"S7, Captain, could you buy me some extra materials?" Felix joined in the fun, reminding her of his much-anticipated list.

"Sure, sure," Cora chuckled foolishly.

Onyx gently took the terminal from Cora's playful hands and began carefully flipping through the report, examining each page. He was slow and meticulous, the specialized data that Scarlett Holland couldn't make sense of presented no barrier to him.

The report had 24 pages, and Onyx took his time, reading every single word.

Then he removed his glasses and pinched the bridge of his nose, his thin lips curling into a faint, mocking smile. This was B-District arrogance at its finest. The people at the Aberrant Bureau had clearly underestimated them.

Even for an S1 Aberrant, a normal analysis report would be over 25 pages. And yet here was Cora Thornton, a rare S7, with a report that they hadn't even bothered to complete properly—just hastily chopped down and passed off as finished. Fooling the uninformed might be easy, but deceiving him was nothing but a pipe dream.

After all, the Arashi Research Institute had developed the R-Type Analyzer capable of conducting genetic analysis. What no one knew was that its creation had been driven by Onyx himself.

—There wasn't a person alive who understood its capabilities better than Onyx de Montclair.

CHAPTER 29

Invitation

Early the next morning, F777 boarded the starship arranged by the Aberrants Bureau and officially set off from Frontier City to the Northern Base.

The silver-white flight terminal streaked across the sky like a meteor, passing effortlessly through the transparent protective shield. Cora clung to the window, wearing a satisfied smile like that of a proud father. This time, they hadn't resorted to tricks or deceit; they had entered District B on their own merit and hard work.

As soon as the starship arrived at the platform, Cora jumped down before it even came to a full stop. A gentle breeze caressed her face, and the air was refreshing as the weather simulation system gradually dispelled the scorching summer heat.

It was Damian's first time entering the city, and he eagerly ran to the railing with Cora to get a better view. Unlike the barren plains that stretched for thousands of miles outside the city, the Northern Base was a city of substance: sky tunnels, floating subways, sleek cars —products of the technological advancements born during the Glory 30-year Era were everywhere.

The towering skyscrapers, staggered and layered, created a visually stunning spectacle. One floor even housed an infinity pool the size of a football field, where several Aberrants were splashing around. Much water-powered Aberrants playfully manipulated the water, sending sparkling droplets falling like rain.

Cora's eyes sparkled with excitement. "Wow..."

Damian echoed, "Wow..."

Just then, a fleet of armed ships flew overhead, with several Aberrants standing confidently on top. One of them, bare-chested and covered in scars, held up the freshly severed, still-bleeding head of a giant beast and waved to the crowd on the platform with a hearty laugh before entering two connected cylindrical towers.

In the distance, a massive leaderboard appeared in the sky, with numbers flashing and shifting until they formed a giant ranking:

"Blue Flame defeated a Level 4 mutant beast: the Black Fang Fish. Real-time score updated."

Cora watched as Blue Flame's ranking climbed two spots, placing them tenth in the Northern Base and 122nd in the New Pacific Alliance. This... this was the Northern Base? The sheer energy of the place was intoxicating.

Svetlana Yevgeniyeva was waiting for them at the platform, beaming with pride at her own dazzling KPI. "Here are your new terminals and the procedures for transferring your Aberrants registration. I'll assign someone to follow up later."

"Now, follow me to see Officer Holland. She's waiting for you at the Aberrants Bureau."

The Aberrants Bureau of the Northern Base was exactly where Cora had seen those two cylindrical towers from earlier.

Svetlana's red heels clicked crisply against the polished floor, echoing around them. Cora and the others followed her, passing by a wall of historical honors that displayed images of the Global Anopower Summit, round table forums, Gene Selectors exchange visits, and joint military exercises with the Galio Empire and the Luse Federation. Over time, Aberrants had become increasingly acknowledged.

Cora realized that this was the stark contrast between the different districts of the Alliance. In the lower districts, awakening as a D-level was cause for celebration, but in the Northern Base or other District B zones, Aberrants—especially those who emerged after the apocalypse—were a common sight.

Cora also noticed that everyone here was a high-level Aberrant, with faint traces of psychic energy swirling around them, though they kept it well-contained.

Along the way, several people subtly observed them, trying to figure out which one of them was the legendary S7. The news that the base had recruited an S-level offensive Aberrant had already spread like wildfire, and Svetlana escorting F777 inside made their identities quite clear.

Under everyone's watchful eyes, they took a fully automated scenic elevator to the upper floors.

Looking at the building, which seemed to have no security measures in place, Cora suddenly had a thought and asked, "What if an Aberrant terrorist attacks?"

Svetlana chuckled softly. "Trust me, the dumbest way to die in this world is to recklessly use Anopower in the building beneath our feet."

She tapped her pearl earrings, and a video clip instantly appeared on the elevator's announcement screen, with the headline— "Safety Tutorial 014."

"This is footage from eight months ago, just after the apocalypse broke out. A newly registered A7-level Aberrant from a lower district, along with twenty-three bandits, stormed the Aberrants Bureau, attempting to kidnap Officer Holland and take over the entire Northern Base."

In the footage, the leader, a corrupt Aberrant, wore an arrogant expression, his chin held high as he barked orders, "Everyone, hands on your heads! Squat down! Don't move!" As he moved forward, the floor, counters, and pillars dissolved into corrosive goo wherever he stepped.

Just as he was about to cross the middle line, the ceiling of the Aberrants Bureau vanished, revealing a deep, spatial rift. Hundreds of black energy cannons appeared, and with a deafening "bang bang bang—" blinding beams of light shot out, instantly turning the bandits into Swiss cheese. When the light finally faded, the only one left standing was the A7-level Aberrant, but he didn't survive for long —he was soon blasted into a pulp.

Literal pulp, with sticky red chunks falling onto the polished floor like rain. The scene was eerily silent, as if under a spell.

The camera panned to a transparent SkyBridge where two young Aberrants in uniform stood. They were tall, with similar features— blond hair, green eyes—and carried an air of casual indifference.

The woman's slender hands rested on the railing as she gazed down at the A7-level Aberrant's remains with the same interest one might show to an ant, while the man leaned against the wall, arms crossed, seemingly asleep, his expression utterly indifferent.

Svetlana coughed lightly, her tone filled with deep sympathy. "Of all the unfortunate criminals in the forty-seven years since the base was established, these were the unluckiest. They just so ran into the Rowin twins returning for their performance review, and we didn't even get the chance to offer them a chance to surrender."

Cora looked surprised. "The Rowin twins?"

"Yes, Wyan and Yvonne Rowin, a pair of fraternal twins. They are the only two S6-level offensive Aberrants in the Northern Base." Svetlana lowered her voice, winking slyly. "They're also Aberrants who were naturalized by the Galio Empire."

Cora glanced back at the footage. The Rowin twins finished handling the crisis and left with an air of indifference.

S-level Aberrants have absolute dominance over all levels below them, and with the two S6s involved, these criminals were indeed extremely unlucky, as Svetlana said.

With Svetlana leading the way, F777 moved unimpeded and quickly reached the second-to-top floor.

In a spacious conference room, they finally met the highest-ranking officer of the Aberrants Bureau, Scarlett Holland... or rather, her holographic image.

The seven of them exchanged subtle glances. Scarlett's claim that she would "personally" meet them had turned out to be in this form. But it was understandable; even though F777 had voluntarily sought them out, Scarlett wasn't so overcome with joy that she let down her guard when facing an S7-level offensive Aberrant and an entire team of A-level Aberrants.

Scarlett was dressed in a deep blue suit, with a pair of black-framed glasses perched on her nose. Her expression was stern and dignified, with two deep lines of nasolabial folds on either side of her nose.

Cora Thornton was reminded of a strict dean she once encountered during her brief stint as a student.

"Cora Thornton, and the members of F777, welcome to the Northern Base," Scarlett began, getting straight to the point. "Two weeks ago, I watched the live broadcast of the Throne Tournament finals in District C83. You are an outstanding team, each member shining in their own way, with impeccable coordination—a team where every individual is indispensable."

Her appreciative gaze swept across the group, accurately calling out the names of Suchat, Damian Blackwood, Charles Franz, and even Yuui Hayashi's real name. Then... she naturally skipped the remaining two.

The two who were confined to wheelchairs exchanged a glance, one smiling slightly, almost flippantly, while the other yawned out of boredom.

Since entering the Northern Base, Onyx and Felix had meticulously restrained their psychic energy, making them appear no different from ordinary people. Thanks to Cora's influence, their identities were officially registered as "accompanying personnel."

Although Scarlett had followed the tournament, she had watched the official broadcast, not the 24-hour surveillance of F777. During the marathon match, Felix had used a mechanical arm the entire time, never revealing his hacking abilities on camera. Onyx was even more discreet; he didn't have a tracking drone, and barely appeared on camera at all. Even when he did, Felix had erased those moments.

In the Northern Base, strength was the only currency, and no one would deliberately hide their identity as an Aberrant. So, Scarlett naturally assumed they were just ordinary people who teamed up with F777... no, just disabled people, not worth a second glance.

Scarlett said nothing, nor did she show any disdain, but Onyx, with his keen insight, could detect her subtle disregard for ordinary people.

"I didn't expect you to break through to S-level in such a short time after the competition and choose the Northern Base," Scarlett said, her expression unchanging.

Cora scratched her head awkwardly.

Jumping from A-level to S7-level was nearly impossible, but Scarlett didn't expose her. Instead, she went along with the fabricated letter Onyx had concocted, giving Cora an easy out. This showed that Scarlett didn't hold Cora's secrecy about her level in Felalakas against her.

"According to the recruitment order, I represent the Northern

Base in offering you five apartments in the central zone, full access to all Aberrant privileges in District B, and a special monthly stipend, along with corresponding living benefits."

Scarlett, with her deep pockets, upgraded the original offer from "free apartment stays" to "ownership of five apartments," along with housing and money, making F777 feel a warm sense of welcome. She then introduced the basic functions of the Aberrants Bureau and the currently available job positions, which were indeed tempting.

Finally, Scarlett turned to Cora, "If you have any requests, ask. After the probationary period, I will make sure they are fulfilled immediately."

"Probationary period?" Cora caught onto the key term.

"The survival rule of the Northern Base is absolute strength," Scarlett nodded slightly. "We implement an elimination system, with the rankings updated monthly. Unfortunately, the bottom 1% of teams cannot stay here."

"Of course, I'm confident that you will pass the probationary period. In a month's time, I look forward to seeing you again." Scarlett smiled. "Perhaps then we can sit down and have a cup of tea, face to face."

Her words carried a hint of deeper meaning, implying that F777 might get the chance to meet her in person next time.

Even when dealing with an S-level Aberrant, Scarlett didn't display any eagerness to keep them. She perfectly embodied the calm and rational demeanor expected of someone in her position, yet she paid close attention to Cora, speaking in a measured tone that clearly showed she valued her opinion.

Cora felt Scarlett seemed like a person full of contradictions.

"This is prepared especially for you." Scarlett turned her head and gave a few quiet instructions.

On Cora's side, the door to the conference room was knocked on softly, and two staff members wheeled in a mobile table displaying a variety of colorful terminals, covering nearly all the popular models in District B.

"We were planning to buy them together," Cora politely declined, thinking they might get a discount through a group purchase.

Scarlett simply stated, "the Aberrants Bureau issues directly All

S-level terminals."

Cora paused, staring at her.

Scarlett was direct. "S-level Aberrants have potential risks, and we need to ensure that we can contact you 24/7. These terminals come pre-installed with a locator and a dedicated communication channel. You can start using them once they're bound to you."

Cora averted her gaze, took a few steps forward, and silently picked one.

As they exited the Aberrants Bureau, Yuui grumbled in dissatisfaction, "What is this, surveillance?"

Charles stroked his chin thoughtfully. "I think there's something off about Officer Holland. Her words and actions don't quite match up."

"She's a pure opportunist," Onyx's calm voice interjected.

The others all turned to look at him.

Onyx continued, "Everything she says and does revolves around the interests of the Northern Base. In her eyes, Aberrants are merely tools to maintain those interests. When she needs you, she'll accommodate you and shower you with praise. But if a conflict arises or you go against her interests, she wouldn't hesitate to discard you."

"However, at least for the Northern Base, she's a very competent leader," Onyx added with a sarcastic smile.

"So, should we even use this terminal?" Cora asked, examining the brooch-style terminal she had chosen, which looked a bit like a small bee.

Onyx shrugged, unconcerned. "Use it. We're not doing anything wrong, so what's there to fear? If we ever need to do something shady, we'll figure out how to hack it then."

Cora sighed internally. Why did Onyx sound so confident about doing something shady?

The first time the terminal was activated, it required an initial binding process. As Cora gently released a bit of her psychic energy, she felt a faint, fleeting sensation, as if something was observing her. She hesitated, realizing that without her experience in the Death Hell, she might have overlooked this subtle feeling.

But the feeling she had was eerily similar to what Felix had described while being bored in prison. Why would a terminal in

District B evoke the same sensation? Cora shared her discovery with her teammates.

Felix's pale fingers took the terminal, and he studied it for a moment, his icy blue eyes reflecting a cold, almost mechanical indifference. "Mild thought integration... as expected, it's her handiwork."

His words were cryptic, but Felix didn't bother to explain further. Instead, he quickly input a series of anti-surveillance codes. "If we tamper with it too much, it'll get noticed. Just wear it for now and avoid using 'privileges' as much as possible."

"Privileges?" Cora was puzzled.

"Yeah, accessing information you don't already have in your mind, or actively seeking knowledge you never possessed—those are considered 'privileges.' While they can be convenient, every time you use them, it deepens the thought integration."

"Oh," Cora nodded obediently. "I don't need to use that. I'll just ask Onyx if I have questions."

Why bother with information or knowledge from a rigid terminal when she had Onyx? The "Alliance Encyclopedia" not only answered all her questions but also adjusted his explanations to suit her understanding, ensuring she always comprehended the answer.

Onyx suddenly smiled, a smile that could melt ice and snow, with a visible pleasure in the curve of his lips.

"Sorry to interrupt, but who exactly is 'she' that you're talking about?" Yuui cautiously asked.

"The Lucas Supercomputer," Felix replied in a flat, emotionless tone. "She's infiltrated the terminal network in District B. She sees everyone."

A chill ran down the group's spines.

Before, they had thought the terminals in District B were just cool and impressive. But now, after Felix's explanation, the idea of being constantly watched felt deeply unsettling.

Still, the issued terminal had its uses, like providing direct access to the mission system.

The seven of them huddled together as Cora opened the system's interface, excitedly navigating through it. Even after deducting the 500,000 points for the entry fee, they still had 200,000 left. The team was feeling pretty wealthy and confident that they'd easily make it onto the leaderboard.

Then reality hit Cora like a ton of bricks.

After the real-time points update, a line of text appeared on the projection: "F777 Current Points: 220,050. Monthly Ranking: 99.99%." "—Unfortunately, your team did not make it onto the leaderboard. Please keep trying!"

Cora desperately scrolled up to see the next team's score. The team above them had 448,888 points—more than double F777's score.

Cora's face fell.

Oh my god, were Aberrants in the Northern Base really this competitive?

CHAPTER 30

Testing

Perhaps because of special instructions from Svetlana, the agent assigned by the Aberrants Bureau was incredibly attentive and enthusiastic. Not only did they quickly complete transferring their registrations, but they also drove them to buy new terminals.

Except for the two "ordinary people," the four A-level members of F777 all switched to the District B terminals. Afterward, they updated their Aberrant information, chose apartments, and received local advice from the agent:

"Don't choose the ground floor; the lighting is poor. And avoid the top floor—too many flying terminals, it'll drive you crazy with the noise."

"I like this one!" Damian pointed out a flashy blue neighborhood, lured in by the over-the-top holographic advertisement featuring 360-degree deep-breathing jellyfish lights, mood-changing algae floors, and an immersive humpback whale soundscape in the bedroom—clearly designed to impress.

The agent shook their head repeatedly. "Many Aberrants in that neighborhood end up depressed, probably because of the prolonged deep-sea environment. You'd be better off choosing a small garden-style house with plenty of sunlight. You could even knock down the walls between two units to connect them."

Although no one said it directly, the observant agent noticed the harmonious dynamic within the F777 team and figured they'd prefer to live close to each other.

Amid the lively discussion, Cora, having nothing better to do, pulled out her terminal for a quick glance. Then... she watched as F777's ranking dropped to another spot.

It was still a public holiday in the Alliance—didn't these people take breaks or sleep? No way, she needed to step up her game too!

The worried captain immediately opened the mission system. Damian ran over to ask her opinion on a house, but she waved him off distractedly. "You guys choose, you buy?"

The mission list refreshed rapidly; new tasks were posted and taken down almost instantly, with restrictions on levels, distances, and eligibility conditions. Cora became increasingly engrossed, fully concentrating on selecting a mission.

[C-level Mission: Clear the infestation of mutant apple snails along the coast of Silver Bay (District C44). Reward: 80,000 points.] This one looked promising! Cora eagerly clicked on it, only to be met with a notification— "This mission is no longer available."

Before she could feel disappointed, another batch of new missions popped up.

[B-level Mission (Urgent): A medium-sized zombie wave has appeared in the coffee plantation area of Mandheling (District C43). Please clear it within 4 hours.] At the bottom, a line of urgent red scrolling text read: Attention coffee lovers, please save Mandheling! This area is a major production site for Mandheling coffee. If the zombie wave breaches it, the entire Alliance's coffee supply will be affected!

Cora took a deep breath. That sounded serious! She didn't drink coffee, but she had a strong sense of justice!

Her fingers flew across the virtual panel as she tried to accept the mission, but perhaps because of the sheer number of coffee enthusiasts, all she got was a notification—"Mission acceptance limit reached."

Cora was stunned. What? It's full already? She, the coffee guardian, hadn't even had time to help!

Feeling down, she scrolled through the panel a bit more and actually found a mission worth 200,000 points that hadn't been taken yet! She quickly clicked it like crazy, but...

"Sorry, your team does not meet the acceptance criteria."

What? What didn't they meet? Cora focused on the details: [B-level Mission: Rebuild the outdoor hot springs at Delta Island (District B15). Engineering Aberrants required; the higher the level, the better!]

Cora was exasperated but determined not to give up!

She kept her head down, furiously attempting to grab a mission. But despite her best efforts, she couldn't land a single one!

She was so focused on the task that she didn't notice when the team had moved far ahead, nor did she see Onyx stop and wait for her. With a "thump," she stubbed her toe on his wheelchair and lost her balance, tumbling forward—right into someone's arms.

Onyx's wheelchair rolled back slightly as he opened his arms, catching her firmly. When Cora looked up, she was met with the perfect curve of his jawline.

Today, Onyx was dressed in a light-colored suit. The open collar revealed a clear view of his collarbone, and his nose was tall and narrow. His lips curved slightly in a smile, and the gold-rimmed glasses with two fine chains dangling from them made him look like a dashing celebrity from a street ad.

Onyx lowered his head, his Adam's apple moving subtly with each breath. Without a word, he pinched Cora's cheeks and shook her head gently from side to side.

"Mmm... squeezing makes me drool..." Cora mumbled incoherently.

Onyx chuckled, a low sound resonating from his chest. Cora, still leaning against him, felt her heart skip a beat.

Her ears felt like they were burning, and she extended two fingers, pressing them against Onyx's chest, pushing herself back a few inches. Then she used his thigh as leverage to swiftly stand up.

Onyx's expression turned slightly amused. "Cora, if you keep touching me like that, things might get out of hand."

Cora protested, "I wasn't... touching." She was just using him for support, after all. How petty.

Feeling indignant, she glanced at Onyx's leg. What's so special about his thigh, anyway? Can't even touch it. Onyx, uncomfortable, placed his right hand on his knee and changed the subject. "What's got you so absorbed?"

When he asked, Cora's frustration resurfaced, and she complained, "I can't grab any missions."

"Let me see," Onyx said, extending his hand.

They were used to sharing a terminal by now, so Cora handed it over without thinking twice. However, the agent ahead of them turned around just in time to witness this, and their eyes nearly popped out of their head.

In District B, terminals were extremely private, as personal as underwear! They were terminals! Devices that could project your thoughts in real-time! How could anyone just hand theirs over so casually?

The agent, speechless with shock, stared at Onyx's strikingly handsome face. Slowly, their disbelief turned into realization. Ah, this pretty boy... with that heart-meltingly gentle smile, no wonder he could still win the favor of an S-level despite being in a wheelchair...

What a world, the agent thought with a sigh. Then they accidentally glimpsed Felix, and their mind went blank. Wait, one wasn't enough? They needed two? Not even bothering with chairs, just sitting down for a game? This new S-level seemed to have... some rather peculiar tastes.

Unaware of the agent's complex thoughts, Cora was only concerned with F777's ranking. "Can you grab any?"

Onyx's fingers flashed across the screen. "With this speed, they're probably using an auto-mission grabbing bot."

"A bot... for grabbing missions?"

Cora's voice trembled with anger. Did they really have to go that far? No wonder her fingers were sore from tapping, and she hadn't secured a single mission.

"What bot? What are you talking about?" Yuui curiously leaned over. When Cora explained their situation, everyone seemed eager to try it. "If it's that competitive, we have to join in too!"

"This is our first mission in the Northern Base. We have to complete it beautifully and make a powerful impression," Suchat said directly. "It's still early. Let's do a mission before heading back."

Onyx tossed the terminal to Felix and said pointedly, "The captain wants to take on a mission. Handle it."

The agent, whose worldview had just been shattered, bit their finger in shock. Th-three people sharing one terminal? This was too much!

Hacking was nothing new to Felix; he had never lost a class registration battle back in Luboni. His fingers flew across the screen, inputting a string of code, and soon a freshly created "random mission interception bot" was running through the vast data sea. A few minutes later, the terminal dinged with a notification: "Mission successfully accepted. Please complete it within the specified time limit."

"What did we get?" The others crowded around, eager to see F777's first mission in the Northern Base.

[B-level Mission (District B10 exclusive): Fishing Expert. The Base's Marine Biology Research Institute is preparing to add new specimens to their collection. Please capture the listed mutant species at Silver Bay (District C44) within 24 hours. The better the specimen's appearance and completeness, the higher the score.]

Friendly reminder: This mission is not suitable for individuals with a fear of elongated creatures.

Cora was confused. What? What elongated creatures...? But time was tight, and there was no time to explain. She quickly rallied her team. "Let's go. Time to tackle the mission!"

Silver Bay was only a two-hour trip by starship from the Northern Base, but by the time F777 arrived, there was hardly any space left on the beach to stand. Just like in Frontier City, Aberrants were everywhere, and the scene resembled a chaotic marketplace.

"Move aside, move aside, we were here first... Don't you understand what I'm saying?"

"Who cares about who came first? If I grab it, it's mine. If you want it, take it back, hah!"

"You #%@??%&, get lost you @#&*??...."

One wind-powered Aberrant took advantage of the situation, stirring the ocean's surface and causing waves to surge forward, turning everything upside down. The mutant creatures hiding beneath were thrown into disarray, revealing a sight that Cora Thornton would rather forget for the rest of her life.

Countless ferocious ribbonfish, three-headed deformed eels, mud eels as thick as an arm, and thousands of furious octopuses and squids rained down like a hailstorm, with the overwhelming stench of decay and sea salt assaulting everyone's senses.

Aberrants rushed forward to snatch the creatures, their dazzling array of powers nearly blinding those nearby. Cora and her team couldn't even get a hand in, barely picking up any scraps.

Well, they could at least get the scraps.

"Thud!" A spiked loach landed at Cora's feet, its jagged teeth latching onto her shoe before she impassively stabbed it through.

"Thud!" A ribbonfish smacked into Yuui Hayashi's shoulder, slapping her hard as it wriggled.

"What the hell," Yuui muttered, stunned. This was the first time in her life that she had been slapped by a fish. Suchat swiftly grabbed the ribbonfish with one hand, releasing a toxic mist that instantly snapped its neck.

"You... okay?" Suchat asked.

Yuui turned her dazed expression towards him, then gritted her teeth. "If I don't wipe out the entire ribbonfish species today, I might as well change my last name."

But talking tough was one thing—actually catching these creatures was another.

Cora fired an arrow, pinning down a Level 3 mutant clam queen, but before she could celebrate, a sand-powered Aberrant swiftly swept up the prize with a wave of sand, leaving nothing behind.

"Thief!" Cora yelled in shock and anger.

Looking around, the beach was a sea of heads—human and mutant alike. There was no way to spot the culprit.

The rest of the team wasn't faring much better. Being decent and fair-minded, they focused on catching and keeping their own fish, while the other Aberrants shamelessly grabbed whatever they could, pocketing everything in sight.

Suchat and Yuui were busy chopping up ribbonfish, only to have their spoils stolen right under their noses. Damian froze an area with his powers, but before his short legs could get there, a space-powered Aberrant swooped in and teleported the catch away, leaving him hopping mad.

As for Felix... he was at least getting something done, using his six mechanical arms to expertly steal other people's prey.

Onyx, however, had retreated far away, his germaphobia in full force, looking utterly disgusted by the chaos.

Cora met his gaze, seeing Onyx leaning weakly against his wheelchair, his eyes full of reproach: You want me to go catch fish? Okay, okay. There was no way Cora could bring herself to make him join in.

After a whole day of hard work, they had barely earned 50,000 points. When they checked their ranking, they saw, with bitter laughter, that they had fallen into two more places.

By the time F777 returned to the Northern Base, everyone's faces were grim, and the starship reeked of a strong, rotten stench.

Their first mission, intended to make a grand impression, had clearly flopped.

Cora sighed quietly. At this rate, was she going to be the first S-level Aberrant in the Northern Base to be eliminated because of low rankings?

"I heard you guys went fishing. Hahaha, and caught nothing?" Svetlana's laughter came through the terminal.

"Don't even mention it," Cora groaned, rubbing her forehead.

"Cora, do you have any connections at the base?" After teasing her for a bit, Svetlana finally got serious.

"The top-tier Aberrants have their own ecosystem here. I've heard that the higher-ranked teams have a private channel. All the high-reward S-level and A-level missions get monopolized by them, so they never make it to outsiders."

"If you know someone, get them to pull you into the channel. It'll definitely be more effective than... haha, fishing."

Connections?

A face slowly came to mind for Cora: wearing a sniper visor, black gloves gripping a gun, with rebellious eyes and a ruby earring glinting on his right ear.

It seemed like she knew someone, after all.

"There's one more thing. Earlier, that... ahem, a family member of yours wanted to meet with Professor Gawin Ming and his wife, right?" Svetlana added.

"Their guest appointment channel has been closed for years, and they haven't appeared in public for a long time. But I found Professor Ming's current address. It's on Antique Street. Let me know when you have time, and I'll go with you."

"Okay, I'll check with them first."

A laboratory filled with various instruments hummed with activity. The "beep beep" of machines filled the air, while slowly rotating gene sequences floated in the void.

Inside an observation chamber lay two living corpses, their skin severely decayed. Upon closer inspection, their eyes were a murky gray—the telltale sign of Fallens captured from Ocean Gate. On the panel beside them, an invisible shadow was steadily eroding their bodies, and one of them had already lost all vital signs.

"Radiation levels?"

"47.75%, we've reached the critical threshold!"

"Psychic energy levels?"

"0."

The upper body of one corpse suddenly jerked upright, arching into a bridge shape as a raspy wail escaped its throat. Then it collapsed heavily, devoid of any remaining life.

"Subject... confirmed dead." The surrounding assistants fell into an uneasy silence.

After a tense two minutes, a hoarse voice finally spoke, "Record this: radiation overload at 47.75%, DNA double-helix rupture, chromosome deactivation, organ dissolution... the primal cells lost their regenerative abilities. The fourth awakening experiment has failed."

"Ninnemann, what should we do with these two failed test subjects?" A man with graying temples and a gaunt face replied quietly, "Destroy them."

Another failure. The number of failures was now too many to count, and the atmosphere in the lab was heavy with despair.

Just then, an assistant in a white coat entered the room, holding a light screen. "Dr. Ninnemann, the Aberrants Bureau, sent over a file. They suspect the subject might have a genetic disorder and would like you to look."

"Do you think I have time for this?" Ninnemann asked, his expression showing irritation.

The assistant hesitated before speaking again. "It's a request from Officer Scarlett."

Scarlett Holland was the lab's principal benefactor. After a moment of silence, Dr. Ninnemann accepted the light screen and skimmed through the file.

What began as a cursory glance soon slowed, his expression growing increasingly serious as he read. Eventually, he lingered on page 17—an enormous mass of shadows engulfed the body in the image, making the recently deceased Fallen from radiation overload seem almost laughable by comparison.

"What is this? A newly discovered mutant zombie?"

"No," the assistant stammered, startled by the image. "This is the new S-level at the base."

"An Aberrant..." Ninnemann flipped back to the report's cover page and read the name aloud, "Cora Thornton."

"Leave the report with me. Tell Officer Holland to arrange for this... Cora Thornton to visit the lab."

"Uh, for what reason?" the assistant asked hesitantly.

"For further genetic testing," Ninnemann replied, pointing to a section of the genetic report.

In a garden apartment in the central district, a tall, slender figure stood before the floor-to-ceiling window.

The man, nearly 6'1" tall, had long limbs and a relaxed posture. His facial features were sharp and well-defined, and when he wasn't smiling, his deep-set eyes and straight lips gave him the appearance of a cold, indifferent deity looking down upon the world.

Charles, who had been rubbing his chin thoughtfully, remarked, "I suppose that's the advantage of being an S-level? You've recovered half a month earlier than I expected."

Onyx turned at the words, his broad shoulders and straight back stressed by the well-tailored suit pants that hugged his long legs. "Thanks to your skilled hands, Dr. Franz, I didn't suffer any lasting damage."

"When are you going to tell the captain?" Charles asked.

"No rush," Onyx replied with a smile, the chains on his glasses swaying slightly with the motion, adding to his air of refined elegance.

He found the wheelchair quite useful. His carefully cultivated "delicate flower" persona seemed to resonate with Cora, often garnering his unexpected support.

"Onyx!" The room door burst open as Cora stormed in, her voice loud and impatient. "Svetlana said she'll accompany us to..."

Onyx's thoughts were abruptly interrupted as Cora barged in, his expression shifting to one of helpless resignation. "Cora, could you at least knock before entering my room?"

But Cora didn't seem to hear him, her mouth forming a perfect 'O' shape.

This was the first time she had seen Onyx standing so effortlessly, without the aid of cumbersome crutches or the urgency of just finishing a painkiller shot. He was simply standing there, using his own two legs, whole and unassisted.

Outside the window, the golden light of dawn cast a warm glow, with countless flying vessels zipping back and forth. Onyx's superior profile stood in the back light, bathed in a radiant halo.

He looked... both familiar and unfamiliar. It was as if he had become someone else—still Onyx, yet somehow not.

CHAPTER 31

Burning

In the living room of the apartment, the entire F777 team had been called together for an impromptu meeting.

"Captain, what's up?" Felix asked, sitting cross-legged on the circular bar counter, his cheeks puffed out. He shot a glance at a certain someone lounging lazily in a wheelchair. The others all turned to look as well, except for Charles, who awkwardly scratched his head, not daring to say a word.

"Stand up," Felix ordered coldly from his perch.

Under the watchful eyes of the team, Onyx gave a couple of "frail" coughs, braced his hands on the wheelchair, and slowly stood up. He took a shaky step forward, his knee seeming to falter slightly, causing his body to wobble.

Suchat instinctively reached out to steady him, but Felix, expressionless, said, "Cut the act." Immediately, Onyx straightened his back, and the wobbling stopped.

"...Well, alright then," Suchat muttered, retracting his arm.

Onyx awkwardly froze mid-motion, then nonchalantly shoved his hands into his pockets when he realized Felix would not help him. He quickly adjusted his posture to optimal condition, his stride becoming smooth and confident. He casually strutted back and forth like a male model on a catwalk, then leisurely sat back down.

In the silence that followed, everyone had just witnessed a top-tier runway show. Suddenly, they were all indignant, pointing fingers at him. "You liar! You had me pushing you around just two days ago!" This came from Damian Blackwood, the free laborer who had been tricked.

"Lame," Felix muttered, rolling his eyes.

"Why didn't you tell us sooner? This whole thing..." Charles tried to smooth things over, attempting to avoid further scrutiny.

Yuui shot him a suspicious glance. "Charles, you're his primary doctor. How could you not know his leg was healed?"

"Uh, well, I..." Charles stammered for a while, but couldn't come up with a coherent explanation.

Yuui dramatically clutched her chest, face full of anguish. "I see how it is. You two conspired to deceive us...to deceive our captain's honest heart!"

Felix nodded solemnly. "Yeah, you—Wait, what feelings?"

He quickly pulled the conversation back on track. "So, what's your plan now?"

"Keep my recovery under wraps. I'll stick to the wheelchair for now," Onyx said, crossing one leg over the other, his suit pants stretching tautly over his legs. His hands rested on his stomach, and his expression was relaxed, without a hint of embarrassment. "Besides, I'm used to it. It's pretty comfortable."

"Right, right," the others grumbled, rolling their eyes but readily agreeing.

Although they had exchanged a few sarcastic remarks with Onyx, everyone understood not to spread the word. After all, when Yuki woke up, they all had their suspicions about Onyx's true identity, but no one had ever confronted him. Everyone has their own secrets that shouldn't be pried into, and teammates should respect that.

Taking the opportunity, Felix brought up that Svetlana Yevgeniyeva was planning to accompany them to meet Gawin Ming and his wife, and asked Onyx to pick a time.

After a moment of contemplation, Onyx replied, "The sooner, the better. Let's do it tomorrow."

"Alright," Felix nodded. "I'll go with you."

"Good." Onyx's eyes curved into a charming smile. "District B is full of danger. It's all my fault for being unwell, constantly causing trouble for everyone. But at least our captain doesn't mind dragging along this dead weight. How could I ever ask for more?"

Felix frowned, feeling that something was off.

Felix twisted his mouth into a frown, turning halfway around to avoid looking at Onyx's fake smile. She quietly pulled out her Little Bee terminal. As the responsible captain, she still had to worry about their current mission.

She pulled up Silver Owl's contact and carefully typed out a message. It was to let him know that she and her teammates had arrived at the Northern Base and to ask if they could be added to the exclusive channel for taking on missions.

As she typed, Onyx got up, casually leaning on the bar with one hand, and rested his chin on her shoulder, staring intently at the message she was writing. From behind, it looked almost like he was half-embracing her.

After about a minute, Silver Owl's reply finally came. Felix opened it, only to find a single location pin and an exclamation mark.

Just as she was about to ask for clarification, another message from Silver Owl arrived. "Come."

"A man and a woman, alone in the middle of the night. Is he looking for trouble?" Onyx's smile turned icy.

Before Felix could respond, another message from Silver Owl came in, likely realizing how ambiguous his earlier message had been. This one was more detailed. "Need a hand. You can come alone. There's an S-class threat on-site. It's dangerous."

Felix felt the weight on her right shoulder. Then Onyx's warm breath hit it. She turned her head slightly. "Should I go?"

"What for? Ignore him," Onyx huffed.

Felix counted Onyx's thick lashes and said seriously, "We need his help. It's called…" She thought for a moment, then said, "Reciprocity."

Onyx couldn't help but chuckle. "You've changed. Who would have thought you'd pick up on things like this so quickly?"

"Do you really have to go?" His deep eyes seemed to peer into her soul, his tone soft and mournful.

"I have to," Felix said earnestly.

They locked eyes for a few seconds, and Felix couldn't help but feel a strange sense of guilt, as if she were a two-timer sneaking off to meet a secret lover behind her partner's back. What was she even thinking?

She shook her head, trying to clear the ridiculous thought.

"Fine, go. But take someone with you." Onyx finally relented with a sigh. "An S-class threat, huh? Who isn't? Just don't take any unnecessary risks and be back early. If you get mixed up in something you shouldn't, I won't let you back in." He ruffled her hair with one hand, reminding her not to forget his warning.

Since he couldn't reveal himself in public because of his "condition," he had to pick someone from the team to accompany her.

Felix Lucas was busy testing out additional parts he'd bought from the black market, tinkering with various gadgets.

Onyx stopped in front of him and nudged an uninstalled mechanical arm with his toe. "Hey, driver, you're coming with the captain for a field mission."

Felix didn't even look up as he refused. "No time."

Onyx dangled a lure. "You'll get an extra shopping trip, within reason."

Felix put down the part he was holding, contemplating the offer. "I want rhenium blocks. No deal otherwise."

"100 grams," Onyx offered.

"500 grams," Felix countered.

Onyx turned to walk away.

Felix sighed and quickly compromised. "300 grams!"

Onyx haggled smoothly, "250."

Felix sneered. "I won't accept that number."

Onyx smirked, "270 grams. Take it or leave it. That's all I've got."

Felix quickly calculated. The amount Onyx offered was just enough to upgrade one mechanical arm, but only if nothing was wasted. It was obvious Onyx had already figured out the exact amount needed, intentionally setting the offer at the edge.

Felix cursed him under his breath for being stingy, but outwardly, he said, "Deal."

Silver Owl's coordinates were on the border between Northern Base (District B10) and Delta Island (District B15). These two regions had a long history of conflict, and Cora had heard plenty of stories about the notorious "North-Delta Feud" during her time in Front City. It was all about petty retaliation—today you poach my top Aberrant, tomorrow I'll steal your S-class contract. One day you stab me in the back, the next I'll trip you up. No one ever let a grudge go.

By the time Felix piloted the armed warship (a vehicle they had secured with S-class clearance) to the coordinates, a fierce battle was already underway. Two groups of about thirty people each were facing off, and flashes of Anopower in different colors flickered across the battlefield.

The poor lighting of the night made it hard to see, but from the faint outline of the ground and the sound of waves crashing against rocks, Cora could tell they were on a tidal flat. Seeing the environment, she felt a headache coming on—she hadn't yet gotten over the shadow of what had happened during the day, and now she was wondering if she'd have to go fishing again.

The warship hovered in a low circle, and Cora quickly spotted Silver Owl among the combatants, though he clearly didn't have time to greet her.

In the dark night, a lightning-wielding Aberrant's hands crackled with electricity, sending countless small orbs of energy flying forward like slithering snakes. Silver Owl dodged and rolled through the electric onslaught with surprising agility, taking advantage of every opportunity to counterattack. Each time he raised his wrist, it was to fire a precisely aimed shot. Even if the lightning Aberrant dodged, the energy would still strike another Aberrant on the opposing side, gradually clearing out an empty zone.

Cora's eyes narrowed slightly. Judging by the emanating energy, Silver Owl was up against an S-class Aberrant.

As the electric orbs danced around, the muscles in Silver Owl's back and shoulders tightened to the extreme. Instead of retreating, he advanced, suddenly charging straight at the isolated S-class lightning Aberrant. Every path he crossed ignited in fierce golden flames. Jennifer provided timely support, spreading her Anopower across the area, while the members of "Tustan" moved in to assist.

Silver Owl executed a slide, his abdominal muscles taut as he leaned back just in time to avoid an electric orb aimed at his face. He got in close and abruptly fired his gun. The opponent quickly dodged, but Silver Owl's lips curled slightly, as if he had expected this reaction. In a split second, he changed tactics and smashed the gun butt into the opponent's temple.

Just as the blow was about to land, four black barriers suddenly descended around them, followed by an endless wave of darkness that rapidly swallowed the area. Everyone within and outside the darkness lost their vision in an instant. A small, gaunt Aberrant dressed in a black cloak floated slowly into view, his cold eyes fixed unblinkingly on Silver Owl.

Cora blinked in surprise—another S-class Aberrant, and a spatial one at that? No, Silver Owl's energy was still present, not erased, just trapped in absolute darkness, his sight stolen away.

A pair of withered hands yanked the lightning Aberrant out of Silver Owl's attack range, and a retaliatory burst of lightning struck back. Silver Owl, unable to see, could only dodge based on instinct, but he still took a heavy hit! His high-topped combat boots gouged a deep trench in the mud as he fell to one knee, clutching his abdomen with his left hand, his knuckles bulging with tension as blood gushed from the wound.

Silver Owl was A9-ranked, naturally at a disadvantage against S-class opponents—especially when facing two of them at once. The usual trace of light-heartedness in his expression was gone, replaced by a stern and solemn focus.

"Jupiter Blade, what's this? You head to Delta Island and suddenly don't recognize an old colleague? Why the heavy hand?" Silver Owl's voice was strained but steady.

"We serve different masters now," the lightning Aberrant, Jupiter Blade, replied in a low voice.

Finally, with the two opponents momentarily at a standstill, Cora found her chance to enter the scene. She signaled to Felix, then leaped from the warship.

Thud—

Dust scattered as Cora landed between the two groups, her hands empty, looking like an innocent bystander who had accidentally wandered into a battlefield while out for a late-night stroll. Yet no one dared underestimate her. Jupiter Blade and the gaunt woman beside him, who looked like she hadn't eaten in days, both eyed her warily, as if facing a formidable opponent.

"Oh, you're here?" Silver Owl greeted her with a bright smile, extending his free right hand. "Mind giving me a hand?"

Cora pulled him up from the ground and glanced down, noticing a nasty electrical burn across Silver Owl's lean, flat abdomen. His flesh was torn, and blood was still oozing from the wound.

But he acted as if it were nothing, patting the injury casually and explaining to Cora in a low voice, "They're all from Delta Island. The guy's Jupiter Blade, S4 lightning type. The woman's Sachiko Nokuma, S3 mystery type—her power is darkness deprivation."

"Help me keep them busy. Don't let them take the creature."

Creature? What creature?

Before Cora could ask, the surrounding darkness receded like a tide, revealing a bizarre sight.

Lying on the tidal flat was the enormous corpse of a beached sperm whale, over fifty meters long, its cylindrical head massive, with two small eyes that were stark white in death. A scarlet crystal hovered above it, surrounded by a faint blue mist, and no one dared approach it—it was a rare level 4 mutant beast.

As the darkness faded, several Delta Island Aberrants were thrown into the air, drenched and disoriented. A woman with delicate features stood in the middle of them, wearing a blue dress. Cora gasped softly; judging by her aura, this was also an S-class. What was going on tonight? Was it an S-class beach party?

Thankfully, Silver Owl spoke up, identifying her. "She's one of ours, Sunny Zhao, S2 water type." Sunny gave Cora a subtle nod in acknowledgment.

"This mutant whale was killed by us, but the other side insists it was on their territory and demands we leave it behind," Silver Owl explained. "its pure thuggery, trying to bully us and slap Northern Base in the face!" one of the "Tustan," members angrily added.

Cora Thornton, who had grown up in a fishing village, vaguely remembered hearing that whales were considered "treasures of the sea." Even in an apocalyptic world, their value for consumption, industry, and research far surpassed that of ordinary creatures— especially a level 4 mutant beast like this one.

It made perfect sense that Northern Base and Delta Island would go to war over the rights of this mutant whale.

Sachiko Nokuma, her voice raspy and thick with a poor command of the Alliance language, threatened, "The mutant whale belongs to us. You get out."

Silver Owl chuckled coldly. "Sorry, when we killed it, it was still in Northern Base's waters."

Negotiation was impossible—no way they could come to an agreement. Since talking was off the table, fighting was inevitable. Though dealing with Sachiko's control-type powers was manageable, the S4 lightning-wielding Jupiter Blade was a significant challenge.

He had once been an Aberrant at Northern Base, but Delta Island had lured him away with better offers. No one could fault him for seeking better opportunities, but what really rankled was how he turned around and used his powers against his former comrades, showing not a shred of loyalty.

Delta Island had plenty of other strong offensive Aberrants, and as an S-class, Jupiter Blade had the right to refuse missions, but he didn't.

Silver Owl leaned close to Cora and whispered, "You handle Jupiter Blade. Rain and I will take care of Sachiko Nokuma. Can you manage that?"

Cora discreetly flashed an "okay" sign behind her back.

Silver Owl then raised his voice to draw the enemy's attention. "Jupiter Blade, did you think Northern Base would fall apart without you? Let me introduce you to our new S-class."

Cora gave a polite bow to the two opposing Aberrants. "Nice to meet you. Please, teach me well." She casually picked up a fallen power line pole.

Jupiter Blade stared at her.

Sachiko Nokuma looked puzzled. "What's this new S-class playing at? Mocking us?"

"It's big," Cora muttered, dissatisfied, "but I suppose it'll do."

Jupiter Blade raised both hands, and the high-voltage electricity from his overpowering mental energy instantly changed the color of the night sky. Sachiko Nokuma lunged at Cora, only to be stopped by water arrows and a hail of bullets, forcing her to engage with them instead.

"Your opponent is me," Rain said icily.

In the lightning-lit sky, thousands of fierce bolts shot toward Cora. Dragging the power pole behind her, Cora stepped onto the mutant whale's corpse and launched herself into the air, hurling the pole with all her might.

A ghostly blue twelve-section whip sliced through the air,

absorbing most of the lightning along the way. It crackled with electricity as it flew toward Jupiter Blade like a relentless viper.

"Here, have it back!" Cora was all about reciprocity.

Jupiter Blade's pupils contracted as he hastily condensed the electricity into a fan-shaped barrier to block the reflected attack. The lightning crackled and exploded against the whale's rotting flesh, sending chunks of decayed tissue flying everywhere.

Cora snapped the whip again, the heavy tip moving with incredible speed in her hands. Like a rattlesnake, it lashed out, striking Jupiter Blade's wrist. He couldn't dodge, and he heard a clear "crack" as his bones fractured.

Jupiter Blade was a long-range fighter, disadvantaged in close combat. But Cora's whip followed him relentlessly, slicing horizontally, slashing diagonally, even tracing complex patterns in midair. She treated his lightning bolts casually—dodging what she could and tanking the rest, her physical resilience seemingly impervious to pain.

Crack—

A bolt struck Cora's shoulder, the faint smell of burned flesh wafting through the air.

Whack—

The whip came down hard on Jupiter Blade's back, causing him to shudder in pain.

The two of them weaved and fought atop the whale's corpse, their mental energy pouring out without restraint.

As Jupiter Blade's vision blurred from the beating, he suddenly realized Cora had vanished!

Damn! Jupiter Blade's head snapped up, just in time to see Cora descending in a cross-shaped leap from the whale's head. His face twisted in shock—he had been so focused on her strange whip technique that he hadn't noticed her closing the distance.

Cora dropped like a cannonball, one hand clamping around Jupiter Blade's throat as she slammed him into the ground.

Boom!

Jupiter Blade's body sank into the sand, the force of the impact sending a wave of air that rustled the whale's decaying skin. Cora moved quickly, wrapping the whip around his hands and tying a dead knot. Then she twisted her arm with brute strength.

First came a sickening "crack" that echoed clearly in the air, followed by Jupiter Blade's agonized scream as his arms were twisted cleanly out of their sockets.

The S-class's howl of pain caused the battlefield to freeze for two seconds.

"What the hell," Silver Owl muttered, hoarse. "I asked you to keep him busy, not cripple him."

Cora grabbed Jupiter Blade by the collar and flung him toward Sachiko Nokuma. Already struggling against Rain and Silver Owl, Sachiko was surprised, tumbling like a bowling ball until she collided with the whale's corpse.

With Delta Island's two S-class leaders out of commission, Northern Base claimed a decisive victory.

The Aberrants behind Silver Owl and Rain burst into victorious laughter. Cora dusted off her hands and was about to head back when she noticed the expressions of the Delta Island group suddenly shift to horror as they pointed frantically at something behind her.

She whipped around—

The beached mutant whale's corpse was rapidly inflating from its abdomen. The excess radiation and the impact of S-class mental energy had caused a buildup of putrid gases beyond the limits of its decomposing skin. The stench of rot and decay filled the air, causing everyone on the tidal flat to wrinkle their noses in disgust.

"Whale explosion! Run for it!" someone screamed, their voice tearing through the chaos.

Whale explosions, often referred to as nature's bombs, were the foulest biochemical weapons in existence. A regular adult whale's explosion was said to be equivalent to ten thousand grenades, and this one was a fifty-meter-long level 4 mutant sperm whale.

Both sides snapped out of their daze and bolted for safety. Silver Owl rushed over to grab Cora's hand, shouting, "Let's go!"

High above, Felix realized the danger and dove the warship down, opening the rear hatch. The Northern Base Aberrants scrambled on board, some barely staying on their feet in the chaotic rush. Amidst the pandemonium, Cora suddenly thought of something and broke free of Silver Owl's grip, shoving him away. "You go first!"

"Hey! Don't run off!" Silver Owl called after her, but the stench in the air was so overwhelming that he turned away to retch. When he looked back, Cora had vanished.

"Cora!" he shouted, only to gag again. The whale's bloated body was now blocking out the sky, the radiation levels spiking dangerously close to the explosion point.

A few seconds later, a tiny figure came sprinting back from the distance. Cora was wildly gesturing at the sky. "Felix, take off!"

The warship took off abruptly, the sudden acceleration causing the Aberrants in the rear cabin to slip and nearly fall out. The hatch slowly closed as Silver Owl grabbed onto a railing with one hand, half of his body hanging out, as he extended his hand to Cora. "Hurry, get in!"

Boom!

The whale's distended belly finally burst.

The contents of its stomach—undigested rotting food, vast quantities of methane, ammonia, hydrogen sulfide gas, and countless microorganisms—erupted in a deluge of blood and tissue, raining down like a toxic storm.

Cora flicked out her whip, securing it around the warship's tail fin. Felix rapidly ascended, using the momentum to pull her up. She shot through the foul-smelling rain and poisonous fumes like an arrow, nimbly flipping into the cabin.

The rear hatch sealed shut just as the blast wave rocked the entire warship, its windows splattered with black, decayed matter.

"Why did you run back?" Silver Owl asked sharply, not even waiting to catch his breath. "Do you know how dangerous that was?"

Cora opened her palm to reveal a crimson level 4 crystal, gleaming brilliantly. "I went back...to get the crystal." Her tone was matter-of-fact, then she added with a hint of reproach, "You guys are so wasteful."

As a captain who had once been very poor, frugality was a virtue she took pride in. Northern Base might be wealthy, but F777 was not, and to think they could just leave behind a precious level 4 crystal!

Silver Owl was momentarily at a loss for words.

"Uh...Captain..." someone began hesitantly, trying to get Cora's attention. But before they could finish, the cabin was filled with the sound of people vomiting.

Cora absentmindedly wiped her face, only to have a piece of rotting whale flesh fall off.

She looked down in shock. In her rush to escape, her jacket had been splattered with many debris from the whale explosion. She gave it a shake, and a chunk fell off.

She shook it again, and two or three more pieces dropped to the floor.

Her first thought was: With Onyx de Montclair's level of cleanliness, would he even let her back inside when he saw her like this?

CHAPTER 32

Survived

"Here, the crystal." Cora handed over the Level 4 crystal she had salvaged. Both Silver Owl and Sunny Zhao declined it. Although they hadn't taken down the mutant whale, at least Delta Island didn't get it either. All things considered, it was a draw.

Since Cora was the one who recovered the crystal, it rightfully belonged to her. Thanks to her violent intervention, Jupiter Blade and Sachiko Nokuma were both trapped under the whale, likely unable to escape easily. While their S-rank physiques meant they wouldn't die, they were definitely in for some suffering—just thinking about the stench during the explosion was satisfying enough. They finally got their revenge.

"You keep it. Thanks for the help. This was an A-rank mission, so I'll transfer the mission points to you as well," Silver Owl said, wanting to help her clean up a bit but hesitating, unsure where to start.

Cora, unaware of his dilemma, was overjoyed internally: 200,000 points instantly in the account—this trip was worth it!

The cockpit door slid open, and Felix Lucas emerged. "Captain, oh honest Captain, please fulfill your promise and take me shopping..." The mixed, unbearable smells from the rear cabin hit them hard.

The exhausted Aberrants sprawled out on the floor, and Felix's wheelchair skidded to a halt as his face contorted in clear disgust. Without stopping, he rolled back inside.

He even reached out and slammed the door shut.

Gritting her teeth, Cora seethed silently. What a teammate—leaving his captain to clean up without even helping and slipping away faster than anyone else.

Sunny Zhao, standing nearby, chuckled. Her demeanor was gentle; you'd never guess she was an S2-ranked Aberrant just by looking at her.

With a slight motion of her fingers, the moisture in the rear cabin coalesced into two elastic water spheres, which gently scrubbed Cora's face and jacket, cooling and cleaning away most of the dirt and debris. Sunny then lifted her delicate arm, and with a single hand, she effortlessly opened the heavy sunroof and snapped her fingers, sending the dirty water spheres flying outside.

Cora sniffed herself—much better. At least the stench was gone.

"Thanks."

"I should thank you for the help. I'm not good at fighting. Without you today, we might have been in real trouble," Sunny whispered.

As an S-rank Aberrant, Sunny Zhao had honed her water powers to perfection. Water could be shaped into any form, from square to round, capable of creating and containing anything. Yet, unlike metal abilities, it lacked the fierce, aggressive force. Sunny's powers leaned more towards a hybrid type, with ice arrows being her only effective offensive technique. Thus, her usual role was controlling the battlefield, providing support, and assisting from the sidelines. She used to fight alongside Jupiter Blade, but now they were on opposite sides.

Cora and Sunny's abilities had similarities in how they could morph into various forms, and the two exchanged tips and learned from each other.

After they finished talking, Silver Owl poked Cora in the shoulder. "Captain Cora, done chatting? Is it my turn now?"

"What?"

Silver Owl sat cross-legged across from Cora, his abdominal wound hastily bandaged, his deep gray eyes fixed on her. "Why didn't you tell me you were coming to the base?"

"Uh…"

Onyx didn't allow it.

"And why didn't you tell me your S-rank?"

"It's a long, long story."

Also forbidden by Onyx.

"If I hadn't heard that the new S-rank at the base shared your name, I'd still be in the dark."

Silver Owl scooted closer, his knee touching Cora's leg, and pressed on. "During the marathon, I thought we fought side by side, at least as friends. Were you planning to use me for free labor from the start?"

"Of course not!" Cora quickly defended.

"Then why didn't you tell me? Planning to freeload off me?" Silver Owl's accusations grew wilder.

"Stop, stop saying that," Cora warned, clenching her fists.

Silver Owl narrowed his eyes slowly. "Could it be... you're avoiding me because I confessed my feelings to you?"

Sunny Zhao looked on with a "this is juicy" expression.

Tustan's team members, enjoying the drama, whistled and cheered.

In the rear cabin, Aberrants outside Tustan's team whispered among themselves, "Damn, Silver Owl's got guts..." "He's chasing an S7, not afraid of getting his head blown off?" "I underestimated Silver Owl. He's a true role model, the wildest wolf in the Northern Base..."

Cora didn't forget her purpose for this trip, and, faced with the growing commotion, calmly said, "Just pull me into the channel first."

Without a word, Silver Owl dabbed the ruby earring and pulled her into the "B10 High-End Talent Dating Convention" channel.

Only then did Cora realize the earring was his terminal—fitting into Silver Owl's flashy and arrogant style.

She double-checked the channel's name several times before she said earnestly, "Focus on your work, don't daydream. There's no chance for us."

Silver Owl stubbornly fired off three questions in a row. "Why not? Why reject me? Because of the guy in the wheelchair?"

Silver Owl rubbed his fists, unwilling to back down. "That sickly guy. What's he got that I don't?"

Silver Owl rubbed his hands together. "Why isn't that coward here today? Let me have a go at him!"

"Or is it you just like someone who looks like him?" Silver Owl rubbed his chin, hesitated for a second, and then scoffed, "But that face isn't even his—it's stolen from Jasper…"

Seeing him ramble on, Cora, unable to take it anymore, thought of nothing else but shutting him up. "Yes! I do like him!"

Silver Owl immediately went silent.

"He's mine. Don't bring up the face thing again."

Cora lied through her teeth, "And his health is weak. If you run into him, don't bully him."

"Bully him?" Silver Owl asked in disbelief, clutching his wounded abdomen, feeling colder and colder inside.

Anger made every part of him ache. Turning around, he noticed countless gossiping eyes staring at him from the rear cabin. "What are you looking at?" Silver Owl roared. "You happy to see me get rejected?"

The Aberrants at the scene quickly averted their eyes, not daring to make a sound. Damn, after witnessing Silver Owl's failed confession, would they need to be silenced, too?

The airship cruised steadily back to the Northern Base, carrying everyone onboard. It was close to midnight by the time they arrived. After parting ways with Felix at the elevator, Cora slipped off her shoes, carefully holding them in her hand as she tiptoed towards the bathroom.

She had expected no one to be in there at this hour. The warm yellow light cast a soft shadow, and from behind the steamed-up frosted glass, she could make out the silhouette of a tall figure... someone was showering.

Cora quietly turned to leave without making a sound. But it was too late.

The water stopped abruptly, followed by the click of the bathroom door opening from the inside.

"Back already?"

"... Yeah." Cora stiffened, not daring to turn around.

"All sorted?"

"All sorted."

A low, almost teasing chuckle sounded. "What are you hiding from? Turn around and speak."

Cora awkwardly turned around, moving in sync with her limbs. Onyx swept his wet hair back, revealing sharp, handsome features and deep, mesmerizing eyes. Water dripped down his body, which was wrapped in nothing but a towel at the waist. His well-defined abs and the narrow line of his hips were clearly visible.

Onyx casually rubbed a towel over his head and asked offhandedly, "Need to use the bathroom?"

"Maybe... or maybe not." Whether it was the steam or something else, Cora's cheeks burned, her heart racing wildly.

Onyx took a step forward, his towering frame leaning down over her, trapping Cora between him and the sink. "There's only one bathroom. If you're not using this one..."

His expression suddenly froze as he lifted a lock of Cora's hair, bringing it close to his nose for a sniff. "What's that smell?"

His face immediately darkened, and he stepped back quickly. "Did you roll around in a pile of zombies again?!"

Cora: How is his nose better than Dorothy's?! She'd stood outside in the wind forever to blow the stink away!

Onyx's brow furrowed deeply. He tried to hold back, but ultimately couldn't resist the urge to wash his hands meticulously.

The cozy atmosphere evaporated instantly. Cora puffed her cheeks in frustration, marched forward, and deliberately bumped into Onyx's shoulder before quickly rubbing her head against him. Then she spun him out of the bathroom, shut the door, and locked it.

Since there's only one bathroom, we'll both stink! Deal with it!

The next morning, Svetlana led Cora and Onyx to the Old Town Street.

Old Town Street was a replica of ancient civilization, a rebuilt street lined with a variety of second-hand shops, specialty restaurants, fortune-telling stalls, and rows of yellow cabs. It was usually bustling, home to regular people with B-district residency.

The three of them weaved through the long street, taking several turns until they reached the end. The constant noise of the crowd gradually faded, and they found themselves in a quiet area filled with three-story villas.

After confirming the house number, Svetlana spoke into the visitor system. "Hello, I'm Svetlana Yevgeniyeva from the Aberrants

Bureau. We'd like to visit Mr. and Mrs. Gawin Ming." She scanned her credentials at the camera. A mechanical voice responded, "Verification in process, please wait."

Ten minutes later, after the homeowners granted permission, the gates automatically opened. "Please come in."

The three walked up the steps, passed through a serene garden, and entered the living room, where a couple was already seated.

Perhaps because of good care, the couple appeared to be in their early fifties. Lucia had her hair neatly pinned up, dressed in a traditional Tang suit, exuding elegance and composure. Floating screens filled with dense academic papers and reports surrounded Gawin Ming.

When Svetlana and the others entered, Gawin Ming put down the paper he was grading, lifting his head to scrutinize them with wise, weathered eyes. "I don't recall the Ming family having any business with the Aberrants Bureau."

Both he and his wife were ordinary people who had immigrated years ago. They lived quietly, unaffected by the apocalypse, and avoided contact with Aberrants.

Gawin Ming had a stern, unsmiling face, his hair streaked with gray. When he looked up, there was a distinct sense of scrutiny, typical of an intellectual. As she pushed Onyx's wheelchair, Cora hesitated, certain she had never met Gawin Ming before, yet something about him seemed oddly familiar. She quickly brushed off the feeling.

Svetlana spoke respectfully. "Professor Ming, I apologize for the intrusion. We're here at someone's request. There's a gentleman who wishes to meet you."

Lucia subtly hinted for them to leave. "Miss Yevgeniyeva, I'm sorry, but my husband and I don't entertain guests."

Onyx rolled his wheelchair forward and politely nodded to the couple. "I'm Onyx de Montclair, a former colleague of your son, Jace Ming. We worked together on the same project at Arashi Research."

At the mention of Jace Ming, surprise flickered across Gawin Ming and Lucia's faces, but they didn't ask them to leave.

"You should talk. I'll wait outside," Svetlana said, tactfully stepping out.

Now that they had stayed, the couple naturally extended their hospitality. Lucia waved her hand lightly, and a robotic butler immediately brought over a tea cart, setting out exquisite tea sets and snacks before them, skillfully brewing and serving the tea.

Lucia sipped the hot tea, her voice tinged with a hint of nostalgia. "It's been a long time since I've heard little Jace's name. You were his colleague? What brings you here to see us?"

Onyx watched Svetlana's silhouette disappear before getting straight to the point. "Do you know where Jace is now?"

Cora's eyes widened slightly in shock. Was he really going to be that direct? No buffer at all?

Onyx had intended for there to be no buffer. People's instinctive reactions are hard to hide, even for the most skilled psychologists. He focused intently on the couple, not missing a single micro-expression.

Gawin Ming's face showed a moment of shock, quickly replaced by anger. Lucia's hand trembled slightly as she held the teacup, but she soon regained her composure.

A slow smile crept across Onyx's face, a flash of understanding in his eyes. It seemed this trip was worth it.

Gawin Ming's tone was sharp and direct. "Jace has been dead for fourteen years. He was blown to bits in Loyak. The news came directly from Arashi. As his colleague, didn't you know?"

"And now you're here, saying this? Are you trying to provoke us?" Gawin Ming's chest heaved with anger, his breathing becoming rapid.

"Professor Ming, please don't get agitated. At first, I believed Jace had died," Onyx remained calm, explaining slowly. "But by chance, I met another survivor from the project. She witnessed Jace's survival."

"According to her, Jace left the research institute alone before the accident." Onyx's expression grew distant. "And he took an important experimental subject with him."

"That's impossible! Jace would never do something like that!" Gawin Ming roared in fury. "He's dead, and you can't slander him."

Lucia nearly lost her grip on the teacup, spilling a few drops of hot tea. "There must be some mistake… Little Jace was an honest, upright child. Stealing an experimental subject would be a crime. He wouldn't do it."

The tea Lucia served had a rich, lingering fragrance that tempted

Cora. As the three of them talked, she stealthily reached out for the plate, intending to take a small sip.

"This is indeed hard to believe, so I brought that witness with me."

Onyx sighed softly, pulling out a light screen from his bag. "If you don't believe me, you can confront her directly."

Witness? In the large living room, besides the four of them, there was only one other person. Gawin Ming and Lucia turned to Cora, one glaring, the other full of disapproval.

Gawin Ming slammed the table with such force that it overturned the teacup, spilling golden tea across the table. He pointed at Cora, "You're the witness? Fourteen years ago, how old were you? Why are you slandering Jace?"

CHAPTER 33

An Old Friend

At the critical moment, Onyx cleared his throat twice, rescuing Cora from the unfair blame. "Professor Ming, this is the actual witness."

The light screen timely switched to a holographic projection, and a woman in a researcher's white coat appeared before the three of them—Yuki Hayashi. It seemed Onyx had briefed her in advance because today she was uncharacteristically serious, sitting upright with a solemn expression.

"Fourteen years ago, Jace Ming and I were both researchers in Group G of the Fire seed Project. Jace was the cultivator, and I was the recorder. The day before the accident..." Yuki began recounting in a calm voice.

Gawin Ming and Lucia listened intently.

Cora, still sulking over not getting any tea and being falsely accused, suddenly found a steaming cup of tea in front of her—Onyx had quietly pushed his cup over to her. She picked it up, sipping contentedly, and closed her eyes in satisfaction at the taste.

Lucia noticed the girl's pitiful expression out of the corner of her eye and instructed the robot to brew another pot of tea, placing it deliberately in front of Cora.

After Yuki finished speaking, the living room fell into a prolonged silence. "You're not lying?" Gawin finally asked coldly after a while.

Yuki looked up, meeting Gawin Ming's gaze—his sharp eyes filled with scrutiny, as if he could see through any lies she might harbor.

"I'm not," Yuki replied firmly.

"How can you be sure you weren't subjected to hypnosis or psychological manipulation? What if you're just fabricating these facts from your imagination?"

Yuki sighed softly. "Professor Ming, I've already died once. What you see now is my backup memory. I never expected to be revived, and I doubt anyone would go to such lengths to alter my memory. So I am very clear-headed and telling the truth."

"Jace Ming wasn't just my colleague; he was also a friend. Like you, I want to know why he did what he did."

The heavy silence in the room deepened, making even the air feel dense.

Gawin slowly removed his glasses, rubbing his temples wearily, his eyes showing a hint of tears. He was a man of integrity and seriousness, and learning that his child had committed a crime shook him to his core.

"This question... I can't answer it. My son, Jace Ming, was intelligent and exceptional. He earned his PhD at 20 and was one in a million, chosen to join Arashi. After he started working, because of the confidentiality of his work, we communicated less, but every time we talked, he seemed stable."

"Whatever he did, he's no longer with us..."

"Professor Ming, allow me to correct you," Onyx interrupted. "Jace didn't die. He took the experimental subject and is likely still alive. I need to know his whereabouts."

"If he's alive, why hasn't he come to see us? It's been fourteen years. We never moved; would he really be so heartless as not to return even once?" Gawin asked, his voice filled with pain.

"And what about you, Professor Lucia?" Onyx suddenly shifted his focus. "I believe... you know where Jace is, don't you?" His words sent shockwaves through the room, even leaving Gawin speechless as he looked at his wife.

Lucia set down her teacup and sighed. "Until you all walked through the door, I believed my child was dead. How could I possibly know?" Onyx remained serious. "I bear no ill will towards Jace Ming himself. But the Fireseed Project is the most classified project in the alliance. From Arashi's perspective, that experimental subject must be retrieved."

Gawin and Lucia were people who understood right from wrong, and upon hearing this, they fell silent.

"What kind of person do you believe Jace Ming is?" Onyx asked Lucia gently, his eyes focused on her. "What do you think his motive was for taking the experimental subject?"

Lucia disliked having the pace of the conversation controlled by others. She calmly glanced at Onyx, then suddenly turned to Cora. "Child, do you really like tea?"

"Huh?" Cora, who had been savoring her tea with closed eyes, was surprised by the shift in attention. She stammered, "Y-yes, I do."

"Few people drink tea these days." Lucia smiled kindly. Tea was a cultural symbol from the old era, and tea trees were difficult to cultivate and produced very little, making tea a rarity that was gradually phased out by modern developments.

"My grandfather also loved tea, but it wasn't as good as yours," Cora said earnestly.

Onyx didn't rush her, patiently waiting.

Lucia seemed to be lost in distant memories. "When Jace was little, he loved animals. He was always bringing home stray kittens and puppies, asking me with his eyes, 'Mom, can I keep them?' I'd say, 'Of course,' and he'd be so happy. But his luck wasn't great; those little things were weak and didn't live long. Jace would cry his heart out every time."

"Eventually, he stopped keeping pets and told me he wanted to study hard so that he could one day help them live longer. On the day he started working, he smiled at me for the first time in a long while and said, 'Mom, I'm going to take care of things again. This time, I won't let anything die.'"

"Sometimes I wish he weren't so kind and sensitive, that he could be a little colder toward the world..." Lucia raised her hand to wipe away a tear, sighing softly.

Onyx lowered his voice, "So you've seen him, haven't you? After the accident, you saw Jace."

Gawin looked shocked. "Lucia, you...?"

"I didn't see him, and I'm not sure if it was him," Lucia denied.

"After we received the news of Jace's death, I fell seriously ill, barely able to get out of bed. The following year, on our wedding anniversary, someone left a bouquet of immortelle at our doorstep, with no signature. I asked the delivery person, but they said it was an anonymous sender with an encrypted address, so it couldn't be traced."

Lucia squeezed Gawin's hand. "You had heart problems those years, so I didn't tell you to avoid worrying you."

Gawin squeezed back tightly. "It's okay. It doesn't matter. I know now."

"The next year, on the same day, another bouquet of immortelle arrived. Then the third year, the fourth year... I never knew who was sending them."

"Until one year, the flowers stopped coming. I waited another year, but there were still no flowers. Year after year, I slowly came to realize that the person sending the flowers might no longer be alive."

Onyx calmly asked, "When did the flowers stop coming?"

Lucia thought for a moment. "In the year 40 of the New Calendar."

Her tone softened. "Child, I know Jace made a mistake, but as a mother, I believe he had his reasons..."

"Finding Jace and retrieving the experimental subject is my personal mission. This matter will not be made public," Onyx solemnly promised.

After leaving the Ming residence, Yuki Hayashi couldn't help but ask softly, "Onyx... um, was the person who sent those flowers really Jace Ming?" Onyx had strictly forbidden her from calling him "Jasper" or "Dr. Montclair," so Yuki had nervously settled on calling him "Onyx."

"Most likely."

"Then, if Jace is still alive, wouldn't he have continued sending flowers to his parents?"

"Not necessarily. Let's go back and see if we can dig up anything from that virtual address."

In the end, Lucia had given Onyx the information about the flower sender. With Felix Lucas on the case, they were bound to find some clues.

Yuki murmured to herself, "...I have such mixed feelings right now. If Jace hadn't stolen the experimental subject, he might have been blown up along with me. But he escaped and avoided the accident.

Professionally, I strongly condemn him! But in my heart, I'm kind of glad he survived."

"Why do you think Jace took the experimental subject when he ran? Why didn't he take the other ones scheduled for destruction, like LAK0117 and LAK0366? Why specifically LAK0017?"

Yuki chattered on. Despite her job, she was still a 23-year-old girl at heart.

Onyx replied, "Jace was the cultivator."

Yuki nodded enthusiastically. "Yes, yes, exactly."

"Do you know what specific experiments were conducted in the Fireseed Project?"

"Not really." As a recorder, Yuki had the lowest level of clearance and wasn't a core member of the Fireseed Project. But she had heard bits and pieces about some of the gene fusion experiments... which were extraordinarily cruel.

"Jace knew," Onyx said calmly. "As a cultivator, he had the clearance to take part in some of the gene fusion experiments. According to Lucia, Jace was highly empathetic. What if, just like with those stray cats and dogs, he developed a 'sympathy' for LAK0017?"

"But that's... that's just an experimental subject!" Yuki exclaimed.

Experimental subjects were mindless, artificially created aberrant beings—how could they be compared to cats and dogs?

Yuki found herself at a loss for words. She suddenly remembered a time during a lunch break when she had seen the handsome young man standing alone in the hallway, lost in thought. She had playfully patted him on the shoulder, saying, "Hey, why are you hiding here slacking off?"

Jace had turned around, and it was only then that Yuki noticed his eyes were slightly red. "...What's wrong?" she asked, following his gaze into the lab, where the observation chamber door was closed, and everything seemed normal.

"It told me today... that it hurt," Jace's voice was almost inaudible.

"Who did?"

"Yuki, what exactly is the Fireseed?"

"The Fireseed is hope, the hope of all humanity."

"Yes... the hope of all humanity, but not for it."

"For the Fireseed itself, it burns again and again, turning to ashes.

It's been in a state of despair all along."

At the time, Yuki hadn't understood the meaning of those words, but now, looking at Onyx's statue-like profile, she fell into a deep silence.

Before meeting up with Svetlana Yevgeniyeva, Yuki Hayashi retreated into the light screen. The three of them made their way back through Old Town Street toward the floating car parking area. Halfway there, Cora's terminal beeped. She checked it.

The message was from the Aberrants Bureau, filled with official jargon that made Cora's head spin. The opening was a lengthy, flowery praise of her excellence, but the gist of it was that, because of her rare S7 ranking, they wanted her to undergo further genetic testing to provide some parameters for their archives, to improve the precision of future Anopower assessments, blah, blah, blah…

Cora read through it twice, unsure of what the Bureau was really getting at, and consulted Onyx.

"Ahhhh—!"

A panicked scream erupted from the street ahead, jolting Cora's head up.

A double-decker bus had suddenly lost control, careening wildly as it smashed through the storefronts along the street. Bystanders who couldn't escape in time were crushed under its wheels. Inside the driver's cabin, the driver's face twitched unnaturally, his pupils clouded over with a deathly white film.

It was a zombie! The apocalypse was still ongoing, radiation was everywhere, and with its accumulation in the body, ordinary people exposed to sunlight could suddenly lose their sanity and turn into flesh-eating monsters.

The previous message on her terminal was replaced by a new one:
「C-Rank Emergency Request (Exclusive to B10 District): A zombie suicide attack has occurred on Old Town Street. Please eliminate the source immediately, protect the civilians, and contain the situation as quickly as possible.」

Aberrants nearby rushed forward, aiming to take down the zombie driver.

However, the swaying double-decker bus drifted around a corner and crashed directly into a high-speed, multi-car floating subway train!

Boom—!!

The bus's massive frame soared into the air, and the resulting impact generated a catastrophic explosion.

Svetlana dashed forward, unleashing her power. A wave of invisible mental energy rippled out, freezing both the double-decker bus and the floating subway in midair, as if someone had pressed the pause button. The passengers inside both vehicles were frozen with terror, their eyes darting around frantically, their mouths moving in slow-motion screams. Svetlana was a gravity manipulator!

But her strength alone wasn't enough to hold them. Within seconds, the ground beneath her feet began to crack and crumble, and the overwhelming force pushed backward her, on the verge of collapsing—

The floating subway wobbled dangerously, plummeting rapidly from the sky!

As luck would have it, Onyx was directly beneath the train's front end. Even if he stood up and ran, it would be nearly impossible to escape the danger zone in time. Onyx tried to steer his wheelchair away, but the panicked crowd jostled him, sending his gold-rimmed glasses flying across the ground.

Boom!

At that moment, a slim figure shot forward like an arrow, blue light flashing from her hands. Instantly, her fists were encased in a layer of metal knuckle dusters as she leaped up to meet the falling train.

Thud! Thud!!

With the aid of Svetlana's gravity manipulation, Cora delivered powerful punches that dented the train's front, each strike filled with formidable strength. Despite the overwhelming force, Cora moved with ease, as if she were merely tossing around a sandbag instead of battling several tons of crashing metal.

The immense impact forced the floating subway back, causing it to curl up like a snake and slowly collapse to the ground. Cora jumped onto the roof, grabbed the hovering double-decker bus, and executed a mid-air shoulder throw, slamming it down on top of the subway.

Bang—!

Dust and debris flew everywhere, and what could have been a disaster that destroyed Old Town Street was effortlessly averted by her. Cora then shattered the driver's seat window, yanked out the still-convulsing zombie driver, and snapped its neck with a single motion.

The once-bustling street fell silent. Aberrants and ordinary civilians alike stared in shock at the savior who had descended from the sky. Cora turned around, and Svetlana gave her an enthusiastic thumbs-up.

With everyone's eyes on her, Cora crouched down to search the ground, picking up Onyx's fallen gold-rimmed glasses. She carefully wiped them clean with a piece of cloth, then returned to Onyx, bending down to place them back on his face.

A pair of dimples appeared on her cheeks as she smiled proudly. "Captain, was that awesome or what?"

Onyx played along and praised her. "Of course, it was awesome. Our captain is the best. This team... ahem, F777 couldn't function without you."

His sweet words completely charmed Cora, her heart swelling with pride as she declared, "When we get back, let's tackle some missions and climb the rankings! Captain, we're aiming for number one!"

As for the message from the Aberrants Bureau, it had long been forgotten...

The news of an S7-ranked assault in Aberrant emerging at the Northern Base quickly spread. The first to react was Delta Island.

Footage of Cora rescuing people and stopping the vehicles on Old Town Street, along with the video of her beating up Jupiter Blade and Sachiko Nokuma at the tidal flats, were placed on the meeting table of B15 District's high command.

"Well, let's hear it. What are your thoughts?"

"This is the first publicly known S7-ranked Aberrant across the entire alliance. Both her reaction time and explosive power are top-tier, but I have a question. If the data is correct, she's an assault type, right? Isn't her physical strength a bit too outrageous? Catching a subway weighing several thousand tons with her bare hands is almost at an S-rank physique level."

"Can we get her Anopower report?"

"That's going to be difficult. The old hag has those S-rank reports well hidden."

"Send in a spy and see what we can find out. Also, I've heard she came up from a lower district and doesn't have strong ties to the Northern Base. We should try to recruit her."

"Understood!"

A1 District, The Central. A reporter was analyzing top-tier Aberrant resources from each district in front of a projection.

"...Overall, the number of Aberrants is showing a steady increase... Resource distribution among districts remains uneven, with the highest-ranked individual currently being the S7-ranked Aberrant at B10 District's Northern Base..." The screen flashed a scene of Cora punching the floating subway and kicking the double-decker bus.

"Stop." An official sitting below suddenly spoke up.

"Commander Park, do you have any instructions?" The reporter asked nervously.

Jae-Woo Park stroked his chin, deep in thought. "This Aberrant... she looks familiar..."

A look of realization slowly spread across his face. Ah, wasn't this the one who killed Bloody Hunter Punk in Deep Woods? The owner of that mad dog is still chasing after him like a rabid beast, demanding he hand over the recording of the incident.

"I want to speak with the person in charge of B10 District," Jae-Woo Park ordered.

"Do you mean General Yevgeniyev?" the secretary beside him asked reflexively.

Jae-Woo Park smiled faintly without answering. The secretary quickly corrected herself, "Understood. I'll contact Commander Holland right away."

CHAPTER 34

New Missions

A month was the deadline, and as long as the team wasn't ranked in the bottom 1%, they could stay—but that was for an average team.

F777 was far from average. As a lively, free-spirited, and united team that was rapidly rising to fame, they had more ambitious goals. Led by a brilliant S-class captain, supported by four A-class stalwarts, and backed by two multi-talented, enigmatic allies, their target was obvious—to shoot to the top!

But before their captain could lead them to glory, Cora had to settle her debts. Specifically, the 270 grams she owed Felix.

Felix had his eye on a piece of rhenium with a purity of over 90% at the black market. It was a rare find, and currently up for auction online. Winning it required not just deep pockets but lightning-fast reflexes.

Cora crouched beside him, clutching her wallet with a heavy heart. It was her first time seeing Felix so engrossed, his six mechanical arms manipulating six screens at once, each filled with rapidly updating data. Meanwhile, he furiously typed away on his terminal, the clattering of keys never ceasing. According to Felix, he had installed an automatic bidding system in the auction's backend, one that could place thousands of bids per minute.

In the ultra-high-definition projection, the auctioneer was passionately describing the item. Cora, however, paid no attention, her eyes glued to the large screen where the numbers jumped higher and higher—one million, two million, three million...

"Ding—" The golden auction gavel finally came down. "How'd it go?" Cora asked anxiously.

"Got it," Felix replied, a proud grin spreading across his face. His silver hair brushed his neck as a flash of something resembling "joy" flickered in his unique eyes. "Time to pay up, Captain."

Cora glanced at the last bid displayed on the screen, her voice trembling as she asked, "Felix, do we really need this?"

Felix's wheelchair slid over to her with a swift "whoosh," and he stared at her unblinkingly. "Onyx said you would buy it for me."

There was a certain determination in his gaze, much like a stubborn child refusing to let go until they got their candy. If she didn't buy it, he'd keep pestering her, seizing every opportunity to plead his case.

Cora glanced at his empty pant legs. Aside from mechanical parts, Felix never asked for anything. All he wanted was a new, shiny leg. He was her teammate, after all—what else could she do?

Gritting her teeth, she declared, "Buy it!"

With a noble air, Cora pulled out her terminal and swiped. The "ding" of the transaction echoed as a notification appeared: "3,300,000 NPA credits have been deducted from your account ending in xxxx."

Three-point-three million! Not three hundred and thirty! For such a tiny piece of metal! This wasn't just a chunk of rhenium; it was a gold-devouring beast! Not just her wallet, but a piece of Cora's soul seemed to vanish.

Felix was thrilled, immediately purchasing additional parts. His joy was so pure and straightforward—a mere 3.3 million was all it took to satisfy him. Cora, meanwhile, rested her chin on the counter, her face filled with despair. As Onyx walked by, he casually asked, "How much did it cost?"

Cora sluggishly lifted her terminal to show him.

"Hm, that's about what I calculated."

Realization dawned on Cora. No wonder Onyx had insisted on buying only 270 grams—no matter how deep their pockets were, they couldn't withstand Felix's spending habits.

Onyx leaned in close to whisper in her ear, "Don't worry, you won't lose out. This is just setting the bait. Give him a little taste of sweetness now, and I'll help you get it all back—with interest—later."

Cora sneaked a glance at Felix, silently lighting a candle for him in her heart. How unlucky he was to have a friend like Onyx—poor guy, really.

The next day, Felix was holed up in his room for hours, and finally, his new arm was complete.

Among his six mechanical arms, one stood out—a sleek silver-white design, as radiant as a starship.

"Does it do anything besides look good?" Charles Franz asked, curiosity written all over his face.

Felix's rhenium arm shot out, tapping the terminals of Charles, Suchat, and Yuui Hayashi in quick succession. To everyone's astonishment, the browsing histories of all three of the previous night appeared before them.

Charles had been poring over old photos and videos of himself with Rao Cheung and Lily. Suchat had been diligently studying public lessons from an Alliance Martial Arts Master—resources he hadn't had access to back in Felalakas. And as for Yuui... she'd been chatting with Jennifer, who, to impress her, had gleefully spilled all the juicy details about her godfather Silver Owl's failed confession attempt, much to their shared amusement.

Yuui pressed a hand to her forehead, gritting her teeth. "... Felix, could you respect people's privacy?" she muttered, stealing a guilty glance at Suchat, who was diligently studying even before bed.

After showing off his new arm's capabilities, Felix finally answered Charles' question. "Rhenium has a hexagonal close-packed crystal structure with excellent mechanical properties. When alloyed, it can become a superconductor. I've combined my Anopower with the arm—it's now a powerful hacking tool that can interface with any machine with basic computational abilities."

"Any machine? Even a starship?" Onyx suddenly asked.

Everyone froze. What did that mean? "The latest model from District B. Can you hack that?" Onyx asked again.

Currently, the missions they could take on were limited by transportation and time costs, confining them to the Northern Base area. If they could switch to the fastest starship in the entire New Pacific Alliance, it would save them a lot of time, allowing for a broader range of mission options.

"No way... You're planning to steal a starship?" Yuui gasped. That was a bold move, especially right after arriving at the Northern Base. "It's not stealing if you return it. We'll just 'borrow' it," Onyx corrected.

Northern Base.

A bustling starship terminal.

A newly serviced starship slowly backed away from the energy column, gliding smoothly along the track toward the boarding gate to pick up passengers.

A group of seven, masked and wearing hats, passed by—men and women, young and old, with two young men in wheelchairs and a girl holding the hand of a bouncing child. They seemed as cheerful as a family heading out for a picnic.

As they passed the unoccupied starship, a silver-white mechanical arm flashed in the air, touching the charging port for a moment before disconnecting. The control panel inside the starship flickered for a second, silently switching its route to high-rail mode and steering it toward an empty platform.

The terminal's floating screen automatically issued an error alert: "Error detected on Train C1011, signal lost!"

A silver-haired young man tilted his head slightly, his ice-blue eyes lighting up with pinpricks of data as it flowed into the panel. Half a second later, the floating screen corrected itself: "Error resolved. Today's weather: sunny."

The starship's doors opened, and the seven passengers calmly boarded, disappearing into the sky moments later, just like any other peaceful morning.

Only the passengers waiting at the original platform were left bewildered: Where was their train? They had bought tickets—so where had the train gone?

The channel Silver Owl had pulled Cora into had a strange name, but the missions listed there were indeed of higher quality than those pushed by the system—and much easier to grab. Before long, they landed on a mission they liked:

[Urgent A-level Mission: A large zombie horde has appeared in Rainbow Town, District C27. Detected zombie numbers are: XX level-3 zombies, XXXX level-2 zombies, and XXXX Aberrant zombies. All nearby Aberrants, please assist immediately. Rewards include points and NPA credits based on the number of zombies killed.]

Killing zombies was F777's specialty. All four engines roared to life as the silver-white streak of a starship shot across the sky.

Rainbow Town was a typical karst landscape, with its central city perched atop a plateau, surrounded by wavelike green terraces. Now, however, the terraces were overrun with a horde of zombies climbing layer by layer. In this crisis, Aberrants, from all directions, rushed to the battlefield, joining the fight.

Although this wave of zombies was massive, it lacked a commander, making it far less dangerous than the time they faced the Zombie Lord.

As the starship's doors opened, F777 arrived above the battlefield in the biting morning wind.

Cora and Suchat, the team's melee fighters, leaped into the densest part of the Aberrant zombies and began slashing through them like a whirlwind. Yuui promptly applied buffs, boosting their speed and strength. With their Ethereal Artifacts in hand, they reaped the zombies like Death's scythe.

Damian tied on his signature headband and started moving like he was doing a workout—raising his arms, kicking his legs. With each movement, a wave of ice spikes swept across the battlefield, precisely piercing zombie skulls, making him the most efficient killer of them all.

Felix controlled the starship with one of his mechanical arms while setting up a heavy machine gun he'd bought from the black market. He and Onyx rained down bullets from above.

Standing in a small elevated area within the zombie horde, Cora overlooked the sea of undead below her. She raised her hand slightly, ready to act, when her terminal suddenly beeped. Cora dismissed the notification, only for it to switch to voice mode. With a slight click of her tongue, she glanced at the sender—it was the Aberrants Bureau again. They had swapped out multiple staff over the past few days, constantly pestering her to undergo "further testing." Annoyed, Cora blocked the number and activated Do Not Disturb mode, finally achieving some peace.

She then flexed her hand, summoning a rapid-fire longbow. "Suchat, lend me some Anopower."

Suchat flipped over with one hand, gripping the bowstring as his mental energy surged. The bow's surface flashed with a cold green sheen—a new attack method they had developed after battling mutant moths in the U-Lab.

Cora stepped back, drew the bow, aimed, and released—twang! The arrow pierced through the skull of a level-3 zombie.

She drew and released again, and another level-3 zombie fell.

One arrow after another, each hit its mark. Cora specifically targeted the level-3 zombies, and under the dual impact of powerful penetration and strong neurotoxins, even the formidable level-3 zombies dropped instantly, with no chance to fight back.

In the terraces below, Charles, carrying a black backpack, darted like a scout along Cora's shooting path, swiftly reaching the fallen level-3 zombies and cleanly extracting the crystals from their skulls.

It sounded ridiculous when said aloud, but why was F777's healer on the battlefield? The others claimed it was because of Charles' unique constitution and precise surgical skills that he had been entrusted with the most critical task—crystal harvesting.

Cora patted his shoulder encouragingly. "No worries, I'll protect you."

Damian grinned. "Uncle Charles, you really should exercise more."

The other Aberrants on the battlefield were stunned by their antics. "What the heck? Where did these people come from?"

"They're only targeting evolved zombies and Aberrant zombies. Are they here just to farm points?"

"Secretary Lee, I need all the information on that team within a minute!"

After resolving the zombie horde crisis in Rainbow Town, F777 immediately headed to their next destination.

[Private A-level Mission: Escort mission. Please protect Mr. Willson and his family from the Silver Kela Shelter to White Town, District B13.]

Private commissions like this were rare gems. The client had to pay a hefty deposit on the mission platform and could set the mission's level themselves. Although the points were calculated at the minimum level, the real draw was the generous NPA credit rewards.

As for Mr. Willson, who commissioned this mission, whether he was just naïve, incredibly wealthy, or had more money than sense, he posted it as an A-level mission! Onyx was right—after getting a taste of success, Felix was more motivated than ever and used his newly upgraded hack to snatch up this coveted commission.

At the entrance of the Silver Kela Shelter, Mr. Willson anxiously paced back and forth. A group of Aberrants in matching tactical gear approached him.

"Are you the client, Mr. Willson?" a gentle female voice asked. Mr. Willson looked up in surprise. The speaker was a charming woman with long, flowing hair.

"You are...?" Mr. Willson asked, puzzled.

Snap! The group in front of him suddenly stood at attention, shouting in unison:

"A thousand miles back home, our hearts stay true—F777 will guide you through!" Damian enthusiastically recited the lines.

"Worry-free service, care beyond measure—F777 ensures your safety beyond leisure." Suchat was resigned to his fate.

"F777, the most reliable guardians in the entire NPA, here to safeguard your journey," Onyx concluded with a smile, hands clasped in front of him.

Cora, standing behind the group with her arms crossed, nodded in satisfaction. She had thought long and hard about that slogan— very good, very imposing.

Were these flashy people reliable? He had specifically requested at least two A-class Aberrants!

"So...which route will we take back?" Mr. Willson asked cautiously.

The cities along the way from the Silver Kela Shelter to White Town were mostly overrun, so Mr. Willson's family dared not travel alone. If this group couldn't come up with a solid plan, he would definitely file a complaint with the platform!

"Honored wallet...ahem, client, your exclusive shuttle is ready," Cora said with utmost seriousness.

Mr. Willson followed her pointing finger, staring in bewilderment, eyes widening in shock. A gleaming starship was parked not far away. These people had got a starship?! And not just any starship—a brand-new model from District B! Was it even legal to use a starship for private purposes? Mr. Willson and his family boarded the starship, still in a daze. Hours later, when they finally stepped onto the soil of White Town, they were still in deep disbelief.

Was it really…over already?

As night fell, the seven spent the night in White Town. During that time, Onyx slipped out for a while. The next day, they resumed their journey, continuing to rack up points. After three full days of non-stop action, F777's points shot up significantly, currently placing them around the 60th percentile.

Three days later, they finally had a rare day off. The Northern Base Garden Apartments.

At five in the morning, Cora, her hair a tangled mess, sleepwalked to the kitchen to grab a drink of water. They had taken on three A-level missions yesterday, and everyone was as exhausted as Dorothy. With her eyes half-closed, she groggily made her way back to bed, but accidentally kicked over the trash can. She glanced down—it was full.

Cora stared blankly at it for a couple of seconds before deciding to take out the trash. Dressed in her pajamas, she stepped out of the apartment, only to hear someone calling her name from behind.

"Cora?"

A man and a woman stood together under the shade of a tree. They looked strikingly similar. The woman eyed her up and down, while the man glanced at her and pulled out a terminal to check some footage. Cora thought they looked familiar, and after a few moments of sluggish recollection, she realized they were the S6-level twins— Wyan and Yvonne Rowin.

As soon as Yvonne called out to her, two more unfamiliar Aberrants emerged from behind Cora, subtly blocking her path. Cora's gaze sharpened as she instantly woke up. Judging by their external aura, these two were S-class as well!

Yvonne sighed. "You were really hard to find."

"What?"

Yvonne pointed to her dark circles and cursed in the Galio Empire's common language. "Your location keeps changing. You're running all over the alliance, and we've been staking out for three days with no sleep."

"You've been staking out... me? For what?" Cora asked, thoroughly confused.

"We'd like you to come with us," Yvonne said.

As soon as the words left her mouth, Wyan and Yvonne moved simultaneously, clearing everything around Cora, including the trash bag in her hand.

The next second, Cora noticed that all the radiation in the vicinity had vanished. It felt eerily similar to what she had experienced below the seventh level of Death Hell—her mental powers couldn't resonate, and she couldn't use her Anopower!

Her limbs were bound by an unseen force, and she couldn't make a sound.

Was this… a restraint-type Anopower? A domain-type?

Cora jerked her head up abruptly, realizing it was the other two S-class Aberrants who had made their move.

The twins each grabbed one of Cora's arms and effortlessly lifted her off the ground. As her feet dangled in the air, Cora's mind filled with question marks. What were these people doing? Were they here to fight? It didn't seem like it.

"Apologies, apologies!" Another A-class Aberrant came rushing out, hands clasped together as he repeatedly bowed to Cora. "We mean no harm, but we're really out of options. The Bureau's been sending you messages that you didn't respond to, voice calls you didn't answer, and even tracking your location, which you blocked. Commander Holland gave strict orders—no matter what, we have to bring you in today."

Cora slowly blinked. Commander Scarlett Holland wanted to see her?

Fine, then. If they wanted to talk, they could've just asked nicely. Why go straight to the rough stuff? And sending four S-class Aberrants? Was that really necessary? Seriously, it wasn't. And could they at least let her change out of her pajamas?

A strong spatial fluctuation surged, and the five of them disappeared from the spot.

Half an hour later, Onyx lazily leaned against Cora's door, knocking softly. "Captain, time to head out." No response.

He shifted his position, casually tidied his hair, and knocked again, twice. "Cora, don't even think about sleeping in." It was so quiet inside, it was as if no one was there.

Onyx's brow furrowed slightly, his casual demeanor fading as he turned the doorknob. "I'm coming in."

The bedroom was empty. Onyx quickly crossed the room, touching the bed with his palm. It was ice cold.

Though his expression remained relatively calm, storm clouds gathered in his eyes, a sense of impending doom looming. His S-class mental power surged outward, covering the area like a tidal wave. In the invisible space, a faint trace of lingering spatial energy was still detectable.

CHAPTER 35

Kidnappers

"What?" "What—what?!" "Cora has been kidnapped?!"

The screams echoed louder and louder throughout the entire garden apartment building.

The entire F777 team was dumbfounded. They had just finished packing up, planning to enjoy a leisurely day off, when Damian sprinted into Cora's bedroom, his little duckling backpack bouncing on his back. He flung open the curtains, yanked open the closet, and even bent over to check under the bed. "Sis—ter!!"

"Our Cora, an S7-level powerhouse, never lost a one-on-one fight, and you're telling me she was... kidnapped?"

Yuui couldn't believe it, pinching her own cheek and then, just to be sure, pinching Suchat's thigh. She still doubted her ears. No matter how she looked at it, this was a fairy tale.

"Are you two lovebirds messing with us? Where exactly is Cora hiding, slacking off?" Suchat, unfazed by the pinch, nuzzled Yuui's back, showing for her to look at someone.

Yuui looked up, and when she saw his expression, she instantly fell silent.

Onyx's expression couldn't be described as just bad; it was downright terrifying. He stood by the bar, one hand in his pocket, clutching the terminal Cora had left on her bedside table in the other. His long, dark lashes hung low as he silently contemplated something, giving off an air that was both brooding and dangerous.

Onyx was known for his calm demeanor, seemingly emotionless, his intellect so high that he found little interest in anything. No one could truly grasp what was going on in his mind.

The rest of F777 had joined for various reasons—some were lone wanderers with nowhere to go, others had goals they couldn't abandon—but Onyx was the first to meet Cora. From their very first meeting, he had been in a wheelchair because of a leg injury and was the only one with "no goal" in mind. No one knew what he was truly thinking or planning.

This was the first time Yuui had ever seen Onyx in a rage. Yes—rage.

Even though he was silent, his pale face emotionless, everyone could feel the terrifying pressure emanating from him. It was the S-level aura that could overwhelm others, and given his awakened mental abilities, the sense of suffocation and dread was nearly unbearable.

He was like a volcano on the verge of eruption—the calmer he appeared, the more terrifying his eventual outburst would be.

"The surveillance footage is up," Felix announced. Everyone quickly shifted their focus to the projection.

At 5 AM, Cora, dressed in pajamas, holding a trash bag, yawned as she strolled out of the apartment building. She turned into a shaded area and then... disappeared.

"Conveniently, the camera was in a blind spot." Felix zoomed in and changed the angle, but nothing under the trees was captured.

He switched to other cameras around the complex, scanning each one. Half an hour had passed since Cora vanished, and apart from a few routine visits by the AI maintenance staff, there were no suspicious figures at all.

This made the kidnapping even more mysterious. No signs, no sounds—a living person just vanished? Suchat said coldly, "The perpetrator scouted the area beforehand and came prepared."

Onyx's voice was hoarse. "She didn't resist immediately, which means the person wasn't a stranger." The group fell silent.

"You're saying Cora knew the kidnapper?" Yuui gasped.

"Not knew, but at least recognized them as non-threatening."

If the kidnapper had been a stranger with malicious intent, Cora, with her sharp instincts, wouldn't have hesitated to fight back. The ensuing battle would have been so intense that the rest of the team couldn't have missed the commotion.

Onyx's fingers tightened around the terminal. "To take her away without a sound, the kidnapper must be an Aberrant, and... most likely has control-type abilities."

"The captain is S-level," Suchat reminded them abruptly.

The words seemed disconnected, but the others immediately caught on right! Cora was an S-level Aberrant—anyone capable of controlling her must also be S-level!

"Probably more than one," Onyx sneered, a hint of sarcasm in his eyes. "If I were the one behind this, to ensure success, I'd send two, three, even four Aberrants, whatever it takes."

As their reasoning deepened, the truth about Cora's kidnapping slowly surfaced, but the more they uncovered, the more absurd it seemed. In the Northern Base, who had the power to mobilize two or more S-level Aberrants?

A name loomed large in their minds—the second-in-command of Sector B10, the top officer of the Aberrants Bureau.

Yuui frowned. "Was it Scarlett Holland?"

Charles Franz was puzzled. "But wasn't she all friendly before? Why would she suddenly turn hostile?"

"I think this is the reason." Onyx pointed to Cora's terminal. Cora had set no permissions, so he easily unlocked it.

Onyx had already checked it once. He had released the Aberrants Bureau from the blacklist and opened the barrage of unread messages in front of everyone, pausing on the words "further examination."

For the past three days, F777 had been swamped with missions, barely having time to breathe. With Cora's personality, she'd probably forgotten all about it, or dismissed it as just some spam messages.

Onyx's voice was grave. "Cora's Anopower report has issues."

The team was taken aback. "What issues?"

"The report that was sent back was missing pages. Someone deliberately erased the gene sequence and radiation stability information."

Onyx had noticed the anomalies in the report early on, but since these two items were just routine checks, and seemingly unrelated to Anopower awakening, he hadn't paid it much attention.

"I was wrong," Onyx sighed.

"Scarlett Holland must have discovered something odd but couldn't confirm it, so she suppressed the issue for the time being, waiting for another chance to question Cora directly." Repeatedly urging her to undergo further tests suggested that this matter was crucial to Scarlett, important enough to risk turning against a powerful S-level Aberrant.

"Could it be that they found out Cora is a dual-powered Aberrant and want to capture her for research?" Charles asked, anxiety clear in his voice. F777 knew well that Cora was an S-level dual-powered Aberrant, but they had always kept it a tightly guarded secret, never revealing a word to anyone.

Onyx clenched the terminal, slowly shaking his head. "Dual Anopowers can't be detected by instruments."

"In theory, dual Anopowers have dominant and recessive traits. For example, Punk's Blood Blast is a dominant Anopower, while his Time Rewind is recessive. On a single timeline, a coordinate point cannot host two Anopowers simultaneously, which means Punk can't use Blood Blast and Time Rewind at the same time. When facing an instrument check, he can choose which Anopower to reveal, which is why he hid it for so long."

"Cora's second Anopower involves physical regeneration, a passive, recessive trait. Unless her heart is seriously damaged, like last time, even the R-type scanners wouldn't pick it up."

Onyx had trusted the R-type scanner's capabilities, which is why he had no qualms about Cora undergoing the gene test. Charles was even more confused. "But if it's not because of the dual Anopowers... why would Scarlett Holland want to kidnap her?"

Gene sequence and radiation stability—Onyx couldn't figure out how these two routine indicators could be problematic. What exactly was it about Cora that even he hadn't discovered?

Yuui snapped her fingers, pulling everyone's attention back. "Now that we know who the kidnappers are, how do we rescue her?"

There were some things they didn't need to say out loud—they all understood. Cora Thornton was the soul of F777, the core that held them together. Yuui didn't ask whether to rescue her, but how to do it.

"Dare to kidnap my sister? I'll kill them!" With Cora missing, Damian's claws were out. His angelic face was dark with fury.

"Storm the Aberrants Bureau headquarters?" Charles rubbed his chin, his thoughts unconsciously turning more violent.

"Not a chance," Felix quickly opposed. "Have you forgotten those safety education videos we watched?"

Suchat's input hit the mark. "The most important thing right now is to pinpoint the Captain's exact location."

Onyx's expression shifted slightly as he opened a contact on his terminal and started a video call. The other end quickly picked up, the voice full of energy. "Good morning, Cora. What's the additional request...?"

"Ms. Yevgeniyeva, it's me. Cora is missing." Onyx coldly cut her off. Svetlana Yevgeniyeva's face showed apparent shock.

Onyx's next words blew her mind. "Do you think she might be in the Aberrants Bureau?"

"What?"

Though Svetlana had a lively personality, her mind worked fast. After the initial shock, she quickly regained her composure. "Mr. Montclair, are you suspecting me?"

Onyx replied, "I suspect everyone equally."

Onyx blatantly hinted, "Perhaps you could use your authority to check if anyone... inappropriate... has entered the building this morning."

Svetlana took a deep breath and switched off the screen. "Hold on."

A few seconds later, she returned, her tone firm. "I've confirmed it. There's been absolutely no unauthorized access to the Aberrants Bureau. We're a lawful institution; we wouldn't detain an S-level Aberrant without reason. Why are you so convinced Cora is here?"

Onyx closely watched Svetlana's micro-expressions. Her face showed anger, indignation, and a sense of being wronged, suggesting she genuinely knew nothing. Onyx curled his lips in a smile devoid of any warmth and abruptly changed the subject. "What's Commander Holland busy with today?"

Svetlana's anger halted abruptly, and a chilling thought flashed through her mind. Maybe... Onyx wasn't truly suspecting her.

"... I'm sorry, Commander Holland's schedule is classified."

Her voice calmed as she added, "But her schedule is packed today, with her attending all meetings. She wouldn't pick this time to... you know, go after Cora."

Being accused of kidnapping so early in the morning only made Svetlana more annoyed. She raised her voice, "Cora and F777 are under my watch at the Northern Base. Don't worry, I'll sort this out and give you an explanation."

With that, she cut the call.

Onyx stared at the blackened screen, then tossed the terminal to Felix. "I need information on all the S-level Aberrants in the Northern Base, including their specific ranks, Anopower types, and... current locations."

Felix didn't take the terminal. A rare flicker of hesitation crossing his face.

Onyx and Felix were the only two in F777 who hadn't upgraded to B-sector terminals. One barely used electronic at all, living like a caveman and occasionally borrowing Cora's devices to catch up on news. The other was immersed in instruments but stubbornly used outdated C-sector models, claiming they were "safe and clean."

Felix lowered his gaze, staring at the little shining bee terminal, his voice flat. "You want me to establish a deep consciousness connection?"

Onyx nodded. "Yes."

To track the location of S-level Aberrants, they would need to breach the B-sector's firewall and hack into its network, meaning Felix could only do it using a B-sector terminal.

"... She'll find me." Felix murmured something cryptic. Onyx was unmoved. "What, six years ago, you could take her down at her peak, and now you're trembling at the thought of facing her?"

Felix's icy eyes suddenly narrowed, veins bulging on the back of his hand, revealing his sharp, aggressive stance.

Onyx met his gaze without backing down, his eyes like the mouth of a deep volcano, ready to erupt with molten lava. "You've been playing chauffeur and tinkering with gadgets for so long that you've started seeing yourself as useless? Have you forgotten—you're also an awakened Aberrant?"

The tension between them was so thick that the others were too scared to breathe. It felt like one more word from Onyx, and Felix would sever ties with him completely.

In the dead silence, Onyx asked, each word deliberately, "Under her nose, can you find Cora, erase all traces of your intrusion, and get out unscathed? Can you still do that?"

Felix's expression was blank as he silently picked up the terminal. The synthetic circuits in his arm flickered as he connected to the data port.

As he moved, the entire living room was instantly flooded with brilliant silver light.

Vast streams of data flowed like a galaxy, stars drifting slowly overhead. The team felt as though they had stepped into a void, surrounded by streams of complex, dancing code.

Damian couldn't help but murmur, "...He looks like a tree."

In a distant city far from the Northern Base, inside a vast, silent greenhouse, a withered giant tree stood alone. Suddenly, it sensed something, its roots emitting a soft pink glow. A pair of inorganic eyes slowly opened, ancient and serene, as a whisper echoed through the stillness.

"——I see you, my child."

But the light flickered and vanished almost instantly, lost in the boundless sea of data, impossible to trace.

Yet, the nearly dead tree glowed. Its branches rustled as if a multitude of children were clapping with joy. Tiny sparks of life emerged, and the gentle pink light shot up into the sky, enveloping the entire city in a soft, hazy radiance.

Back at the garden apartment, Felix Lucas still had his eyes closed, but the information of the eight S-level Aberrants in the Northern Base, aside from Cora, was now clearly displayed.

Thanks to the special terminals issued by Scarlett Holland to the S-level Aberrants, and the habit of B-sector residents to carry them at all times, none of these individuals could hide from top-tier hacker Felix Lucas's tracing:

Kenn Oda: S2-level Engineering Aberrant, located ten kilometers away in the Ocean District.

Wyan Rowin and Yvonne Rowin: S6-level Powerhouse Aberrant twins, currently at the Aberrants Bureau building, there for their scheduled performance review.

Sunny Zhao: S2-level Water Aberrant, located thousands of kilometers away in Sector C.

Jirgalang: S3-level Restriction Aberrant, somewhere within the city.

Heize: S3-level Domain Aberrant, also somewhere within the city.

The remaining two unidentified S-level Aberrants were located at the Governor's residence, which had the highest level of firewall protection. Felix didn't waste time trying to break through it further.

The answer was already clear.

Jirgalang and Heize—one a Restriction Aberrant, the other a Domain Aberrant—were both currently at the same location. S-level Aberrants were territorial. Unless they were twins like the Rowin siblings, they rarely gathered together outside of missions.

Dozens of scenarios where these two could have used their powers in tandem to catch Cora off guard flooded Onyx's mind.

"Where is this?" he asked in a low voice.

"The map doesn't label it specifically. It's only marked as a controlled zone with a risk level of H (High Danger)," Felix replied.

Onyx straightened up, slowly exhaling the stale air from his lungs. "Let's move. We've always relied on the Captain to save us; this time, we're the ones rescuing her."

Suchat hauled a crate of Ethereal Artifacts out of a room, quickly strapping them to his arms and legs.

Charles Franz pulled out a few bags of heavy weapons they had specifically purchased for missions, clumsily trying to assemble them. Felix silently took over, his six arms moving in a blur as he pieced them together in an instant.

Onyx led the five of them out of the apartment, with the others following behind him, fully aware:—he wasn't in a wheelchair.

In a brightly lit laboratory, Cora was being dragged along by the Rowin twins, floating through a long corridor. Since there was no chance of escape for the time being, she closed her eyes to rest. Though she appeared to be asleep, she was actually pretending to lull the enemy into a false sense of security while secretly using her mental powers to monitor her surroundings.

A few moments later, Cora was brought into a sealed capsule

room. The room was completely empty, without even a chair or table; the staff had been informed that she could materialize objects with her Anopower, so they had cleared everything out in advance.

Through the transparent glass, Yvonne Rowin opened her terminal, and on the other end, Scarlett Holland's holographic image appeared.

"Cora, I have another meeting, so I'll make this brief. Dr. Ninnemann is an expert in genetic engineering. He'll be conducting a thorough examination of you while ensuring your safety. I need you to cooperate, no matter what."

Scarlett Holland spoke with the authority of someone used to being in charge, her tone a mix of soft coercion. Cora found it somewhat annoying. Internally, she couldn't help but think: Cooperate? I'm already captured by you, with S-level Aberrants watching me like hawks—how is that not 'cooperation'?

Scarlett quickly ended the call, clearly very busy.

The Rowin twins completed their task and left the scene with an A-level Spatial Aberrant, leaving only Jirgalang and Heize behind. The two of them used their powers in tandem, never letting up for a moment, their eyes vigilant as they stood guard outside the chamber.

Cora dawdled for a bit, then slowly yawned and sat down cross-legged.

Bored, she looked around to her left, then her right. Suddenly, a faint glimmer caught her eye, causing her to pause and lift her head. In the completely sealed, small space, a glaring light shone directly down from above, with a tiny red dot flickering on and off high up—it was the surveillance camera.

Cora gazed at it for a while, lost in thought. Her pupils, shrinking under the intense light, appeared as dark as ink against the stark white background, making her eyes seem impossibly black.

CHAPTER 36

The Ruler

The laboratory doors slid open automatically, and a group of researchers in white lab coats entered. Leading them was a middle-aged man with graying temples. He looked like he hadn't slept in a long time, with a tired expression and large dark circles under his eyes. The assistant beside him respectfully called out, "Dr. Ninnemann."

Through the glass, Dr. Ninnemann glanced at Cora Thornton, who was sitting on the ground, then lowered his head to review the Anopower report on the display.

After a few seconds, he looked up again. Seeing her in person, Cora appeared so normal that no one would suspect she harbored radiation levels twenty times higher than the average person, as if she were carrying a ticking nuclear bomb, yet casually walking around as if nothing were amiss.

Dr. Ninnemann pressed the intercom button and calmly said, "I'll be conducting a radiation tolerance test on you. I hear you're S7-level?"

Cora's dark eyes fixed on him. "Yes."

Dr. Ninnemann nodded with satisfaction. "Good. Your physical condition meets the requirements. The testing process will be grueling, so try to endure it as best you can. Your vital signs will be monitored throughout. If it becomes too much, just raise your hand, and I'll stop."

Feigning concern, Cora rolled her eyes dramatically.

Dr. Ninnemann remained unbothered. "Begin."

Inside the capsule chamber, four overhead embedded RF lamps switched on, causing Cora to instinctively squint against the bright light.

Dr. Ninnemann waited in place for a moment. "Radiation levels?"

"23%... 35%... 41%... 48%!" The assistant's voice gradually shifted in pitch. His surprise was understandable—the data had already surpassed their highest recorded levels, previously achieved by a Fallen, with a critical point of only 47.75%.

Cora sat quietly in the capsule chamber, cross-legged, as if completely unaffected by the increasing radiation. The nausea, vomiting, bleeding, and decay that should have manifested were entirely absent.

Dr. Ninnemann turned to the resonance spectrometer. The images showed that Cora's organs were functioning normally. The only notable aspect was the massive amount of radiation within her chest, which seemed to be greedily absorbing energy.

"Mental power levels?" he asked.

"Stable at 12,000," the assistant reported.

For an S7-level Aberrant, mental power typically fluctuated between 8,000 and 13,000, meaning that the current radiation increase had no significant effect on Cora's mental strength.

"Increase the radiation levels," Dr. Ninnemann instructed calmly.

The assistant, nervous, carefully operated the machine without the slightest error. Following Dr. Ninnemann's orders, he adjusted the levels to 50%, then pushed it to 90%, paused briefly at 100%, and finally cranked it up to 120%.

"Stop," Dr. Ninnemann raised his hand.

Cora felt a vague discomfort, but it wasn't the increasing radiation that bothered her. It was the oppressive atmosphere of the environment—the glaring lights overhead, the flashing red indicators, the white-coated researchers bustling in and out. Her eyes lost focus, and she experienced auditory hallucinations, a voice screaming hysterically in her ears, like some desperate, dying animal.

Taking a deep breath, Cora irritably stood up, covering her ears with her hands and pacing back and forth in the narrow space.

"Record: Radiation exceeded 120%. The subject shows significant anxiety, pacing behavior. DNA double helix normal. Organ functions normal. Mental power... huh?" Dr. Ninnemann's eyes widened slightly in surprise. "Mental power is at 14,000."

The surrounding assistants collectively gasped. Not only was the subject unscathed by the terrifying radiation levels, but her surging mental power had already reached S8 levels!

A strange gleam appeared in Dr. Ninnemann's eyes as he clenched the display, unable to resist stepping closer to the glass, his nose almost touching it. "Record: Radiation exceeded 120%. The subject is showing signs of a second awakening."

"Increase the radiation!"

"Doctor..." the assistant stammered, "The radiation is at 130%, the dial is maxed out."

The machine they were using had a limited gauge, with the maximum setting at 130%. Yet, astonishingly, even at the highest level, Cora seemed to have no upper limit to her radiation tolerance.

The discomfort in Cora's body intensified. Under the extreme radiation, her skin burned as if on fire, her cells dying off in massive quantities only to rapidly regenerate. Something within her seemed eager to burst out, to take control of her body. Her limbs spasmed, and she stumbled forward a couple of steps.

Bang—!!

A thunderous crash echoed through the chamber as Cora slammed her fist into the glass. Blood gushed from her hand, but despite the glass being specially reinforced, it didn't shatter. However, the entire laboratory floor trembled violently, the force of the impact causing the researchers outside to retreat in fear.

Bloodshot veins surfaced in Cora's eyes as she pressed her face against the glass, staring unblinkingly at the people in white coats. Dr. Ninnemann glanced at the spectrometer—the radiation in Cora's body was being absorbed at an alarming rate, with all her organ functions becoming erratic.

"Stop," Dr. Ninnemann ordered.

The assistant, relieved, quickly pressed the pause button.

Dr. Ninnemann spoke slowly. "Record: Radiation exceeded 130%. The subject's anxiety increased, emotions nearing the point of losing control. Mental power level... 18,000."

The room fell into a dead silence. After a long pause, the sound of someone gulping could be clearly heard.

18,000—what did that number mean? It was theoretically an S9 level. If Cora wanted to, she could not only crush them like ants, but she could also effortlessly destroy an entire city.

As the radiation in the capsule stabilized, Cora's mental power gradually decreased back to 12,000, and her other vitals returned to normal.

"Administer the nutrient solution," Dr. Ninnemann ordered quietly.

A small hatch opened in the ceiling, dropping a bag of liquid onto the floor. Cora didn't touch it. She curled up in a corner like a wary young beast, her eyes wide open—watching everyone.

Dr. Ninnemann fell into deep thought, his expression unusually hesitant. "Professor? Is something wrong?" the assistant asked.

"Her physique is too unique. Is there any way we can convince her to cooperate with us for long-term experiments?"

"But Commander Holland said... this 'examination' is a onetime thing," the assistant reminded him cautiously, swallowing nervously,"After all, she's an S7-level Aberrant. Just getting her here once was no small feat."

Though he said this, the assistant couldn't help but secretly think: Sure, Commander Holland requested the examination, but your approach was a bit too harsh. You didn't even give her a heads-up before subjecting her to a radiation test. If this S7 doesn't come after you for revenge, it's practically a miracle.

Dr. Ninnemann also realized the slim chances. "Then have Commander Holland replace this machine with one that has a higher gauge."

The assistant blinked. "...Now?"

Dr. Ninnemann's expression remained impassive. "If she wants results, then yes, now."

Before the assistant could react, several Aberrants in security uniforms rushed into the lab. "Dr. Ninnemann, the laboratory is under attack! You need to evacuate immediately!"

"Attack?" Dr. Ninnemann repeated incredulously. "Didn't you say when you brought me here that this place had security second only to the Aberrants Bureau?"

Outside the laboratory, F777 was tearing through the defenses with full force.

A blizzard raged overhead, a disorienting fog that would confuse anyone who stepped into it, coupled with shadows moving like deadly phantoms. Bright flashes of Anopower struck precisely into the crowd, and even though many high-level Aberrants were guarding the lab, this fearless six-person team was unstoppable.

"How much longer?" Onyx asked.

"Two minutes," Felix replied.

The laboratory's protective door was made of special materials, impervious to both fire and water. Even when Suchat struck it with all his might, it only left a faint mark. Felix quickly hacked through the firewall, and two minutes later, the door creaked open slightly. F777 fought off the security that rushed out and quickly entered the facility.

"Time is short. The Aberrants Bureau has already received the alert. Reinforcements are expected to arrive in ten minutes," Felix reminded them.

"Find Cora first," Onyx ordered decisively. They headed straight for the laboratory, catching Scarlett Holland off guard. By the time she realized what was happening, it would be too late for her to escape.

In the bright hallway, security personnel shouted desperately, "Quick! Notify Dr. Ninnemann to evacuate!"

A gust of wind blew by, and the shouting man fell to the ground, clutching his head and writhing in agony as a searing pain tore through his mind.

A young man dressed in black crouched down, his cold eyes staring at him. "The Dr. Ninnemann you mentioned... that wouldn't be Ninnemann Ninnemann, would it?"

The security guard's face showed shock, as if wondering: how did you know? Onyx's expression remained inscrutable as he stepped over the guard and quickly made his way deeper into the lab.

"Dr. Ninnemann, you need to leave now!"

"You go ahead. I need to retrieve the research data."

"No data is worth more than your life, Doctor! Your safety comes first!" urged one of the security guards, growing anxious.

"What do you know? Without the data, the research can't proceed. If we had the data... if we had the data, I wouldn't still be stuck doing basic tests!" Dr. Ninnemann's voice rose sharply, his chest heaving with frustration.

Click, click, click—

The steady sound of footsteps echoed like a death knell in Dr. Ninnemann's ears, as a tall figure walked against the light in the hallway, stopping in front of him.

The security guard beside him reacted with panic, raising his gun to aim at the intruder, but in a flash, Suchat appeared behind him and swiftly disarmed him with a few quick moves.

Screams filled the air, alarms blared, and the sound of hurried footsteps fleeing the scene echoed through the corridor.

Holding a stack of documents, Dr. Ninnemann was also shaken, his nerves on edge. He looked up, startled when he met the stony gaze of the young man in black. "Long time no see, Dr. Ninnemann," Onyx spoke calmly.

"Old Montclair?" Dr. Ninnemann blurted out, but then his eyes hardened as he quickly corrected himself. "No, Old Montclair is dead... It's you."

Dr. Ninnemann's expression grew dazed. "You're still alive. You're actually... still alive?"

Onyx stopped in front of him. "Where is Cora?"

Dr. Ninnemann covered his face, torn between laughter and tears. "If I'd known you were still alive, I wouldn't have bothered with all this..."

"Dr. Ninnemann, we can catch up later. Where is Cora?"

"Cora?" Dr. Ninnemann looked puzzled for a moment before it clicked. "You mean the S7 that Scarlett Holland sent over?"

Onyx nodded. "Whatever you've done, release her immediately."

To his surprise, Dr. Ninnemann refused outright. "I can't release her! Not right now."

"She just underwent a radiation tolerance test. Her accumulated levels are too high. Even the slightest stimulus could push her over the edge."

"Radiation test?" Onyx's eyes darkened with concern.

Uncertain of Onyx's relationship with Dr. Ninnemann, the scientist shared everything without hesitation. He handed over a display showing Cora's complete Anopower report. "You're an expert.

Take a look by yourself. Given her condition, these tests were necessary, and the sooner, the better."

"Setting aside the unknown source of her excessive radiation, just the hidden gene sequences—if we don't figure out where they came from, you know very well what could happen if they erupt someday."

Outside the capsule chamber, Jirgalang had been resting with his eyes closed. The moment he noticed the person beside him stand up, he immediately questioned, "Where are you going?"

Heize shrugged nonchalantly. "I'm bored. Just stretching my legs."

"Don't forget our mission," Jirgalang warned sternly.

"Mind your own business," Heize retorted sarcastically. Though both were S3-level Aberrants, Jirgalang was nearing middle age, while Heize was only twenty, with a promising future ahead. He considered himself far superior to the older man.

Heize swaggered over to Cora, tapping on the glass with no manners. "Hey, what kind of freak are you to survive such high radiation? Or do you have some trick up your sleeve to resist it? Spill it—I'm all ears."

Cora stared at him, her dark eyes unblinking.

Heize found her gaze unsettling, but more than that, he felt a twinge of jealousy. So what if she was S7? She was still a prisoner, dragged into some ridiculous experiment.

Dr. Ninnemann's assistants had already fled in a panic, and no one remembered to turn off the machines. Heize, with his hands in his pockets, sauntered over to the radiation meter and, without warning, pressed the activation button, sending the radiation levels back up to 130%.

"Are you out of your mind? Who told you to mess with that?!" Jirgalang roared in anger.

"Just having some fun. It's not like she's affected," Heize countered, blocking Jirgalang's punch with a smirk. He activated his domain and turned to Cora with a mocking grin. "The doctor told you already, right? If it gets too much, just raise your hand—raise it nice and high."

"Shut it down!" Jirgalang demanded, unleashing his mental power, which Heize met with equal force.

Inside the capsule chamber, the radiation that had just stabilized shot back up to its peak. Cora's dark eyes grew more intense, her cells burning with fiery energy. The chaotic screams in her ears became deafening, and her ability to think was slipping away.

On the spectrometer, unnoticed by anyone, Cora's previously stable DNA double helix mutated rapidly, forming an entirely unfamiliar structure, grotesque as the skull of a wild beast. Meanwhile, her mental power levels had already broken through 20,000!

Cora slowly raised her hand. Behind Jirgalang and Heize, the instruments levitated, bathed in a ghostly blue light, morphing into a fierce sword. The sword's blunt edge struck the glass with a resounding clang, creating an almost imperceptible crack.

The two men who had been fighting abruptly stopped, staring at her in shock.

It was just a tiny, tiny crack, but it was enough. A dam is broken by the smallest leak. Cora pressed her palm against the glass, and with a surge of mental power, she pushed outward—

The entire glass wall shattered with a thunderous crash, crumbling into fine debris.

Onyx's gaze deepened as he scanned Cora's report, which was nothing short of unbelievable.

Dr. Ninnemann watched his face closely and sighed deeply. "Genes are truly amazing. Back then, no one believed you two were father and son. Now... well, anyone with eyes wouldn't mistake it."

Onyx ignored the remark and instead furrowed his brows, asking, "How much over-radiation did you use on her?"

Dr. Ninnemann hesitated before answering, "Uh... 130%."

Onyx let out a cold laugh. "130%? That's about the maximum capacity for standard equipment, isn't it? I've heard Scarlett Holland sponsored this lab. Are you working for her? What exactly are you researching here—'Project Fireseed' or 'Plan Eternity'?"

Dr. Ninnemann fell silent.

"Forget it. I'm not interested in the details. Now, take me to see Cora."

Bang—!!

As they spoke, the ceiling above them suddenly cracked and collapsed. A slender figure plummeted down, pinning another person to the ground with a sickening crunch as bones shattered. Blood gushed from the victim's mouth and nose, and his lifeless face slowly turned toward them—it was Heize, the S3-level Domain Aberrant who had provoked Cora.

"Sister!!"

"Captain?"

The members of F777 were about to rush forward in relief, but their steps halted abruptly.

Something was clearly wrong with Cora. Her eyes were pitch black, devoid of any warmth or expression. She held her sword, blood dripping from her hand, and without hesitation—she plunged it into Heize's heart!

"Ahhh—!!"

The powerful mental force Heize released in his dying moments shattered the glass in the hallway. Thud! As everyone stared in shock and disbelief, another body fell from the ceiling. Jirgalang, though in slightly better shape than Heize, was in a terrible state. His mental field was shattered, blood pouring from his mouth as he weakly crawled away, desperate to escape.

Cora stood up, her sword pointing coldly at his throat.

At that moment, reinforcements from the Aberrants Bureau arrived, unleashing their powers without hesitation, all aimed at Cora. "Cora! Stop!" Scarlett Holland's holographic image flickered to life, shouting in a commanding tone.

Cora, like a bloodthirsty warrior from a nightmare, spun her sword, spraying fresh blood as she swiftly cut down on her enemies. F777 members still couldn't fully grasp the situation, but with their captain in battle, how could they stand by and watch? Without hesitation, they joined the fray.

"From now on, pretend you don't know me," Onyx whispered, shoving Dr. Ninnemann away from the center of the fight.

Cora had gone berserk, leaving a trail of bodies in her wake. Blood dripped continuously from the tip of her sword, and every step she took left a crimson footprint behind. Only a handful of Aberrants were still standing, all of them retreating in fear.

Felix quickly assessed the situation. "Three S-level Aberrants, including Scarlett Holland's personal vehicle, are on their way. If we don't leave now, we won't make it."

"Cora, let's go, okay?" Yuui called out urgently, but the lone figure standing amidst the bloodbath gave no response.

Onyx stepped over the bodies and pools of blood, resolutely approaching Cora. She noticed him from the corner of her eye and suddenly raised her sword, pointing it coldly at him.

"Cora," Onyx's voice was gentle, "it's me, Onyx. Calm down, inspect me." "Do you remember?"

Cora stared at him silently, neither lowering her weapon nor speaking. In her dark eyes, a small reflection of Onyx appeared. The piercing screams in her ears continued unabated, and she couldn't stop the hallucinations from distorting her vision.

Who was it?

It was her.

It was her banging on something—was it a door? Or glass? She couldn't remember. All she knew was that a proud young man was sitting with his legs crossed outside, grumbling nonstop. "Finally found a quiet place..."

"You won't let me work on the project, and I'm stuck memorizing data every day."

"Are you even my real dad? How am I supposed to memorize all this in a single day?"

Bang, bang, bang! She pounded on the door, trying to get his attention.

"Be quiet." The young man turned his head, glaring at her with those beautifully shaped eyes full of irritation. But she was in so much pain—so much pain that she couldn't help but bang even harder. Bang, bang! Bang, bang, bang!

The young man clicked his tongue in annoyance and slowly walked over, crouching in front of her. His slender fingers flashed over the control panel. A bunch of colorful nutrient packs dropped from the ceiling, thudding down, many of them hitting her on the head.

"There, that should keep you quiet, you little thing."

At first, she was confused, but then she quickly tore open the packaging and started devouring the contents. Whether it was real or just her imagination, the pain in her body seemed to ease, just a little.

"Inspect—what an ugly thing you are."

The young man propped his chin on his hand, scrutinizing her before quickly turning away in disdain. "... Is this batch spliced with lizard genes or something?" Her eating paused for just a moment—ugly. What did that mean?

Unaware of her reaction, the young man yawned and leaned back, flipping through some documents with a bored expression. His posture was lazy, his demeanor nonchalant. On his flawless profile, a teardrop mole near the corner of his eye gleamed brightly.

"Cora, it's me, Onyx." He continued softly, "Look at me—just look. You remember, don't you?"

Somewhere deep within her, it felt like someone was calling out to her from afar.

"Onyx..." Cora's hoarse voice slowly uttered the words, and the dark haze in her eyes lifted as her consciousness returned to her body.

Onyx exhaled in relief, stepping forward to wrap his arms tightly around her bloodied form. "It's me. Everything's okay now. Don't be afraid." He soothed her as if calming a frightened child, gently patting her back.

The screams in her ears faded away, and the burning sensation in her cells gradually subsided. Cora looked down at her blood-soaked hands, only now beginning to realize what had just happened.

Aberrants surged into the hallway, surrounding the remaining members of F777. Under protecting the Rowin siblings, Scarlett Holland appeared at the rear of the crowd, her face dark with anger.

She glanced at the convulsing forms of Heize and Jirgalang on the ground and erupted in fury, "All I asked was for you to cooperate with the examination, Cora! You've defied orders and harmed your own kind. Are you trying to get yourself expelled from the Northern Base?"

Cora met her gaze squarely. "Examination—I cooperated."

Scarlett's lips tightened into a thin line. "This is what you call cooperation?" She raised her hand, about to say something more.

"Shing—"

A sword whizzed past her ear, and in a flash, Cora charged through the ranks of Aberrants toward Scarlett with lightning speed. The Rowin siblings were taken aback and hastened to stop her, but Felix's mechanical arms and intercepted the Suchat, who shadowed their every move.

Cora's raw power yanked Scarlett out of the crowd, slamming her to the ground by the throat, her face rapidly turning a deep shade of purple. "Have you lost your mind...?" Scarlett choked out, "You dare to assassinate..."

The aftereffects of the cellular firestorm hadn't entirely subsided. Cora's expression remained stony as she raised the sword high, its blade reflecting Scarlett's terrified face—no longer calm, but filled with sheer terror. "I really cooperated."

The blade tip slowly pierced Scarlett's chest, Cora's hand steady and unwavering, her expression deadly serious.

"When I first arrived here, you said that in the Northern Base, strength is everything." She stared down at Scarlett, her voice icy. "You're just a B-level, aren't you? Why wouldn't I dare kill you?"

Scarlett's pupils contracted sharply, her face turning ashen.

"Wait—"

At the critical moment, a powerful and unfamiliar S-level Aberrant strode in from outside. His arm, as strong as steel, gently deflected Cora's blade. He looked at her calmly, saying, "Please, hold on."

Cora studied him for a couple of seconds before rising to her feet and pulling the sword from Scarlett's chest without a hint of hesitation. "Ugh!" Scarlett groaned in pain.

The stranger helped Scarlett up before turning his attention to both sides in the standoff in the hallway. His authoritative voice echoed, "Everyone, stand down."

F777 didn't move, but the Aberrants from the Bureau obeyed immediately, retreating a few steps, including the Rowin siblings.

The man silently activated his terminal, and a holographic image appeared—a venerable old man leaning against a window, his profile as stern as a statue. His voice was steeped in experience and age.

"I heard from Svetlana that a young S7 Aberrant arrived at the base recently—hardworking, disciplined, and with a genuine talent for combat. She's been going on about it so much that I've become curious myself. Scarlett, I've sent Chu Bai to fetch her—no objections, I presume?"

Scarlett, clutching her neck, bowed her head respectfully.

The old man nodded. "The term 'Aberrant' doesn't emphasize the 'Aberrant' part but the 'Human' part. They are flesh and blood, just like the countless citizens of this base. Never forget that this is our foundation—don't lose sight of what's important."

Scarlett dared not argue, bowing even lower. "Yes, I will remember your teachings."

The old man sighed softly, then looked at Cora, who was standing silently in the corner. "You must be Cora Thornton. I'm Dmitri Yevgeniyev. I'd like to meet you and your friends in person. Would you be willing?"

Cora didn't respond immediately. The elder's tone was polite, and he didn't press her, patiently waiting for her answer.

After a long pause, Cora slowly nodded. "Alright."

"Let's consider today's incident closed, then. Bai, bring her back." The elder's image faded from the air, leaving behind an unspoken tension that gripped everyone.

Was Scarlett powerful? As the second-in-command of the Northern Base and the top officer of the Aberrants Bureau, she could manipulate things in Sector B10 to her will, even forcibly dragging a powerful S-level Aberrant into human experiments.

But one thing had been ingrained in everyone since the Northern Base was established:

—The true rulers of this city bear the name Yevgeniyev.

CHAPTER 37

Resolution

Chu Bai was a man of few words, as quiet as Suchat. At least, since Suchat joined the team, he had become somewhat more talkative. But on the way to Dmitri Yevgeniyev's residence, Chu Bai didn't say a single word, perfectly embodying the phrase "silence is golden."

The hover car sped along the suspended SkyBridge, cutting through the bustling city center and heading toward the outskirts.

Inside the car, Charles used his Anopower to treat Cora's wounds, a soft white glow illuminating the area as the minor fractures in her joints healed seamlessly.

Damian, lying carefully across Cora's lap, looked up at her with wide eyes. "Sister, do you remember Little Diamond now?"

The others also looked at her with concern. Cora's earlier state had been terrifying, as if she was lost in a trance, unable to recognize anyone, consumed only by the urge to kill.

Cora patted Damian's curly hair, finding its texture soothing. "It's alright. I've remembered everything," she reassured softly, prompting a collective sigh of relief from everyone.

In the quiet, Cora stole a glance at Onyx. She then noticed that Onyx was also watching her, his deep, focused gaze unwavering.

Cora felt her breath hitch. She glanced away, but after a moment, she couldn't resist sneaking another glance, only to find him still staring at her.

A blurry image flashed through her mind, but all she could recall was the phrase, "Be quiet." She couldn't remember anything else.

She wasn't even sure whose memories those were, as nothing from her life in District F199 matched these scenes.

Cora's frequent glances didn't go unnoticed. Onyx took her hand and gently smoothed her palm, discreetly tracing the word "later." Cora understood; it wasn't the right time to talk.

Two hours later, the F777 arrived at the Governor's residence.

To everyone's surprise, Dmitri Yevgeniyev lived in an unassuming three-story villa. Although the property was expansive, the house itself was low key and simple, blending in with the surrounding modern skyscrapers of the Northern Base.

The security here was surprisingly ordinary—nothing like the fortress-like Aberrants Bureau under Scarlett Holland's control, or as secure as Rainer Ninnemann's lab.

Onyx's only comment was, "The more a person lacks something, the more they flaunt it."

Scarlett Holland, being only a B-level Aberrant, was extremely insecure, which was why her office building was as impenetrable as a fortress. When they first met her, she only dared to communicate via hologram.

What did this mean? Was Dmitri not lacking in security? At first, the group didn't quite understand Onyx's remark, but the answer soon became clear.

As the hover car entered the villa's grounds, they were greeted by Svetlana Yevgeniyeva, dressed in her Aberrants Bureau uniform. She nodded at Chu Bai.

"Shouldn't you be at work at this time, Miss Yevgeniyeva?" Onyx asked casually as he stepped out of the car.

"Thanks to you, the Bureau is in chaos today, so I've been forced to take the day off," Svetlana replied with a sigh that was somewhere between sincere and sarcastic.

"Yevgeniyeva... Yevgeniyev..." Yuui repeated the names, hesitantly asking, "So, General Yevgeniyev is your...?"

Svetlana smiled wryly. "Yes, he's my grandfather."

Yuui suddenly understood. No wonder Svetlana, merely an administrative secretary, held such chief authority in the Northern Base. Not only could she independently manage Aberrant recruitment, but she could also easily fulfill their requests. It turned out she was an unassuming but powerful third-generation official—a description meant entirely as a compliment.

"Please come in; my grandfather is waiting for you," Svetlana said.

As they passed by her, Cora softly murmured, "Thank you." Based on what Dmitri had said in the lab, his willingness to meet them was likely because of Svetlana's influence.

Svetlana smiled. "I told you, I'd give you an explanation."

Chu Bai led them through the corridors into an old-fashioned study, where Cora finally met the true master of the Northern Base.

Dmitri Yevgeniyev was dressed casually. At nearly 90 years old, his hair was white and neatly combed, his eyes sunken, and his weathered face etched with deep lines and spots, like a map of the life he'd lived. Despite this, his eyes held a calm that came from seeing everything the world offered. His back was straight, and he carried himself with a soldier's discipline—a remnant of surviving both war and time.

But that wasn't what shocked Cora the most. She had seen elderly people before. What stunned her was that Dmitri was an S-level Aberrant! He wasn't intentionally suppressing his power, but he also wasn't in an aggressive stance. Instead, his aura flowed naturally, like breathing, yet the sheer force of it, coupled with the inherent dominance of an S-level, made those around him instinctively lower their heads in submission.

"General, I've brought them," Chu Bai said respectfully before quietly exiting the room.

His use of "General" wasn't just for show. Unlike someone like Ne Kon, who was all bluster, "General" was the highest title in Woodlands, reserved for those truly deserving. Dmitri Yevgeniyev was a genuine military man. He had fought with a gun, bled in battle, dug trenches, and commanded troops during the Old World era.

Dmitri had witnessed the fall of the Old World, the rise of the New Pacific Alliance, and now, the dawn of the apocalypse. His life was like a thick, ancient tome, covered in the dust of time but still holding immense value.

In recent years, due to declining health, Dmitri had gradually retreated from public view.

The Northern Base, where strength reigns supreme. Cora

suddenly recalled this saying. No wonder Dmitri didn't need extensive security. He himself was the most impenetrable shield, even in his old age.

Meeting such a legendary figure made Cora feel awkward, unsure of where to place her hands and feet.

Dmitri broke the silence. "Is that a sword you've got there?" he asked, gesturing to the blade strapped to her backpack. "May I look?"

Cora quietly removed it and handed it over to him.

Dmitri's hands were old, his thick joints barely able to bend. He gently caressed the blade, sighing softly. "I never thought I'd see a young person using something from the Old World. I figured it would be buried with us old folks."

He made a small joke, and although no one laughed, the tension in the room eased a bit.

Despite being in a position of power, Dmitri was nothing like Scarlett Holland. He didn't carry that air of arrogance, but exuded the humility of a seasoned elder. When he spoke, he made direct eye contact and listened with patience.

He slowly spun the sword in his hand and then abruptly asked, "Do you have a terrible impression of the Northern Base?"

Cora remained silent for a moment before nodding sincerely.

Dmitri smiled. "You don't seem to talk much."

Onyx stepped forward to stand beside Cora. "General Yevgeniyev, with all due respect, our captain may not be talkative, but that doesn't mean she should be mistreated. Scarlett Holland unlawfully detained an S-level Aberrant and even resorted to violence. How do you intend to handle this?"

"I'd like to discuss this matter calmly with you," Dmitri replied, handing the sword back to Cora. "Scarlett indeed made a mistake. She's the kind of person who gets stuck on things. I'm not excusing her behavior, but her initial intention was to have you examined, to understand your unusual condition. The situation escalated because you nearly killed two S-level Aberrants. Do you understand the gravity of this?"

Dmitri pressed a switch on his desk, and a holographic display appeared, showing live footage and several reports. Jirgalang was shown in a coma, critically injured and still unconscious. Heize, although barely clinging to life, had suffered severe consequences.

The latest tests showed that because of the disruption of his magnetic field, his rank had dropped to A9. This was the first recorded case of an S-level falling in rank, and once the news broke, it would undoubtedly cause an uproar within the Alliance.

"A few months ago, a dual-type S-level Aberrant was killed in District C. The inspection team is still tracking down the culprit. In these apocalyptic times, every S-level Aberrant is a valuable strategic resource. Scarlett has always valued Aberrants highly. The fact is, you disabled two of her people, so naturally, she's going to hold you accountable."

Cora remained expressionless. District C, a dual-type S-level Aberrant... It sounded vaguely familiar, as if it might have been her doing.

"Do you intend to hold us accountable too, General Yevgeniyev?" Onyx's face was devoid of any humor.

Dmitri waved his hand and sighed. "I've always believed that seeing isn't believing. Cora, I want to hear your side of the story. Why did you try to kill Jirgalang and Heize?"

Cora looked into the old man's calm eyes. After weighing her options, she recounted how Heize had provoked her and deliberately activated the device.

Dmitri nodded thoughtfully. "If that's the case, you've certainly endured quite a bit. How do you wish for me to handle this?"

"General Yevgeniyev, are you aware that Scarlett Holland has been secretly funding illegal research?" Onyx suddenly changed the topic. "With all due respect, she's not a suitable leader. She's extreme in her actions and deeply prejudiced. On one hand, she exploits Aberrants, and on the other, she can discard them without a second thought. Have you considered the consequences of continuing to support her?"

Onyx's words strongly implied that letting Scarlett run things would spell disaster for the Northern Base.

But Dmitri replied, "Scarlett is currently the most suitable person for the job. She has the ability and ambition. Even if she can't make things better, at least she can maintain the status quo."

Onyx noticed that Dmitri emphasized "currently" and "maintain the status quo."

"Do you know what people outside call the Northern Base?" Dmitri asked. "—'The last hope of humanity.'" He spoke each word with deliberate gravity.

"This world will only get harsher, and the despair it brings will grow. Who knows, one day, it might all come to an end." Dmitri's gaze grew distant but firm.

"But even if that day comes, I hope the Northern Base can still serve as a last refuge for countless people. That's the reason I built this city."

"I'm old. I could embrace death at any moment, but I don't want to see my life's work go to waste."

Dmitri let out a deep sigh. "Until we find a suitable successor to fully entrust the Northern Base to, Scarlett can't be removed from her position, despite her mistakes."

Dmitri gazed at the girl in front of him. As a fellow S-level Aberrant, he could more keenly sense Cora's strength. She was like a sword unsheathed, her edge sharp and invincible. Most importantly, her blade would never be turned against her own people.

This was the rarest trait in an S-level Aberrant. Unfortunately, Scarlett Holland couldn't see that.

In a voice weathered by time, Dmitri asked, "Cora, could you give the Northern Base another chance?"

Cora blinked in surprise.

"From now on, report directly to me about your team's affairs. You won't have to answer to the Bureau of Aberrants anymore. If you have any issues in your daily life, talk to Svetlana. And if you ever face any more injustices, this old man will see to it."

"After all..." Dmitri's tone grew cold, "I may be old, but I'm not dead."

Cora recalled the conversation she had with Onyx aboard the F777 on their way to the Northern Base. She had asked him what kind of person had founded the base.

Onyx had replied, "Someone worthy of respect."

She looked at Dmitri, his hair silver with age, and after a long moment, she slowly nodded.

After leaving the villa, Yuui grumbled, "Two weeks of suspension for Scarlett Holland? That's way too lenient."

"Exactly!" Damian chimed in, "That old witch! I curse her!"

But Cora's expression remained unusually calm. "It's because I'm not strong enough."

If she were stronger, back at the apartment entrance, even if both Jirgalang and Heize had attacked, she shouldn't have been subdued so quickly. Thinking back to the fight on Manzoni Street with Punk, if she had killed him outright, he wouldn't have had the chance to use a time reversal.

Cora looked down at her palms. She had been too confident all along.

The direction in which Aberrants awakens varies, and their methods of attack are often unexpected. If she encounters the same situation again, if even more S-level Aberrants come after her, will she be as helpless as she was today?

—Absolutely not.

Though the intense radiation brought unbearable pain, it also awakened new power within her. Cora suddenly remembered Dr. Ninnemann, his hair streaked with gray. In the fight's chaos, she wondered if that guy had survived.

Back at the apartment, Onyx followed Cora into her room.

His expression serious, he pulled out a holographic screen. "Now, let's talk about your physical condition."

Cora glanced down at it, her eyes signaling. I don't understand.

Onyx paused for a moment, then shifted to another topic. "Your grandfather—do you have any photos or videos of him?"

CHAPTER 38

His Mysteries

"Photos of Grandpa?" Cora shook her head honestly. "No, I don't have any."

"Not even one?" Onyx asked, slightly surprised.

Cora began counting on her fingers. "Grandpa didn't take photos, didn't do 'v-r-o-g,' and didn't have a phone." As for a terminal? District F didn't have such things.

Onyx cleared his throat and couldn't help but correct her pronunciation. "V-l-o-g."

Cora puffed out her cheeks. "...Oh." She had learned the Alliance language late, so her poor pronunciation wasn't really her fault.

Onyx continued, "Do you still remember what your grandfather looked like?"

Cora nodded. "Of course I do."

"Then describe him, and I'll draw him." Onyx grabbed a pen, crossed his long legs as he leaned against the window, and began sketching.

"Grandpa was about as tall as Dr. Franz. His forehead was round, his nose was straight on top, but curved a little at the bottom... He had wrinkles here and here, and he had little hair." Cora struggled to describe with her limited vocabulary. "He enjoyed wearing hats. His health wasn't good; he coughed a lot."

About ten minutes later, Onyx put down his pen and turned the holographic screen toward Cora. "look—does it look like him?"

"Mmhmm!" Cora gave him a thumbs up. "It's super accurate!"

Onyx looked at her with mild exasperation. "Really accurate, or are you just being nice? I need the truth."

"It's really accurate," Cora affirmed.

Onyx frowned as he stared at the sketch on the screen. Based on Cora's description, he had drawn a frail old man with drooping eyes and a slightly hunched back, appearing to be around seventy years old but lacking the vitality of someone like ninety-year-old Dmitri Yevgeniyev.

"Cora," Onyx said, sitting down beside her, switching the screen to projection mode. "Did you have any serious illnesses when you were a child? Did you ever go to the hospital?"

"I don't get sick," Cora shook her head. She'd always been robust, rarely even catching a cold.

"Look, this is your genetic report. I've highlighted some missing nitrogenous bases in your DNA, as well as broken polypeptide chains that affect two copies. It's possible there were issues during meiosis or translocation, but this unknown sequence is different..."

As Onyx explained, Cora's eyes glazed over. She pulled a granola bar from her pocket and started munching on it mechanically. The crisp sound of her chewing abruptly interrupted Onyx's analysis.

He twisted his head to see Cora with her cheeks full of food.

They stared at each other for a moment before Cora quickly swallowed, like a student caught daydreaming in class, and sheepishly apologized. "Sorry, I don't understand."

Onyx sighed. "...No, it's my fault."

He quickly adjusted his approach. "In short, your genetic makeup has some issues, and I suspect..." He hesitated to say the rest. I suspect your grandfather might have taken you for genetic modification.

But he couldn't bring himself to say it. Cora was an orphan who had grown up with only her grandfather. To say something like that would be like stabbing her in the heart.

Onyx raised his hand, resting it on Cora's cheek for a moment before finally patting her head. "Genetic issues are like hidden mines. Just because you've made it through the last nineteen years without problems doesn't mean you're safe for the future. Let's sort this out, okay? Don't worry, there won't be any more radiation tests like today.

I'll accompany you to every checkup."

Ninnemann's lab would take a few more days to rebuild, and it had top-tier research facilities and equipment in District B. The only concern was the potential leak of information because of his dealings with Scarlett Holland, but Onyx could negotiate that with other leverage.

For Cora's upcoming tests, he would have to personally oversee every step. Onyx's handsome profile was lost in thought, the furrow between his brows deepening. Cora extended a finger and slowly smoothed out the wrinkle.

Although she didn't believe she had any "genetic defects," she still nodded. "Okay."

In the next room, Yuui was busy searching the Lucas Network for information on Rainer Ninnemann. As expected, with the high clearance of District B's terminal, pages of information quickly flooded the screen.

After flipping through a couple of pages, Yuui's eyes widened in disbelief. "This Ninnemann is actually a genetic engineer as famous as Jasper M.! He officially joined Arashi Research in Year 19 of the New Era."

She tapped the screen lightly and called out, "Hey, Yuki, come out, quick!"

A holographic projection flickered to life, showing Yuki Hayashi sitting up in bed, wrapped in a blanket and muttering sleepily. "Why are you calling me? I stayed up late watching dramas last night. I'm exhausted."

"Come on, an AI can't get tired," Yuui laughed.

"I'm simulating sleep to create an atmosphere, don't you get it?" Yuki retorted.

"Not really," Yuui rolled her eyes, then asked eagerly, "Hey, do you know Rainer Ninnemann?"

"Dr. Ninnemann? I've heard of him, but never met him. Why?"

"He seems to know Onyx de Montclair," Yuui said, a mischievous grin spreading across her face.

"You mean Jasper or Onyx?" Yuki asked, eyeing her sister skeptically.

"Uh..." Yuui hesitated, still unclear about the exact relationship between the two.

"If you mean Jasper, then it's not surprising they know each other —they're colleagues. But..." Yuki suddenly chuckled, "They're supposed to be rivals in the academic world."

Yuui's curiosity was piqued. "What do you mean?"

"He has a nickname—'The Eternal Runner-Up.' As long as Jasper is around, he's always the second-best. He joined Arashi a year later, got promoted to professor slower, published one less paper in top journals, and even lagged in getting married and having kids. Last I checked, he was still single when I was decommissioned!"

"What?! Onyx—I mean, Jasper is married?"

"Yep, it was quite the sensation back then. The news was all over about the 'Golden Couple, a cross-disciplinary union.' And the bride had a very influential background. But in the end, no one could dig up her name or any photos..."

After her rant, Yuki yawned and returned to her "atmospheric sleep." Yuui stared at her terminal, murmuring, "I'm now convinced our teammate is truly a man of mystery."

Suchat, who had been silently observing the entire conversation, finally spoke up. "Why are you suddenly interested in this?"

"Why? Because I'm curious, obviously," Yuui replied, as if it were the most natural thing in the world.

"I thought..." Suchat hesitated before stammering, "I thought you, uh, you and the captain... this isn't right."

Yuui burst into laughter, completely unbothered by the idea. "You didn't think I was interested in him, did you?"

Suchat had no response to that.

"Why would I be?" Yuui stared at him with a teasing smile, covering her mouth in a mock flirtatious gesture. "I clearly prefer innocent little puppies. I thought you knew that."

The knife that Suchat had been twirling between his fingers froze mid-spin. He looked up at her, saying nothing, lips pressed tightly together.

Yuui's red lips curled into a smile. After teasing him, she retreated to her rocking chair, comfortably settling in to manage some remote work. Feeling the intense gaze boring into her back, she pretended not to notice, humming a lighthearted tune:

"I like~ like the smile of a puppy, like a gentle rain~ pouring into my heart." After all, it was her own song, so she could change the lyrics as she pleased.

Her chat notification pinged, and Jennifer sent a heart emoji, followed by a photo of a table adorned with rose petals and a sweet voice message. "Darling~ I've booked a table at the Galaxy Restaurant. Would you do me the honor of joining me for a starlit dinner tonight?"

Yuui glanced over at Suchat, who had seen the message and was now frowning, his ears practically standing on end. Yuui deliberately typed out her reply. "Why the sudden invitation?"

Jennifer replied almost instantly, "Because you're my savior~ My dad always says, 'Repay a drop of water with a bucket of water.'"

Yuui smiled. "The phrase is 'Repay a drop of water with a gushing spring,' but since we're friends, you don't need to be so formal."

Jennifer's melodious tone faltered, and she responded in her normal voice, "Oh, actually that line was taught to me by that illiterate Silver Owl. I'm very cultured myself. And since we're friends, I just want to see you. I want to be your best girlfriend."

The sound of a high chair scraping harshly against the floor cut through the air. Suchat suddenly stood up. "I'm going to train," he muttered, shoulders hunched as he stormed out of the room.

Yuui leisurely sent a voice message, "Sorry, Jennifer, I can't have dinner with you alone. My little puppy is upset, and I need to calm him down." Jennifer sent back a crying emoji and said, "Let's talk business then. Have you checked the commission group? Are you guys interested in the top mission posted today?"

In the living room, Damian was deeply absorbed in his drawing when Charles walked by and took a glance. "Yao, you're quite the abstract artist."

Damian had drawn a twisted-faced witch that looked like the White Bone Demon from a storybook, being thrashed by a group of Aberrants. One of them, a muscular figure, was unleashing a fierce blizzard, with colorful text beside it that proudly labeled him as "The Three-Meter-Tall Hero, Damian."

As he colored the picture, Damian huffed, "This is that old witch Scarlett, and this one here is my sister, who's the strongest. And the tallest one is me! We teamed up to defeat the old witch!"

Charles rubbed his chin, regarding the drawing for a while. "There's something wrong with your picture." Damian immediately turned to him. "What's wrong with it?"

"What about me?" Charles pointed to himself. "You even drew Toto. Where am I?"

Damian blinked a few times, then jumped off the barstool, grabbed his drawing board, and ran off to his room, muttering under his breath, "You don't even fight."

Charles rolled up his sleeves, playfully threatening, "You little rascal, getting cheeky, huh? Who says I can't fight? I'm the one who picks up all the crystals!"

As the two were roughhousing in the living room, Suchat emerged from Yuui's room and silently sat on the couch. Damian looked up at him with his big, expressive eyes, silently asking, What's wrong with him?

Charles, still catching his breath from the chase, shook his head as if to say, How would I know?

A moment later, Cora and Onyx came out of Cora's room. Onyx casually asked, "Where's Felix?"

Charles replied, "He went out—said something about dyeing his hair?"

Right on cue, the apartment door slid open, and a familiar wheelchair rolled in. But the person sitting in it looked strikingly different.

His once light hair was now a sleek, jet-black, falling neatly to his neck. The young man's eyes had been altered to a clear tea-brown, and a pair of thick, black-rimmed glasses rested on his nose. His face, pale from lack of sunlight, bore a calm expression as he gazed at the stunned group. "I'm back."

Cora glanced at his empty legs, then back at his face, finally realizing who he was. "F-F-F-Felix!"

Felix adjusted his glasses, responding with a haughty, "Hmm."

Cora, shocked, slipped into her native tongue, "Why did you change like this?"

Felix cast a quick glance at Onyx before lifting his chin and saying, "I caused a bit of trouble by hacking into the District B terminal. Of course, I erased all traces and did it flawlessly, but for safety's sake, and learning from someone's past mistakes, I disguised myself."

"Oh..." Cora nodded in full understanding. She snuck a glance at Onyx and couldn't help but blurt out, "You two have some pretty similar hobbies, huh?"

Yuui emerged from her room, holding her terminal. Noticing the gathering in the living room, she squeezed through to get a look and burst into laughter. "Well, well, the brothers in misfortune—first the wheelchairs, now the glasses and RPGs?"

Onyx and Felix exchanged a look, then spun away from each other in mutual disdain.

Yuui waved over Cora. "Cora, come check out this commission. Should we take it?" Cora quickly trotted over.

As the group dispersed, Onyx stood beside Felix and asked seriously, "Did you find any leads on that anonymous IP?" He had handed Felix the sender's address he'd gotten from Lucia for investigation.

Felix replied, "The guy was pretty cautious, encrypting his own programs. But it was all for nothing—I cracked it in under five minutes. Based on the last signal source, he's likely in the eastern part of the Alliance."

"But there's something odd. He didn't connect using a terminal; he was using a low-level local area network. I mean, isn't that kind of relic long obsolete? Also, his outer IP was fixed, but the inner one kept changing. I estimate he's using at least 1,500 devices."

Felix's glasses slipped down as he spoke, and he adjusted them awkwardly before continuing. "If the network wasn't so low grade, I'd almost think someone from your side was running a 'junk network test.' Aside from a research lab, who else would need so many devices?"

"No," Onyx suddenly interjected, "there's another possibility."

"—He's in an internet cafe."

Felix looked puzzled.

Having grown up in District B4, Grass Pit, surrounded by the latest computer technology, the term was completely foreign to him. But Felix wasn't about to reveal his ignorance. His fingers twitched as he quickly searched the term on his terminal.

"With 1,500 devices, that would make it a large internet cafe, which makes it easier to stay hidden."

"In some of the more backward districts, like District D or F, it's common for people to use this method to sneak onto the Lucas Network..." Onyx trailed off, suddenly piecing together the clues in his mind. An anonymous sender... Ming... District F... internet cafe...

In a flash, all the threads connected, leading to an idea that seemed almost too wild to believe.

Cora saw the commission that Yuui had mentioned in the "District B10 High-Talent Matchmaking" channel.

Several major rehabilitation, nursing, and food supply companies from District B had jointly issued an S-level commission: "As of 11:00 PM yesterday, the Ministry of Foreign Trade in District A5, Elder Nation, has been out of contact for twenty-one days. Direct communication lines have failed, and all related cooperation has ceased. Teams of Aberrants with A-level or higher are requested to go to District A5 to assess the situation. Those who accept the commission will receive 48-hour supplier access rights."

Cora froze for a moment. This was the first commission she had encountered concerning District A!

She quickly gathered everyone for a meeting, starting with a sincere, "Thank you."

Today had been the most chaotic day in Cora's nineteen years of life. From being kidnapped in the early morning, subjected to radiation tests, losing her mind and entering a killing spree, to being rescued by her teammates, having Dmitri Yevgeniyev mediate, and then the meeting at the Governor's residence—everything had unfolded in a whirlwind of turmoil.

Thankfully, she had returned to her senses, and the F777 was safe.

"Starting tomorrow, we keep pushing for the top of the rankings," Cora said with determination. "Scarlett Holland's actions today won't go unanswered."

"I agree," Charles said. "Scarlett dared to act against you because, first, she holds immense power in District B10, where she's used to controlling S-level Aberrants. And second, she looks down at us. We're just a bunch of unknown A-levels, low on the rankings—nothing but nobodies in her eyes."

Yuui crossed her arms and sneered, "Then let's show her. Not only is Cora an S7, but we're also F777."

Damian banged on the table. "We'll charge up to the top of the Northern Base rankings and take down that old witch!"

Suchat nodded silently, showing his support.

"No," Cora shook her head, her eyes filled with a determined resolve. "Not just first in the Northern Base."

"We're aiming for first in the entire Alliance."

CHAPTER 39

Elder Nation

Northern Base, Outskirts of Foresight City

A helicopter slowly descended, the massive rotors vibrating with a loud hum, forcing pedestrians to step back from the strong gusts.

The cabin door opened, and a team of Tustan operatives in black combat uniforms dropped a swaying rope, gripping it with bare hands as they rappelled down in swift succession, their movements so sleek it felt like a scene from an action movie.

The first to touch the ground was a tall young man wearing aviator sunglasses, with a ruby earring that sparkled brilliantly, exuding a vibe that screamed he didn't care about anyone else. He waved at the group waiting across from them. "Hey, Captain Thornton, got stuck in the morning rush. Sorry we're two minutes late."

Silver Owl's grayish eyes peered through his shades, taking in the large vehicle parked on the roadside. His eyebrows arched slowly. "Well, well, a Lucas starship from B4 District. No wonder you had the confidence to call us over for a meetup."

No doubt, the other group waiting on the spot was F777. They had pulled another stunt this morning, "borrowing" a starship once again. "Yuu~ Yuu~"

Jennifer had just landed, her deep crimson curls bouncing flirtatiously as she eagerly rushed towards Yuui with outstretched arms, ready to pull her into a hug.

Suchat expressionlessly stepped in, blocking her path with a foot. Jennifer glared at him. "What are you doing? I want to hug the beauty."

Suchat remained immobile, his tone as cold and hard as iron. "No hugging fans. Please maintain a safe distance."

She had worked so hard to set up this joint operation between the two teams.

Oh, wait... the alliance between the two teams, and this man's stony face, was ruining everything!

"Let's get on board. We're short on time," Cora coughed twice, raising her voice.

The two teams quickly boarded the starship. The hatch closed as the silver flying craft slipped away quietly amidst the bustling crowd heading toward the Northern Base, bathed in the glow of dawn and morning mist.

Inside the starship, the twelve Tustan members spread out, searching for seats.

Silver Owl moved with long strides, heading straight for Cora, only to find someone already seated beside her—a man dressed in white casual wear, with golden-framed glasses giving him a refined look as he read from a holographic screen, his profile as perfect as a painting.

Silver Owl scoffed inwardly. Onyx was such a fool. Wearing all white on a mission? Not afraid of getting bloodstains on that?

He casually dropped into the seat opposite the two, dismantle and reassembling his "Hellcat," the cold metallic parts gleaming ominously.

Onyx glanced up at him briefly, showing no emotion.

Once everyone was seated, one of Tustan's members spoke up loudly, "Captain, none of us have ever been to A District. We know next to nothing about the Elder Nation. Can you give us some background on this mission?"

Silver Owl clicked the last piece of Hellcat into place, setting it down in front of Onyx before standing up at a leisurely pace. "Sure—"

"No need," Onyx cut him off, smoothly maneuvering his wheelchair past Silver Owl and into the aisle, coming to a stop in front of the group. "I'll handle it."

Silver Owl made a grand gesture with his hand, signaling "please," then leaned back with folded arms, an amused look on his face.

Onyx nodded coolly. "I'm F777's technical advisor. I'll brief you on the mission details. Ask questions if anything is unclear."

Someone whistled lightly from the back, teasing him for stealing the spotlight, but there was no malice behind it. Onyx remained unbothered, activating his screen to project a map of the New Pacific Alliance:

"The New Pacific Alliance currently has five A Districts, each representing the highest authority in different sectors: The Central in A1 District is the political hub, Amyra in A2 District is the military command center, Coin Tower in A3 District governs the economy, Luboni in A4 District is the cultural and educational heart, and finally, Elder Nation in A5 District serves as a welfare paradise for the elderly. Except for the Elder Nation, the other four districts don't offer residency; entry and exit require special permissions. Despite that, 90% of the Alliance's population will never set foot in any A District in their lifetime."

Onyx's explanation was simple and structured, his voice carrying a strange, persuasive power. The members of Tustan gradually dropped their dismissive attitudes, becoming more focused and serious.

Cora, chin in hand, listened intently. Silver Owl watched her face, his fingers twitching slightly, feeling an odd itch. He pulled out a bottle of special-issue grapefruit-flavored energy drink from his tactical backpack and nuzzled it towards Cora.

"The idea of the Elder Nation originated from the famous utopian thinker Smyrna," Onyx continued in a steady tone. "He believed that those who had made significant contributions to humanity deserved to enjoy their retirement in the best possible environment, with the most comprehensive welfare. Smyrna attempted to mobilize the entire Alliance to build a retirement home akin to paradise, dedicated to these honored individuals."

Hearing this, whispers started in the rear compartment, "Doesn't sound too bad…"

"If someone's really done great things for humanity, worked their whole life, they deserve a peaceful retirement." "This expert's suggestions aren't half bad."

Onyx's crow-black lashes lowered, the smile at the corner of his mouth turning cold.

"Smyrna's original intention wasn't wrong, but sadly, he didn't account for human nature."

"The best environment and the most comprehensive welfare always protect the privileged. As long as you have enough power, enough status, and enough wealth, even a crying infant or a bloodstained criminal could knock on the Elder Nation's door and enjoy the finest infrastructure and care in the entire Alliance."

"An A5 District residency is like a free pass in life. Once you have it, you'll never have to struggle again, standing high above everyone else. As various interests flooded in, it gradually lost its original function, becoming a playground for the rich and powerful."

"And Smyrna, the creator of the Elder Nation, was thrown into Death Hell, sentenced to a hundred years of imprisonment."

"Damn! Using our tax money to support a bunch of parasites?"
"You were just an electrician before the apocalypse. How much tax did you pay? I run a company; this is bleeding me dry!"

Two Tustan members who had joined after the apocalypse gritted their teeth. Though the others remained silent, they felt a complex mix of emotions, lamenting both the fate of Elder Nation and Smyrna's downfall.

In the quiet atmosphere, the occasional drift of clouds passed by the portholes. They had already left the Northern Base's perimeter and were speeding northward towards the Alliance's northern regions.

Onyx lightly tapped the screen, switching to the mission briefing page. "Back to the task at hand. Since the residents of the Elder Nation don't produce or work, all resources are supplied externally. Their only administrative department is the Ministry of Foreign Trade, responsible for vetting suppliers and procurement. This department has been out of contact for a full twenty-one days, cutting off the flow of resources. It's understandable that our client is getting anxious."

What Onyx didn't mention was the subtle oddity of the situation. The difficulty of public commissions is determined by the system, and all the clients requested was for them to investigate Elder Nation. So why was this mission rated as an S-rank?

Did Elder Nation fall to a zombie horde or a wild beast wave?—Absolutely impossible.

Not to mention its unique geographic location, Amyra, the strongest military force, oversaw the city defenses of Elder Nation, making it virtually impenetrable.

After understanding the mission's background, everyone felt more confident. Elder Nation is in the Endless Sea in the northernmost part of the Alliance, bordering both the Galio Empire and the Luse Federation. Even with the B District starship at full speed, it would still take about five days to reach their destination.

Onyx returned to his seat, smiling gently and affectionately at Cora Thornton. "Did you catch all that? If anything's unclear, I can explain it in more detail."

Cora proudly lifted her head. "I got it, all of it."

"That's good." Onyx completely ignored Silver Owl across from him. Just as he sat down, he noticed an extra bottle of pink drink on the table.

Without changing his expression, he picked it up, unscrewed the cap, and took a sip. "Thanks, that's thoughtful of you. You knew I'd be thirsty after talking."

Silver Owl barely had time to react. "Hey, that was for Cora!"

"Was it?" Onyx turned to Cora, looking forlorn. "I accidentally drank your drink. You're not mad at me, are you?"

Cora waved it off generously. "It's fine, drink up."

Onyx turned back, his peach blossom eyes curving into a smile as warm as a spring breeze.

He had never seen such a shameless man in his life!

Meanwhile, with the starship entering a stable flight, the Tustan members eagerly started chatting. "This mission has fifty spots, and we're the smallest contingent from the Northern Base, just three teams."

"The other team is Blue Flame, right? Wait, come to think of it, didn't Heize go? Doesn't he usually never miss an S-rank commission?" "Didn't you see the official statement from the Aberrants Bureau yesterday?" "... I was out shopping with my wife yesterday. What happened?"

"An enormous wave of wild beasts attacked Jirgalang and Heize during a mission, and among them was a rare Level 5 Beast. They almost didn't make it. Heize's mental power shattered, dropping his rank back to A9. Commander Holland was suspended because of it."

"What the hell? An S-rank Aberrant getting demoted? That's big news! How did I not hear about it? Am I the only one who didn't know? Hey, F777, did you guys know?"

The F777 member from the "Wild Beast Tide" squad barely kept their smile intact. "Hehe... no, we didn't."

Damian wore an expression of innocent curiosity. "Uncles and Aunties, we were resting yesterday, just sleeping at home all day."

A rare Level 5 Beast...

Five days Later.

The Endless Sea, Northern Region of the Alliance.

Early in the morning, Felix disengaged the autopilot and summoned the control panel, switching the starship to low-orbit mode.

Then he pressed the cabin intercom, his tone flat and emotionless. "Wake up, everyone. We've reached the Doom Sea. I'll be manually piloting the starship through the drifting zone. Friendly reminder: fasten your seatbelts, or suffer the consequences."

Outside the portholes, the sky was ablaze with dawn, casting a golden sheen over the sea. The water's gentle undulations resembled a tranquil, welcoming elder. Although Cora was a fisherman's step-daughter and had grown up by the sea, this expanse gave her a completely distinct feeling. Beneath its calm surface, there seemed to be an undercurrent of hidden danger.

Curious, she turned her head and asked, "Why is it called the Doom Sea?"

Silver Owl, who had just finished freshening up and was returning with a toothbrush in his mouth, casually answered her question. "Because this place brings doom. Every year, hundreds of planes and ships disappear here, and no one's figured out the scientific reason."

"Oh." Cora nodded in sudden understanding. Just then, Felix's morning announcement sounded, and her expression changed as she quickly fastened her seatbelt. The other members of F777 heard Felix was switching to manual control and immediately rushed back to their seats, all wearing similarly serious expressions.

Charles even gripped his armrests tightly, swallowing almost imperceptibly.

Silver Owl hesitated for a moment. His instinct, honed by years of living on the edge of danger, kicked in. He narrowed his eyes slowly, and without a word, tossed away his toothbrush, took a long stride, and leaped into the seat opposite Cora, fastening his seatbelt with a click.

The Tustan members remained blissfully unaware, still laughing and chatting as they strolled around leisurely. Jennifer lounged lazily at the mobile dining table, sipping iced coffee with her pinky extended.

The next second, the entire starship flipped mid-air, the engines roaring violently like a wild horse as it hurtled toward the endless sea. "What the f—!" Jennifer was drenched in coffee, her once-beautiful face now a total mess, but she wasn't the worst off.

The Tustan members standing in the aisle didn't have time to react before the ship's sudden movement sent them tumbling head over heels, spinning and crashing into each other like bowling pins.

In the cockpit, Felix was fully focused, pushing the energy system to its limit. The previously calm sea revealed its treacherous nature, with dark clouds swirling overhead, lightning flashing, and thunder crashing. Massive waves splashed against the front windows, while black, ominous fog closed in from all directions.

Even though the navigation system had long since failed, Felix relied on the mechanical coordinates he had memorized in advance, confidently twisting the controls. The massive starship plowed through the obstacles like a ship cutting through stormy seas, advancing rapidly!

The rear cabin echoed with cries of distress. Jennifer, her hair in disarray, clung to a bar counter like a koala.

But when she glanced up, she saw Silver Owl sitting there comfortably, securely strapped in, laughing heartily at their misfortune.

Jennifer's anger flared. "Silver Owl, abandoning your girl in a crisis, what kind of man are you?!"

Others weakly chimed in, "Yeah, Captain, you... you're really not... ugh!"

Thirty minutes later, the starship finally stabilized, but the sound of retching filled the rear cabin. Onyx softly reminded them, "We've arrived."

Cora eagerly looked out the porthole.

The sky was clear, seagulls soared, and in the middle of the vast sea, a breathtakingly beautiful, dreamlike island stood serenely. This was one of the five A Districts of the Alliance and the destination of their mission—Elder Nation.

CHAPTER 40

Risks

"Prepare for landing."

The starship's announcement sounded again, but this time, without Felix needing to remind them, everyone in the rear cabin promptly clicked their seatbelts into place.

As they approached the island's perimeter, a transparent barrier appeared in the sky, and a holographic sign lit up: "Please proceed through the Supplier Lane."

Next, a small highlighted square area came into view: "Please present access credentials here."

Felix slowed down and adjusted the starship's direction, bringing it to a neat hover over the highlighted area. Cora and Silver Owl activated their terminals and brought up the temporary access permissions they had received after accepting the mission. Two seconds later, the barrier opened a passage just wide enough for the starship to pass through.

The aerial sign also transformed into a clear navigation map: "Please continue along the current route for three kilometers and land at Radiant Hall."

There was no doubt that the Elder Nation's visitor system was very well-organized, but... there was an oddly coercive undertone to it. They had no choice but to follow the route provided by the system, with no possibility of making a detour or exploring elsewhere first.

The top of Radiant Hall featured a luxurious landing pad. Felix found an empty spot and brought the starship down smoothly. As soon as he secured the landing, the ground platform folded open, and the entire starship was gradually drawn inside the building, transferred to a temporary parking level.

After disembarking, the two teams could only take the scenic elevator, which had just one button: "Visitor Hall." "Ding—" The doors opened to reveal a spacious banquet hall. Surprisingly, there were already quite a few people present.

Cora briefly scanned the area and was immediately taken aback—these people were all Aberrants! The chaotic mental energy in the room felt like walking into a crowded marketplace. "Why are there so many people?"

"Fifty teams, of course. Some arrived before us," Onyx explained. The Northern Base was quite far, and even with their non-stop journey, it had taken them a full five days to get here.

"Not just the Alliance," Silver Owl pointed in two different directions. "The Galio Empire and Luse Federation have people here too."

Cora followed his gaze. Although she wasn't sure what permissions the other two nations used to enter, their appearance distinctly divided into three groups, easily distinguishable the Aberrants in the hall.

The Luse Federation, with 90% of its cities in icy regions, had Aberrants who were tall and lean, with deep-set features and a formidable presence. Among them, the most striking pair was a close-looking couple—the man was nearly two meters tall with a build like a powerful polar bear, while the woman, also quite tall at about 6'3", had shoulder-length brown hair and a stern expression.

The Galio Empire group, being a nation of immigrants, displayed a wide variety of skin tones and eye colors, making it hard to discern their origins at a glance.

"What are they doing here?" Jennifer scoffed, her disdain clear.

Silver Owl chuckled. "Girl, your grandfather was from the Galio Empire. Aren't you being a little ungrateful?"

Jennifer wasn't ashamed; in fact, she looked proud. "But my dad made a wise decision to break from tradition. I'm a born-and-bred Alliance citizen."

Onyx, glancing at the three distinct factions in the hall, smiled meaningfully. "Elder Nation is at the junction of the three nations' sea territories. The residents aren't just from the Alliance, so it makes sense they'd want to get involved when they heard the news."

"Sis…" Damian suddenly tugged at Cora's sleeve, his gaze fixed on someone across the hall.

It was a young Aberrant from the Galio Empire, clearly quite young, with freckles dotting his face, thick curly auburn hair, and strikingly clear sea-blue eyes. Despite his age, he was already nearly 5'7", surrounded by people like a minor star.

Tustan's resident electrician leaned over to share some gossip. "His name's Dylan. He's pretty famous."

Damian blinked. "Why is he famous?"

"Dylan is the youngest S-rank Aberrant not only in Galio, but in the entire world. He reached S2 rank at just ten years old. His power is in the mysterious category, known as 'Nightmare Descent', which can put someone's body to sleep while keeping their mind awake, creating something like sleep paralysis."

Damian's mouth fell into a pout.

His pride took a major hit. He had been thrilled about taking on an S-rank mission, but here was Dylan, an S2 at just ten years old, while Damian was only A1 at eleven. Dylan was also nearly 5'7", while Damian guzzled milk every day just to barely reach 4'3".

In terms of powers, and height, and height, and height, Dylan completely outclassed him. It was infuriating!

Damian was officially depressed.

"Silver Owl?" A few Aberrants from the Alliance walked over, led by a short-haired woman with a clean, efficient demeanor who greeted them warmly. "The Northern Base is so far away; I thought you'd arrive tomorrow at the earliest."

"I hitched a ride," Silver Owl grinned, lifting his hand to place it on Cora's shoulder, but thinking better of it, he switched to a friendly pat instead.

"This is F777's captain and my friend, Cora Thornton."

"Glory Ku, captain of Peace Dove squad from Jade Grove (B16 District)."

"The Peace Dove squad," with a man sporting rainbow-colored hair at the back, exclaimed loudly, "F777? Never heard of them.

They're probably not even ranked in the Alliance. Are you guys really that short on people at the Northern Base, pulling together a random team just to fill numbers?"

"We do have a rank," Cora responded earnestly. "We're currently ranked 235,706."

"How much?" Rainbow Hair was stunned for a full three seconds, even digging at his ear before bursting into laughter with his teammates. "Hahaha! Did you all hear that? What rank did she just say?"

"235,706!" Rainbow Hair's exaggerated tone caught the attention of several others. "With a rank like that? Are you sure you didn't just pull together an A-rank to freeload? Are you an A-rank?"

"No," Cora shook her head honestly.

Rainbow Hair then turned to Felix Lucas. "What about you? Are you A-rank?"

Felix didn't even bother looking at him and coldly replied, "No."

"Whoa, and there's even someone in a wheelchair." Rainbow Hair shifted his attention, laughing at himself. "Are you guys holding a disabled person's meetup? Are you A-rank?"

Onyx clasped his hands together and politely said, "Of course not. How could I possibly be A-rank?"

The four A-rank members of F777 exchanged bewildered looks.

Silver Owl and the others who knew Cora's true rank were equally speechless. This Rainbow Hair character was something else. On the one hand, his luck seemed terrible, as he hadn't guessed a single A-rank correctly. His luck was astonishing, as he somehow targeted only the S-ranks every time. Truly, his luck was... unparalleled.

"Enough, Bryan Young. If you say one more word, I'll send you back to Jade Grove," Glory Ku scolded sternly. Bryan mimed, zipping his lips shut.

Silver Owl chuckled, choosing to ignore him. "Why is everyone gathered here?"

"Because we can't leave," Glory dropped a bombshell calmly. "Elder Nation's weather simulation system has malfunctioned."

Weather simulation system? Cora quickly glanced at Onyx—why did the name sound so familiar?

Glory pulled out her terminal and brought up the environmental stats. "You guys came in via the aerial route, right? So you wouldn't have felt it, but the current temperature outside is very high, the sunlight is blinding, and the radiation levels are over thirteen times higher than the normal post-apocalyptic standard. Staying outside for too long could lead to mutations."

"Someone just tried to go out. Within five minutes, their mental energy went berserk, so they had to retreat." Silver Owl asked, "Did you report the issue?"

"We've already contacted Arashi Research, but..." Glory sighed, "We've lost many high-level repair specialists since the apocalypse. The earliest they can get someone here is in two days."

"Why bother telling them?" Bryan rambled again, unable to keep his mouth shut. "What, you think they can fix it?"

Glory took a deep breath and rolled her eyes behind his back. "Bryan. Young."

"Alright, alright, I'll stop talking," Bryan instantly backed down. Glory nodded at Cora in apology, "Sorry about him. He's got a sharp tongue and loves to argue, but he's not a bad person."

Cora frowned slightly. Their access was limited to 48 hours—two days would be too late.

"Wait a minute, if the radiation outside is that bad, what about the residents? Did they all turn into zombies?" someone from the Tustan team asked in confusion.

"Do you think they're idiots? If they noticed something was wrong, they would've hidden immediately—basements, bunkers, whatever—and sent out a distress signal," their teammate replied logically.

"The problem is..." Glory said in a grave tone, "We have received no signals, and we can't contact any of the local institutions." The group fell into a stunned silence, expressions of disbelief crossing their faces.

Suddenly, someone in the corner stood up. An Aberrant, ignoring the protests of his companions, insisted on going outside, muttering, "What's there to fear? Radiation doesn't cause mutations 100% of the time. It's all about probability. I'll come back before my mental energy goes haywire."

Glory quickly explained, "They were one of the first teams to arrive. They were hoping to secure the lead, but now that more people are showing up, they're getting impatient."

Nearby, the couple from the Luse Federation glanced at the man, exchanged a few low words, but made no move.

The man shattered the floor-to-ceiling window, jumped onto the balcony, then leaped onto the opposite floating bridge, striding into the sunlight with his head held high. His figure vanished in an instant. About seven or eight minutes later, he strolled back nonchalantly, hands in his pockets. "I scouted around the area. There's no one in all of Radiant Hall."

He spread his arms, basking in the sunlight, and smiled casually at his teammates. "See? I'm perfectly fine, and my mental energy is stable. I told you, radiation is a probabil—"

"Plop—" His body suddenly swayed, and a piece of rotten flesh fell from his face. "Captain!!" his team shouted in panic.

The man wiped his face in confusion, only for more rotten flesh to fall off. Under the intense radiation, his pupils rapidly turned gray, his teeth began to bleed and fall out, and he quickly started transforming into a zombie.

"How… could this…?" Before he could finish his sentence, his last shred of sanity disappeared, and he completely turned into an Aberrant zombie, letting out a low growl as light flared in his palms, lunging at his teammates.

From the moment he left to when he returned, the entire process had taken less than ten minutes, yet in that short time, he had gone from human to a ferocious zombie. "Bang! Bang!" The other Aberrants in the building quickly took him down.

The martyr's body lay quietly on the ground, and after this incident, no one dared to venture outside.

Someone smartly sent the situation back to the system platform, and after consulting with the client, the Alliance teams received a new notification: "New Side Mission Added: Please restore A5 District's Elder Nation's ecological environment as soon as possible. Rewards for this mission will be calculated separately."

Cora quietly moved to the side and beckoned Onyx over with a gesture, signaling him to come closer.

"T014." Like a street spy, Cora whispered the code.

This was the serial number for the malfunctioning weather simulation system in Flower City. Back then, only Cora and Onyx had been there, and only they knew the details.

Onyx immediately understood. "Elder Nation's T001 is a first-generation model, the earliest simulation system deployed in an A District. You want me to shut it down, right?"

"Can you shut it down?"

"I can." Onyx smiled. "I know the location of T001's central hub. If we get Felix to do it, it won't take over fourteen days."

"But the real challenge isn't the simulation system. I'm sure there are other hacker-type Aberrants here as well. The key issue is the radiation outside..."

As he spoke, he suddenly looked up, staring intently at Cora. "Cora Thornton, you're not thinking of..."

"What's the radiation level right now?" Cora dodged the question. The formula for calculating radiation levels was extremely complex, but Onyx glanced at the environmental data and gave an answer almost instantly: "About 30% higher than standard."

Cora nodded, then pointed to herself. "I'll go find the central hub."

She wasn't being reckless. The radiation test at Ninnemann Lab had been painful, but it had also given Cora a deeper understanding of the changes in her powers. As long as the radiation didn't exceed 100%, her body wouldn't suffer any damage, and her mental energy would actually increase slightly.

This side mission was practically tailor made for F777!

"The abnormal radiation and unknown gene in your body still haven't been fully analyzed," Onyx hesitated for once. "If something goes wrong in that high-radiation environment..."

Cora patted his shoulder. "Don't worry. I know my condition."

Onyx de Montclair recalled the test report from Ninnemann Lab. Based purely on the data, the 30% excess radiation would indeed have almost no effect on Cora Thornton; her actual tolerance threshold was over 130%.

Onyx remained silent for a while, prompting Cora to gently pat him once, twice, and then a third time. "Let me go."

"Fine, but take the communicator with you and stay in constant contact." Onyx, unable to resist, grabbed her wrist and lightly scratched her palm. "And don't linger—get in and get out quickly."

"Got it." Cora made an 'OK' sign with her other hand.

When they returned to the group, Cora announced her decision to venture outside to find the T001 central hub. Shock rendered both the Tustan and F777 speechless:

"What?!"

"Captain Thornton, don't be rash!"

Silver Owl frowned. "Cora, this is a very unwise decision. If you're that concerned, we can push Arashi to speed things up."

Tustan's members also chimed in, trying to dissuade her. "Yeah, Captain Thornton, you don't need to sacrifice yourself. We're all stuck here, anyway; no one's completing the mission. Hey, F777! Aren't you going to stop your captain?"

Cora hoisted her backpack and zipped up her jacket to the top. "Don't worry. Just wait here." Silver Owl, realizing something, quickly asked, "You have a way to resist the radiation?"

Cora nodded slightly. She didn't intend to share the secret of her body with anyone outside of Onyx and her teammates.

After their initial shock, the F777 members regained their composure.

Damian scratched his head, his thoughts muddled. T001? T014? Memories he thought were long forgotten resurfaced. He instinctively glanced at Onyx, and Yuui and Charles did the same. Cora wasn't the type to act recklessly, and even if her idea was immature, Onyx would surely have stopped her.

Then they noticed Onyx give a barely perceptible nod.

There they go again, keeping secrets from us.

The team quickly returned to normal. Charles sat back down on the sofa and began reviewing treatments for radiation sickness, while Yuui pulled out sunglasses, a hat, and sunscreen gloves from her bag and started outfitting Cora.

Onyx turned to Felix. "Once we get to T001's central hub, how long will it take you to crack it?"

Felix scoffed. "A first-gen system? Half an hour, tops."

"Pfft." Cora couldn't help but laugh, sneaking a glance at Onyx and awkwardly pulling her hat down further.

In a rare moment, Onyx's face showed a hint of embarrassment.

His brown eyes blinked, realizing something. "Did you try cracking the firewall before? How long did it take you?"

Onyx turned his head away coldly. "Prepare for action."

Felix, relentless, leaned closer. "How long did it take? A day? A week? Why didn't you tell me? It must have taken you age, right?"

"Shut up."

"I just remembered!" Damian suddenly shouted. "Is T014 the one you took fourteen days to fix?"

Felix chuckled.

His mood visibly brightened, and his mechanical arm lifted and lowered as he cheerfully walked off.

Onyx narrowed his eyes, glaring at Damian. Damian, feeling a chill down his spine, quickly ran to hide behind Cora.

Five minutes later, Cora was fully geared up with her hat, sunglasses, and earpiece, heading toward the shattered window. She stepped over the body on the ground, waved back at her teammates, and then—under everyone's watchful eyes—leaped outside!

Dylan's sea-blue eyes flashed with a sneer. "Idiot. Adults always overestimate themselves."

The couple from the Luse Federation exchanged a glance, and the tall man spoke in a deep voice. "Veronica, did you sense anything from the person who just went out?"

The S5-ranked foresight of Aberrant Veronica looked grave as she slowly shook her head. "Vladimir, I couldn't see through her level, but she is the 'Chariot.'"

A tarot card suddenly appeared at Veronica's fingertips: The Chariot, in its upright position. The Chariot symbolizes strength and is closely associated with power. In the upright position, it signifies overcoming obstacles and achieving success.

Vladimir bowed his head and made the sign of the cross over his chest.

One Hour Later

Bam! Bam! Bam!

The main doors of Radiant Hall were pounded upon, the sound echoing through the grand space, causing the Aberrants inside to freeze, instantly preparing for battle. Silver Owl casually walked to the center of the room, gripping a powerful energy shotgun with ease, aiming it at the agitated crowd.

"Everyone, relax. Take it easy. It's just our friend returning."

"Are you sure it's still your 'friend' coming back?" one of the Galio Empire Aberrants asked coldly.

"Of course," Silver Owl replied, chambering a round with a friendly smile. "She's knocking, isn't she? Very polite."

Felix swiftly deployed his six mechanical arms, operating the control panel before anyone could react, opening the main doors.

Blinding sunlight poured in, forcing everyone to retreat into the shadows, and then they all looked up sharply.

A massive machine, over two meters tall and wide, slowly "walked" into the hall, crashing onto the floor. From behind the bulky device, Cora Thornton emerged, her cheeks flushed red and forehead beaded with sweat, but her eyes were bright and clear.

"I'm back... so tired."

Cora panted heavily, even though she had followed Onyx's instructions to strip the machine down to its core components. The material it was made from was incredibly dense. She had carried it all the way back, worried about damaging it, and was utterly exhausted.

The hall fell silent, the Aberrants staring in disbelief. She had spent a full hour under radiation thirteen times the normal level, and she was perfectly fine?

Cora caught her breath and then walked over to the Tustan and F777 teams, her expression serious. "Something's not right outside."

"What do you mean?" Silver Owl asked.

"Go out and see for yourselves, and you'll understand."

One of the Aberrants recognized the machine as the control core of the weather simulation system and stepped forward. "Hey, need some help? I'm an A7-rank hacker-type, I could try cracking it."

"No need. We have a faster way," Felix said as he activated the T001 core, tapping on the panel joints. "Come on, I need authorization."

Onyx shot him a distant look before assisting with fingerprint and iris scans.

Felix's fingers flew over the controls as he hummed something under his breath. If you listened closely, you could hear him singing, "Fourteen days, it took fourteen days..."

Onyx's temple twitched. "That's enough. Use your strength to overcome their weaknesses—what's there to be smug about?"

Felix didn't even pause. "Fourteen days~"

Twenty-two minutes and twenty seconds later, Felix entered the last line of code, and T001 was slammed down.

Bryan Young watched the entire process, covering his face in disbelief. "Oh, my god! Is my mouth cursed or something?"

The three people he had mocked for not even being A-rank had all proven him wrong, each delivering a metaphorical slap in the face. What was up with this F777 team? Why did they so easily handle something that no one else could?

"Glory, do you think it's too late if I apologize now?" Bryan asked, looking miserable.

Cora tapped her terminal to submit the mission, and F777's points skyrocketed, earning them a proud spot... in the top 200,000 of the Alliance rankings.

As T001 shut down, the weather outside changed dramatically.

The bright sunlight vanished, the temperature plummeted, and a cold sea wind howled, chilling everyone to the bone despite it being the height of summer.

All the Aberrants stood up and left Radiant Hall. A light drizzle fell, the rain carrying the distinct salty tang of the sea.

Cora and her team walked to the edge of the ribbon bridge, looking down at the entire island.

The city of Elder Nation was undeniably the pinnacle of the Alliance's urban planning. Many of the buildings were unlike anything they'd ever seen: floating cinemas, private care centers, immersive restaurants, and theme-changing simulated parks, all surrounded by various types of flying craft.

The entire city was in perfect order; all the infrastructure was functioning normally. Yet—there were no people. No signs of life, no indications of an invasion—everything was as it should be, yet there was an inexplicable eeriness hanging over it.

This dreamlike island, the A5 District's Elder Nation, was nothing but a deserted city.

Cora looked up at the sky as cold raindrops fell on her cheeks. She suddenly realized that after T001 was shut down, all the seagulls had disappeared. On a nearby rooftop, a sensory-type Aberrant suddenly issued a warning: "Something's coming towards us!!"

Cora sensed it too, raising her gaze to the horizon.

A speedboat was approaching from the sea, carrying a group of Aberrants who shouted at them from a distance, "Hey—we're late! Is the mission done? Can we still get a piece of the action?"

The island's Aberrants remained silent, no one answering.

The man on the boat cursed, "Damn Doom Sea! If it weren't for that drifting, we would've been here ages ago!!"

"Sister, look over there!" Damian pointed to a spot in the distance where continuous shadows were rapidly moving, causing the waves to swell and the sea to rock.

Suddenly! A group of whale sharks, their bodies covered in gray spots, burst from the sea. Their massive bodies flipped through the air, and one of them sank its teeth into the speeding boat!

"Ahhh—!!"

The driver didn't have time to escape; his body was bitten in half at the waist, while the others frantically fell into the sea, desperately unleashing their powers.

But the ocean was not a battlefield for humans.

Another group of hideous creatures broke through the surface, their decaying bodies moving with eerie agility as they swam, chasing and tearing apart the floundering Aberrants. Blood spurted, turning the water deep red in an instant.

Cora swallowed hard as she got a clearer look at the creatures. "Can you guys... swim?"

CHAPTER 41

Side Quest

Cora felt an overwhelming sense of unease, as if the tragedy before her was a harbinger of something far worse.

"Can you all swim?" she asked, turning to her companions.

"I can do all kinds of strokes!" Damian, who, like Cora, had grown up in District F199, answered enthusiastically. Most kids from the coast were naturally excellent swimmers. "Yes," Suchat, hailing from the Rainy Forest, responded. His rigorous training had included swimming as a basic survival skill.

Cora felt slightly reassured but then looked over at the two in wheelchairs, Felix and Onyx.

"I used to," Felix admitted, always direct about his limitations. "But now, I might need a moment to adjust." Since losing his leg, he'd been thrown into Death Hell and hadn't had the chance to swim since.

Onyx, reclining in his wheelchair, glanced disdainfully at the blood-stained sea. "Swimming isn't exactly my favorite activity…"

"Oh really? Didn't you rent out the heated pool at the dorm for ten years straight? Spent a fortune on it too," Felix shot back, mercilessly exposing his former classmate's hypocrisy.

Onyx's smile remained unchanged, but his tone shifted. "… But I'm still pretty good at it."

Among the rest of the group, Charles shook his head honestly. "No, I never had time to learn. Too busy with work."

The surprise came when Yuui awkwardly laughed, "Well, um, I

can't either."

"Hm?" Cora's eyes widened slightly. "Didn't you shoot that underwater photo series?"

Cora vividly remembered the promotional music video that had been looped on every flower boat and billboard in Felalakas, showing Yuui swimming gracefully like a mermaid in crystal-clear waters.

"It was all special effects," Yuui confessed, clutching Cora's shoulder, her expression pitiful. "I'm a complete landlubber and terrified of water. Cora, you can't let me go in there!"

Cora was silent for a moment, lamenting how fake the entertainment world could be. "Then wear a life jacket."

Onyx retrieved lifejackets from his storage space and handed them out. "Better safe than sorry. Everyone, put them on."

As they donned the jackets, the group discussed their situation. "Why did so many sea monsters suddenly appear?" someone asked.

"Because we shut down T001," Onyx replied, looking up at the gloomy sky. "Its intense radiation used to repel them. Sea creatures naturally avoided this area, but now that everything's back to normal and with so many Aberrants gathered here, they were drawn to the scent."

The ribbon bridge surrounding Elder Nation's island, known as the "Island Scenic Line," gradually rotated, bringing them closer to the ocean's surface. The scene before them slowly came into focus.

Zombie whale sharks and grotesque giant flounders leaped into the air, desperately ramming into the island. Although an invisible barrier stopped them, the ground beneath the group shook violently.

The Aberrants on the island quickly responded to the threat.

On Tustan's side, Silver Owl had set up a mortar, activating his "Weakness Detection" Anopower. The crimson explosive shell arced through the air, landing precisely on a zombie whale shark that had just surfaced, blasting its eye socket into a bloody crater. Shrapnel shredded its brain, and its massive body fell back into the sea with a splash that sent water shooting up over fifty feet.

Jennifer and the other area-effect Aberrants unleashed a barrage of attacks. Fire, lightning, wind, and fog erupted across the water's surface, covering a wide area. However, the sea monsters proved cunning, diving deep to avoid the damage as soon as they sensed the attacks coming.

Glory Ku, an A5-ranked control Aberrant from Peace Dove, had a unique Anopower called "Convergence," which could draw enemies into a specific area, making her a valuable asset against zombie hordes.

As Glory weaved her fingers through the air, a vortex appeared on the water's surface, sucking nearby monsters into it. She glanced over at Tustan's side and shifted her focus, drawing another wave of creatures toward them, allowing the area-effect of Aberrants to land a solid hit. "Thanks, Glory!" Tustan's teammates shouted from afar.

The Aberrants from the New Pacific Alliance were highly skilled, with several S-ranked individuals standing out in the fray.

Meanwhile, over on the Galio Empire and Luse Federation's side, the most striking duo was the Icefield Couple, Vladimir and Veronica from "Kazan Locomotive." Vladimir's Anopower, "Distortion," coupled with his skills as a boxer, made him a formidable force. Despite not being able to enter the water, he raised his scar-covered right hand, clenched his fist, and twisted.

A giant flounder twisted into a grotesque shape, its hundreds of broken bones piercing through its flesh, turning it into a bloody, impaled mess in an instant.

Everyone fought fiercely, except for... those who looked suspiciously idle from F777.

From Bryan Young's perspective, this group seemed like cowards. They'd put on life jackets early, and the entire team appeared to be slacking off. The only one who had done anything was a kid! He immediately regretted his earlier apology. He hadn't been wrong—their low ranking of 235706 was well deserved. They might be good at fixing machines, but for fighting sea monsters, they were utterly useless.

[F777]

Charles, designated as Slacker No. 1, usually handled collecting crystals. But with the current situation, there wasn't much for him to do. Slacker No. 2, the brothers in wheelchairs, were in charge of logistics and transportation, only stepping in when absolutely necessary. That left the two passive slackers, Cora and Suchat, standing around, looking at each other with uncertainty.

They were both melee fighters, and jumping into the ocean to fight wasn't exactly an option. The monsters were swarming, and the various Anopowers flying around could easily hit them by mistake. Bored, the two idly shot their ethereal crossbows into the water, not expecting much.

Damian was in his element. He started doing calisthenics, and with the water amplifying his ice Anopower, his strength surged. A simple stretching motion froze the water's surface instantly, and a kick sent ice spikes flying, skewering several fish at once.

Damian glanced over at Dylan, his face full of smug satisfaction. "Nightmare's Descent" couldn't control the sea beasts, and Dylan was visibly frustrated, practically hopping with irritation.

Yuui was also contemplating new possibilities. Her Anopower required lyrics to activate, with different lyrics giving different buffs on various targets. But these sea monsters didn't understand human language, so her singing had lost much of its impact.

Closing her eyes, Yuui hummed a melody without lyrics, her ethereal voice echoing over the sea. When the song ended, nothing had happened. Yuui felt a twinge of disappointment—she had tried to communicate, but it was clear the sea beasts couldn't understand her.

Bryan Young couldn't believe what he was seeing.

What was going on? They were doing exercises and singing? Were these people on vacation? Could they take this seriously, please?

After more than half an hour, with everyone working together, the sea monsters were finally defeated, their floating corpses drifting away with the waves. The crisis in Elder Nation had been averted.

The Aberrants prepared to conduct a thorough search of the island. Just before leaving, Cora glanced back at the blood-red sea. Had the crisis truly been averted?

Six hours later.

"Click—"

Cora popped open a can, letting the sweet corn juice flow down her throat, warming her entire stomach. The weather was dreary with continuous rain. She blew into her hands, but her fingers remained cold.

Elder Nation's streets were dotted with colorful little kiosks, mobile restaurants with varied styles and flavors. They required no payment or verification; anyone passing by could grab hot, freshly prepared food from the machines inside.

Such facilities would be impossible in District F199; they'd be smashed to pieces and looted by desperate vagrants on the first day. But in District A5, where residents lacked for nothing, it seemed they preferred to use such "generosity" to showcase their "noble" morality.

With T001 deactivated, the paradise-like facade of the Elder Nation had been torn away, revealing its true nature. The island was shrouded in a gray mist. Visibility was poor, and the roads were slippery. The constant drizzle was enough to drive anyone crazy after a while.

A group of Aberrants passed by, their whispered conversation carried to Cora by the wind. "The entry restriction is almost up. Damn, where the hell are all the people here?!"

"Maybe we should bail? S-rank missions are tough enough as it is, and this place is creepy. Captain, let's just get out of here." "Yeah, let's go. No point staying in this ghost town."

The group headed toward Radiant Hall, ready to call it quits. Cora watched them leave, took another sip of her warm corn juice, and turned away from the kiosk.

Two meters away, inside an empty cafe, Onyx asked quietly, "Any progress?"

Suchat whiffed his head. "This island is structured differently from a typical city. There are no bomb shelters or basements—no safe havens. I checked all the residential buildings and public places. There's no one here."

"Is that so? Interesting..." Onyx propped his chin on his hand, his gaze growing distant. Suchat hesitated, then spoke up. "This place feels... off."

"What feels off?" Onyx raised an eyebrow.

"It's too clean, too orderly. It doesn't look like the residents were attacked. It's more like... they just vanished." Suchat knew his theory sounded absurd, but it was what he believed: the residents of the Elder Nation had simply disappeared.

"You're not wrong," Onyx nodded calmly. "I suspect they left voluntarily." His statement dropped like a bomb.

"What?" Yuui exclaimed in disbelief. "Why would they leave voluntarily? Elder Nation is the most privileged city in the entire

Alliance. Why would they abandon a life of luxury to suffer in lower districts?"

"That makes little sense, right? There are a lot of residents here. If they really left, how come there's no word of it?" Charles voiced his doubts.

The local population of the Elder Nation was around a million. Compared to the Alliance's thirty billion, it was a drop in the ocean. But for a million people, especially the privileged class, to disappear without a trace? That seemed impossible.

This S-rank mission was becoming more and more mysterious. What were the residents of the Elder Nation hiding, and where had they gone?

"Exactly. A million people can't just vanish." Onyx tapped his fingers on the table, his gaze growing colder. "Which is why I suspect the Central Council knew about this all along, and maybe... this is part of one of their plans."

Everyone was baffled, just about to ask Onyx to elaborate.

"Something's not right." Suchat spoke up, his keen senses on high alert. "What is it?" The others tensed immediately.

"When we left Radiant Hall, I marked a reference point," Suchat pointed to a spot below them. "The position of that tree has changed."

Yuui looked over blankly and then back again, equally confused. "I see nothing. What do you guys think?"

Onyx frowned at the news. "It's not the tree that's moving; it's us."

All around them was nothing but an endless expanse of ocean, making it easy to lose one's sense of direction.

Felix quickly pulled up the map to confirm their location. "Wow, here's some bad news: since we landed, Elder Nation's absolute position has shifted by thirty nautical miles."

With no one noticing, the entire island had been drifting across the sea. The group was stunned into silence. "..."

Innocently, Damian asked, "Is this island... alive?"

"Maybe it's because of magnetic attraction..." Onyx mused for a moment. "Can you determine the direction of movement?"

Felix's fingers flew across the keyboard, then paused. "An even worse piece of news: it seems we're heading toward the Doom Sea."

"At this rate, we'll enter the Doom Sea's triangular zone in fifteen hours."

The Doom Sea triangle, a legendary sailor's nightmare, a place from which no one returns. Fifteen hours—that's less than a day.

Cora was about to say something when she suddenly noticed movement out of the corner of her eye.

A two-meter-long emperor crab was scuttling toward them, its eight long legs raised high—

Cora reacted in a flash, throwing a knife that pierced its shell and pinned it to the ground!

The zombie emperor crab's beady, gray eyes twitched a few times before it vomited up a puddle of foul-smelling pus.

"Yikes, that's terrifying!" Damian nimbly jumped onto a chair, pointing toward the street. "Cora, there's more out there!"

Cora snapped her head up. And sure enough, there were a dozen more of the same monsters scurrying through the muddy puddles in the street.

"Ah—!!" A sharp scream echoed from the distance.

Swarming hordes of pale, flesh-colored sea rats wriggled out from the corners, like giant turnips with long tails, rolling and squirming across the damp ground. Cora's face paled—these creatures definitely didn't belong in the Elder Nation. How had they breached the barrier?

From above, the sound of engines revving up filled the air. A fully armed supersonic ship was taken off from the rooftop helipad of Radiant Hall. It must have been the team that had planned to leave earlier. Cora watched as the ship ascended smoothly into the sky.

Then, something bizarre happened. All four burning engines suddenly cut out. The ship wobbled, nose-diving straight down and crashing into the sea!

Cora's eyes widened in shock. For a moment, it felt like she was back in Blossomville, witnessing that starship fall like a meteor shower all over again.

Felix was equally stunned. "The power failed? No, the Sora Wings were drained!"

All Alliance flying terminals relied on Sora Wings, an alternative energy source that allowed them to hover. The Lucas Starships were even built entirely using this technology. Without Sora Wings, they could only fly short distances, needing to stop frequently to recharge, much like when they had escaped from Death Hell.

Onyx quickly scanned the environmental indicators. "The magnetic field's gone haywire." Just as he spoke, Cora's can of corn juice tipped over on the table, spilling its thick, creamy contents.

Suddenly, the ground shook violently. A low rumble from deep beneath the ocean reverberated upwards, sending shockwaves rippling through the earth.

"Crack—!"

A deep, bottomless fissure opened up beneath their feet. Yuui nearly split into a full split, but Suchat grabbed her with one arm, leaping them both over to where Cora, Charles, and Damian were standing.

But the crack continued to widen, splitting deeper and broader, until the island itself was being torn apart right before their eyes. Cora and her six companions stood in stunned silence.

Elder Nation had literally split in two!

The tremors continued beneath the ocean. After the first crack, countless smaller ones branched off, rapidly shattering the island into pieces. Large and small fragments of land tumbled from the heights.

Snap!

Cora stumbled, bracing herself on the ground as she watched the section of island holding Onyx and Felix slip away.

In a split second, Felix's six mechanical arms shot out, embedding themselves in the opposite piece of land. His entire body, wheelchair and all, flew across, barely making it to the other side. The force was too much, though, and he tumbled out of his wheelchair. Charles and Suchat rushed to help him up.

Onyx wasn't as lucky. He was closest to the fissure, and as the ground tilted, his wheelchair careened downward. If he fell, it didn't matter if he could swim—he'd be crushed by the debris.

Cora took two steps back, then bolted forward. Leaping through the air, she lunged toward the cliff's edge. In one swift motion, her hand transformed into an ethereal short blade, which she drove into the ground. With her other hand, she grabbed Onyx just as he was about to plunge into the abyss!

Onyx dangled in midair, swinging amid the falling debris. He reached up and gripped her arm. Cora's feet slipped forward, and she gritted her teeth, her face flushed with effort. With a final, powerful yank, she pulled Onyx up. The momentum sent them both tumbling across the ground, rolling to safety.

As soon as they stopped, Cora scrambled to her feet, kicking Onyx's leg and roaring like a dragon. "Stop faking it, you cripple! Get up! Run!!"

Onyx winced in pain, hissing, "Cora, you're giving me too much credit."

Was he pretending to be a cripple to avoid running? He'd been in a wheelchair for almost a year now—he really was a frail researcher. No matter how fast his mind worked, his body just couldn't keep up.

The two of them stumbled back to where Yuui and the others were, finding refuge on a relatively intact piece of the island. Cora, still panting heavily from the adrenaline, suddenly froze in place, her eyes wide.

Emerging from one of the massive fissures was a gigantic head covered in large, dark blotches. Its eyes were clouded over with a gray film, and its mouth hung open slightly as it swallowed several falling Aberrants whole.

As the colossal creature moved, Cora could finally make out its full form. It was over a hundred meters long, and aside from its head, limbs, and tail, its entire body was covered in dark green armor. Its back was coated in a horrifying forest of barnacles that would make anyone with trypophobia scream.

With a great splash, the beast's enormous front limbs rose from the water, paddling like oars as it slammed into the island fragment they stood on. The ground shook violently once again; the cracks widening beneath their feet. Cora suddenly understood—this creature had shattered the Elder Nation!

Her terminal beeped urgently. A new notification flashed across the screen:

New Side Quest (Urgent): Eliminate the Level-5 Zombie Beast—Leatherback Sea Turtle—threatening District A5, Elder Nation.

CHAPTER 42

A Weak Spot

According to the World Universal Zombie Biological Guide issued post-apocalypse: Evolved zombies are classified from Level 1 to Level 4, with Level 4 Zombie Lords keeping some human intelligence but lacking full consciousness.

The levels of Anopowered Zombies fluctuate with their original host's strength decreasing proportionally, and never exceeding Level 4. A Level 4 Anopowered Zombie is equivalent to an S-level Aberrant; however, such a creature has yet to be encountered globally.

Only zombies and mutated beasts exist within Levels 1 to 5. Among them, Level 5 mutated beasts pose a severe threat to an entire region. Though their intelligence can't compare to humans or even Zombie Lords, each one possesses devastating combat power.

The suppliers remotely monitoring the mission from District B4 were evidently unprepared for the appearance of a Level 5 beast in the Elder Nation.

Their original commission was merely an investigative task, intended to recover a massive debt. But as the Aberrants ventured deeper, facing extreme radiation, swarms of oceanic creatures, and now the emergence of a Level 5 leatherback sea turtle, the situation spiraled beyond their expectations.

These suppliers deeply regretted their involvement—Elder Nation was a death trap. No wonder the system automatically rated it as an S-level danger zone!

Bang! Bang, bang!!

The leatherback sea turtle continued its relentless assault, causing buildings on the island to collapse with resounding crashes. Debris slid down in heaps, and though Elder Nation's vast area temporarily withstood the devastation, the situation remained dire.

In the midst of the upheaval, Felix Lucas opened the map. "Its speed is increasing. In four hours, we'll enter the Doom Sea Triangle." Cora looked up, scanning the surroundings. On the uneven terrain, the Aberrants launched their attacks. Some close-combat specialists found their positions and leaped onto the turtle's shell, landing firmly.

Against the massive leatherback sea turtle, Glory Ku's "Gathering" technique was rendered useless, and other group attack abilities were equally ineffective. Jennifer's flames extinguished before igniting, quenched by the sea. Damian's ice spikes struck the turtle's back, but caused no harm; instead, they merely scraped off a few barnacles.

Silver Owl, his expression cold and stern, quickly ascended a collapsing hospital rooftop and set up a mortar, aiming for the turtle's eyes.

It's said that turtles live for centuries, and this one had likely survived for countless years, showing remarkable intelligence. As the shell exploded near its head, the turtle flapped its flippers furiously, propelling itself forward. Boom!! The explosive shell missed by a hair, only leaving a scorched mark on its impenetrable shell.

Silver Owl cursed under his breath.

Unless an Anopower attack was instantaneous and lethal, the turtle could easily evade it. With its tough shell and oceanic domain, the battle against the leatherback sea turtle became increasingly challenging.

The tall tower where the "Kazan Locomotive" was stationed was the last remaining vantage point amid the ruins. Veronica's eyes lit up as her brown hair fluttered, and a tarot card slowly materialized in her palm: the reversed Tower card—signifying impending disaster and total collapse.

Veronica's trembling hand brushed across the card's surface as she murmured, "Mbl yMpeM. (We are doomed.)"

Vladimir cradled her head, their foreheads touching. "God is with us, Veronica. Wait for my return."

With that, he turned and left. His massive, muscular frame descended from the rubble, leaping onto the turtle's shell, his fists crashing down with immense force. Thud! The ground rocked, and even the Level 5 beast's relentless assault faltered momentarily.

Dylan's blue eyes flared with anger as he focused on the turtle's pale gray eye. Activating his "Nightmare Arrival" Anopower, the beast's movements suddenly froze, its forelimbs locked in place on the sea's surface, trapped in a state of "sleep paralysis."

Damian, watching from the side, pouted. He was no match—his attempts only tickled the turtle, while Dylan effortlessly immobilized it with a single move.

Cora exchanged a glance with Suchat, their Ethereal Artifacts gleaming in their hands. This battle clearly spelled doom, but if they didn't kill the leatherback sea turtle, death was their only outcome.

"You all take care of yourselves," Cora urged her companions, giving an extra glance at Onyx.

Suchat silently looked toward Yuui, his lips moving slightly as if to say something.

Yuui strode closer, rising on her tiptoes to pat his head. Her soft fingers slid to the back of his neck, pressing lightly as Suchat obediently lowered his head. Their noses brushed together, and Yuui smiled, "I'm not interested in raising another puppy, so... stay safe, okay?"

Suchat's breath hitched, but Yuui quickly released him, stepping back. She turned and shouted at Charles, "Old Franz! Can you check if I'm wearing my life vest correctly?!"

Suchat steadied himself, following Cora. The two of them leaped onto the leatherback sea turtle's back with a heavy thud.

Bryan Young was already on the shell, swearing as he hacked at the barnacles, trying to break through. When he saw them, his eyes widened. What was an F777 slacker doing here? Shouldn't they be hiding?

Bryan shot up, hands on his hips, and advised, "Hey, don't throw your lives away. Leave it to your big brother Bryan...!" But Cora ignored him, and she and Suchat flew over the hundred-meter-long barnacle forest, disappearing from view.

"Big brother Bryan can't save you now."

On their path forward, a man halted Cora. The man, resembling an arctic bear, was a Luse Aberrant who quickly spoke to her, "@#%&*....!"

Cora: What language was that?

Luckily, her terminal had a built-in translator. She quickly activated it, and the man, seeing her action, repeated himself swiftly. "I'm Vladimir, an S5-level close-combat specialist. This beast is hard to kill; I want to team up with you."

In critical moments like this, strong Aberrants needed to unite more than ever. Vladimir gazed down at the slender girl before him. Veronica had called her the "Chariot," and her divinations had never been wrong.

Cora twirled her blade elegantly, then pointed to her eyes, signaling that they should attack the beast's head. Vladimir responded, "#@%*&.... (Let's move together; I'll take on its forelimbs.)"

Cora glanced at the translator, nodded, then raised her fist with a serious expression, "Charge!!"

Vladimir pounded his chest with his fists in response.

The three of them split up. Cora leaped near the leatherback sea turtle's head. The water here was already up to her thighs, making movement difficult. She slashed her long blade, which gleamed with a dark green light, immediately drawing the beast's attention as its massive head slowly turned.

On the other side, Suchat feigned an attack at the turtle's eye. The leatherback sea turtle used the same tactic as before, powering its forelimbs to leap forward. But just then, Suchat made a sudden turn, redirecting his blade to strike at the thin membrane behind the turtle's ear—an expertly executed feint!

Cora, who had already swum ahead and was waiting, took advantage of the moment. With a powerful kick, she leaped out of the water, her Ethereal Artifact glowing blue in her palm. With precision and steadiness, she drove it straight into the beast's right eye!

Almost simultaneously, a blast shot from afar, taking advantage of the turtle's momentary stiffness to hit its left eye dead on.

Cora looked up abruptly to see a young man on the rooftop of the ruined hospital, wearing sniper goggles and giving her a thumbs up.

The leatherback sea turtle, its eyes injured, thrashed in agony, its limbs convulsing as it let out a sharp wheezing sound. It suddenly opened its mouth, and a powerful jet of air shot out, sending towering waves into the sky and flipping many Aberrants into the water.

Splash, splash! Both Cora and Suchat fell into the water, but they had created the perfect opportunity!

Vladimir, lurking in the sea, was already in position. He grabbed the leatherback sea turtle's muscular forelimbs, activating his "Distortion" Anopower!

In an instant, the ten-meter-long forefinger twisted into a mangled mess of flesh, with thousands of bone spurs piercing through the shattered meat. Vladimir held his breath, bubbles escaping his lips, and with a mighty push of his powerful legs against the turtle's shell —under his terrifying strength, the entire forefinger was torn off.

The other Aberrants followed suit, attacking the remaining three limbs exposed outside the shell. Various Anopowers rained down on the turtle, and although they couldn't tear the limbs apart like Vladimir, they still inflicted jagged wounds.

Dylan sprinted across the island's debris, finally circling around to face the leatherback sea turtle. Staring into its one good eye, he attempted to trigger "Nightmare Arrival" again, but this time, whether because of its blindness or developing resistance, it failed to take effect.

Wham! The enraged turtle thrashed wildly, its hardened shell colliding with the debris. The ground beneath Dylan's feet crumbled, and he nearly plunged headfirst into the water, only to be caught just in time by his black-clad bodyguard.

With its forelimb severed, the leatherback sea turtle swayed in agony, entering a frenzy. It suddenly leaped out of the water, its hundred-meter-long body performing a full 360-degree spin. The Aberrants on its back were all thrown into the sea, and the waves swept Vladimir up, sent soaring tens of meters into the air before plummeting uncontrollably.

The leatherback sea turtle, its gray-white eye oozing foul blood, quickly locked onto Vladimir as its target for revenge. With a powerful thrust, its hard shell's edge slammed into Vladimir's chest, blood splattering as a chunk of his flesh was brutally torn away!

"No—!!"

Veronica clutched the railing of the lofty tower, screaming in anguish.

Her eyes suddenly blazed with intensity as dark clouds gathered behind her, lightning flashing and thunder roaring. The sea around Elder Nation erupted with fierce winds and towering waves, shocking everyone. This... was this a weather-based Anopower? The ability to forcibly change local weather, to summon storms—an Anopower only an S-level Aberrant could possess!

The leatherback sea turtle's pursuit was abruptly halted as it struggled to maintain its balance amid the monstrous waves.

Veronica was an S-level dual-powered Aberrant who had hidden her second Anopower well. But seeing Vladimir on the brink of death, she could no longer hold back, desperate to save her beloved.

Frantically, Veronica tried to summon a new tarot card, but the divination had a cooldown period. Though she was anxious, it was no use. Moments later, she cursed under her breath and began descending the tower, leaping into the sea to rescue Vladimir.

With its target lost, the leatherback sea turtle began smashing the island in a frenzy. Its hind leg swiped, shearing off another chunk of debris, leaving the Aberrants with even less space to stand. Soon, there would be nowhere left to hide.

Felix shouted through the blinding wind, "Hey! You're an S-level first awakened. Can't you control it?"

Onyx yelled back at the same volume, "Even if I did, I can't kill it!"

This leatherback sea turtle wasn't as easy to deal with as the Cockroach King in Blossomville. Its hide was tough, and its defense was nearly maxed out. Onyx could indeed use his psychic powers to control it, but he couldn't kill it in one strike.

Besides, after being controlled once, the turtle would be on guard. Just now, Dylan's second attempt had failed, so his psychic piercing was best saved for the critical moment to coordinate with Cora's attack.

Cora and Suchat both plunged into the water, their heads breaking the surface for a deep breath before diving back down, chasing after the leatherback sea turtle.

Through the murky water, Cora noticed they had reached the turtle's underbelly, its softest and least defended by a weak spot. The pale pink flesh was smooth and unscarred. Suchat blew a stream of bubbles, gesturing toward her. Cora understood—he suggested that if they could hold out, they should launch their attack from below.

Cora nodded, expelling a few bubbles herself. She could manage underwater for seven to eight minutes without a problem.

Grasping a sinking a piece of building debris, Cora's hand flashed with blue light, summoning two serrated saw blades with icy teeth. She gently pushed one toward Suchat, who grabbed it. They kicked their legs and quickly closed in on the turtle.

The island, already on the verge of collapse, was further battered by the raging storm and the turtle's frenzied rampage, making the situation even more dire.

On the small remaining high ground, Onyx stood soaked to the bone, his white, casual clothes clinging to his chest, looking a bit disheveled. He removed his glasses, drenched with water droplets, and pushed his hair back.

Suddenly, he looked up toward the vast, stormy sea. "What... what now?" Charles clung to Felix's mechanical arm, his voice trembling with fear.

"This isn't good," Onyx said, his face more serious than ever before.

Below, Suchat's saw blade cut through the turtle's underbelly in several strokes, allowing the poisonous mist to seep in quickly. He turned and gestured to Cora. "Retreat! Retreat! Retreat!"

The two of them swiftly retreated, and just seconds later, the leatherback sea turtle performed another 360-degree spin, the chaotic waves throwing them both another ten meters away. However, the turtle's wound festered rapidly because of the spreading toxin. Cora's eyes lit up—this could work!

She was about to suggest another attempt to Suchat when her eyes suddenly widened.

The water was quickly filling with blood—both the turtle's and the Aberrants'. The intense scent of blood had attracted other predators nearby. From the murky depths, a swarm of mutated great white sharks came speeding toward them.

Their pupils were vertical slits, their wide-open jaws brimming with serrated teeth, targeting the Aberrants in the water. Among them, two particularly aggressive sharks were riddled with radiation and were likely Level 4 beasts.

Cora felt a wave of despair—when it rains, it pours! A Level 5 leatherback sea turtle was bad enough, and now there were two Level 4 mutated great white sharks?!

The Aberrants closest to the sharks were the first to be attacked. They had no time to dodge before the sharks tore them apart, devouring them within moments. One of the Level 4 sharks swam toward the leatherback sea turtle's underbelly, viciously tearing into it.

The sharks moved with incredible speed, and in no time, they were circling around Suchat.

Fighting underwater was challenging, and Suchat was in a dire situation. The poisonous mist surrounded him, and although he fought back with all his strength, the sheer number of sharks was overwhelming. A momentary delay in his movement allowed one shark to bite down on his arm.

Cora grabbed a piece of building debris, transforming it into a ghostly blue spear, which she thrust forward with force, piercing the attacking shark. The shark recoiled in pain, releasing Suchat, who seized the chance to escape. But Cora wasn't done—the spear, like a boomerang, continued to slice through the water, cutting into the massive, spindle-shaped bodies of the sharks. Black blood gushed out, and the shark formation was thrown into disarray.

Suchat pursued Cora, swimming away while he pulled out a bandage, tightly wrapping his wound to prevent more blood from attracting the monsters.

Thud, thud—thud, thud—

The island fragments were relentlessly pounded as the ferocious sharks poked their heads out of the water, eyeing the Aberrants on land with predatory intent.

To make matters worse, a thunderous roar suddenly came from the direction of the Doom Sea, a seismic shockwave triggering a destructive tsunami. "What kind of cursed mission is this?" Yuui wailed in despair, "First the leatherback sea turtle, then the sharks, and now a tsunami too?!"

Under the triple assault, the once-mighty Elder Nation finally crumbled and collapsed entirely. All the Aberrants were plunged into the water!

Yuui, who couldn't swim, shut her eyes tight as she hit the water with a splash, her arms and legs flailing desperately, but she couldn't stop herself from sinking. Frantically, she checked her life vest, only to find that it had been torn by debris during her fall—just her luck.

Yuui gasped as water filled her lungs, her oxygen rapidly depleting as her heartbeat slowed. Was she... going to die? In her next life... she'd definitely learn how to swim...

Her vision blurred, and just as she was losing consciousness, a massive shadow swam toward her.

The tsunami triggered by the shockwave swept up all the beasts and Aberrants alike.

Cora was caught in the whirlpool, tossed and turned, unsure of where she was being carried. She struggled to break free, and just as she shook off the dizziness, a Level 4 great white shark, having just finished two Aberrants, locked its vertical gray-white pupil on her. Its forked tail flicked, propelling it straight toward her.

Cora quickly changed direction, kicking her legs hard, but as a ruler of the ocean, the shark was clearly faster in its hunting motions. In the blink of an eye, it was at her leg, biting down—

But it didn't succeed. Its snout was caught.

A long, triangular military dagger had appeared on Cora's calf, wedging itself in the shark's mouth. The pain of the dagger piercing it made the shark thrash violently, its serrated teeth scraping against Cora's leg, sending waves of excruciating pain to her brain. But instead of pulling back, she twisted and pushed, driving the military dagger deeper into the shark's snout, causing black blood to spurt out!

The Level 4 beast, with its low-level intelligence, retreated, flapping its dorsal and tail fins in fear as it tried to escape Cora's grasp.

Bitten me and now you want to run? Cora's upper body quickly followed, both hands gripping the dagger as she plunged it into the shark's dead white eye, slashing out a cross! With a sickening sound, the shark's entire head split open, revealing a pigeon-blood red crystal gleaming among the decaying flesh.

Cora swiftly sliced the crystal free and pocketed it. The shark gradually stopped struggling. She then climbed inside its mouth, unfastened the military dagger from its bindings, and slowly retracted her leg. With a last kick, she sent the shark's heavy body sinking to the seafloor.

Cora looked at her right leg. From her shin to her ankle, the flesh was mangled and bloody. The pain was bearable, but there was another sensation, one that had been growing since earlier—a vague, unsettling shiver that seemed to come from deep within her soul.

The aftermath of the 30% overexposure to radiation appeared to be manifesting only now. Cora's entire body felt like it was burning. The agony of her genes tearing apart caused her to scream silently, and the searing pain on the back of her neck was drilling down into her bones.

A few seconds later, Cora was horrified to discover that scales were growing on the back of her hands!

She looked around frantically, finding a place to hide in the coral reef. She huddled tightly, trying to hide her hands.

What's happening? Could that shark have some kind of infection?!

Cora anxiously felt her leg. Luckily, her secondary Anopower was kicking in, with her cells regenerating and the wound healing steadily.

It's okay... it's okay... I'll be fine soon, she reassured herself, blowing out a stream of bubbles. She'd been underwater for nearly seven minutes and needed to surface for air.

Cora checked her leg once more, feeling that it had mostly healed, and slowly swam out of the coral reef.

Then she suddenly froze, looking down at her legs.

No, they weren't legs at all. Her legs had vanished! From the waist down, Cora's lower body had transformed into a long, serpentine tail covered in tiny scales, with the forked tip radiating a poisonous glow.

Cora couldn't believe her eyes. She flung the massive tail into the air, trying to shake it off. But it wouldn't go away—what had happened to her legs?!

Whack—the forked tip struck the coral reef she'd been hiding in, instantly draining its vibrant red color to a lifeless gray, followed by a resounding crack as it shattered. What... that powerful? Cora's jaw dropped in shock, water rushing into her mouth. She quickly spat it out in bubbles.

In the distance, she saw a figure swimming toward her. Cora raised her head, eyes full of wariness.

CHAPTER 43

Famous

While everyone else was still lost in the astonishing scene before them, Onyx quickly regained his composure and was the first to hit the "Complete Mission" button.

Cora, who had been comfortably coiled in her wheelchair, noticed his action and was so surprised that she straightened up slightly, causing the blanket to bunch up over her legs—an obviously unnatural position for human legs.

Next to her, Damian's mouth formed an "O," his eyes wide with shock.

Onyx's brow twitched, but he remained unfazed, calmly pressing the blanket back down. He brought a long finger to his lips, signaling for both of them to stay quiet.

The two nodded in unison.

No matter what had happened in Elder Nation, F777's primary goal was to complete the S-level mission, and turning it in to earn points was the most important thing. Everyone was still somewhat dazed and confused, but Onyx's mind had already connected all the dots, revealing the truth.

Since the original mission was an investigation, they would need to submit a detailed report explaining everything to the client. But with Onyx around, such matters would be handled smoothly, especially since he had once volunteered to work with Svetlana using "Cora's voice."

Utopia eventually came to a halt high in the sky, resembling a massive floating ship. The chaotic magnetic fields around it calmed, and the mutated fish turned, its endless wings flapping as it leaped thousands of miles away in an instant, carrying them out of the Doom Sea.

No, it's not a fish but a whale!

Yuui slowly leaned down, her cheek pressed against the whale's back, and sang a haunting melody. The mutated whale seemed to understand her murmurs, lifting its head to let out a sorrowful cry before diving into the sea and transforming into countless large fish.

Wave after wave of shocks had numbed the Aberrants' nerves. Even witnessing Yuui's "brainwave communication" with the whale, they only blinked dully, their faces saying, "F777? How many more surprises do you have in store for us?"

Soon, they returned to where the Elder Nation had once stood, but now there was nothing left except the vast, empty sea.

With T001 deactivated, the natural weather had become completely chaotic. It was as if there was a clear boundary—on one side; the sky was bright, while on the other, thunder rumbled in the darkness, as black as the deepest night.

The weary and bewildered Aberrants, too exhausted to think, lay down where they were waiting for rescue.

An hour later, three large starships arrived overhead. Spotting the giant creatures in the sea, the pilots didn't dare land. They could only hover low, carefully lowering gangways for the Aberrants to evacuate. Damian wheeled into the cabin for Cora, who was panting with the effort.

As they departed, Yuui glanced back. The mutated whale let out a low, mournful cry, as if bidding her farewell, before flipping over and disappearing from sight.

The harrowing day finally ended. Too tired for any social interaction, everyone quietly took their seats to rest. After bidding farewell to Silver Owl, Glory Ku, and the others, F777 specifically chose the most secluded booth on the starship. They entered silently, and Felix casually installed a signal jammer by the door to prevent eavesdropping.

After a moment of mutual silence, the room erupted into a chorus of voices:

"Sister, your blanket was—&@??*~ What's going on!!"

"What was with that fish?"

"Let me tell you, I had the worst luck today. That damn life vest actually ripped!"

"How many points did we get? Let me see."

"We lost the starship; how are we supposed to get back?"

The room was chaotic, with everyone talking at once, and no one could make out what the others were saying. They fell silent for a second before all speaking again simultaneously: "#@$*%&.....!!"

Cora raised her fist, "Stop! One at a time!"

Yuui raised her hand elegantly, gesturing for the "captain to go first."

Cora responded by dropping a deep-sea torpedo. She dragged back the blanket. "You all need to stay calm, okay?"

A long, black snake tail slid down from the wheelchair, quickly filling the entire space. The cold, serpent-like aura brushed past their noses, while the poisonous forked hook at the end of the tail twitched slightly, emanating a chilling menace.

Yuui's pupils dilated, and she was left speechless. Felix's expression remained indifferent, but his mechanical arm shot out involuntarily. Charles had the most dramatic reaction, staggering back a step and clinging tightly to the cabin door.

After a moment of stunned silence, Damian's eyes sparkled with excitement: "Wow... that's so cool."

"Sister, sister, that's amazing! Can I touch it?" His voice was sweet as honey. "Just one touch, maybe two!"

Cora was surprisingly generous. "Don't touch the hook. Anything else is fine."

Damian carefully pressed a hand against the tail, then quickly withdrew it. The texture was rough, and the scales felt prickly against his palm, making it itch. It was like he had discovered a fascinating new toy and was about to reach out again when—

Onyx stepped over the winding tail, grabbed Damian by the collar with one hand, and disdainfully tossed him over to Charles.

"Cora's condition is complicated. My preliminary assessment is that there's a genetic issue. I'll take her for a thorough examination as soon as we get back. Meanwhile, everyone else should help cover for her."

The signs weren't as obvious in the water, but now, out of the combat environment, it would be easy for others to notice something was wrong if they weren't careful. The group nodded in agreement, all pledging to protect their captain without hesitation.

Finally, Suchat found his chance. "You and that whale..."

Yuui waved dismissively, unconcerned: "That's not important. What I want to know is what exactly Utopia is."

Onyx sat down close to Cora, lazily crossing one leg over the other. He activated the terminal's speaker and began drafting the report. "The truth is already quite clear."

Cora unconsciously shifted her tail, loosely coiling it around him, encircling him like a protective barrier. The tip of her tail rested on his knee, making it look as though Onyx was seated on a snakeskin sofa.

"The conclusion of this S-level mission is obvious: the residents of the Elder Nation didn't disappear mysteriously—they went to Utopia. Have you heard of the 'Ark'?"

Onyx freed his left hand, skillfully massaging the tail on his lap like a seasoned therapist, hitting all the right spots. The gentle electrical pulses sent waves of pleasure to Cora's brain, making her relax into her wheelchair, her eyes narrowing slightly, while the tip of her tail twitched in contentment.

"The Old Civilization's Bible mentioned a mortal named Noah. Following divine instructions, built a massive ship called the 'Ark' to protect the world's creatures from God's wrath."

"The Alliance..." Onyx's voice was soft and measured, his one-handed typing steady and deliberate.

"It wasn't just the Alliance. Galio and Luse also took part in this plan. Together, the three nations built an 'Ark,' which is Utopia, and issued 'tickets' to a select few."

Yuui was surprised. "Are you saying the residents of the Elder Nation willingly left District A5 because they received these so-called 'tickets'?" Felix casually interjected, "Maybe right now they're popping champagne in Utopia, saying, 'Oh my God, look at those foolish groundhogs down there—they'll never know our joy.'"

That joke didn't land, and everyone shot Felix a blank stare.

"I still don't understand," Yuui said slowly. "Leaving aside why they would so firmly abandon Elder Nation for the seemingly unattainable Utopia, how could they keep this a secret? Even if we hadn't taken this mission, wouldn't the rise of such a massive airborne city have exposed everything?"

"Because Utopia has already risen," Onyx replied calmly, though there was a distinct edge to his voice. "Twenty-one days ago, Elder Nation's Ministry of Trade went silent. I believe that's when they preemptively moved to the underwater Utopia, waiting for the right time to launch."

Everyone was stunned.

"And even if it had been exposed, it wouldn't have mattered. No one could have stopped them—once their aim was achieved, it was too late."

Onyx opened the Lucas Network, where a video shot by an Aberrant had already gone viral, sparking widespread outrage. Most people didn't understand what had happened and were just jumping on the bandwagon to condemn the global powers of their conspiracy.

"But didn't you say that Smyrna's theory was unachievable?" Charles stroked his chin, deep confusion in his eyes. "So why did the Alliance go through with this? When did they plan? And how did they make the floating city a reality?"

Onyx patted Cora, signaling her to shift. "Let's rewind the timeline, back to where it all began."

"The New Pacific Alliance was formed after the war to rebuild the nation. Because of nuclear warfare, living conditions on the surface became increasingly harsh, with extreme weather occurring frequently. This led to the creation of the weather simulation system. Yet, even with that, the Alliance might have long recognized that this land was no longer suitable for survival. They needed to find or create a new home."

"And things only got worse after the apocalypse," Cora added, straining to think and offer a constructive suggestion.

"That's right, the captain has a point." Onyx's hand slid slowly down her tailbone, carefully checking for any wounds inch by inch.

The post-apocalyptic world, with its hordes of zombies, savage beasts, scarce resources, and abandoned cities, made human survival increasingly precarious.

"As for when Utopia was constructed, it might have been before

Smyrna was sentenced to Death Hell, or perhaps when the First Council rejected the Utopia proposal—that's when the Alliance might have taken action." Onyx smiled knowingly. "After all, 'Rome wasn't built in a day.' A project of this magnitude would have required a lengthy period of preparation."

Felix opened a map, circling a familiar area.

"The Endless Sea is the perfect factory. At the junction of three nations, its unique geographic position makes it an informal 'no-man's-land.' If anything goes wrong, the various national powers can quickly intervene. Plus, the natural magnetic disturbances in the Doom Sea make it difficult for instruments to detect any activity. And since the construction took place underwater, secrecy wasn't a concern."

Onyx nodded slightly, an unusual sign of agreement. "After considerable effort, Utopia was finally completed. The only remaining challenge was how to send it into the sky."

"That's easy," Felix immediately countered, "as long as there's enough Sora Wings."

Sora Wings, an alternative energy source discovered in the early century, was originally monopolized by the Lucas family in the Grass Pit for extraction and purification. Later, the Lucas family voluntarily handed the technology over to the Alliance, which led to the explosive development of flight terminals. During the Glory 30-year Era, Lucas Starships (upgraded by Felix in Year 32 of the New Calendar) became a symbol of brilliant civilization.

Yuui raised a concern.

"But I've read reports that the world's supply of Sora Wings is limited. The energy needed to lift Utopia into the sky must have been enormous. How did they gather so much?"

"I know," Cora suddenly spoke up, "because the Sora Wings from the lower districts... they were all reclaimed."

In the fall of Year 46 of the New Calendar, just one week after the apocalypse began, Cora traveled alone from District F177 to Blossomville. She had once witnessed a meteor shower of starships crashing from the sky—a harrowing sight that she would never forget. From that day forward, all starships in the lower districts ceased to function, making inter-district travel nearly impossible.

She couldn't understand why, but now it all made sense.

Perhaps in the Round Table meetings at The Central (District A1), the 155 lower districts (CDEF Districts) outside of Districts A and B were expendable. After all, the people there didn't even have full access rights and might never glimpse the true nature of the world. They were like a bundle of discarded firewood in a corner—ready to be burned whenever needed.

Felix scoffed. "I just checked the news from the other two nations. After the apocalypse, the failure rate of flight terminals skyrocketed there as well."

It didn't need to be said—the missing Sora Wings from Galio and Luse were also used to power Utopia.

Onyx chuckled softly. "Fast forward to today, and after everything was in place, they chose this day as Utopia's 'birthdate.' And all the anomalies we experienced—T001's malfunction, the disappearance of Elder Nation's barrier, the sudden appearance of Level 4 and 5 beasts—were all caused by the intense seismic activity underwater, disrupting the local ecosystem."

Yuui sighed, massaging her temples. "We really had terrible luck... No, actually, those suppliers had it worse, losing both their goods and money..."

"I can't speak for everyone, but at least F777 isn't the unluckiest," Onyx remarked, typing the last characters. A graduate of Luboni's finest academy, he had just completed a meticulously written, well-argued, and thoroughly detailed report. He took Cora's hand, cradling her index finger as they ceremoniously pressed the "Submit" button together.

If the report passed the review, this S-level mission, along with the two side quests, would earn them an astonishing amount of points.

Onyx's deep, almond-shaped eyes narrowed slightly, a hint of cold indifference gracing his handsome features. "The storm is coming."

"As for what happens next, let the bigwigs fight it out. After all, we're just an ordinary, ordinary squad trying to make a living by earning points occasionally, right?"

No sooner had he finished speaking than he was abruptly proven wrong.

"Beep, beep." The terminal's notification chime sounded

incessantly. Inside the "District B10 High-Tier Talent Dating Event," channel, countless people were searching for them.

"OMG!! Has anyone seen this video on the Lucas Network? Here's the link." "Saw it. Who's F777? Are they from the Northern Base?"

"Yeah, they just joined the group recently. I'll tag their captain @CoraThorntonIsTheBest." "I don't believe it. That video must be fake." "I was there, the video is legit." "@SilverOwlLockedHeart@SilverOwlLockedHeart, were you on the scene?"

Curious, Cora clicked on the link, and was immediately greeted with a first-person view of the sea battle. The main title was extremely flashy: "Shocking! A Video That Will Leave Men Speechless and Women in Tears: The First-Ever Level 5 Beast, Leatherback Sea Turtle, Defeated in the Alliance!"

The subheading glowed brightly: "Who on Earth Is F777, Ranked 235,706?" Below that, a line in red text declared— "You're not a loyal member of the Alliance if you don't watch this."

CHAPTER 44

A Surprise

Onyx clicked his tongue softly, his knuckles tightening around the snake's tail. He dragged the progress bar back and pressed play from the beginning, forcing everyone to watch those three flashy lines of text again.

The video appeared to have been recorded using a ring terminal, with a limited field of view that occasionally wobbled. The person filming likely hadn't expected what would happen next. At first, they were absentmindedly filming the empty streets of Elder Nation, but soon the ground cracked open with a thunderous roar. The camera shook violently, plummeting downward as if it were on a free fall ride, inadvertently capturing the ocean surface—a massive beast's head suddenly emerged!

The realism of the disaster was overwhelming, the golden opening scene executed flawlessly, making it no surprise that the video went viral, instantly capturing the audience's attention. Many people on the island were filming. Some Aberrants were even connected with their clients, keeping them informed of the situation.

But when Elder Nation collapsed and the leatherback sea turtle began its rampage, everyone was thrown into a fierce battle, too occupied to care about recording. However, this guy didn't just keep the camera rolling—he even switched to motion capture mode, enhancing the image quality.

A line of text slowly appeared on the screen: "The real action begins now."

Yuui chuckled, "Oh, there's even post-production."

"Whoosh! Whoosh!" Two agile figures landed in the center of the screen—Cora and Suchat materialized out of thin air, like twin stars in orbit, weaving through the barnacles as they charged toward the leatherback sea turtle's head.

The cameraman let out a startled "Holy sh—" and stumbled along behind them, tripping multiple times before finally catching up to the action, just in time to witness their brilliant teamwork.

A blue light flared up as Cora and Suchat, one appearing real, the other an illusion, simultaneously thrust their Ethereal Artifacts with unstoppable force. Combined with the distant firepower support, they instantly blinded the leatherback sea turtle! The intense background music kicked in, followed by the adrenaline-pumping text: "First blood!" "Double kill!"

"Whoooaaa!!" The cameraman let out an excited scream, the voice vaguely familiar.

Cora's face showed a hint of surprise. After a moment, she dredged up a memory from the depths of her mind—that voice belonged to none other than the chatty rainbow-haired Bryan Young!

Onyx paused the video, rewound it, and watched again. Cora's genes hadn't yet shown any issues; her silhouette was still agile, and her legs could be clearly seen as she ran.

The leatherback sea turtle launched a 360-degree counterattack, knocking Bryan into the water. The camera bobbed up and down, the suffocating pressure of the deep sea making it hard to breathe. He eventually climbed back onto the turtle shell, wiping away the water droplets from the lens, only to find that Cora had vanished from view.

In the distance, a group of mutant sharks appeared. Bryan gathered his Anopower, bravely charging forward while muttering non-stop, "If I die, this will be my last words video. But no worries, twenty years later, your bro Bryan will be back!"

Yuui rested her chin on her hand, her expression slightly worried. "If he keeps filming like this, won't he capture Cora's tail?"

Cora, startled, quickly retracted her snake tail, curling it tightly into a large spiral.

Felix calmly shook his head. "If he really caught something, the

Lucas Network wouldn't be so quiet right now."

So far, online discussions had covered every topic, except for any mention of a "snake tail."

"Keep watching," Onyx said in a low voice.

The video continued. By now, Cora's snake tail had already grown, and everyone in the private box straightened up, focusing intently on the screen.

Bryan's bad luck continued. Just as he climbed back onto the turtle shell, he turned around and ran straight into a Level 4 mutant shark. The creature opened its gaping maw, ready to bite his head off, when —suddenly—it froze!

"Triple kill!"

Cora appeared from the side, her hands executing a deadly cross-slash. "Slash!" She tore open the beast's skull, dark blood splattering across the lens, instantly darkening the screen as if drenching the viewers in the scene. Then, a blood-red crystal caught everyone's attention.

Onyx slowly replayed the frames, and as the mutant shark's snout was pierced, a faint dark light flashed by. He zoomed in with two fingers, holding the hooked fork on Cora's tail, and pulled it up to compare with the projection. "Can you see it?"

Charles leaned in for a closer look. "I would just assume it's a blade."

Suchat agreed, "Hard to tell." The others shook their heads as well. Cora's attack was swift and clean, leaving no traces, and nothing unusual could be seen in the video.

Next came the scene where Cora faced off against the leatherback sea turtle alone. Bryan's position was a bit too far, and even with the zoom at its maximum, the camera was still slightly out of focus.

This was the most likely moment of exposure—when Cora was launched into the sky, her tail, which wasn't fully covered, could be caught on film!

However, when the kill scene appeared, everyone in the private box fell silent.

Bryan had manually added special effects, with rainbow laser lights swirling around Cora, making her look like she was standing under the rotating lights of a low-end disco.

The effect was so blinding that it could have made anyone squint. But that wasn't the best part—he had also exaggerated the size of the trident, so all that could be seen was a massive, colorful orb and an over-the-top trident descending from the sky, stabbing through the leatherback sea turtle's head.

"Quadra kill!" "Aced!"

As soon as the Level 5 crystal appeared, Cora was bathed in a shower of golden light (added in post-production), resembling the famous giant Buddha statue in Cloud City. In this kind of scene, not only was her tail hidden, but even if she had sprouted wings and taken flight on the spot, it would have looked perfectly natural.

Cora sincerely praised, "Wow… that looks awesome."

Yuui was incredulous. "You think that looks good?"

Cora blinked, unsure, and mumbled, "It's... it's pretty nice."

"I shouldn't have asked. You and that rainbow-head have the same taste." Yuui sighed, rubbing her forehead.

Bryan had really outdone himself, accidentally giving Cora some cover.

But Bryan wasn't done yet. He recorded Utopia rising and Yuui riding the whale, both scenes filled with the same bling-bling effects. However, because the mutant whale was so large, he couldn't capture it all on screen, so he opted to add a voiceover: "My savior is F777's greatest heroine. One day, she rode a giant fish to rescue me."

After F777's highlight reel ended, Bryan still stretched the video out for another twenty minutes, rambling on about his thoughts and feelings that no one wanted to hear until the rescue finally arrived and the video came to a close.

Yuui was at a loss for words, "Well, at least it drew some fire away from the Captain. I don't have any dirt, so they can dig all they want."

Onyx asked coldly, "Can the video be deleted?"

Felix replied, "Not entirely. The spread is too fast and downloads have already exceeded two hundred million."

Though it ended on a low note, Bryan's "First Video of an Alliance-Level 5 Beast Kill" had enough hype and just enough quality to be decent. In less than two hours, it had spread across all of District B.

"Even if it's deleted, as soon as others share their local files, it'll just resurface—like weeds that won't stop growing no matter how much you burn them," Felix remarked in a flat, pessimistic tone.

Onyx closed his eyes for two seconds before snapping them open. "Then deal with the source file." The edited video showed nothing unusual, but the original footage might be a different story. Bryan had noticed nothing wrong yet, but if he ever reviewed it carefully, he might just realize something was off.

Bryan Young's "Peace Dove" squad was on the same starship as F777. Onyx, Felix, and Suchat pushed the door open and stepped out, the three stern-faced young men walking through the rear cabin and stopping in front of another private room. Even through the door, Bryan Young's incessant chatter could be heard.

"Hey, Sister Glory, do you think I'm gonna be famous? Maybe I should switch careers and become an influencer. Your bro Bryan's got a bright future ahead of him."

"Shut up, Bryan! Can't you ever be quiet?"

"Knock, knock—" Onyx politely knocked on the private room door, and without waiting for a response, he yanked it open—Suchat stood at the forefront, his six-foot-three frame filling the doorway, eyes dark and a ghostly blue dagger spinning in his palm.

Sure enough, Bryan Young had a ring on his left middle finger, a skull-headed Gothic piece that somehow matched his offbeat personality.

Onyx pushed up his gold-rimmed glasses, his demeanor refined and gentlemanly, like a corrupt, elite lawyer.

"Captain Glory, I'm the appointed lawyer for F777. Your team member has unlawfully recorded and distributed a video without my client's consent, severely infringing on our image rights and reputation. Of course, our Captain Thornton is magnanimous and doesn't intend to claim the original compensation of 40 million NPA credits. All we ask is that the infringing evidence be destroyed."

"Image... reputation... what??" Bryan stammered, rattled by the mix of threats and legal jargon, "You-you-you can't just bully me because I don't know the law! Forty million? Are you robbing me? I wouldn't have that much if you sold me!"

Onyx smiled nonchalantly, a distant glint in his eyes. "We just want to make a quiet fortune, but you're making that really difficult."

"Sorry about that," Glory Ku, who was reasonable, apologized.

"We didn't mean to cause you trouble. Bryan, delete the video."

Suchat pressed the knife's tip against Bryan's nose. Shaking, Bryan gingerly removed the ring and placed it on the knife. Suchat flipped it back over his shoulder, and Felix's bionic arm moved in sync, copying the source file, then effortlessly crushed Bryan's copy, ensuring that even an S-rank hacker couldn't restore it.

"Well then, sorry to bother you. Have a pleasant journey back." Onyx flashed a courteous smile before shutting the door with a loud "bang."

Bryan sat there, defeated, his wild rainbow-colored hair drooping. "... Sister Glory, I've thought it over. Becoming an influencer is way too dangerous. It's even riskier than being an Aberrant. I think your bro Bryan should just stick to the basics."

After dealing with Bryan Young, the trio returned to their private box. Felix sent the copied source file to Cora's terminal while Onyx carefully reviewed it.

With the major issue resolved, only minor matters remained.

Suchat finally found his chance and asked Yuui for the third time, "You and that fish...?"

Charles was also curious. "Yeah, how did you communicate with a wild beast?" Cora and Damian Blackwood turned their heads, their eyes bright as they looked at Yuui.

Yuui casually flipped her hair and gave a sultry smile, covering her mouth as she laughed lightly. "I thought you guys weren't interested? Well then, let me tell you all about my legendary story."

Before Elder Nation collapsed, Yuui had sung a song on Ribbon Bridge, infusing it with a faint amount of mental power. She hoped to communicate with the sea creatures, but she wasn't sure if the frequency was off or if the wild beasts, despite their intelligence, lacked sentience. There was no response, so she assumed her attempt had failed.

It wasn't until she was on the brink of drowning, her life jacket torn, that the mutant whale saved her. At that moment, she was disoriented and thought she was hallucinating. It wasn't until she broke through the water's surface, coughing violently, that she realized she had indeed witnessed a miracle.

Through the whale's low hums, Yuui learned it wasn't a native creature of the Endless Sea. Because of its unique vocal frequency, it had never communicated with others of its kind and had spent countless days and nights wandering alone in the eastern and northern seas of the Alliance. That day was the first time it had heard —and understood—a "kinder spirit" song.

Yuui still found it unbelievable. "I can't explain why, but I really could communicate with it—using mental power." She added softly, "I don't think it's a wild beast."

After hearing Yuui's account, something flashed through Cora's mind. "I've seen a strange wild beast, too."

She recalled encountering a strange bird at the martial arts hall on Mount Yue after the apocalypse. She was covered in blood, a murderous aura emanating from her, yet the bird simply observed her quietly from the windowsill with no intent to attack.

Onyx spoke slowly. "Humans can mutate into zombies or Aberrants. Animals affected by radiation also mutate in different ways. The creatures you encountered wouldn't exactly be called 'wild beasts.' Perhaps we could call them 'animal Aberrants.'"

Cora's eyes lit up with sudden inspiration. "Not-so-wild beasts?"

Onyx coughed awkwardly. "Close enough. As long as you understand, the name isn't important."

"Alright then, if there's nothing else, you can all rest now. Questions?" Onyx asked.

"I do." Felix quietly raised one of his bionic arms. "The starship we 'borrowed' from the Northern Base is missing. The Trojan I implanted is about to expire soon. Have you thought about what might happen when it does?"

"I know! We'll be wanted," Damian answered enthusiastically.

What was going on? From Sin City to Deep Woods and then to the Northern Base, they were law-abiding citizens—so how had they ended up on a blacklist wherever they went? Onyx rubbed his temples in exasperation. "...I'll contact Svetlana Yevgeniyeva."

District B7, Northern Yard.

In the empty office, a woman's silhouette merged with the darkness, resembling a silent statue, as she gazed intently at the floating light screen before her. On the desk behind her lay a gilded invitation, with the name at the bottom reading: Utopia. It was a pass, or more accurately, a "ticket"—an entry pass to board Utopia.

Even though the message could have been delivered through a terminal, the person who sent the invitation chose the oldest method —a paper letter. It was as if they wanted to leave a last trace of their existence in the world they were about to abandon.

Few people knew of Utopia's existence, and even fewer would refuse such a precious "ticket." If there had been no unforeseen circumstances, the woman before the screen should have long been enjoying a new life in Utopia. Yet, she had not once glanced at the desk. Instead, her eyes remained fixed on the video, repeatedly pressing pause at the same point.

It was when the leatherback sea turtle self-destructed—a subtle pause caused by the massive body—a tiny detail that could easily be overlooked. But the woman was certain that it was the work of a mental-type Aberrant.

A blurry shadow flickered at the edge of the frame. No matter how many times she paused the video, the figure's appearance remained indistinct. Even when zoomed in, all that could be seen were scattered pixels.

The video focused on Cora Thornton, who single-handedly took down the Level 5 wild beast. No one paid attention to the unremarkable bystanders, especially when this person's face was unclear.

The woman dragged the video back again and again, replaying those brief two seconds.

The room's lights gradually illuminated the woman's striking face. Though no longer in her prime, traces of her once extraordinary beauty were still clear. Besides her appearance, her long tenure in a prominent position had imbued her with an imposing aura that made her difficult to look at directly.

The woman slowly parted her lips, her slightly hoarse voice echoing in the room. "Can this video be deleted?"

The person on the other end of the holographic projection responded with utmost respect, "Sorry, General, I'm afraid... it can't be completely erased."

"Then suppress its popularity, bring it down as low as possible."

"Yes."

"Send Captain Anderson from the Eleventh Squad over."

"Understood."

Before long, a tall young man in uniform appeared. Captain Vincent Anderson removed his cap, holding it in the crook of his arm, and bowed respectfully. "General."

It was none other than Vincent Anderson, a former member of the Azure Force's Eleventh Squad.

The woman nodded slightly, her tone indifferent as she said, "I've read your report. You mentioned the F777 team in it."

Vincent was slightly surprised. F777 wasn't directly related to their mission, so he had only briefly mentioned them. He didn't expect the General to recall the name after all these months—her memory was astonishing.

"Yes, Captain Wolf... had some dealings with them." The mention of Jeremy Wolfgang's name caused a surge of grief and anger, like a dormant volcano erupting within Vincent, making his voice waver slightly.

The woman pressed the play button remotely, restarting the video that had looped countless times. "Do you recognize any of these people?"

Vincent focused, carefully identifying them. "Cora Thornton, Damian Blackwood, and I've seen two others at U-Lab—Yuui Hayashi and Suchat." As for Charles Franz, whom he hadn't met, and Felix Lucas, who didn't appear in the footage, Vincent naturally couldn't recognize them.

Something suddenly came to Vincent's mind, but he wasn't sure if that person counted as a member of F777. After all, it was difficult for Aberrants and ordinary people to form a team based on mutual trust. Who knew if they had already parted ways?

"There was another person with Cora—a man in a wheelchair who claimed to be a senior maintenance engineer for the weather-mimicking system."

"And his name?" the woman asked, her posture betraying a barely perceptible pause.

"His name... was Onyx de Montclair." In the end, Vincent spoke the truth.

"What did you say?" The woman's figure froze ever so slightly.

"Onyx de Montclair."

"He said his name was 'Onyx de Montclair'?"

"Yes." the woman's reaction puzzled Vincent, but he still replied firmly, "We verified his credentials. He indeed came from the Arashi Research Institute, and his work ID had the name Onyx de Montclair."

A deathly silence fell over the office. After a long pause, a faint sigh echoed through the room.

The dim moonlight from outside filtered onto the desk, casting a soft glow on the top of the invitation.

— (Honorable General Arashi Sheen, we sincerely invite you to Utopia...)

CHAPTER 45

A Reward

"That's ridiculous!!!"

On the other end of the communication line, Svetlana's voice roared with such intensity that it made everyone's ears ring in the room.

Cora twisted down the volume. The righteous third-generation government official was clearly shocked by their outrageous stunt, her voice trembling at the end of her sentence:

"You... You're an S7-level, all-A rated Aberrant team. How could you... How could you steal a starship?!"

"Onyx said that borrowing intending to return isn't stealing..." Damian muttered softly, betraying his teammate without hesitation.

Svetlana's sharp ears caught the remark, and she immediately shot back, "That's still 'completed theft,' at most it counts as turning yourselves in. Besides, did you even return it?"

"Last time, we did," Captain Thornton stepped forward, owning up to their mistake with sincerity. "This time, there was a small, unexpected incident." The starship's Sora Wings had been sucked away by the ascending Utopia, and the vessel itself had long since been shattered into pieces in the underwater vortex.

"What?! There was a last time?!" Svetlana nearly choked.

Cora let out a small "Oops," covering her mouth guiltily.

Svetlana sighed deeply, trying to persuade them earnestly. "If you needed a starship, you could have told me. I could have helped you apply for one."

Yuui retorted coldly, "By the time your Bureau of Aberrants' approval process is complete, we'd be late to the party."

Svetlana was speechless. The starship was the Alliance's most advanced flight terminal, with 100% automated navigation on all public routes. But if used for private travel, the unpredictable routes required a dedicated pilot, and the application process was notoriously lengthy. Sometimes, just waiting for an appointment could take half a month.

"But you still shouldn't have stolen it..." Svetlana sighed in resignation. "Fine, fine. I'll handle the damaged starship. I'll also apply for a private one for you guys. Without a pilot, the approval should be much quicker. And with my grandfather backing you, it's not really bending the rules..."

"Miss Yevgeniyeva, how's the progress in the lab we discussed?" Onyx suddenly interjected.

"Oh, I've already arranged it. Once you land, Chu Bai will take you there. Don't worry, no one will dare to kidnap you this time." Svetlana vaguely knew that something was wrong with Cora's condition. The fallout between F777 and Scarlett Holland was related to this. So, when Onyx requested an independent lab, she didn't ask many questions, and agreed without hesitation. Her efficiency was top-notch, arranging a location in less than a day.

Cora made a "stiff-backed grandpa" gesture across the room. Onyx understood and replied, "Thank you. Once we've handled our current tasks, we'll meet General Yevgeniyev right away."

After the call ended, Onyx's expression darkened.

It had been over 24 hours since Cora's snake tail appeared. During that time, they had tried everything—scaring her, mental stimulation, Cora even had Suchat cut her tail, but it still wouldn't revert.

Afterward, Charles gave them a stern lecture, scolding them for being reckless just because they had a healer on hand to fix the wounds.

However, for Cora, this kind of mutation was extremely dangerous. Genes had their own recognition patterns; if they accepted the snake tail as the norm and solidified it, the consequences would be unimaginable. Onyx was desperate to get her to the lab for a restoration experiment.

Even though, in theory, he could handle the matter on his own, he didn't dare take risks with Cora. After a moment of contemplation, he dialed another number.

The next morning, everyone, still half-asleep, heard the good news.

The report Onyx submitted had passed the supplier's review, and the long-overdue rewards for the S-level commission had finally arrived.

Whether it was shutting down the Weather Simulation System, killing the leatherback sea turtle, or uncovering the truth behind the Elder Nation's communication blackout, F777 played a crucial role. They were the biggest winners of this mission, with their points soaring to several million!

As for the ranking that Cora was most concerned about, F777 had finally made a breakthrough, jumping from an awkward middle position to 52nd in the Northern Base and 1,314th in the New Pacific Alliance.

Five days later, at the Starship Port in Tustan, Northern Base.

No matter the time, this place was always bustling. Those eager to join District B4 rushed about, while intermediaries called out enthusiastically. The seven members of Cora's team disembarked from the starship, quickly blending into the crowd under the dim evening sky.

They had deliberately chosen to get off one stop early to avoid running into Tustan. If Silver Owl Jennifer and her overly enthusiastic father suddenly suggested continuing their mission, it would be a real headache.

At the exit, Yuui turned around, half her face hidden behind a mask. "Let's head back to the apartment first." After Bryan Young's video spread, it was safe to assume that everyone in the Northern Base knew about F777. It was best to keep a low profile.

Felix waved his mechanical arm. "Let's hope the Captain comes back with an extra leg."

Cora was already immune to his dark humor. "I'll do my best, really."

Onyx pushed Cora toward Chu Bai, who was waiting on the side. Seeing that the person in the wheelchair had changed, Chu Bai didn't seem surprised at all. The two got into the hover car. F777 had made quite a name for themselves this time, and an ordinary person would have jumped at the chance to gossip or pry for insider information, but Chu Bai remained silent the entire trip.

It wasn't until they got out of the car that he finally spoke. "Do you need me to wait for you?"

"No, thank you," Cora politely replied.

Chu Bai paused for a moment and, surprisingly, added, "Miss Yevgeniyeva bought this place. I've already disabled the surveillance inside." Whatever they did in the lab wouldn't be discovered.

Cora mentally gave Svetlana a thumbs-up. She was truly reliable. She had only mentioned "arranging" the lab, but it turned out she had bought it outright.

After saying goodbye to Chu Bai, Onyx entered the password Svetlana had provided. The main door slowly opened, and the two of them took the elevator down to the basement level.

With no one else around, Cora let herself go completely, sliding off the wheelchair as her long snake tail unfurled across the corridor, silently gliding forward. The only sound echoing through the empty hallway was the steady, unhurried steps of Onyx following behind her, careful not to step on her tail.

However, Cora was used to walking on two legs, and after spending days cramped in the starship's cabin with no opportunity to practice, she could hardly maintain the S-shaped balance required for reptilian movement. She hadn't slithered more than a few steps before —thud—she landed face-first on the ground.

"Ow!" Tears welled up in Cora's eyes as she whimpered, holding her nose. Suddenly, a pair of long legs appeared in front of her. Onyx squatted down, trying to help her up, but Cora, feeling embarrassed, protested, "I can do it myself!"

She pressed her fingertips to the ground, attempting to lift herself, but the floor was too smooth. Her snake tail kept slipping, and as soon as she got up, she wobbled and fell again. Smack! A crisp slap echoed as Onyx's gold-rimmed glasses slipped off his face.

Cora stared at the clear red mark on his cheek. "Uh..."

The lab was eerily silent, with the polished floor reflecting the harsh lights above.

Onyx lowered his gaze, his expression unreadable. But it took little imagination to realize that this young master had probably never been slapped in his life. Cora felt a wave of guilt, wishing she could disappear into the floor. "Sorry about that."

"It's fine." Onyx sighed and simply sat down on the floor. "Cora, we need to talk."

Cora straightened up, "Okay."

"Epigenetics—you know what that is?" Cora looked blank, her eyes clearly saying, "Do I look like I know?"

Onyx adjusted her hair gently, switching to a simpler explanation. "Basically, different species have obvious differences in chromosome numbers and genome sequences. Even if a DNA sequence is identical, minor changes in regulatory mechanisms can significantly affect gene expression."

Cora nodded earnestly, moving closer and placing her hands on the ground, ready to listen. Onyx subtly shifted his knees, effectively encircling her.

"After the New Era began, humanity achieved 100% genome sequencing, meaning our DNA is more transparent and complete than any other species. But you're not like that; about 16% of your genes are unknown."

Cora hesitated, then nodded.

"Although humans and snakes share 85% homology, a normal person wouldn't suddenly turn into a snake—don't argue, not even half a snake. You get it?"

Cora grudgingly shut her mouth and nodded again.

"So, I suspect that you..." Onyx trailed off, gazing at the girl in front of him, sinking into rare silence.

"You suspect that I'm an experiment." Cora lifted her head and calmly finished his sentence.

Onyx was taken aback, not expecting Cora to come to that conclusion herself.

Cora wasn't naïve. Ever since Onyx had reviewed her full Anopower report, he had been troubled by something. She had lived through the apocalypse, seen and heard so much—could she really be oblivious to her abnormalities? No. In fact, she had a vague sense of it.

This suspicion had been irrefutably confirmed when she inexplicably grew a snake tail.

Onyx nodded slightly. "I suspect you were part of a gene fusion experiment, but you have no memory of it. So, where it happened, when, who conducted it, and how to reverse it—we can't be sure yet. We need to decode those unknown genes."

"Will decoding them give you the answers?" Cora blinked.

"Yes." Onyx took her hand and slowly brought it to his forehead. "Here lies all the data on gene experiments, down to every log, every sequence, every success or failure."

"As long as we can detect those unknown sequences, I can figure out your origin and stabilize you." There was a deeper concern in Onyx's mind, but he decided not to share it with Cora until he was certain.

"What exactly will the experiment involve?" Cora asked, poking his forehead lightly with her finger.

"We'll need to attach sensors, inject some reagents, run some scans, and... there might be a little radiation."

Cora's tail flicked impatiently. "I don't like being locked up." The memory of that last experience with excessive radiation was too awful; she loathed the idea of being confined in a narrow capsule.

Onyx grasped her cheeks, gently shaking them from side to side. "I won't lock you up, absolutely not."

He suddenly smiled, his deep eyes rippling with amusement. "To be honest, though I'm well-versed in theory, this will be my first time conducting a real experiment. To make sure everything goes smoothly, do you think you could?"

"Do you want a pre-reward?" Cora mumbled in a confused tone.

"Do you think you could advance me some points?" Onyx whispered, his light-colored eyes filled with mirth, his handsome face practically glowing.

"Huh?" Cora's heartbeat slowed as she didn't fully grasp his meaning. But somehow, her blood suddenly surged, rushing to her head.

Before she could react, Onyx leaned in.

It was a kiss, light as butterfly wings, carrying Onyx's scent.

Her heart pounded so loudly it was deafening, and goosebumps prickled down her back. Cora was frozen in place, too dazed to resist. Her fingers curled in, and her long tail coiled tighter and tighter, her scales involuntarily spreading out.

Yet, she felt an unexpected happiness, and her tail swayed on its own.

Onyx's hand slid from her cheek to the back of her head, ready to deepen the kiss when—

"The equipment is ready. Seriously, what's taking you two so long to get in here?" A sudden voice broke through from the end of the hallway.

The intimate moment shattered. Onyx closed his eyes, his brow twitching in frustration.

Cora's eyes snapped wide open when she saw who it was. She shoved Onyx away and flicked her forked tail, wrapping it around the intruder's neck. Rainer Ninnemann's face turned beet red, his feet lifting off the ground as he was hoisted into the air, choking violently.

Onyx, with his back to them, ran a hand through his hair, exhaling a deep breath to calm himself. "Cora, I asked him to come." Cora loosened her grip slightly, her eyes still wary, ready to strike if Rainer made any wrong move.

Onyx shifted uncomfortably, his voice low and laced with gritted teeth. "Dr. Ninnemann, I'm in a very bad mood right now. You better start explaining yourself."

CHAPTER 46

Transformation

Rainer Ninnemann still looked as though he hadn't slept in days—his temples streaked with gray, his expression fatigued, and his drooping eyes fixated on Cora's snake tail. "I know you hate me, but tonight... cough... I'm not your enemy."

He clutched at the bruises on his neck, his voice hoarse and dry. "Cough... This kid made a deal with me, so I'm here tonight as his assistant for the experiment."

Rainer, a heavyweight in the field, acting as an assistant to the unknown Onyx de Montclair? If word got out, it would shock everyone.

"Aren't you Holland's man?" Cora narrowed her eyes, clearly suspicious of his words.

Rainer was about to reply when a chill suddenly ran down his spine, a cold sensation of being watched by a predator. He looked up slightly and noticed that Cora's eyes had already turned into vertical slits—a sign that her mutation was deepening.

"I belong to no one," Rainer sighed. "Scarlett wanted my research results, so she provided me with money and equipment. I needed a team and space to conduct independent experiments, so I accepted her protection temporarily. It's a mutual exchange, nothing more. That last time, it was my idea to have her bring you in, but I didn't expect her to use such extreme methods."

"Scarlett is skilled at political maneuvering but clueless for academia. She thought I wanted to use you for human experiments, like those with the mutant zombies, but she was wrong." Rainer's eyes gleamed with a certain fanaticism as he took a step forward, unable to suppress his excitement.

"From the moment I saw your Anopower report, I had a feeling that your ability to withstand high radiation would be the key to a breakthrough in my research."

These researchers were never quite normal, and Rainer's stubbornness and madness surpassed the average person. Startled, Cora swiftly raised her hand, throwing a ghostly blue dagger that pinned Rainer's shoe to the ground, causing him to stagger back and fall with a thud.

"Rainer, she's not your lab rat," Onyx slowly stood up, retrieved his glasses, and put them back on, issuing a cold warning.

"I get it. I promised I wouldn't target her anymore, but you'd better keep your word, too." Rainer seemed rather wary of him.

"Why did you bring him?" Cora grumbled, bumping her head against Onyx.

"Sorry, I..." Onyx apologized readily, but hesitated slightly in his tone.

Rainer struggled to pull himself up using the wall for support and casually commented, "Reverse genetic experiments are full of risks. If something goes wrong, it could spiral out of control. This kid wasn't confident, afraid you'd get hurt, so he brought me in as backup."

Cora paused, remembering Onyx's earlier comment about it being his "first time." She had been too flustered to pay much attention to it.

Onyx uncertain? He always seemed so composed, as if everything was under control. Could he really be afraid because he wasn't sure? Or was it because she was the subject of the experiment that he didn't dare take any risks?

Rainer, finally prying the dagger out of his shoe, handed it back to Cora. "And I—I've been involved in the 'Spark' and 'Plan Eternity' projects. My current research is also closely related to genetic engineering. You won't find anyone more experienced or suitable in the entire Alliance."

"Besides, I'm still with the Arashi Research Institute. When he was a kid, I even—"

"Ninnemann, some things are better left unsaid," Onyx interrupted him.

Rainer waved a hand dismissively. "Alright, your condition can't be delayed. Let's get started." Cora remained wary, not moving.

Rainer sighed again. "Even if you don't trust me, trust this kid beside you, right? I promise, whatever happens here tonight, no one else will ever know."

Onyx quickly traced an "S" on Cora's palm.

Cora immediately understood and nodded silently. Rainer was just a regular person; coming here alone meant he was taking on far more risk than they were. After all, against two S-level Aberrants, they could kill him effortlessly.

Cora swayed her tail awkwardly as she moved through the corridor, and the three of them entered the lab's inner chamber. Onyx didn't even glance at the enclosed capsules, instead choosing the most spacious examination room and moving the equipment inside.

The room was kept at a cool temperature, and Onyx dimmed the lights to a soft glow—bright enough, but not harsh. He then pulled out a soft leather recliner, removing the restraining straps. Cora propped herself up with one hand and hopped onto it, coiling half her tail while the rest hung down to the floor.

On the large, cluttered experiment table, various instruments were laid out. Rainer was about to adjust some equipment when Onyx stopped him. "I'll handle it."

Onyx gazed at the equipment for a moment, rapidly recalling the relevant information in his mind. His brow furrowed slightly as he struggled to decide where to begin.

Rainer smirked and couldn't resist reminding him, "Start with the blood centrifuge. Draw the serum—400cc from each arm."

Onyx coldly retorted, "Why do you need so much? You don't feel sorry since it's not your blood, huh? 400cc in one go is more than enough."

Rainer's mouth twitched, thinking that this rookie couldn't possibly manage with no loss. He'd have to make up for it later, anyway.

But Onyx executed the task flawlessly, even more precisely and skillfully, than the assistant who had worked with Rainer for four or five years. Rainer had no more objections.

One by one, the sensors were attached along Cora's tail. Curious, she poked at them while Onyx approached with a syringe. "Blood draw—are you scared?"

Cora shook her head, rolled up her sleeve, and confidently extended her arm.

Onyx carefully filled the 400cc syringe, his movements delicate. Just as he removed the needle and prepared to press a cotton swab to the wound, the injury had already healed. His hand froze mid-motion, the cotton still between his fingers.

Too slow—the second Anopower had already kicked in.

Onyx's expression remained unchanged as he casually handed her the cotton. "Press it down yourself. Don't let it bleed."

Cora stifled a laugh, playing along with his act. "Okay."

The blood test results came in quickly, showing that Cora's vital signs were essentially normal. Onyx focused on the gene spectrometer, inputting the decryption program and patiently waiting as it compared the data against a vast database.

Watching from the side, Rainer Ninnemann sighed quietly. This kid, hands in his pockets, expression blank—didn't he know that crucial bandwidth data needed to be recorded? Rainer opened a holographic screen and dutifully began the assistant's work, though he couldn't resist bringing up another topic.

"Last time, you asked me whether my research was part of the 'Spark' project or 'Plan Eternity.'"

"I told you I wasn't interested." Onyx shot him a glance.

"It's neither," Rainer replied to himself. "Neither one... What I'm researching is a third path."

Cora, who had a silver helmet on her head that made her look like she was getting her hair permed, asked, "What's the difference between Spark and Plan Eternity?" She had never fully understood the connection between the two. Onyx seemed somewhat neutral when talking about "Spark," but he always looked displeased when "Plan Eternity" was mentioned.

Rainer explained, "Spark was an independent gene project developed by Arashi, with Jasper as the core figure. The initial goal was to stabilize human genes through selective fusion, reducing disease rates and extending average life expectancy."

Less sickness and longer life? Cora nodded, half-understanding. That sounded good—she herself was healthy and rarely got sick.

"I joined Arashi a year late. By the time I was qualified to join the core team, the Loyak incident had occurred, and the Spark project was declared a failure. The Alliance reclaimed all research rights."

"And Plan Eternity was the gene project 2.0 started by the Alliance later," Rainer continued, his tone dropping. "Their ambitions were too great—not only did they want to achieve eternal life, but they also wanted to awaken powerful Anopowers in humans. But the catch was that all the benefits would only serve a select elite."

"The original intent of Spark was completely distorted, and since Plan Eternity involved live biological experiments, I withdrew."

"But my research is version 3.0. After the apocalypse, the first round of selection was completed, and the evolution of Aberrants was a foregone conclusion. Now, by finding the optimal gene ratio and radiation threshold, I could enable all Aberrants—no, all of humanity..." Rainer's excitement grew as he spoke.

"What? Scarlett Holland isn't satisfied with her current lifespan?" Onyx retorted coldly.

Scarlett, outwardly fair and just, was secretly a self-serving elitist, someone who saw herself as superior to others. It made sense that she would secretly fund Rainer's research to merge her position.

Rainer shook his head. "I'm not defending Scarlett, but she might not be doing this just for herself. You know that 'he' isn't in good health—especially this year... It's only thanks to his S-level physique that he's still holding on. My research has been stalled, and she's getting desperate."

He... Cora blinked. Rainer must be referring to General Yevgeniyev, right? Was General Yevgeniyev's health really that bad?

Beep beep—

Their conversation was interrupted as the spectrometer displayed the results.

Onyx focused on the screen. "As I suspected, this isn't ordinary snake DNA—it's from a Hooked Serpent." The Hooked Serpent was a mythical beast from ancient texts, over twenty meters long, amphibious, with a bifurcated, venomous tail used to prey on animals and humans.

"A Serpent?" Rainer was astonished. "That's a replicated gene."

Replicated genes referred to those of species long extinct, revived through artificial means. The original samples of such genes were extremely rare and preserved by specialized organizations. Rainer vaguely recalled a name like "Monad One" or "True—."

"I don't know about other organizations, but Arashi once purchased replicated genes in bulk—at least forty-seven branches, including U-Lab, stored copies," Onyx accurately reported.

Rainer glanced at him. "You've got an excellent memory."

After thinking for a moment, Rainer added, "Replicated genes are hard to remove. If you just want to revert to normal, reverse radiation can temporarily suppress them."

"What's the threshold?" Onyx asked.

"Fifteen to twenty percent. Snake genes have low activity... Oh, and the radiation intensity can be adjusted next door."

Onyx stood up and, before leaving the room, warned coldly, "Don't touch the equipment."

Once Onyx had walked away, Rainer muttered under his breath, "Looks like old man Montclair, but with a temper, just like his mother."

Cora's ears perked up. "Mother?"

Onyx had never mentioned his parents before.

Rainer flipped through the holographic screen nonchalantly, saying, "Back then, a bunch of armed thugs stormed the lab to kidnap him. That's when we found out this kid had dropped out of Luboni and was working for old Montclair. He even lied to him, saying he was on vacation—it made him furious..."

Onyx had a rebellious past like that? Cora listened intently, but she suddenly realized something. "Thugs?"

"Yeah, his mom's men—a bunch of big guys in military uniforms, all Aberrants. Back then, Aberrants were so valuable. Using them to capture a runaway kid was a complete waste," Rainer said, sounding pained.

Aberrants... military... Cora stared at Rainer in silence. The man didn't seem to realize how shocking his words were.

Snap! Cora's tail coiled around his neck again, tightening slightly.

"Stop. Don't talk about him. Not another word."

"Not a single word!"

When Onyx returned, the examination room was eerily quiet. Rainer Ninnemann had moved as far away as possible, and the bruises on his neck looked even darker.

Onyx paid no attention to him. After adjusting the settings, he pulled down the partition screen, blocking Rainer out and joining Cora inside to monitor her condition. Even though 15% overexposure to radiation was something a normal person couldn't endure, an S-level Aberrant like Cora could withstand it for a while.

Leaning against the counter, Onyx looked down at Cora. "The reverse radiation test will emit different frequency bands. We need to find the one that triggers your reversion."

Cora nodded, "Okay."

A faint radiation enveloped them both, and with each change in frequency, Onyx would inform Cora. After twenty minutes, her snake tail twitched, and the scales faded.

Onyx's eyes curved into a smile, but it quickly disappeared as something occurred to him. Swiftly, he pulled a blanket from his spatial storage and covered Cora entirely. After a moment, two feet poked out from under the edge of the blanket.

"I've changed back!" Cora's muffled voice came from beneath the blanket, and her toes wiggled nimbly.

Onyx turned his back to her, his expression slightly awkward. "Cora, uh, you should... put your pants on first."

The sound of rustling clothes filled the room as Cora quickly dressed. "Okay, okay, you can look now!"

Onyx turned around slowly, seeing Cora happily examining her legs, touching them as if to confirm they were real. A faint smile played on his lips; she was finally back to normal.

Outside, unaware of what had transpired inside, Rainer knocked on the protective glass. "Hey, come out and look at this."

After shutting off the radiation and raising the partition, Onyx walked over to the equipment. "What is it?"

Rainer's expression was grave as he pointed to the instrument's screen. "Look here, this is the Hooked Serpent's frequency band—it's weakened. But now, we're seeing new curves emerging. From a rough estimate, there are four distinct segments."

Onyx's eye twitched. New frequency bands meant... new unknown genes.

Inside the room, Cora felt an itch at the tip of her nose and suddenly sneezed. Then she noticed the sensor pads on the "hair-perming machine" above her head.

They glimmered and swayed, captivating her gaze. An inexplicable longing surged within her.

It was as if she were entranced, her hands lightly pressing against the floor as her body shifted low, her waist and hips raised high. Her leg muscles tensed, ready to spring, and faint brown spots appeared on her skin, resembling those of a feline predator.

Her ears twitched slightly. Just as Onyx looked up, he noticed something was wrong. A sense of dread washed over him. "Cora—!"

Startled, Cora's sensitive ears perked up!

Thud!

She sprang up, leaping nearly six meters into the air, grabbing onto the dangling sensor pad—and simultaneously crashing through the ceiling.

Dust and debris rained down as the examination room filled with swirling particles. Onyx could only cover his face in exasperation.

On the spectrometer, the analysis of the second unknown gene had just completed—Caracal.

The caracal was known in nature as being the highest-jumping and most ferocious wild cat.

Cora cautiously poked half her head through the hole she had made, clearly still under the influence of the caracal's instincts, her only thought being to grab the shiny object. A few more pieces of debris fell, landing at Onyx's feet as he looked up and locked eyes with her.

CHAPTER 47

A New Life

"Come down."

The room was filled with dust, making it hard for Onyx to breathe. He raised his hand to unbutton the collar that was pressing against his throat.

Cora, aware of the trouble she had caused, shrank back into the hole she had made, leaving only her fuzzy head peeking out.

Realizing his tone was too harsh, Onyx quickly softened his voice to coax her. "I'm not mad at you. Just come down."

Who could be mad at a little kitten? Even if it was a wild one.

Cora hesitated for a moment, then cautiously extended half of her body out, giving him a wary glance. Finally, her spine stretched out gracefully, and she landed silently on the floor, as if her feet had soft, cushioned pads. In her hand, she still clutched the shiny sensor pad.

Fortunately, the lab was underground, so Cora had only broken through one layer of the ceiling. Otherwise, if anyone outside had seen her, they'd be on the news again. But considering the new lab had already been wrecked like this, a scolding from Svetlana Yevgeniyeva was inevitable.

Onyx lowered his gaze to inspect her. The spots on Cora's body had mostly faded, and though her limbs were slender, they were covered with a thin layer of muscle, making her look almost like her old self. The caracal genes that had manifested this time differed greatly from the Hooked Serpent's, merely inheriting the biological traits with no external physical mutation.

Because Cora had damaged the power lines, some of the equipment had stopped functioning, including the gene spectrometer. Onyx used the remaining instruments to conduct a rough examination and found that her vital signs had returned to those of a normal Aberrant.

"The caracal genes appear to be more stable." Rainer's voice was hoarse as he glanced at the spectrometer. Since the power was cut, the last two genes had not been decoded successfully. "I suggest we maintain the current state, wait until the Hooked Serpent genes become recessive, and then switch to another frequency band."

"If you want to fully understand her DNA structure, you'll need to consider the issues of stabilization and radiation. It's best to space out each experiment by at least a week."

The unknown genes in Cora's body were like opening a blind box —you never knew what would come next. If it was something relatively stable, like the caracal, that was fine. But if it turned out to be something highly mutated, like the Hooked Serpent, it could affect their actions for some time.

After all, reverse radiation caused irreversible damage to the body's magnetic field, and even an Aberrant couldn't withstand it continuously. They had to take it slow.

"Here, I've compiled the frequency band data from earlier," Rainer said, handing over a holographic screen.

"No need," Onyx glanced at it and casually declined, "I've already memorized it."

Rainer frowned, clearly disapproving. "Don't joke around. You can't be careless with experiments. A tiny mistake could—"

Onyx promptly recited a string of data, and Rainer immediately recognized it as the log from the critical decryption points.

When he checked the corresponding lines on the screen, they were exactly the same. Although he had heard rumors, seeing it firsthand was still unbelievable—this kid's memory was astonishing!

Rainer's gaze grew more fervent as he looked at Onyx. "My work here is done. What about what you promised me?"

"You're struggling with the uncontrollable nature of high-dose radiation, right?" Onyx asked.

"The rejoining of DNA strands after double-strand breaks under high-dose radiation leads to single nucleotide polymorphisms," Rainer quickly explained. "I remember old de Montclair conducted a specialized study on this in 2027? Or was it 2028?"

Onyx only needed a few seconds to think. "New Era 2028, the second phase of the Spark Project's predictive experiments, focused on genetic mutations caused by radiation. I'll send you the relevant data."

As they spoke, Cora busied herself cleaning up the room, righting the overturned equipment, pushing the leather recliner back into place, and even mopping the floor. Onyx helped, and after they finished tidying up, he prepared to take her home.

Rainer stopped him, speaking in a dry voice. "You've memorized all the data from the central system, haven't you? I don't know how you managed it, but what about the rest of the Spark Project data? Are you just going to let it gather dust forever?"

The air froze.

"The Spark Project has already failed," Onyx replied flatly. "That data is meaningless."

It was as if a drop of water had fallen into hot oil. Rainer's eyes reddened as he lost control of his emotions completely.

"How can you say it's meaningless? You don't understand the importance of the Spark Project!"

"Even if it failed, knowing which steps failed and why is valuable experience and knowledge. If it could be shared, it would prevent all of us from blindly stumbling around. It's something that could benefit all of humanity! If old de Montclair were still here, he would definitely do it!"

Onyx's fists clenched suddenly, his straight spine tensing into a rigid line. He turned around, his expression cold to the extreme. "—Benefiting all of humanity has nothing to do with me."

Rainer was stunned.

"I'm not him. I'm a morally deficient, selfish person—I'm no saint."

Onyx lazily slipped his hands into his pockets, using his height to look down on Rainer. The light-colored eyes behind his glasses were devoid of warmth.

"Ninnemann, the Spark Project, has no relevance anymore. Whether you want to pursue 3.0 or 'benefit all of humanity,' I sincerely suggest you ask your former colleagues for the Plan Eternity data. From a broader perspective, that direction is more likely to yield results and won't leave you empty-handed."

Rainer was at a loss for words, unable to respond.

"We're leaving now. Don't bother seeing us out," Onyx said, his usual casual demeanor returning as he turned away.

On their way out of the lab, Cora silently glanced at Onyx's sharp jawline.

Onyx unexpectedly lowered his head, catching her gaze before she could look away, a hint of teasing in his eyes. "Did I scare you?"

Cora shook her head. "Were you serious?"

Onyx had a habit of lying as easily as he breathed, so Cora couldn't be sure of his true thoughts. But when in doubt, she asked—after all; he had promised never to lie to her.

"Which part?" Onyx asked with interest.

"The part about all of humanity having nothing to do with you," Cora replied honestly.

"Of course it's true. If someone wants to play savior, let them—I can't do it." Onyx gave her a brilliant smile. "I can't take care of everyone. Just monitoring you is enough of a handful."

He took her hand, intertwining their fingers in a firm grip. "Wild cats are creatures that don't like to settle down. I need to keep a close watch."

Cora bared her teeth at him playfully but didn't pull her hand away.

In Tustan, the two walked through the busy streets, masks covering their faces. Cora pulled up her hood, blending in with the crowd. The night market was bustling, colorful hover cars zipping through the sky, and people agitating the Northern Base Aberrant rankings.

They boarded a hover bus bound for the inner city. The bus was driverless, with only a few passengers inside. As it departed, the cool night breeze blew in through the windows, and the people below grew smaller and smaller until they looked like tiny ants.

"Let's visit Professor Gawin Ming and his wife tomorrow," Onyx suddenly suggested.

Cora mentally calculated the dates. Tomorrow was Gawin Ming

and Lucia's wedding anniversary. "Okay."

"Remember to bring some flowers," Onyx said, patting her head.

Jace Ming's flowers had been cut, so someone needed to replace them.

A dedicated starship cut through the night and docked smoothly at the platform.

Scarlett Holland, dressed in a dark gray suit, stepped out briskly, her expression stern, bringing a sharp wind with her as she walked. Her newly appointed administrative secretary followed closely behind, saying, "Commander Holland, welcome back."

During the two weeks of her suspension, Scarlett had taken a trip, but no one knew what she had been doing.

"Four S-level Aberrants will arrive tomorrow. Arrange for their registration as soon as possible," Scarlett ordered as she walked.

"Understood," the secretary replied, internally amazed.

Since Jirgalang was seriously injured and Heize had dropped to an A-level, the number of top Aberrants at the Northern Base had sharply decreased.

Who would have thought that Scarlett would personally recruit four S-level Aberrants on this trip, making such a significant move upon her return?

Scarlett continued walking swiftly, giving more instructions. "Any recent developments at the base?"

"Uh... F777 has returned," the secretary reported nervously. "They just killed a Level 5 beast in the Endless Sea..."

"I already know that. So?" Scarlett interrupted.

"So... General Yevgeniyev has appointed Svetlana as their direct contact from now on," the secretary hesitated for a moment, then said, "It was the General's direct order."

Scarlett paused briefly but then resumed walking as if nothing had happened. "The General's orders will be followed as they should be," she said, her tone indifferent. The secretary breathed a sigh of relief, patting her chest.

"How is the General's health lately?"

The secretary scratched her head, unsure how to answer. After all, how could a lowly administrative secretary like her have any insight into General Yevgeniyev's health? Scarlett gave her a sidelong glance;

the new secretary wasn't very sharp and would need time to be trained.

Scarlett took another step forward, looking down from her high vantage point at the brightly lit city below. The Northern Base was home to millions of high-level Aberrants and countless civilians. It was the largest human settlement in the Alliance, and also the safest fortress.

It was just like countless other quiet nights in the past. However, Scarlett knew that with the rise of Utopia, the post-apocalyptic peace was unraveling.

A storm was coming.

At the Garden Apartments, the sound of the door opening caused the five people in the living room, who were watching the news, to look up.

"Sister!" Damian, who had been sneakily pulling out Charles's gray hair, flipped over and hugged Cora's leg as he stood up. "You're better!"

"Any lasting side effects?" Yuui asked, her face covered with a mask, as she touched Cora's waist.

"Probably not," Cora replied, laughing as she dodged the ticklish sensation. Onyx followed her in, saying, "Her condition has stabilized for now, so don't worry. I'll take her for regular check-ups."

"What are you watching?" Cora asked curiously. Suchat made room for her, and Cora tiptoed over to sit down lightly.

"News about Utopia has spread," Felix said, enlarging one screen.

After a few days, the Utopia incident had reached a fever pitch. Several governors issued a joint manifesto, demanding an explanation from the Central Council. Protests broke out across various districts, and some even resorted to violent checkpoints. Unfortunately, any flight terminal that approached the floating city was mercilessly shot down.

Videos of Utopia went viral on the Lucas Network, overshadowing the attention F777 had gained from killing the leatherback sea turtle.

The existence of the floating city had disrupted the ecological balance, causing global climate changes, with coastal areas being the hardest hit. Delta Island (District B16) experienced three major tsunamis, and White Town (District B13) was devastated by tornadoes, leaving the city in ruins.

On the high-definition projection, images of severe natural disasters ravaging multiple cities made Cora's expression turn somber.

"And there's more bad news, though it seems like no one's paying attention to it."

Felix pulled up footage from a terminal in District C. "The aggression of zombies and beasts in the lower districts has increased."

The zombie hordes were becoming more frequent, and the beasts more ferocious. These post-apocalyptic creatures seemed to have become stronger in some intangible way. "It's unclear whether these changes are caused by Utopia, but the situation is dire."

The seven discussed the current state of the Alliance for a while, realizing there was little they could do about it. They could only take things one step at a time. "Let's get some rest. Tomorrow, we'll go see General Yevgeniyeva," Cora decided.

Yawning, she stood up and, as she passed by a row of lush potted plants, sneezed twice. "Ah-choo! Ah-choo! What are these?"

"Oh, some new variety the AL management sent over. They said it's a special feature of the Garden Apartments," Yuui replied casually. Cora sniffed the air lightly, feeling another sneeze coming on, and hurried away.

A small glowing tag fell from one pot, with a warm reminder from AL management. "Actinidia polygamy, a kiwi plant. Not recommended for households with cats."

"Let's go! Time to head out!" Early in the morning, Cora stretched energetically, full of life.

"Hey, Captain, looks like you slept well last night," Yuui commented as she came out, yawning and rubbing her sleepy eyes, with none of her usual celebrity composure.

"Yep! Slept like a log!" Cora's cheeks dimpled into a small smile—the first truly restful sleep she'd had in two weeks.

The only odd part was waking up to find the blanket tucked in so tightly around her it took her a while to wriggle free.

Before long, the members of F777 gathered together. Charles glanced around and muttered softly, "Where's our Princess Onyx?"

Onyx had earned the nickname "Princess" because of his severe cleanliness habits, along with his picky and demanding nature with living conditions. Of course, this was a nickname everyone only dared to use behind his back.

Click.

The bedroom door opened.

Onyx emerged, surrounded by an aura of low energy, his face dark with displeasure. He stopped in his tracks when he saw Cora's innocent and curious expression.

His eyes were bloodshot, with dark circles marring his usually handsome face, ruining his ever-present elegance.

"Did you not sleep well?" Cora asked, concerned.

"No," Onyx replied, his feelings mixed.

As he passed by the balcony, Onyx precisely picked up one of the potted plants, glanced at its label, and coldly tossed it into the trash can.

To Be Continued...

About Me

This is Jennifer. I have a deep passion for young adult romance and science fiction, with a penchant for weaving in the extraordinary, like zombies, into the ordinary.

About the Series

"Ethereal Artifacts" was originally serialized via a web novel platform. It's my first long series with all elements I like in my life: post-apocalypse, zombies, dystopian, cyberpunk, and of course, strong female leads.

Please Review

Your opinions matters! It is important for authors to improve themselves.